CW00327219

Best Short Stories 1994

Best Short Stories 1994

EDITED BY GILES GORDON AND DAVID HUGHES

HEINEMANN : LONDON

This collection was first published in Great Britain 1994
by William Heinemann Ltd
an imprint of Reed Consumer Books Ltd
Michelin House, 81 Fulham Road, London SW3 6RB
and Auckland, Melbourne, Singapore and Toronto

A CIP catalogue record for this title
is available from the British Library

ISBN HB 0 43400164 3
      PB 0 434 00043 4

Typeset by Deltatype Limited, Ellesmere Port, Cheshire

Printed and bound in Great Britain
by Clays Ltd, St Ives PLC

Contents

Introduction

This is the ninth volume of our best short stories of the year and we have selected the by now usual count of twenty-five narratives from sources that include national newspapers, little magazines published anywhere from Newcastle to New Zealand, broadcasting, the weeklies and monthlies, and any American journal that includes work by British or Commonwealth authors.

Our spread of source is wide, as naturally is our range of subject and style. We have now and then been castigated for describing our choice as 'the best'; we have always answered by saying that the subjective judgements of two independent editors, who like each other but are unalike, make a quorum but not a committee. Our main purpose has been to provide pleasure in many forms. We have never leant on the established at the expense of the unknown. We have considered no type of story alien to us, if within its genre – science fiction, romance, the thriller, ghost stories, the avant-garde however that is defined – it has not been bettered within the given year.

If we ask anything of readers, as if we could or should, it is to concentrate less on any point of controversy an introduction of ours might raise than on the considerable sweep and variety of the fiction we have gathered between these covers.

Giles Gordon and David Hughes

The Dream Lover

WILLIAM BOYD

'NONE OF THESE girls is French, right?'

'No. But they're European.'

'Not the same thing, man. French is crucial.'

'Of course . . .' I don't know what he is talking about but it seems politic to agree.

'You know any French girls?'

'Of course,' I say again. This is almost a lie, but it doesn't matter at this stage.

'But *well*? I mean well enough to ask out?'

'I don't see why not.' Now this time we are well into mendacity, but I am unconcerned. I feel good, adult, quite confident today. This lie can germinate and grow for a while.

I am standing in a pale parallelogram of March sunshine, leaning against a wall, talking to my American friend, Preston. The wall belongs to the Centre Universitaire Méditerranéan, a large stuccoed villa on the promenade at Nice. In front of us is a small cobbled courtyard bounded by a balustrade. Beyond is the Promenade des Anglais, its four lanes busy with Nice's traffic. Over the burnished roofs of the cars I can see the Mediterranean. The Baie des Anges looks grey and grimy in this season: old, tired water – ashy, cindery.

'We got to do something . . .' Preston says, a hint of

petulant desperation in his voice. I like the 'we'. Preston scratches his short hard hair noisily. 'What with the new apartment, and all.'

'You moved out of the hotel?'

'Yeah. Want to come by tonight?' He shifts his big frame as if troubled by a fugitive itch, and pats his pockets – breast, hip, thigh – looking for his cigarettes. 'We got a bar on the roof.'

I am intrigued, but I explain that the invitation has to be turned down as it is a Monday, and every Monday night I have a dinner appointment with a French family – friends of friends of my mother.

Preston shrugs, then finds and sets fire to a cigarette. He smokes an American brand called 'Picayune' which is made in New Orleans. When he came to France he brought two thousand with him. He has never smoked anything else since he was fourteen, he insists.

We watch our fellow students saunter into the building. They are nearly all strangers to me, these bright boys and girls, as I have only been in Nice a few weeks, and, so far, Preston is the only friend I have made. Slightly envious of their easy conviviality, I watch the others chatter and mingle – Germans, Scandinavians, Italians, Tunisians, Nigerians . . . We are all foreigners, trying hard to learn French and win our diplomas . . . Except for Preston, who makes no effort at all and seems quite content to remain monoglot.

A young guy with long hair rides his motorbike into the courtyard. He is wearing no shirt. He is English and, apart from me, the only other English person in the place. He revs his motorbike unnecessarily a few times before parking it and switching it off. He takes a T-shirt out of a saddle bag and nonchalantly pulls it on. I think how I too would like to own a motorbike and do exactly what he has done . . . His name is Tim. One day, I imagine, we might be friends. We'll see.

Monsieur Cambrai welcomes me with his usual exhausting, impossible geniality. He shakes my hand fervently and shouts to his wife over his shoulder.

'Ne bouge pas. C'est l'habitué. L'habitué!'

That's what he calls me – l'habitué, l'habitué de lundi, to give the appellation in full, so called because I am invited to dinner every Monday night without fail. He almost never uses my proper name and sometimes I find this perpetual alias a little wearing, a little stressful. 'Salut, l'habitué', 'Bien mangé, l'habitué?', 'Encore du vin, l'habitué?', and so on. But I like him and the entire Cambrai family; in fact I like them so much that it makes me feel weak, insufficient, cowed.

Monsieur and Madame are small people, fit, sophisticated and nimble, with neat spry figures. Both of them are dentists, it so happens, who teach at the big medical school here in Nice. A significant portion of my affection for them owes to the fact that they have three daughters – Delphine, Stephane and Annique – all older than me and all possessed of – to my fogged and blurry eyes – an incandescent, almost supernatural beauty. Stephane and Annique still live with their parents. Delphine has a flat somewhere in the city, but she often dines at home. These are the French girls that I claimed to know, though 'know' is far too inadequate a word to sum up the complexity of my feelings for them. I come to their house on Monday nights as a supplicant and votary, both frightened and in awe of them. I sit in their luminous presence, quiet and eager, for two hours or so, unmanned by my astonishing good fortune.

I am numbed further when I consider the family's disarming, disinterested kindness. When I arrived in Nice they were the only contacts I had in the city and, on my mother's urging, I duly wrote to them citing our tenuous connection via my mother's friend. To my surprise I was promptly invited to dinner and then invited back every Monday night. What shamed me was that I knew I myself could never be so hospitable so quickly, not even to a close friend, and what was more I knew no one else who would be, either. So I cross the Cambrai threshold each Monday with a rich cocktail of emotions gurgling inside me: shame, guilt, gratitude, admiration and – it goes without saying – lust.

Preston's new address is on the Promenade des Anglais itself –

the 'Résidence Les Anges'. I stand outside the building, looking up, impressed. I hve passed it many times before, a distressing and vulgar edifice on this celebrated boulevard, an unadorned rectangle of coppery, smoked glass with stacked ranks of gilded aluminium balconies.

I press a buzzer in a slim, freestanding concrete post and speak into a crackling wire grille. When I mention the name 'Mr Fairfield' glass doors part softly and I am admitted to a bare granite lobby where a taciturn man in a tight suit shows me to the lift.

Preston rents a small studio apartment with a bathroom and kitchenette. It is a neat, pastel coloured and efficient module. On the wall are a series of prints of exotic birds: a toucan, a bataleur eagle, something called a blue shrike. As I stand there looking round I think of my own temporary home, my thin room in Madame d'Amico's ancient, dim apartment, and the inefficient and bathless bathroom I have to share with her other lodgers, and a sudden hot envy rinses through me. I half hear Preston enumerating the various financial consequences of his tenancy: how much this studio costs a month; the outrageous supplement he had to pay even to rent it in the first place; and how he had been obliged to cash in his return fare to the States (first class) in order to meet it. He says he has called his father for more money.

We ride up to the roof, six storeys above the Promenade. To my vague alarm there is a small swimming pool up here and a large glassed in cabaña – furnished with a bamboo bar and some rattan seats – labelled 'Club Les Anges' in neon copperplate. A barman in a short cerise jacket runs this place, a portly, pale faced fellow with a poor moustache whose name is Serge. Although Preston jokes patronisingly with him it is immediately quite clear to me both that Serge loathes Preston and that Preston is completely unaware of this powerful animus directed against him.

I order a large gin and tonic from Serge and for a shrill palpitating minute I loathe Preston too. I know there are many better examples on offer, of course, but for the time being this shiny building and its accoutrements will do nicely as an approximation of The Good Life for me. And as I sip my sour drink a sour sense of the world's huge unfairness crowds ruthlessly in. Why should this guileless, big American, barely older than me, with his two thousand Louisiana cigarettes, and his cashable first-class air tickets have all *this* . . . while I live in a narrow frowsty room in an old woman's decrepit apartment? (My straitened circumstances are caused by a seemingly interminable postal strike in Britain that means money cannot be transferred to my Nice account and I have to husband my financial resources like a neurotic peasant conscious of a hard winter lowering ahead.) Where is *my* money, I want to know, *my* exotic bird prints, *my* pool? How long will I have to wait before these artefacts become the commonplace of my life? . . . I allow this unpleasant voice to whine and whinge on in my head as we stand on the terrace and admire the view of the long bay. One habit I have already learnt, even at my age, is not to resist these fervent grudges – give them a loose rein, let them run themselves out, it is always better in the long run.

In fact I am drawn to Preston, and want him to be my friend. He is tall and powerfully built – the word 'rangy' comes to mind – affable and not particularly intelligent. To my eyes his clothes are so parodically American as to be beyond caricature: pale blue baggy shirts with button-down collars, old khaki trousers short enough to reveal his white-socked ankles and big brown loafers. He has a gold watch, a zippo lighter and an ugly ring with a red stone set in it. He told me once, in all candour, in all modesty, that he 'played tennis to Davis Cup standard'.

I always wondered what he was doing in Nice, studying at the Centre. At first I thought he might be a draftee avoiding the war in Vietnam but I now suspect – based on some hints he has dropped – that he has been sent off to France as an obscure punishment of some sort. His family don't want him at home: he has done something wrong and these months in Nice are his penance.

But hardly an onerous one, that's for sure: he has no interest in his classes – those he can be bothered to take – nor in the

WILLIAM BOYD

language and culture of France. He simply has to endure this
exile and he will be allowed home where, I imagine, he will
resume his soft life of casual privilege and unreflecting ease
once more. He talks a good deal about his eventual return to
the States where he plans to impose his own particular
punishment, or extract his own special reward. He says he will
force his father to buy him an Aston Martin. His father will
have no say in the matter, he remarks with untypical
vehemence and determination. He will have his Aston Martin,
and it is the bright promise of this glossy English car that really
seems to sustain him through these dog days on the Mediterranean littoral.

Soon I find I am a regular visitor at the Résidence Les Anges,
where I go most afternoons after my classes are over. Preston
and I sit in the club, or by the pool if it is sunny, and drink. We
consume substantial amounts (it all goes on his tab) and
consequently I am usually fairly drunk by sunset. Our
conversation ranges far and wide but at some point in every
discussion Preston reiterates his desire to meet French girls. If I
do indeed know some French girls, he says, why don't I ask
them to the Club? I reply that I am working on it, and coolly
change the subject.
   Steadily, over the days, I learn more about my American
friend. He is an only child. His father (who has not responded
to his requests for money) is a millionaire – real estate. His
mother divorced him recently to marry another, richer
millionaire. Between his two sets of millionaire parents
Preston has a choice of eight homes to visit in and around the
USA: in Miami, New York, Palm Springs and a ranch in
Montana. Preston dropped out of college after two semesters
and does not work.
   'Why should I?' he argues reasonably. 'They've got more
than enough money for me too. Why should I bust my ass
working trying to earn more?'
   'But isn't it . . . What do you do all day?'
   'All kinds of shit . . . But mostly I like to play tennis a lot.
And I like to fuck, of course.'

6

'So why did you come to Nice?'

He grins. 'I was a bad boy.' He slaps his wrist and laughs. 'Naughty, naughty Preston.'

He won't tell me what he did.

It is spring in Nice. Each day we start to enjoy a little more sunshine and whenever it appears within ten minutes there is a particular girl, lying on the plage publique in front of the Centre, sunbathing. Often I stand and watch her spread out there, still, supine on the cool pebbles – the only sunbather along the entire bay. It turns out she is well known, that this is a phenomenon that occurs every year. By early summer her tan is solidly established and she is very brown indeed. By August she is virtually black, with that kind of dense, matt tan, the life burned out of the skin, her pores brimming with melanin. Her ambition each year, they say, is to be the brownest girl on the Côte d'Azure . . .

I watch her lying there, immobile beneath the invisible rain of ultra violet. It is definitely not warm . . . even in my jacket and scarf I shiver slightly in the fresh breeze. How can she be bothered? I wonder, but at the same time I have to admit there is something admirable in such singlemindedness, such ludicrous dedication.

Eventually I take my first girl to the Club to meet Preston. Her name is Ingrid, she is in my class, a Norwegian, but with dark auburn hair. I don't know her well but she seems a friendly, uncomplicated soul. She speaks perfect English and German.

'Are you French?' Preston asks, almost immediately.

Ingrid is very amused by this. 'I'm Norwegian,' she explains. 'Is it important?'

I apologise to Preston when Ingrid goes off to change into her swimming costume, but he waves it away, not to worry he says, she's cute. Ingrid returns and we sit in the sun and order the first of our many drinks. Ingrid, after some prompting, smokes one of Preston's Picayune cigarettes. The small flaw that emerges to mar our pleasant afternoon is that, the more Ingrid drinks, so does her conversation become dominated by references to a French boy she is seeing called Jean-Jacques. Preston hides his disappointment; he is the acme of good manners.

Later, we play poker using cheese biscuits as chips. Ingrid sits opposite me in her multicoloured swimsuit. She is plumper than I had imagined, and I decide that if I had to sum her up in one word it would be 'homely'. Except for one detail: she has very hairy armpits. On one occasion she sits back in her chair, studying her cards for a full minute, her free hand idly scratching a bite on the back of her neck. Both Preston's and my eyes are drawn to the thick divot of auburn hair that is revealed by this gesture: we stare at it, fascinated, as Ingrid deliberates whether to call or raise.

After she has gone Preston confesses that he found her unshavenness quite erotic. I am not so sure.

That night we sit on in the Club long into the night, as usual the place's sole customers, with Serge unsmilingly replenishing our drinks as Preston calls for them. Ingrid's presence, the unwitting erotic charge that she has detonated in our normally tranquil, bibulous afternoons, seems to have unsettled and troubled Preston somewhat and without any serious prompting on my part he tells me why he has come to Nice. He informs me that the man his mother remarried was a widower, an older man, with four children already in their twenties. When Preston dropped out of college he went to stay with his mother and new stepfather. He exhales, he eats several olives, his face goes serious and solemn for a moment.

'This man, his name's Michael, had three daughters – and a son, who was already married – and, man, you should have seen those girls.' He grins, a stupid, gormless grin. 'I was eighteen years old and I got three beautiful girls sleeping down the corridor from me. What am I supposed to do?'

The answer, unvoiced, seemed to slip into the Club like a draught of air. I felt my spine tauten.

'You mean – ?'

'Yeah, sure. All three of them. Eventually.'

I don't want to speak, so I think through this. I imagine a big silent house, night, long dark corridors, closed doors. Three bored blonde tanned stepsisters. Suddenly there's a tall young man in the house, a virtual stranger, who plays tennis to Davis Cup standard.

'What went wrong?' I manage.

'Oldest one, Janie, got pregnant, didn't she? Last year.'

'Abortion?'

'Are you kidding? She just married her fiancé real fast.'

'You mean she was engaged when – '

'He doesn't know a thing. But she told my mother.'

'The, the child was – '

'Haven't seen him yet.' He turns and calls for Serge. 'No one knows, no one suspects . . .' He grins again. 'Until the kid starts smoking Picayunes.' He reflects on his life a moment, and turns his big mild face to me. 'That's why I'm here. Keeping my head down. Not exactly flavour of the month back home.'

The next girl I take to the Club is also Scandinavian – we have eight in our class – but this time a Swede, called Danni. Danni is very attractive and vivacious, in my opinion, with straight white-blonde hair. She's a tall girl, full breasted, and she would be perfect but for the fact that she has one slightly withered leg, noticeably thinner than the other, which causes her to limp. She is admirably unselfconscious about her disability.

'Hi,' Preston says, 'are you French?'

Danni hides her incredulity. 'Mais, oui, monsieur. Bien sûr.' Like Ingrid, she finds this presumption highly amusing. Preston soon realises his mistake, and makes light of his disappointment.

Danni wears a small cobalt bikini and even swims in the pool, which is freezing. (Serge says there is something wrong with the heating mechanism but we don't believe him.) Danni's fortitude impresses Preston: I can see it in his eyes, as he watches her dry herself. He asks her what happened to her leg and she tells him she had polio as a child.

'Shit, you were lucky you don't need a caliper.'

This breaks the ice and we soon get noisily drunk, much to

Serge's irritation. But there is little he can do as there is no one else in the Club who might complain. Danni produces some grass and we blatantly smoke a joint. Typically, apart from faint nausea, the drug has not the slightest effect on me, but it affords Serge a chance to be officious and as he clears away a round of empty glasses he says to Preston, 'Ça va pas, monsieur, non, non, ça va pas.'

'Fuck you, Serge,' he says amiably and Danni's unstoppable blurt of laughter sets us all off. I sense Serge's humiliation and realise the relationship with Preston is changing fast: the truculent deference has gone; the dislike is overt, almost a challenge.

After Danni has left, Preston tells me about his latest money problems. His bar bill at the Club now stands at over $400 and the management is insisting it be settled. His father won't return his calls, acknowledge telegrams and Preston has no credit cards. He is contemplating pawning his watch in order to pay something into the account and defer suspicion. I buy it off him for 500 francs.

I look around my class counting the girls I know. I know most of them by now, well enough to talk to. Both Ingrid and Danni have been back to the Club and have enthused about their afternoons there, and I realise that to my fellow students I have become an object of some curiosity as a result of my unexpected ability to dispense these small doses of luxury and decadence: the exclusive addresses, the privacy of the Club, the pool on the roof, the endless flow of free drinks . . .

Preston decided to abandon his French classes a while ago and I am now his sole link with the Centre. It is with some mixed emotions – I feel vaguely pimp-like, oddly smirched – that I realise how simple it is to attract girls to the Club Les Anges.

Annique Cambrai is the youngest of the Cambrai daughters and the closest to me in age. She is only two years older than me but seems considerably more than that. I was, I confess, oddly daunted by her mature good looks, dark with a lean, attractive face, and because of this at first I think she found me rather aloof, but now, after many Monday dinners, we have become more relaxed and friendly. She is studying law at the University of Nice and speaks good English with a marked American accent. When I comment on this she explains that most French universities now offer you a choice of accents when you study English and, like ninety per cent of students, she has chosen American.

I see my opportunity and take it immediately: would she, I diffidently enquire, like to come to the Résidence Les Anges to meet an American friend of mine and perhaps try her new accent out on him?

The next morning, on my way down the rue de France to the Centre I see Preston standing outside a pharmacy reading the *Herald Tribune*. I call his name and cross the road to tell him the excellent news about Annique.

'You won't believe this,' I say, 'but I finally got a real French girl.'

Preston's face looks odd: half a smile, half a morose grimace of disappointment.

'That's great,' he says, dully, 'wonderful.'

A tall, slim girl steps out of the pharmacy and hands him a plastic bag.

'This is Lois,' he says. We shake hands.

I know who Lois is, Preston has often spoken of her: my damn-near fiancée, he calls her. It transpires that Lois has flown over spontaneously and unannounced to visit him.

'And, boy, are my Mom and Dad mad as hell,' she laughs.

Lois is a pretty girl, with a round, innocent face quite free of make-up. She is tall, even in her sneakers she is as tall as me, with a head of incredibly thick, dense brown hair which, for some reason, I associate particularly with American girls. I feel sure also, though as yet I have no evidence, that she is a very clean person – physically clean, I mean to say – someone who showers and washes regularly, redolent of soap and the lingering farinaceous odour of talcum powder.

I stroll back with them to the Résidence. Lois's arrival has temporarily solved Preston's money problems: they have cashed in her return ticket and paid off the bar bill and the next quarter's rent which had come due. Preston feels rich enough to buy back his watch from me.

Annique looks less mature and daunting in her swimsuit, I'm pleased to say, though I was disappointed that she favoured a demure apple-green one-piece. The pool's heater has been 'fixed' and for the first time we all swim in the small azure rectangle – Preston and Lois, Annique and me. It is both strange and exciting for me to see Annique so comparatively unclothed and even stranger to lie side by side, thigh by thigh, inches apart, sunbathing.

Lois obviously assumes Annique and I are a couple – a quite natural assumption under the circumstances, I suppose – she would never imagine I had brought her for Preston. I keep catching him gazing at Annique, and a mood of frustration and intense sadness seems to emanate from him – a mood of which only I am aware. And in turn a peculiar exhilaration builds inside me, not just because of Lois's innocent assumption about my relation to Annique, but also because I know now that I have succeeded. I have brought Preston the perfect French girl: Annique, by his standards, represents the paradigm, the Platonic ideal for this American male. Here she is, unclothed, lying by his pool, in his club, drinking his drinks, but he can do nothing – and what makes my own excitement grow is the realisation that for the first time in our friendship – perhaps for the first time in his life – Preston envies another person. Me.

Now that Lois has arrived I stay away from the Résidence Les Anges. It won't be the same again and, despite my secret delight, I don't want to taunt Preston with the spectre of Annique. But I find that without the spur of his envy the tender fantasy inevitably dims; for my dream life, my dream love, to flourish, I need to share it with Preston. I decide to pay a visit. Preston opens the door of his studio.

'Hi stranger,' he says, with some enthusiasm. 'Am I glad to see you.' He seems sincere. I follow him into the apartment.

The small room is untidy, the bed unmade, the floor strewn with female clothes. I hear the noise of the shower from the bathroom: Lois may be a clean person but it is clear she is also something of a slut.

'How are things with Annique?' he asks, almost at once, as casually as he can manage. He has to ask, I know it.

I look at him. 'Good.' I let the pause develop, pregnant with innuendo. 'No, they're good.'

His nostrils flare and he shakes his head.

'God, you're one lucky – '

Lois comes in from the bathroom in a dressing-gown, towelling her thick hair dry.

'Hi, Edward,' she says, 'what's new?' Then she sits down on the bed and begins to weep.

We stand and look at her as she sobs quietly.

'It's nothing,' Preston says. 'She just wants to go home.' He tells me that neither of them has left the building for eight days. They are completely, literally, penniless. Lois's parents have cancelled her credit cards and collect calls home have failed to produce any response. Preston has been unable to locate his father and now his stepfather refuses to speak to him (a worrying sign) and although his mother would like to help she is powerless for the moment, given Preston's fall from grace. Preston and Lois have been living on a diet of olives, peanuts and cheese biscuits served up in the bar and, of course, copious alcohol.

'Yeah, but now we're even banned from there,' Lois says, with an unfamiliar edge to her voice.

'Last night I beat up on that fuckwit, Serge,' Preston explains with a shrug. 'Something I had to do.'

He goes on to enumerate their other problems: their bar bill stands at over $300; Serge is threatening to go to the police unless he is compensated; the management has grown hostile and suspicious.

'We got to get out of here,' Lois says miserably. 'I hate it here, I hate it.'

Preston turns to me. 'Can you help us out?' he says. I feel the laugh erupt within me.

★

I stand in Nice station and hand Preston two train tickets to Luxembourg and two one-way Icelandair tickets to New York. Lois reaches out to touch them as if they were sacred relics.

'You've got a six-hour wait in Reykjavik for your connection,' I tell him, 'but, believe me, there is no cheaper way to fly.'

I bask in their voluble gratitude for a while. They have no luggage with them as they could not be seen to be quitting the Résidence. Preston says his father is now in New York and assures me I will be reimbursed the day they arrive. I have spent almost everything I possess on these tickets, but I don't care – I am intoxicated with my own generosity and the strange power it has conferred on me. Lois leaves us to go in search of a toilette and Preston embraces me in a clumsy hug. 'I won't forget this, man,' he says many times. We celebrate our short but intense friendship and affirm its continuance, but all the while I am waiting for him to ask me – I can feel the question growing in his head like a tumour. Through the crowds of passengers we see Lois making her way back. He doesn't have much time left.

'Listen,' he begins, his voice low, 'did you and Annique . . .? I mean, are you – '

'We've been looking for an apartment. That's why you haven't seen much of me.'

'Jesus . . .'

Lois calls out something about the train timetable, but we are not listening. Preston seems to be trembling, he turns away, and when he turns back I see the pale fires of impotent resentment light his eyes.

'Are you fucking her?'

'Why else would we be looking for an apartment?'

'What's going on?' Lois asks. 'The train's leaving soon.'

Preston gestures at me, as if he can't pronounce my name. 'Annique . . . They're moving in together.'

Lois squeals. She's so pleased, she really is, she really really likes Annique.

By the time I see them onto the train Preston has calmed down and our final farewells are sincere. He looks around the modest station intently as if trying to record its essence, as if now he wished to preserve something of this city he inhabited so complacently, with such absence of curiosity.

'God, it's too bad,' he says with an exquisite fervour. 'I know I could have liked Nice. I *know*. I really could.'

I back off, wordless, this is too good, this is too generous of him. This is perfect.

'Give my love to Annique,' Preston says quietly, as Lois calls loud goodbyes.

'Oh, don't worry,' I say, looking at Preston. 'I will.'

Sentiment in Drag

MADDO FIELD

BEFORE WRITING A LETTER a man I knew rubbed wild lavender across his page. He used a sachet specially ordered for the purpose, covered in the same leather as his writing-set. On opening a letter from him, a light hurrah of scent would instantly recall his voice to me, his face. It was a delicate stamp of ego and an alluring olfactory refinement.

I had told Sai Morita, my boss at *Rampant*. He was impressed. 'Artful. Don't tell anyone else. I'll copy it.' Sai's correspondents were equally impressed with his lavender-perfumed missives. A recipient had complimented him in my presence. 'Wunnerful, wunnerful. How'd you think of that?' Humble shrug of Sai's shy left shoulder, his hoodwinker eyes looking into the past, past me. You visualised the generations-long line of ancestral lavender-rubbers from whom he'd nonchalantly descended. He jumped into his honest present. 'It's just one more reason to hate faxes, isn't it? First, they busy up one's day tremendously. Second, they can't even be lavenderised,' he sighed twice for effect. Try to beat Sai doing wistful.

He was Japanese (born) Australian (educated – 'if that's not a contradiction in terms', as Bobbi, my co-worker at *Rampant* and a latent Sydney-sider, would add at introductions). Sai received a steady income from his Osaka grandfather. He loved travel and the new. 'I'm rejuvenated by anything I haven't seen before.' When he found somewhere he decidedly liked he would settle there for a year or so, augmenting his income with what he called 'chips from the publishing game'. In Switzerland, for example, he had written and published *Guide for the Walking Gourmet*.

'It was a forest pedestrian's Michelin, lovie,' he told me. 'Those Swiss are born walkers. They love hiking the picturesque. So did I. In Australia it's too tropicano to hike but a daffodil pleasure in Switzerland. Even the cows are pretty.' See his 'fabulous scenics': green lines of pine, bright poppies in wild red fields, blue hills, the white glisten of peaks. Sai had walked the Roman paths from Geneva to Lugano, staying nights in 'utter charms of country inns or grand lac hotel grandeurs'.

'Food landscaped to the views, wherever ya was: silvery trout and mountain streams, tended valley and tender veal. Some stunneroo restaurants. Mm-mm-mh. The number of terraced vines I watched and drank.' Sai had dined and wined himself from arbiter Girardet to agrarian Ticino, 'taking drunken notes on all the good stuff, some of the bad, and then I published what I'd sussed out. It originated as a guide for gourmet English hikers but it was a real goer. Everyone who ever walked in Switzerland seemed to buy it. Now it's been translated into French, German, Italian. Who'da thought? A market niche.' He loved the phrase, and he loved finding one, wherever he was. 'Viable' was a vocabulary must in the world Sai inhabited then, before he went to Tuscany to die good-humouredly. It jolted me hard like that too. I can't let you down any softer than I could myself at the time, or even now. So I'll just continue, heavy-penned, a red-eye special.

We were forbidden to phone him: 'Too much pathos and bathos, I'll call you.' Everyone at the office on tenterhooks, Sai a tender hook in our hearts.

'I'm already in Forte dei Marmi, bella I-t-a-l-i-a,' he trilled down the line, rrrolling r's and l's, lilting vowels. Then, brisk and managerial for effect, 'How's business?'

'Short or long answer?' I said.

'Short,' said brief Sai. 'Mirabeau's right. *Le diable est dans les détails, n'est-ce pas?*'

Sai loved showing off anyone's knowledge. 'So, shoot toot sweet, sweet,' he said. I told him business was thriving.

'Great. And thanks. Thanks to all of you. I appreciate your work. You earn it there. I spend it here: "*La vie en soft*". You'll never guess whose that is, try.'

'Sai, please.' Before he was dying, I used to hate not being able to trounce his French allusions.

'Give up? It's not even literary. I saw it in a Louis Feraud advert. I wish I'd thought it up myself. But then who'll know I didn't, outside France?' hooted Sai. 'Did you get my letter?' he asked, lowering his voice for seriousness.

'Yes, and we've all read it.'

'Did it still smell?'

'Redolently, Sai, redolently.'

Picture pale wood shutters, a dark cool room, the outside bright Italian light. Sai on a death-bed: I wrote him that the image filled me with despair. He wrote back: 'Don't go Renaissance on me, kiddo. I'm not in bed and I'm nowhere near dead yet. I've got some vignette months to go, albeit celibately. When I do die sugar-pie, I'll be your dead friend. You can scatter me over the sea, like Tawaraya Sotatsu, god of the wind.'

All my friends will be dead soon. 'Good title that,' Sai mused. ' "All My Dead Friends".'

He had met me on the street, then employed me off the cuff in San Francisco, where he had started his dual-language magazine for gays. Sai reading this would rage at me, throw pens for emphasis. 'No, no, no. Don't say "gay". Don't. Does Tennessee? Does Quentin Crisp? Please pretty please use "homosexual". *That* only became a word in 1892. I wish we were still "sexual inverts". Far more elegant. Who is GAY? Is Enola Gay? Get me out of these lingual double binds.' I can hear him in my mind, see his storm-black look in my mind's eye. 'Breederina, what would you know?'

'Breeders' is the term homosexuals use to describe hetero-sexuals. At *Rampant* I told them: 'I wish you wouldn't. Humans aren't the only species reproducing: it makes us sound so animal.' Everybody would laugh, I'd be offended. I wasn't even a compulsive heterosexual, much less a breeder. 'And my heterosexual friends don't reproduce, thank you, they adopt.'

'Only because it's fashionable,' our copy editor, Paul, had said. That was sort of true. My friends with infant Thais were either chic or had Fallopian tube problems, sometimes both. 'But take it back, Paul, they're not yuppie scum.'

'Homosexuals don't reproduce, either,' said Sai. 'But there are still millions of us.'

'Homosexuality isn't genetic, it's frenetic,' said Paul.

I don't have his or Sai's gift for words, but I do have Sai's letters. On his written paysage, light and sunshine landed deftly: 'What I love best here is the olive groves – could anything be more *calming*? My nurse told me they were planted as close together as possible, to improve the yield. What it also does is improve the dapple.'

That was very early stages, he'd just been diagnosed. So he'd settled *Rampant* business, taken a Pisa flight, Hertzed it to his paradise on the Ligurian coastline, the small resort town of Forte dei Marmi. 'My last resort,' he'd grinned.

Sai loathed pain. 'No, not pain. I can't escape dying, but pain yes. Thank Dog for morphine serenities.' Once he'd arranged his perfect death he was no longer perturbed about dying; he was matter-of-fact. 'I've adored living,' he said.

'How can you be so cavalier? Is it a Japanese tradition or something?' I thought he was over-extending the samurai ethos. What of fear? 'Are you Buddhist, Sai?'

'No, I just clap like one. Breederina, listen. It's death, it's ghastly. But check out the party I made of my life. Everybody came: the best booze, the best sex, the best drugs. I don't see how I could've improved upon it. Not just the fun part; all of it was perfect. I've never been poor in my pocket or heart. How's that for luck? Solid rabbit's foot. Ask me about malice:

I can count the nasties done to me on one hand. Who else do you know?' Indeed, he hadn't invoked much of his world's malevolence, or he didn't notice it. 'Solid rabbit's foot again. And no bleakness. Drear measured by the minute hand, then it was over' (he gave the Buddhist clap) 'and I was into zing again.' Laughter, voice, sparkle; he was champagne by telephone.

'Don't effervesce on me, Sai. You're dying.'

'But not of boredom. Keep your shirt on. Better still, buy one like mine,' he guffawed. He's dying, I thought, he's dying and he's guffawing.

There he is, alive and well, his Mighty Kings shirt and its embroidered shout: LIVE WILD OR DIE MILD. 'C'mon,' Sai screamed at me, 'c'mon. Stop the morbid, lovie. You know I lived wild. And I still get to die mild. It's *rare* that one can do both. Remember all those tequila sunrises? Now I'm quaffing vintaged wine in the Tuscan sunsets of my life. Tell me the opposite of reminiscing.'

At inception, his dual-language magazine attracted attention – I think – because of the Japanese calligraphy on its cover. Sai had chosen its name; it was a good choice, an eyecatcher. Or maybe people just wanted to know how 'rampant' looked in Japanese. The black-and-white, half/half spread was an effortless way to have a hint of eastern culture and a quirk for the unusual becomingly displayed in one's Edwardian wicker.

Rampant was a contacts gazette for homosexually inclined males. (Better Sai?) Apart from lonely heart advertisements, personal messages, personal massages, friendship/love sought and bought, we ran a column of local interest, a what's-on-about-town piece, play and movie reviews, restaurant drubbings. *Rampant* wasn't ageist, racist, sexist. We had an openline for readers to phone in anti-homosexual activities or activists, verified their reports, then published them. You know the genre and Sai did it well. It had just that little bit of difference to make it distinctive, so you shelled out, what the heck.

In those pre-Toyota and corporate takeover times Japan had allure. There was cachet in those lissom boys: there had been since the 30s. Distingué J. R. Ackerley recorded his preference for their sinewy, sinuous love to his common and guardsmen London variety. The historian Seidensticker described a certain quarter of Shinjuku as 'the homosexual capital of the world'. Dainty in his writing, though perhaps not in his sexual habits – or perhaps so, if you subtract the publicity – Truman Capote later told us that Tokyo was 'heaven'.

What did Japanese Sai think? 'A graceful meat-market. Very nice if you like oriental trade. It's not my taste. The baths in Yoshiwara used to be called "Toruco" – get it, Turkish baths in Japanese – until a righteous Turk objected. Then they were renamed "soaplands".' He chortled. '"The Soaplands of Yoshiwara", another winner huh?' I loved Sai's goblin laugh, ungoblin humour, all his titles.

His Japanese readership seemed more than pleased to have a guide to San Francisco in their own language. It made them feel insiders. Sai often received memorably pretty ricepaper letters to the editor, bearing what looked like exuberant references to *Rampant* in excelsior script.

Where *Rampant* differed from the usual (his coinage) 'lusto-press' was that Sai started to publish the most wonderful stories of male homosexual love affairs. Each excerpt was prefaced with Gore Vidal's immaculate definition: 'Although there is no such thing as a homosexual or a heterosexual person, there are, of course, homo- or heterosexual acts.'

Sai's tales described the connoisseurship of boy love in 17th-century Japan in three different categories of sexual aestheticism: the love betweeen warriors and boys in the samurai town of Edo; between priests and acolytes, in the Buddhist tradition of mutual spiritual enlightenment; and between young actors in Kabuki theatres and their middle-aged patrons. The tales were honed, delicious, fascinating. They emphasised in all three categories the causative, aching bonds of loyalty between these lovers, their beloveds. None of the stories was explicitly erotic. They were sexual adventures set in the colour and movement of another world in another time. The idealism of love, its shine, the wish of it we all have; man, woman, child: shrink to fit.

21

'It's gonna sell like hot cakes,' Sai had predicted in his dual happy role, author/publisher of 'Boy Monde', the title of his series. He hit the spot. Circulation wild-fired. Overnight a cottage (well, a spacious-parqueted-apartment-with-separate-ground-floor-offices) industry became a real money-spinner. Advertisers quadrupled, so did income, and Sai needed more staff. I'd previously desktopped the mag and babied it through the presses. Sai had done the accounts, handled the books and advertisers, and had an assortment of free-lancers who wrote the copy he didn't.

'Boy Monde' had escalated *Rampant*'s readership up along the West coast, across and down the East one. Sai newly employed two full-time writers, a secretary, an official accountant ('I chose him by tie – it was the Hermès skier. He must have a sense of humour and order'), other part-time advertising staffers, a gofer or two. We were dedicated workers to our employer's ongoing success, or rather, *Rampant*'s. We were literary, artistic, genuine, sensitive, high-minded, high-cheekboned, high-assed.

We sucked immensely, but it took us ten years to find out. Sometimes I still shudder: I was insufferable. We all were, except you-know-who; perfect then, perfect now, perfectly delightful Sai. He counted in my youth, he influenced my life. He was my rarest sound track. I can hear him now in my left ear, in my here and now, warbling out-of-key Dinah to me: '"Forgettable, that's what I am, forgettable, near you or far." Dee-ah-dee-ah-da. It doesn't rhyme in first person singular, but you know what I mean, my darling young one.' Yeah, Sai, I know. But I don't know what the opposite of reminiscing is. I got rid of Dinah Washington's version and I got rid of Aretha's version too. I can't rid myself of the memory of my Sai or what his memory does. Sai would fume, hiss *'Tu me fais vomir.* Get on with it, don't wallow.'

Rampant showcased new talent and revered old ones; the photography was superb, *avant la lettre* in blatant black-and-white, an unstyled style, and the intellectual chicness of a foreign language no one needed to pretend they knew or could speak. We were inalienably proud of ourselves: *Rampant* was becoming a literary achievement quietly, without slick. 'We're rising like a Japanese sun fron the rank ranks of the lusto-press, kiddos!' Sai toasted us all and himself. He was proud of his feat. 'I'm standing tall in my proud literary feet,' he said.

When the guests were gone, Sai told me: 'I'll only admit it to you, but what I love best is feeling so across-the-board cosmopolite. Bobbie saw *Rampant* being read in the the the THE Japanese restaurant of Paris. We're not cross-dressing, we're cross-pressing. Who's done that before?' Then, nobody had. A few detractors demeaned his need for research: they considered he already knew the samurai stuff without too much delving; like we know backwoods legends, tea parties, Cherokees. Maybe. I thought his writing had a quality of authenticity to the point of scholarship. I was no more *au courant* with 17th-century Japan than any *Rampant illuminato*, but his tales seemed real McCoy to me, meticulous.

We wanted to know if Sai's 1660 Japan bore any similarities to now. I wonder if he was the right person to ask. He wasn't much of a fan of his country, or if he was, it was in the literal sense – one of those gauzy wax-paper numbers that frailer pillow-talkers whisper behind. 'Take kimonos,' he said. 'Modern Japanese, my dumplings, are not instilled with any of the old teachings. Not just the "Boy Monde" ones. Even the women are losing their traditions.' (Get his 'even'.) 'Takeko had to return to Osaka to learn the art of kimono-tying. Shame, shame.'

This was only half true. His sister Takeko was also a traveller by nature and had been living happily between the States and Europe. By accident, she fell in love with a German she had met in Brussels. He fell in love with her by design, because he loved all things Japanese. He had specifically become a packaging expert with the intention of finding work in Japan, where it was considered a Western speciality. She had pleasantly lived with him for three years. Then the subsidiary who employed him in Frankfurt decided to send him to their parent company in Osaka for two years, renewable. Dieter was ecstatic, she was down-hearted.

'Japan is awful if you're native and live with a foreigner. My family will die. We will have to get married when we live there, just to save my face. That's how it is in my ex-country. Respectful, clannish, provincial. Dieter is dying to go, I can't say no. It's only for two years.' So she had stoically gone with him, pretending not to be grim.

It was Dieter who wanted her to be more traditional, more Japanese-ish when she was there, hence the kimono school. 'Imagine,' she said. 'It's so stupid. Seven yards of material in one piece. When I wear heels and stretch my neck I'm five feet tall. It takes hours. But Dieter is ravished, he thinks I'm gorgeous. I think I look like a geisha without the flour.'

'I can't even take my cats, you know. That's Japan.' She had two little beauties. 'They would be killed by neighbours. Everyone in Japan hates cats. I will have to find a Western-style house, with an enclosed wall so they are protected.' She did, against Dieter's protests: he wanted a Japanese bathroom and kitchen. 'He is ridiculous. I am *not* bathing and cooking over hot stones,' she said, outshining her cats' own eyes.

Takeko wasn't so impressed with Sai's samurai tales. She wasn't very impressed with anything Japanese, really. 'God-awful,' she said, with the true citizen's true contempt. 'Let me tell you,' she told me, finger emphatic, an index wing on her bird-like hand, 'every female's name ends in "ko" – you know what that means? "Little doll." Yukky-yuk.' The hands flew fiercely to the table. I thought she'd snap her chopsticks in hara-kiri anger. She stared into their inlay of black pearl, a Black Pearl herself. 'Everything good we got from the Chinese, and everything bad. We're a dialect people. Take it from me. Copy everything.'

I lent her my apartment once for a short stay and when I returned coloured pieces of paper were in small separate piles everywhere: near the phone, on the kitchen bench, on the balcony table. In the garbage miniature peacocks, cranes, kingfishers, your complete paper aviary: 'I do it when I'm thinking,' she explained. 'It helps me objectify. But it's the only ethnic thing I really like, except for Wasabi sauce.' Her brother was right. It was a shame; Takeko looked so resplendently Japanese.

Sai did when he wanted to, but he could only love his country as an epic: the tales proved that. He said they didn't prove anything but his publishing shrewdness. He had no patriotism. He didn't have any sentiment for his native land, except when he could embody it with his own interpretation, a pleasing one of dignity and bearing, of Bushido honour and Kabuki art. 'Those things no longer exist in Japan in their pure form,' he said.

Galleys sent off, we'd been celebrating with Sai and his usual bottle of favourite Goldwasser. Bobbi took a vintaged sip and a snipe or two at her boss's non-love of his country. She adored the place and the people.

'Do you know that Japanese sommeliers are among the best in the world, Sai?'

'No I didn't. Put it down to their industriousness. That's the only thing the Japanese should be famous for.'

'What about their watches?'

'Anyone serious wears Swiss, Bobbi.'

'What about how the Japanese banned the use of guns for three hundred years, Sai? Enlightened.'

'Look, I hate weaponry as much as the next person or Mishima. But the fact, Bobbi, f-a-c-t, is that guns were banned because feudal lords had to get them out of uprising civilian hands. Peasants only had bamboo spears against the steel swords of Kanemuto. Ineffectual – until they got guns. Then they popped off those samurai like flies. *That's* why guns were outlawed.'

Does the voluntary exile recall his country fondly? Does he prefer the land he inhabits in its stead? At *Rampant* I was the only staffer born and bred in San Francisco. Everyone else had moved there: Paul from Amsterdam, Bobbi from Sydney, André from Paris, etc.; displacees. Do you prefer it here? I'd ask. Why did you leave there? Yes and boredom, they'd reply. Sai didn't. He said, 'I didn't feel at home in my own country, that's all.' I think voluntary exile is a studiable phenomenon.

His Kabuki stories always centred on the choice between

25

duty and compassion. '*Giri* and *ninjo*, they call it,' he said. 'Not much of a choice, is it? It's no choice. Duty must prevail. If it doesn't, Mr Hero has to die.' 'Yes, and he always does in your stories. Usually by his own hand, right?' Sai looked puzzled. 'Is there a better way to go?' he'd asked. Had I stirred some muddy samurai atavism?

Sai never mentioned his background or family and neither did we, his or ours. Parents were parents. I do not know if it was because we were immersed in things besides ourselves or due to the blow-up poem on his office wall. A terse little piece, 'This be the verse':

> They fuck you up, your mum and dad.
> They may not mean to, but they do.
> They fill you with the faults they had
> And add some extra, just for you.

'One's family is not a congenial topic of conversation,' I said. 'Yaddayaddaya, you, me, Philip Larkin,' said Sai. 'You can't pick your parents but you can your friends.' He did not have the familial bonds that tied us in knots and we were envious. It gives one such a freedom, disowning one's parents physically and mentally. As Sai put it, 'They're only interesting financially, really.'

Like Kabuki plays, his stories often had a central action that was incompatible with compassion. Not a morsel of it. If the hero was compassionate instead of dutiful, his gentleness would drive him into taking actions he ought not to take. His lenity would be punished. These tales were not for the squeamish. They were often voluminous oriental dramas in the Maupinesque mode. Dilemma abounded. There were long scenes with characters doing nothing but dialogue or monologue, very restrained, amiably ominous. Then restraint's converse: an explosion of violence, death on the page, sparse prose, concentric ripples of action, gleaming pre-1945 virtues described. 'Just say they're soaps, 17th-century soaps,' said Sai.

A homoerotic shimmer mixed with Loyalty (personal loyalty clashing with official loyalty in the desolate persona of a samurai who remains loyal to his lord, fully realising that his lord's opponents are far more worthy of support); the heroics of love and death, the chaos they create for both hero and villain – this was the stuff of Sai's stories and each one was a 'minor masterpiece', the critics blurbled.

Hey, Sai, I wish you were alive-and-well-and-living anywhere. Or I wish I was religious: failing, ailing Buddha told his grieving animals, 'Look at the moon. As the dying moon renews herself, I too will be renewed by dying.' Sure, sure. Like some bastardised Native American in a cowboy comic strip, I count the moons there've been since I last saw Sai. Many moons, man: six full ones. Not counting the gibbous, the harvest, the crescent, or the three in which I saw his half-moon face. Now this, Sai would detest: mooning of any sort, for anyone.

'Stop it!' he'd scream.

'Nobody's worth it. If they're alive, go get 'em! If they're dead, forget 'em.' That was the full capacity of his emotional circuitry. Although in *Rampant* he didn't bellow it. 'Too much of a crowd-pleaser, sentiment,' said Sai. 'We can't dismiss it, but we can represent it minimally.'

Rampant's articles were implacably redacted by Sai, self-designated Sentiment Editor. Contributors to all sections knew his rigorous 'mush quota' and PWA (People with AIDS) reportage was concernedly treated, but no emotionalism showed, no earnestness. 'We're all too old for that,' Sai strictured. Love, emotion, sentiment, he was suspicious of those unctuous gamuts.

Know what he called the Quilts? 'Sentiment in drag.'

'You'll be skinned alive if you put that in *Rampant*, Sai,' Paul had warned him. We were covering the White House story for our readers and that was Sai's suggested title. It was taking remorseless too far, jesus. Paul blasted: 'Listen, Sai, the quilts are a political statement, they're an effective device to gain the attention of the general public to the AIDS situation and, Cold Heart, they're a mosaic of tribute to all dead PWAs, including the unbeknownst infused or transfused.'

Sai played an imaginary, haunting violin. 'The quilts are a

mosaic of lament. They're a plea for pity, aimed at everyone's sympathetic jugular. We're screaming for public compassion. Majority condolence for sad minority us. It's sentiment in drag, baby duckling. We do NOT need sympathy. Let's not smother all those great cavorting memories in a quilt,' deplored indignant Sai.

'Would you prefer a futon?' spat Paul.

'Didn't we just adore our glorious, sexually vagrant lives? Did we or didn't we?' He always felt sorry for heterosexuals: 'Drab poor buggers by anyone's standards,' was his opinion.

Certainly, the way Sai saw them. 'Look at breeders and their sad, long, slow lives. Truly dismal: a few fucks, a marriage, kids, mid-life, depression, young secretaries, old age. Oh, my. Think of the tons of gorgeous trade I've had; we've had. Who'd swap? Who Who Who?' in Japanese crescendo, kimonoed sleeve hovering in our stunned silent air, a sparrowhawk descending for the kill. He scrunched Paul's text with fisted hand. 'Kill it,' he said. 'I'm publishing life, not death . . .'

'Instead of a handmade quilt, let's have a loud hand of long-standing applause for the passionate living we've done. No grandmama quilts. You wanna say "gay" so be it. Be it. Remember the ball we made of our lives, all the hundreds of fabulous balls, smooth/black/rough/white/yellow we've held in our hot little hands. Now let's die, fellas, as gaily as we know we lived. Sexual heroes with short, happy lives. Who wants to see forty-eight anyway? Knock knock, who's there? Death. I want laughs, not bleeding hearts, no mawk, no sentiment.'

Rampant's ads were another story: they oozed. Sticky-icky messages of true love lost and found, all-is-forgiveness, tender spots, raw feelings, coronary slush.

'Where would we be without them?' I indicated our columns and columns of multiple insertions.

'They pay the bills, but I hate them, really,' Sai would grimace. 'It makes me shudder: all that love with capital ells.'

'I'm asking you, Sai, where would anyone be without sentiment?'

'Ask yourself,' crisped Sai. 'I've been without it all my life.'

From the pages of his own life Sai had impassively edited sentimentality, even if *Rampant* published it for money. He had been dining out with gusto in some of his high-preference Florentine locales. 'I figured out with Doc that I've got three months left of palate,' he told me. He had always relished food, and I relished dining with Sai immensely. He could give you a roaring appetite with a gleam of his eye and a wave of a menu'd hand. His manner of eating was wondrous: he ate with natural rapture. 'That boy's not a gourmet, he's a gourmand,' a lover once told me. 'He's both,' I replied. He loved the gentle flavour of delicately fried zucchini blossoms; together once in Mantova, Sai ordered – and we ate – a goldened crop. A true gourmet, he did recall in fastidious detail all his impeccable meals.

Listen to his zest: 'I want to die eating panzanella,' he told me by phone. '*Il dottore* winces, but he's so s-e-e-rious. Or maybe he doesn't appreciate his own regional foods. He's not too imaginative about culinary delights. I can't quite figure him.' I could. I don't think Sai's doctor had encountered a death-sentenced patient so full of life and its left pleasures. 'I won't be able to eat later because of the wall-to-wall morph, so I'm scheduling lots of last meals while the going's good. Life's a pig when you're dying, I guess. But at least I can finally forget about fucking cholesterol.'

He was a smoker who enjoyed cigarettes. He never coughed, he could puff the occasional after-lunch cigarette or else haze two packets in smoke-ring party chains. He didn't have an ounce of flab but never exercised. 'Except the eyes, of course: twelve ups, twelve downs, twelve lefts, twelve rights. For my equilibrium,' he'd explained. He phoned to tell me, among other things, that he'd tripled his quota of eye gymnastics. 'I need much more equilibrium now. Strange, isn't it? I seem to require more for dying than I did for living. Work that out. I'da thought the reverse would be truer.'

Bravery: we haven't needed that for decades. Now, again, we need it desperately. Fine old bravado or handsome bravura aren't strong enough or tall enough any longer. Maybe Sai's antique tales in *Rampant* were so successful because in a way they called us all to arms. Each other's and to the embrace of courage and samurai strength. A theatrical Kabuki light shone through his stories of life and death as double acts, both played out in eloquent gestures of the hand, movements of the head. Mind and body as graces in tangent, beating down the evil spirits of fear, cowardice, the faint heart. No trembling, please, this is war. Assemble into plague formation.

'Call me No-Flinch,' Sai joked on the phone. 'My heart is a tiger. Don't worry, I'm coping. It's much easier than suiciding, you know. I'm dying a natural death, don't forget.' No one at *Rampant* had seen it like that. Blood cells rioting, circulation running amok, the seditious, insubordinate brain, organs caving in, the immune system in utter collapse – revolt and revolution in one's own body. No side to take. 'I'm my own disaster area,' Sai said.

Mine's my memory of him. It won't dissolve in tears, in flawless dry Martinis, in crystalline mini-Matterhorns of good cocaine. Insoluble Sai.

He had continued sending us stories for *Rampant*, two full disks. 'He's a samurai himself,' we said. Sai had discussed everything with us before leaving for his Tuscan last-splurge and death. Paul was replacing Sai ('Rein in that sentiment, Paul, remember'), with André and myself as second/ secondess. The 'Boy Monde' stories would cease, of course, after we'd published the contents of the disks he'd sent.

On Sai's rigid instructions there was to be no mention of him, no obituary in *Rampant*. 'Low profile. No tea, no sympathy,' Sai admonished us. I'll repeat his lines for emphasis. 'I did have one of the best lives of anyone I know. Food, wines, men, song. The only stormy weather in it belonged to Lena Horne. Note I get to die in Tuscany. Your vast majorities don't even get to live there,' he'd wisecracked in delight. My farceur Sai.

He was as jokester dead as alive: we were five o'clock-Friday sitting in the office, *mood relaxé*, another edition off to press, celebrating our well-done job with a bottle of Sai's

Goldwasser. He'd willed specific stocks for *après*-galleys *dégustation*. 'Here's to us, fuck them' was Sai's pet toast in English and we always used it when we splashed his wine and clinked.

It was like television: our goblets raised and sparkling in the sun's last evening rays, an imperiously pressed buzzer, a suited stranger enters left, a process served in aghast close-up silence. *Rampant* was being sued by the University of California for plagiarism of its publication, 'Tales of Male Love in Pre-modern Japan'. The injunction stated that the publication was a scholarly translation of a work by Yasuro Tsujitani (1642–87), appearing in English for the first time, and that 'Boy Monde' was its mirror image.

We were shattered. Plagiarist Sai? We disbelieved it. He wasn't the type, we thought. But as Bobbi logicised it, 'Possums, we don't know enough plagiarists to make a comparison. *Monsieur* either stole that translation or re-penned the Jappo original. Either way, it wasn't Sai's or Sai's imagination.' Bobbi's hand extended out and up, weighing the matter in her palm, gold bracelets flashing down her wrists in gravity and up again as she grabbed her glass; grave, bamboozled Bobbi. 'I don't get it,' she said. 'Where's the why?'

I didn't know then and I don't now. The tales of spiritual enlightenment, the connoisseurship of loyalty and love and samurai valour of the stories we'd published in *Rampant* hung in the room clouding our memories. Sai himself had never been particularly proud of 'his' stories; only pleased how well they helped sell the mag. Neither had he gone 'author' on us, not once: no blighted muse, blocked pen, blank page acedia.

His hatred of sentiment was spot-on though, I must say. Take a good hard look at all of us there as we were, *avant avant-garde*, being sentimental musho that dead cherub Sai could be a plagiarist. We didn't have a Dadaist bone in our bodies, that's for sure.

We were obliged immediately to stop publication of 'Sai's' series: our excerpts were practically indistinguishable from 'Tales of Male Love in Pre-modern Japan'. 'Boy Monde' was a much better title, said ambivalent Paul, the first to recover. The rest of us were speechless for days. I didn't know what to think, although it's usually one of my habits. Sai himself had intimated nothing, pre- or post-death.

'Maybe he thought the folks at Berkeley would never see it and then we'd never find out. What makes plagiarists plagiarise anyway? I would be frightened to take the chance, myself,' said Andrè *deçu*.

Dead Sai had swizzled us. He'd made us unhappy fools. In and with our hearts, we'd trusted him. I could see us all comforting our intellects: our lack of knowledge of Japanese culture forestalled our worrying that he'd also tried to defraud our minds. 'He couldn't have done it with Western stuff,' we decided, huffy and hurt. But he could have if he'd selected wisely. Like all literati, our reading fields were narrow. Sai certainly could have ploughed up plagiarisable material if he'd just taken a detour around our chosen plantings.

When I think about his plagiarism I see it as Sai's little laugh on death, a funny, money-spinning joke. He'd caught us red-handed with our sentiment and red-eyed with our sadness. How could anyone we loved like that be a plagiarist? How could he leave us with the University of California on our backs? Unhonourable Sai-san. *A la fin*, it was excellent publicity for anti-establishment *Rampant* and UC Berkeley. There was a TV-news-generated rush for authentically intellectual editions of the 'Tales of Male Love', everyone happy and gay about owning the non-porno version, leaves from a tree of life and sex blossoming in the academe grove. I even miss him as a plagiarist.

Oh, Sai. I think of you at sundowner time, moonriser time. 'I personally taught those Tuscans the habit. They weren't serious tipplers. Didn't know the drinker's sundown/moon-up rule. Although everyone loves a new excuse, don't they? I told them it was an ancient Japanese tradition.' He's forged his own in my heart. I sip my moonriser, irenic me on Sai's iridescent balcony, sharing conceptual space with his memory and the glistening bay. I tried to see him as he said he'd be, a tiny cloud of 'my ash-grey ashes cruising' the bright July seas.

Sentiment's struck off my record, I spurn it now as Sai did always. Tawaraya Sotatsu whistles and laughs in the willow-reed chimes that arrived from Osaka two Sai-less weeks after his death. My god of the wind, I promise you, no sentiment. All I want to say is how I feel: irreparable.

My plangency would infuriate Sai, because he'd given me the benefit of the doubt. He'd held my left ear lobe in his Japanese beautiful hand, promised me he was going to die gaily. I've absolutely ruined my mourning gaily role but let's let it pass and let him pass, onto paper and outa my heart. Sai, Sai.

Mlle. Dias de Corta

MAVIS GALLANT

You MOVED INTO my apartment during the summer of the
year before abortion became legal in France; that should fix it
in past time for you, dear Mlle. Dias de Corta. You had just
arrived in Paris from your native city, which you kept
insisting was Marseilles, and were looking for work. You said
you had studied television-performance techniques at some
provincial school (we had never heard of the school, even
though my son had one or two actor friends) and received a
diploma with 'special mention' for vocal expression. The
diploma was not among the things we found in your suitcase,
after you disappeared, but my son recalled that you carried it
in your handbag, in case you had the good luck to sit next to a
casting director on a bus.

The next morning we had our first cordial conversation. I
described my husband's recent death and repeated his last
words, which had to do with my financial future and were not
overly optimistic. I felt his presence and still heard his voice in
my mind. He seemed to be in the kitchen, wondering what
you were doing there, summing you up: a thin, dark-eyed,
non-committal young woman, standing at the counter,
bolting her breakfast. A bit sullen, perhaps; you refused the
chair I had dragged in from the dining room. Careless, too.

There were crumbs everywhere. You had spilled milk on the floor.

'Don't bother about the mess,' I said. 'I'm used to cleaning up after young people. I wait on my son Robert hand and foot.' Actually, you had not made a move. I fetched the sponge mop from the broom closet, but when I asked you to step aside you started to choke on a crust. I waited quietly, then said, 'My husband's illness was the result of eating too fast and never chewing his food.' His silent voice told me I was wasting my time. True, but if I hadn't warned you I would have been guilty of withholding assistance from someone in danger. In our country, a refusal to help can be punished by law.

The only remark my son Robert made about you at the beginning was 'She's too short for an actress'. He was on the first step of his career climb in the public institution known then as Post, Telegrams, Telephones. Now it has been broken up and renamed with short, modern terms I can never keep in mind. (Not long ago I had the pleasure of visiting Robert in his new quarters. There is a screen or a machine of some kind everywhere you look. He shares a spacious office with two women. One was born in Martinique and can't pronounce her 'R's. The other looks Corsican.) He left home early every day and liked to spend his evenings with a set of new friends, none of whom seemed to have a mother. The mis-teachings of the seventies, which encouraged criticism of earlier generations, had warped his natural feelings. Once, as he was going out the door, I asked if he loved me. He said the answer was self-evident: we were closely related. His behaviour changed entirely after his engagement and marriage to Anny Clarens, a young lady of mixed descent. (Two of her grandparents are Swiss.) She is employed in the accounting department of a large hospital and enjoys her work. She and Robert have three children: Bruno, Elodie, and Félicie.

It was for companionship rather than income that I had decided to open my home to a stranger. My notice in *Le Figaro* mentioned 'young woman only', even though those concerned for my welfare, from coiffeur to concierge, had strongly counselled 'young man'. 'Young man' was said to be neater, cleaner, quieter, and (except under special circumstances I need not go into) would not interfere in my relationship with my son. In fact, my son was seldom available for conversation and had never shown interest in exchanging ideas with a woman, not even one who had known him from birth.

You called from a telephone on a busy street. I could hear the coins jangling and traffic going by. Your voice was low-pitched and agreeable and, except for one or two vowel sounds, would have passed for educated French. I suppose no amount of coaching at a school in or near Marseilles could get the better of the southern 'O', long where it should be short and clipped when it ought to be broad. But, then, the language was already in decline, owing to lax teaching standards and uncontrolled immigration. I admire your achievement and respect your handicaps, and I know Robert would say the same if he knew you were in my thoughts.

Your suitcase weighed next to nothing. I wondered if you owned warm clothes and if you even knew there could be such a thing as a wet summer. You might have seemed more at home basking in a lush garden than tramping the chilly streets in search of employment. I showed you the room – mine – with its two corner windows and long view down Avenue de Choisy. (I was to take Robert's and he was to sleep in the living room, on a couch.) At the far end of the Avenue, Asian colonisation had begun: a few restaurants and stores selling rice bowls and embroidered slippers from Taiwan. (Since those days the community has spread into all the neighbouring streets. Police keep out of the area, preferring to let the immigrants settle disputes in their own way. Apparently, they punish wrongdoers by throwing them off the Tolbiac Bridge. Robert has been told of a secret report, compiled by experts, which the Mayor has had on his desk for eighteen months. According to this report, by the year 2025 Asians will have taken over a third of Paris, Arabs and Africans three-quarters, and unskilled European immigrants two-fifths. Thousands of foreign-sounding names are deliberately 'lost' by the authorities and never show up in telephone books or computer directories, to prevent us from knowing the true extent of their progress.)

I gave you the inventory and asked you to read it. You said you did not care what was in the room. I had to explain that the inventory was for me. Your signature, 'Alda Dias de Corta', with its long loops and closed 'a's showed pride and secrecy. You promised not to damage or remove without permission a double bed, two pillows, and a bolster, a pair of blankets, a beige satin spread with hand-knotted silk fringe, a chaise longue of the same colour, a wardrobe and a dozen hangers, a marble fireplace (ornamental), two sets of lined curtains and two of écru voile, a walnut bureau with four drawers, two framed etchings of cathedrals (Reims and Chartres), a bedside table, a small lamp with parchment shade, a Louis XVI-style writing desk, a folding card table and four chairs, a gilt-framed mirror, two wrought-iron wall fixtures fitted with electric candles and light bulbs shaped like flames, two medium-sized 'Persian' rugs and an electric heater, which had given useful service for six years but which you aged before its time by leaving it turned on all night. Robert insisted I include breakfast. He did not want it told around the building that we were cheap. What a lot of coffee, milk, bread, apricot jam, butter, and sugar you managed to put away! Yet you remained as thin as a matchstick and that great thatch of curly hair made your face seem smaller than ever.

You agreed to pay a monthly rent of fifty thousand francs for the room, cleaning of same, use of bathroom, electricity, gas (for heating baths and morning coffee), fresh sheets and towels once a week, and free latchkey. You were to keep a list of your phone calls and to settle up once a week. I offered to take messages and say positive things about you to prospective employers. The figure on the agreement was not fifty thousand, of course, but five hundred. To this day, I count in old francs – the denominations we used before General de Gaulle decided to delete two zeros, creating confusion for generations to come. Robert has to make out my income tax; otherwise, I give myself earnings in millions. He says I've had more than thirty years now to learn how to move a decimal, but a figure like 'ten thousand francs' sounds more solid to me than 'one hundred'. I remember when a hundred francs was just the price of a croissant.

You remarked that five hundred was a lot for only a room. You had heard of studios going for six. But you did not have six hundred francs or five or even three, and after a while I took back my room and put you in Robert's, while he continued to sleep on the couch. Then you had no francs at all, and you exchanged beds with Robert, and, as it turned out, occasionally shared one. The arrangement – having you in the living room – never worked: it was hard to get you up in the morning, and the room looked as though five people were using it, all the time. We borrowed a folding bed and set it up at the far end of the hall, behind a screen, but you found the area noisy. The neighbours who lived upstairs used to go away for the weekend, leaving their dog. The concierge took it out twice a day, but the rest of the time it whined and barked, and at night it would scratch the floor. Apparently, this went on right over your head. I loaned you the earplugs my husband had used when his nerves were so bad. You complained that with your ears stopped up you could hear your own pulse beating. Given a choice, you preferred the dog.

I remember saying, 'I'm afraid you must think we French are cruel to animals, Mlle. Dias de Corta, but I assure you not everyone is the same.' You protested that you were French, too. I asked if you had a French passport. You said you had never applied for one. 'Not even to go and visit your family?' I asked. You replied that the whole family lived in Marseilles. 'But where were they born?' I said. 'Where did they come from?' There wasn't so much talk about European citizenship then. One felt free to wonder.

The couple with the dog moved away sometime in the eighties. Now the apartment is occupied by a woman with long, streaky, brass-coloured hair. She wears the same coat, made of fake ocelot, year after year. Some people think the man she lives with is her son. If so, she had him at the age of twelve.

★

What I want to tell you about has to do with the present and the great joy and astonishment we felt when we saw you in the oven-cleanser commercial last night. It came on just at the end of the eight-o'clock news and before the debate on hepatitis. Robert and Anny were having dinner with me, without the children: Anny's mother had taken them to visit Euro Disney and was keeping them overnight. We had just started dessert – crème brûlée – when I recognised your voice. Robert stopped eating and said to Anny, 'It's Alda. I'm sure it's Alda.' Your face has changed in some indefinable manner that has nothing to do with time. Your smile seems whiter and wider; your hair is short and has a deep-mahogany tint that mature actresses often favour. Mine is still ash-blonde, swept back, medium-long. Alain – the stylist I sent you to, all those years ago – gave it shape and colour once and for all, and I have never tampered with his creation.

Alain often asked for news of you after you vanished, mentioning you affectionately as 'the little Carmencita', searching TV guides and magazines for a sign of your career. He thought you must have changed your name, perhaps to something short and easy to remember. I recall the way you wept and stormed after he cut your hair, saying he had charged two weeks' rent and cropped it so drastically that there wasn't a part you could audition for now except Hamlet. Alain retired after selling his salon to a competent and charming woman named Marie-Laure. She is thirty-seven and trying hard to have a baby. Apparently, it is her fault, not the husband's. They have started her on hormones and I pray for her safety. It must seem strange to you to think of a woman bent on motherhood, but she has financial security with the salon (although she is still paying the bank). The husband is a car-insurance assessor.

The shot of your face at the oven door seen as though the viewer were actually in the oven, seemed to me original and clever. (Anny said she had seen the same device in a commercial about refrigerators.) I wondered if the oven was a convenient height or if you were crouched on the floor. All we

39

could see of you was your face, and the hand wielding the spray can. Your nails were beautifully lacquered holly-red, not a crack or chip. You assured us that the product did not leave a bad smell or seep into food or damage the ozone layer. Just as we had finished taking this in, you were replaced by a picture of bacteria, dead or dying, and the next thing we knew some man was driving you away in a Jaguar, all your household tasks behind you. Every movement of your body seemed to express freedom from care. What I could make out of your forehead, partly obscured by the mahogany-tinted locks, seemed smooth and unlined. It is only justice, for I had a happy childhood and a wonderful husband and a fine son, and I recall some of the things you told Robert about your early years. He was just twenty-two and easily moved to pity.

Anny reminded us of the exact date when we last had seen you: April 24, 1983. It was in the television film about the two friends, 'Virginie' and 'Camilla', and how they meet two interesting but very different men and accompany them on a holiday in Cannes. One of the men is a celebrated singer whose wife (not shown) has left him for some egocentric reason (not explained). The other is an architect with political connections. The singer does not know the architect has been using bribery and blackmail to obtain government contracts. Right at the beginning you make a mistake and choose the architect, having rejected the singer because of his social manner, diffident and shy. 'Virginie' settles for the singer. It turns out that she has never heard of him and does not know he has sold millions of records. She has been working among the deprived in a remote mountain region, where reception is poor.

Anny found that part of the story hard to believe. As she said, even the most forlorn Alpine villages are equipped for winter tourists, and skiers won't stay in places where they can't watch the programmes. At any rate, the singer is captivated by 'Virginie', and the two sit in the hotel bar, which is dimly lighted, comparing their views and principles. While this is taking place, you, 'Camilla', are upstairs in a flower-filled suite, making mad love with the architect. Then you and

40

he have a big quarrel, because of his basic indifference to the real world, and you take a bunch of red roses out of a vase and throw them in his face. (I recognised your quick temper.) He brushes a torn leaf from his bare chest and picks up the telephone and says, 'Madame is leaving the hotel. Send someone up for her luggage.' In the next scene you are on the edge of a highway trying to get a lift to the airport. The architect has given you your air ticket but nothing for taxis.

Anny and Robert had not been married long, but she knew about you and how much you figured in our memories. She sympathised with your plight and thought it was undeserved. You had shown yourself to be objective and caring and could have been won round (by the architect) with a kind word. She wondered if you were playing your own life and if the incident in Cannes was part of a pattern of behaviour. We were unable to say, inasmuch as you had vanished from our lives in the seventies. To me, you seemed not quite right for the part. You looked too quick and intelligent to be standing around with no clothes on, throwing flowers at a naked man, when you could have been putting on a designer dress and going out for dinner. Robert, who had been perfectly silent, said, 'Alda was always hard to cast.' It was a remark that must have come out of old café conversations, when he was still seeing actors. I had warned Anny he would be hard to live with. She took him on trust.

My husband took some people on trust, too, and he died disappointed. I once showed you the place on Place d'Italie where our restaurant used to be. After we had to sell, it became a pizza restaurant, then a health-food store. What it is now I don't know. When I go by it I look the other way. Like you, he picked the wrong person. She was a regular lunchtime customer, as quiet as Anny; her husband did the talking. He seemed to be involved with the construction taking place around the Porte de Choisy and at that end of the Avenue. The Chinese were moving into these places as fast as they were available; they kept their promises and paid their bills, and it seemed like a wise investment. Something went wrong. The woman disappeared, and the husband retired to that seaside

41

town in Portugal where all the exiled kings and queens used to live. Portugal is a coincidence: I am not implying any connection with you or your relations or fellow-citizens. If we are to create the Europe of the twenty-first century, we must show belief in one another and take our frustrated expectations as they come.

What I particularly admired, last night, was your pronunciation of 'ozone'. Where would you be if I hadn't kept after you about your 'O's? 'Say "*Rhône*",' I used to tell you. 'Not "*run*".' Watching you drive off in the Jaguar, I wondered if you had a thought to spare for Robert's old Renault. The day you went away together, after the only quarrel I ever had with my son, he threw your suitcase in the back seat. The suitcase was still there the next morning, when he came back alone. Later, he said he hadn't noticed it. The two of you had spent the night in the car, for you had no money and nowhere to go. There was barely room to sit. He drives a Citröen BX now.

I had been the first to spot your condition. You had an interview for a six-day modelling job – Rue des Rosiers, wholesale – and nothing to wear. I gave you one of my own dresses, which, of course, had to be taken in. You were thinner than ever and had lost your appetite for breakfast. You said you thought the apricot jam was making you sick. (I bought you some honey from Provence, but you threw that up, too.) I had finished basting the dress seams and was down on my knees, pinning the hem, when I suddenly put my hand flat on the front of the skirt and said, 'How far along are you?' You burst into tears and said something I won't repeat. I said, 'You should have thought of all that sooner. I can't help you. I'm sorry. It's against the law and, besides, I wouldn't know where to send you.'

After the night in the Renault you went to a café, so that Robert could shave in the washroom. He said, 'Why don't you start a conversation with that woman at the next table? She looks as if she might know.' Sure enough, when he came back a few minutes later, your attention was turned to the stranger. She wrote something on the back of an old Métro ticket (the solution, most probably) and you put it away in your purse, perhaps next to the diploma. You seemed to him eager and hopeful and excited, as if you could see a better prospect than the six-day modelling job or the solution to your immediate difficulty or even a new kind of life – better than any you could offer each other. He walked straight out to the street, without stopping to speak, and came home. He refused to say a word to me, changed his clothes, and left for the day. A day like any other, in a way.

When the commercial ended we sat in silence. Then Anny got up and began to clear away the dessert no one had finished. The debate on hepatitis was now deeply engaged. Six or seven men who seemed to be strangling in their collars and ties sat at a round table, all of them yelling. The programme presenter had lost control of the proceedings. One man shouted above the others that there were people who sincerely wanted to be ill. No amount of money poured into the health services could cure their muddled impulses. Certain impulses were as bad as any disease. Anny, still standing, cut off the sound (her only impatient act), and we watched the debaters opening and shutting their mouths. Speaking quietly, she said that life was a long duty, not a gift. She often thought about her own and had come to the conclusion that only through reincarnation would she ever know what she might have been or what important projects she might have carried out. Her temperament is Swiss. When she speaks, her genes are speaking.

I always expected you to come back for the suitcase. It is still here, high up on a shelf in the hall closet. We looked inside – not to pry but in case you had packed something perishable, such as a sandwich. There was a jumble of cotton garments and a pair of worn sandals and some other dresses I pinned and basted for you, which you never sewed. Or sewed with such big, loose stitches that the seams came apart. (I had also given you a warm jacket with an embroidered Tyrolian-style collar. I think you had it on when you left.) On that first day, when I made the remark that your suitcase weighed next to nothing, you took it for a slight and said, 'I am small and I wear small sizes.' You looked about fifteen and had poor teeth and terrible posture.

43

The money you owed came to a hundred and fifty thousand
francs, counted the old way, or one thousand five hundred in
new francs. If we include accumulated inflation, it should
amount to a million five hundred thousand; or, as you would
prefer to put it, fifteen thousand. Inflation ran for years at
twelve per cent, but I think that over decades it must even out
to ten. I base this on the fact that in 1970 half a dozen eggs were
worth one new franc, while today one has to pay nine or ten.
As for interest, I'm afraid it would be impossible to work out
after so much time. It would depend on the year and the
whims of this or that bank. There have been more prime
ministers and annual budgets and unpleasant announcements
and changes in rates than I can count. Actually, I don't want
interest. To tell the truth, I don't want anything but the
pleasure of seeing you and hearing from your own lips what
you are proud of and what you regret.

My only regret is that my husband never would let me help
in the restaurant. He wanted me to stay home and create a
pleasant refuge for him and look after Robert. His own parents
had slaved in their bistro, trying to please greedy and difficult
people who couldn't be satisfied. He did not wish to have his
only child do his homework in some dim corner between the
bar and the kitchen door. But I could have been behind the bar,
with Robert doing homework where I could keep an eye on
him (instead of in his room with the door locked). I might
have learned to handle cash and cheques and work out tips in
new francs and I might have noticed trouble coming, and
taken steps.

I sang a lot when I was alone. I wasn't able to read music, but
I could imitate anything I heard on records that suited my
voice, airs by Delibes or Massenet. My muses were Lily Pons
and Ninon Vallin. Probably you never heard of them. They
were before your time and are traditionally French.

According to Anny and Marie-Laure, fashions of the
seventies are on the way back. Anny never buys herself
anything, but Marie-Laure has several new outfits with softly
draped skirts and jackets with a peasant motif – not unlike the
clothes I gave you. If you like, I could make over anything in

the suitcase to meet your social and professional demands. We could take up life where it was broken off, when I was on my knees, pinning the hem. We could say simple things that take the sting out of life, the way Anny does. You can come and fetch the suitcase any day, at any time. I am up and dressed by half past seven, and by a quarter to nine my home is ready for unexpected guests. There is an elevator in the building now. You won't have the five flights to climb. At the entrance to the building you will find a digit-code lock. The number that lets you in is K630. Be careful not to admit anyone who looks suspicious or threatening. If some stranger tries to push past just as you open the door, ask him what he wants and the name of the tenant he wishes to see. Probably he won't even try to give you a credible answer and will be scared away.

The concierge you knew stayed on for another fifteen years, then retired to live with her married daughter in Normandy. We voted not to have her replaced. A team of cleaners comes in twice a month. They are never the same, so one never gets to know them. It does away with the need for a Christmas tip and you don't have the smell of cooking permeating the whole ground floor, but one misses the sense of security. You may remember that Mme. Julie was alert night and day, keeping track of everyone who came in and went out. There is no one now to bring mail to the door, ring the doorbell, make sure we are still alive. You will notice the row of mailboxes in the vestibule. Some of the older tenants won't put their full name on the box, just their initials. In their view, the name is no one's business. The postman knows who they are, but in summer, when a substitute makes the rounds, he just throws their letters on the floor. There are continual complaints. Not long ago, an intruder tore two or three boxes off the wall.

You will find no changes in the apartment. The inventory you once signed could still apply, if one erased the words 'electric heater'. Do not send a cheque – or, indeed, any communication. You need not call to make an appointment. I prefer to live in the expectation of hearing the elevator stop at my floor and then your ring, and of having you tell me you have come home.

L, U, C, I, E

NADINE GORDIMER

MY NAME'S LUCIE – no, not with a 'y'. I've been correcting
that all my life, ever since my name was no longer vocables I
heard and responded to like a little domestic animal (*here, puss,
puss*) and I learnt to draw these tones and half-tones as a series
of outlines: L, U, C, I, E. This insistence has nothing to do
with identity. The so-called search for identity bores me. I
know who I am. You know well enough who you are: every
ridge in a toe-nail, every thought you keep private, every
opinion you express is your form of life and your responsi-
bility. I correct the spelling because I'm a lawyer and I'm
accustomed to precision in language; in legal documents the
displacement of a comma can change the intention expressed
in a sentence and lead to new litigation. It's a habit, my
pedantry; as a matter of fact, in this instance simply per-
petuates another orthographic inaccuracy: 'I am named for my
father's Italian grandmother, and the correct Italian form of
the name is Lucia. This had no significance for me until I saw
her name on her tomb: LUCIE.

I've just been on holiday in Italy with my father. My mother
died a few months ago; it was one of those journeys taken after
the death of a wife when the male who has survived sees the
daughter as the clone woman who, taken out of present time

and place to the past and another country, will protect him from the proximity of death and restore him to the domain of life. (I only hope my father has understood that this was one-off, temporary, a gift from me.) I let him believe it was the other way round: he was restoring something to me by taking me to the village where, for him, I had my origin.

He spent the first five years of his life dumped by poor parents in the care of that grandmother, and although he then emigrated to Africa with them and never returned, his attachment to her seems never to have been replaced. By his mother, or anyone else; long after, hers was the name he gave to his daughter.

He has been to Europe so many times – with my mother, almost every year.

'Why haven't you come here before?' I asked him. We were sitting in a sloping meadow on what used to be the family farm of his grandmother and her maiden sisters. The old farmhouse where he spent the years the Jesuits believe definitive had been sold, renovated with the pink and green terrace tiles, curly-cue iron railings and urns of red geraniums favoured by successful artisans from the new industrial development that had come up close to the village. The house was behind us; we could forget it, he could forget its usurpation. A mulberry tree shaded the meadow like a straw hat. As the sun moved, so did the cast of its brim. He didn't answer; a sudden volley of shooting did – stuttering back and forth from the hills in cracking echoes through the peace where my question drifted with the evaporating moisture of grass.

The army had a shooting range up there hidden in the chestnut forests, that was all; like a passing plane rucking the fabric of perfect silence, the shots brought all that shatters continuity in life, the violence of emotions, the trajectories of demands and contests of will. My mother wanted to go to art galleries and theatres in great European cities, he was gratified to be invited to speak at conferences in Hong Kong and Toronto, there were wars and the private wars of cartels and, for all I know, love affairs – all that kept him away. He held this self hidden from me, as parents do in order to retain what they consider a suitable image before their children. Now he wanted to let me into his life, to confirm it, as if I had been a familiar all along.

We stayed in the only albergo in the village and ate our meals in a dark bar beneath the mounted heads of cerf and mountain goats. The mother of the proprietor was brought to see my father, whom she claimed to remember as a small child. She sniffled, of course, recollecting the three sisters who were the last of a family who had been part of the village so long that – that what? My father was translating for me, but hesitantly, not much is left of his Italian. So long that his grandmother's mother had bred silkworms, feeding them on mulberry leaves from her own trees, and spinning silk as part of the home industry which existed in the region before silk from the Orient took away the market. The church square where he vividly remembered playing was still there and the nuns still ran an infant school where he thought he might have been enrolled for a few months. Perhaps he was unhappy at the school and so now could not picture himself entering that blue door, before us where we sat on a bench beside the church. The energy of roaring motorcycles carrying young workers in brilliantly studded and sequinned windbreakers to the footwear and automobile parts factories ripped his voice away as he told me of the games drawn with a stick in the dust, the cold bliss of kicking snow about, and the hot flat bread sprinkled with oil and salt the children would eat as a morning snack. Somewhere buried in him was a blue-pearl, translucent light of candles that distorted 'like water' he said, some figures that were not real people. In the church, whose bells rang the hours tremulously from hill to hill, there were only the scratched tracings of effaced murals; he thought the image must have come from some great event in his babyhood, probably the local saint's day visit to a shrine in a neighbouring town.

We drove there and entered the chapels along the sides of a huge airport-concourse of a basilica – my mother was not a Catholic and this analogy comes to me naturally out of my experience only of secular spaces. There were cruel and mournful oil paintings behind the liquid gouts of votive candlelight; he dropped some coins in the box provided but did not take a candle. I don't know whether the dingy representation of the present snuffed out his radiant image or whether his image transformed it for him. We had strong coffee, and cakes named for the shrine, in an arcade of delicious-smelling cafés opposite. He had not tasted those cakes for fifty-eight years, since Lucie bought them as a treat; we had found the right context for the candles that had stayed alight inside him all that time. The cafés were filled with voluble old men, arguing and gesticulating with evident pleasure. They were darkly unshaven and wore snappy hats. I said: 'If you'd stayed, you'd be one of them' and I didn't know whether I'd meant it maliciously or because I was beguiled by the breath of vanilla and coffee into the fascination of those who have a past to discover.

At night he drank grappa in the bar with the proprietor and picked up what he could of the arguments of village cronies and young bloods over the merits of football teams, while the TV babbled on as an ignored attraction. These grandchildren of the patriarchs blew in on a splendid gust created by the sudden arrest of speed as they cut the engines of their motorcycles. They disarrayed themselves, flourishing aside tinsel-enamelled or purple-luminous helmets and shaking out haloes of stiff curls and falls of blond-streaked locks. They teased the old men, who seemed to tolerate this indulgently, grinningly, as a nostalgic resurrection of their own, if different, wild days.

No women came to the bar. Up in my room each night, I leant out of my window before bed; I didn't know how long I stayed like that, glitteringly bathed in the vast mist that drowned the entire valley between the window and the dark rope of the alps' foothills from which it was suspended, until the church clock – a gong struck – sent waves layering through the mist that I had the impression I could see undulating silvery, but which I was feeling, instead, reverberating through my rib-cage. There was nothing to see, nothing. Yet there was the tingling perception, neither aural nor visual, that overwhelms in the swoon before an anaesthetic whips away consciousness. The night before we went to the cemetery, I was quite drunk with it. The reflection of the moon seeped through the endless insubstantial surface, silence inundated this place he had brought me to; the village existed out there no more than it had ever done for me when I had never sat in its square, never eaten under the glass eyes of timid beasts killed in its chestnut forests and mountains, or sat in the shade of its surviving mulberry tree.

We had four days. On our last afternoon, he said 'Let's walk up to the old cemetery'. My mother was cremated – so there was no question of returning painfully to the kind of scene where we had parted with her; still, I should have thought in his mood death was too close to him for him to have found it easy to approach any of its territory. But it seemed this was just one of the directions we hadn't yet taken on the walks where he had shown me what he believed belonged to me, given in naming me.

We wandered up to this landmark as we had to others. He took a wrong turning into a lane where there were plaster gnomes and a miniature windmill stood on a terrace, and canaries sang for their caged lives, piercingly as cicadas. But he retraced our steps and found the right cartographical signals of memory. There was a palatial iron gateway surmounted by a cross, and beyond walls powdery with saltpetre and patched with moss, the black forefingers of cypress trees pointed. Inside: a vacuum, no breath, flowers in green water, withered.

I had never seen a cemetery like that; tombs, yes, and elaborate tableaux of angels over grave-stones – but here, in addition to a maze of these there were shelves and shelves of stone-faced compartments along the inner side of the walls, each with its plaque.

Were the dead stored, filed away?

'When there's no room left for graves, it's usual in this country. Or maybe it's just cheaper.' But he was looking for something.

'They're all here,' he said. We stepped carefully on gravelled alleys between tombstones and there they were, uncles and

aunts and sons and daughters, cousins who had not survived
infancy and other collaterals who had lived almost a century,
lived through the collapse of the silkworm industry, the
departures of their grown children to find an unknown called a
better life in other countries, lived on through foreign
occupation during a war and through the coming of the
footwear and automobile parts factories – all looking out from
photographs framed under convex glass and fixed to their
tombstones. No face was old, or sick, or worn. Whenever it
was they had died, here they consorted in the aspect they had
had when young or vigorously mature.

There were many Albertos and Giovannis and Marias and
Clementinas, but the names most honoured by being passed
on were Carlo and Lucia, apparently those of the first
progenitors to be recorded. Five or six Lucias, from a child in
ringlets to fat matrons inclining their heads towards their
husbands, many of whom were buried beside them; and then
we came to – he came to – her grave. Her sisters were on either
side of her. I couldn't read the rest of the inscription, but
LUCIE was incised into the ice-smooth black marble. I leant
to look. Go on, he said, giving me the example of bracing his
foot on the block that covered her. Under her oval bubble of
glass the woman was composed and smooth-haired, with the
pupil-less gaze of black eyes, the slightly distended nostrils
and straight mouth with indented corners of strong will, and
the long neck, emphasised by tear-drop earrings, of Italian
beauties. Her eyebrows were too thick; if she had belonged to
another generation she would have plucked them and spoiled
her looks. He put his arm on my shoulder. 'There's a
resemblance.' I shrugged it off with his hand. If your name is
on your tombstone, it's definitive, it's not some casual
misspelling. Why wasn't she Lucia, like the others?

'I don't really know – only what I was told by my father,
and he didn't say much . . . parents in those days . . . the
sisters kept their mouths shut, I suppose, and in any case he
was away working at the docks in Nice from the age of
eighteen . . . Apparently she had also gone to work in France
when she was very young – the family was poor, no

opportunity here. She was a maid in a hotel, and there's something about her having had a love affair with a Frenchman who used the French version of her name . . . and so she kept it, even when she married my grandfather.'

While he was talking a dust-breeze had come up, sweeping its broom among the graves, stirring something that made me tighten my nostrils. The smell of slimy water in the vases of shrivelled flowers and the curious stagnant atmosphere of a walled and crowded space where no living person breathed – what I had taken in when we entered the place was strengthened by some sort of sweetness. With his left foot intimately weighted against her grave, the way a child leans against the knee of a loved adult, he was still talking: 'There's the other version – it comes from *her* mother, that it was *her mother* who was a maid in Nice and my grandmother was her illegitimate child.' I was looking at the foot in the pump-soled running shoe, one of the pair he had kitted himself out with at the market in Cuneo on our way to the village. 'She brought the baby home, and all that remained of the affair was the spelling of the name.' Dust blew into my eyes, the cloying sweetness caught in my throat and coated my tongue. I wanted to spit. '. . . what the maiden sisters thought of that, how she held out against them? God knows . . . I don't remember any man in the house, I would have remembered . . .'

The sweetness was sickly, growing like some thick liquor loading the air. We both inhaled it, it showed in the controlled grimace that wrinkled round his eyes and mouth and I felt the same reaction pulling at my own face muscles. But he went on talking, between pauses; in them we neither of us said anything about the smell, the smell, the smell like that of a chicken gone bad at the back of a refrigerator, a rat poisoned behind a wainscot, a run-over dog swollen at a roadside – the stench, stench of rotting flesh, and all the perfumes of the living body, the clean salty tears and saliva, the thrilling fluids of love-making, the scent of warm hair, turned putrid. Unbearable fermentation of the sweetness of life. It couldn't have been her. It could not have been coming to him from her, she had been dead so long, but he stayed there with his foot on her stone as if he had to show me that there was no stink in our noses, as if he had to convince me that it wasn't her legacy.

We left saunteringly, ignoring the gusts of foulness that pressed against us, each secretly taking only shallow breaths in revulsion from the past. At the gate we met a woman in the backless slippers and flowered overall that the local women wore everywhere except to go to church. She saw on our faces what was expressed in hers, but hers was mixed with some sort of apologetic shame and distress. She spoke to him and he said something reassuring, using his hands and shaking his head. She repeated what she had told him and began to enlarge on it; I stood by, holding my breath as long as I could. We had some difficulty in getting away from her, out beyond the walls where we could stride and breathe.

'A young man was killed on his motorbike last week.'

What was there to say?

'I didn't see a new grave.'

'No – he's in one of the shelves – that's why . . . She says it takes some time, in there.'

So it wasn't the secrets of the rotting past, Lucie's secrets, it was the secret of the present, always present; the present was just as much there, in that walled place of the dead, as it was where the young bloods, like that one, tossed down their bright helmets in the bar, raced towards death, like that one, scattering admiring children in the church square.

Now when I write my name, that is what I understand by it.

The Mantris Woman

RUSSELL HOBAN

'THIS IS AZNUL HAZAKH, the mantris High Priestess,' she said. Outside the rain was beating down, thunder crashed, lightning flashed, the deep blue night was heavy with drama. For what seemed quite a long time she'd been flinging down her unstretched canvases one after another before me like a rug merchant while Charlie Norton, like the rug merchant's boy, carefully removed each one after it was shown.

I wasn't there to buy paintings; Charlie, whom I'd never met until tonight, had been unable to come to my reading at the State Library in Sydney the evening before but he'd sent me a book of his poems and a dinner invitation via this woman. I'd thought I was coming to his place but it turned out to be her flat in Iron Cove. The room in which the paintings were stacked was lit by a bare light bulb and had nothing else in it but a spattered table cluttered with tubes of paint and a variety of crusted vessels with brushes standing in them. The floor was covered with a drip cloth as if the ceiling were being painted.

The subject of her pictures was always the same: praying mantises singly or in groups, all of them with human faces. Aznul Hazakh, as she now looked up at me from the floor, seemed to be speaking either a prayer or a curse which issued from her head in the characters of some unknown alphabet. She and the other mantises were always seen in a desolation of glistening greys and yellowish greens; the paintings had the authority of obsession and the look of them was like a taste in the mind of something from another time, another place better forgotten.

'These are very strong,' I said. 'You call them mantrises because they speak mantras to you?'

'Yes.'

'What's this one saying?'

'It's nothing I can interpret for you. Maybe if you look at Aznul Hazakh for a long time she will speak to you of the plains of desolation and the deserts of darkness that she and I have crossed.' Her name was Viki Sooma, she was somewhere between fifty and sixty. Her slitted eyes were small and beady, her face was hard and shiny, the skin drawn tight over the big cheekbones and jaw. Her hair was like brass wire and it stood out from her head as if electrically charged. Far away in the rain a dog was barking. Coming there in the taxi I'd passed patches of waste ground, rusting iron, tall brown grasses swaying in the salt wind.

'Do these sell?' I said.

'Not these. Earlier ones sold for five thousand, ten thousand. But when I got into the mantris world nobody wanted my pictures.'

'Could you do a few of the old kind just for money?'

She looked at me from a great distance. 'I'm not there any more. I can only paint from where I am. Dealers who used to beg me for paintings are always out now when I call them on the phone. But I send to them in the night and they remember me, yes. They don't forget me.' Her eyes seemed to sink into her head and grow dim.

'What do you send them in the night?'

'I send Aznul Hazakh and her sisters.'

'Dreams, you mean?'

'If you say.'

'These mantrises are your familiars?'

'Familiars! You think I'm a witch?'

'Are you?'

'But of course I am!' Suddenly she was all bright and sparkly like a celebrity on a television chat show. 'I'm Estonian, you know. My grandmother taught me how to tie the winds up in a knotted handkerchief and let them out when needed.' There was a tremendous flash of lightning followed immediately by a clap of thunder that rattled the windows. The rain was beating down harder than ever. 'You hear that?' she said. 'I called up this storm as a welcome for you. Ask Charlie about the times we've been to the Sabbath.'

'Viki has changed my life,' said Charlie. 'Working with her has opened the doors of perception for me. She's taken me so far beyond the little mind-tricks of the written word.' As well as writing poetry Charlie reviewed books, ran a fiction workshop, wrote radio and film scripts, and in general did whatever would pay the bills. His wife Cindy, busy in Viki's kitchen as we spoke, was a schoolteacher. They had no children.

In the other room there were one chair and a mattress on the floor and a coffee table on which were set out hummus, olives, several kinds of cheese, bean salad, and Italian bread. I'd brought some wine and there'd been a little interval of hospitality before the viewing of the paintings.

'I borrowed the table and the chair and the dishes,' said Viki with great glee. 'My house has nothing in it but emptiness and mantrises.'

'And all that wind from your grandmother,' I said.

Charlie and Cindy didn't seem to belong in the same story with Viki. Charlie was tall and bony with round spectacles and a clean-shaven American Gothic face. He had a soft California way of speaking and reading his poems. Cindy was also American, very ample and comfortable-looking. She seemed quite happy about Viki's opening of the doors of perception for Charlie. I wondered when and how Viki had entered their lives and their economy.

'What Charlie and I have,' said Viki while Cindy carried on with her kitchen duties, 'is a marriage of true minds. We live among the animals of the spirit and they speak to us.'

'They teach us how to be with them and with each other,' said Charlie.

'Show him your black dogs, Charlie,' said Viki. 'Charlie only started painting a few months ago but he's doing marvellous things.'

'For years I've had these black dogs running in my mind,' said Charlie, 'but I never could find the self that could run with them until Viki showed me how.' He modestly took an unstretched canvas from his own small stack of paintings and laid it on the floor. 'In this one,' he said, 'I've tried for the running of the black which comes before the dog and contains it.' The painting, reminiscent of Inuit art, was quite haunting – there *was* the running of the black and it *did* contain the dog with its wild yellow eyes.

'We ran together when he painted this,' said Viki, 'the two of us running on the plains of desolation and the deserts of darkness, running the manyness of the Now of us. It was like nothing else we'd ever known; we feel very lucky to have had that.' She eyed me narrowly. 'You think all this is bullshit, don't you.'

'Never!'

'Pasta's ready,' said Cindy's voice from the kitchen. We went into the other room where we ate some very thick undercooked spaghetti. Then Charlie said, 'I'll do the black dog on the didgeridoo.'

The didgeridoo is a cut-off part of the trunk or branch of a tree that has been hollowed out by white ants, termites. The one Charlie had was from a yellow box-gum and was decorated with aboriginal designs in red and yellow ochre; it was a little less than four feet long and the end that he was blowing into was two inches across. The didgeridoo has no reed, nothing in it but emptiness. It is played by letting the lips vibrate loosely, as in doing a raspberry, while keeping up a steady blowing. For this the cheeks are used as a bagpiper uses the bag, so that air is continually expelled even when the player is breathing in. The sound of the didgeridoo is a peculiarly elemental buzzing and droning, varied by such whooping, barking, or articulation as the player fancies.

Whoever the player, the voice of the didgeridoo is its own ancient self, the voice of limitless space and time, the voice of the continuous undifferentiated moment, the voice of forever and the soul of the white ant.

The deep blue night around us was still crashing with thunder and flashing with lightning and the rain was still beating down wildly as Charlie played the didgeridoo. He gave himself to it and it gave itself to him, buzzing, droning, barking, and howling the long and lonesome black-dog didgeridoos of itself.

'You hear that?' said Viki to me. 'That's the voice you need to listen to. It's the voice of the black running of the manyness of Now and you must open yourself to it.'

'What makes you think I'm not open?'

Her eyes were bright with conviction. 'I've been watching you and I can see that you live in a bubble, you've closed yourself off. You looked *at* my paintings but you held yourself back from entering them. You need to open up, you need to let in the world and the night and all the voices that are waiting to speak and sing to you.'

'Viki,' I said, 'you remind me of those Jehovah's Witnesses who come to my door and presume to instruct me. What in the world makes you think you know anything I don't know?'

All the sureness seemed to go out of her. 'Everyone knows *something* no one else knows,' she faltered. 'I was only offering what I've struggled very long and hard to learn.'

'Lots of us have struggled long and hard and perhaps learned something but we don't talk about it endlessly.'

Her face crumpled and became very red and even more shiny. 'All right then, I promise not to say anything more.'

'Thank you,' I said, feeling an utter monster as she huddled herself together and became very small.

'The rain has stopped,' said Cindy. We got about five minutes of conversation out of that, then I phoned for a taxi, thanked Viki for her hospitality, said my goodbyes, and was out of there.

I enjoy airports; I move through them as a phantom with an American Express Card. In the act of packing I had already become the person who had been here and now was gone, and by the time I checked in at Sydney International I was well on the way to London. I bought earrings for my wife, T-shirts for our sons, and a didgeridoo with a tape and book of instructions at a shop called *The Rainbow Serpent*. Then I hummed and shuddered, taxied down the runway, roared into the air, watched the safety demonstration, drank mineral water, and received

CRUMBED PERCH *with* TARTARE SAUCE
HAZELNUT BAVAROIS *with* CARAMEL
CHEESE *and* CRACKERS
COFFEE   TEA

which, upon being uncovered, revealed itself as

SOMETHING YOU EAT ON A PLANE

Flying time from Sydney to Bangkok was about nine hours with an hour and a half stopover in Bangkok. I stayed on the plane, savouring the in-betweenness of this part of my life.

Once more aloft I enjoyed my second meal of SOMETHING YOU EAT ON A PLANE, chose not to watch a film called *Something You Watch on a Plane*, read two or three short stories by Naguib Mahfouz, brought my diary up to date, and didn't think very much about anything. We did Bangkok to London in less than twelve hours with the help of a tailwind, approaching Heathrow in good order as thousands of square metres of rumpled pillows and blankets, eyeshades, all kinds of rubbish, messy toilets, and heads and feet dangling in the aisles. Alerted by the captain, we pulled ourselves together, attempted to make the blood flow once more through our bodies, and manifested ourselves as ambulatory arrivals filing off the plane. Once home I embraced my family, rejoined my desk, ate dinner at breakfast time, and prepared to sleep for two or three days.

That was when the singing began, the singing of Aznul Hazakh and her sister priestesses. Oh the desolation of it, the tiny sharp mantra of it far away and close, singing in the blood its words that I am always just on the point of understanding when I wake – if indeed I ever was asleep – and begin again. I'm not sure whether it's the waking or the sleeping when they sing but I don't think there's much sleeping and I always have to begin again. So great and commanding she is, Aznul Hazakh. So great and green, with her little sharp human face singing her want and her need, singing her mantra that I must obey with my soul and my body, my body of a small brown male mantis. Ah, the thrill as she clasps me to her and I penetrate her and my seed goes into her, yes, yes, yes as she bites my head off and consumes me. It's always very quick, the mating and the death. Then I wake or sleep, whichever, and the singing begins again.

I don't know what prices Viki's asking these days but I don't think I can afford not to buy a painting. Or perhaps several.

Political Economy

MARGARET HORNER

I ASKED THE old man why he called his bitch Malthusa.

At first, he replied, I gave her no name at all. She answered to commands such as 'sit' or 'down'. I am more or less nameless myself. I long ago stopped being aware of my name. This is because I have no occasion to use it. I have no part in society. I earn nothing and spend nothing. I pay no taxes and receive no benefits. I have no address. If I have a National Insurance number I do not know what it is. Nor does anybody else. When in hard weather I go to night shelters I'm not asked for a name. I'm addressed as 'old chap' or 'my friend' or 'brother'. Young workers from the Charity Action Group sometimes call me 'sir'. So I had no thought of naming the bitch. She understands words and whistles.

How did she come to be called Malthusa?

I am an educated man. Not highly educated. No college or university. But good schooling. I was well taught. I read heavy books. Before I had the bitch I spent time in public libraries, partly for the shelter, as many of my kind do, but mainly for the reading. The library assistants were not always sympathetic to my presence, but they had to put up with it because I was a genuine reader. I read mostly books on history and political economy. But once I took up with the bitch this reading had to end. I could not take her into the library and she would not agree to be left outside. I tried tying her to a lamp-post a couple of times, but her howls were heart-rending. She drew a crowd. Cruelty, I was accused of. The police called me out to attend to her. There ended my use of public libraries.

You must regret having adopted the animal?

No, I don't regret it. I had no choice. In this homeless world homeless dogs attach themselves where they can. At first I resisted. I was determined that I would not make myself responsible for another creature beside myself. It's a painful business, being homeless, and I felt that an animal's pain would double my own. The most painful sight I know is the anguish in the eyes of dogs who have attached themselves to vagrant alcoholics. They get beaten and kicked and slashed with broken bottles. But still they stay with the hand that feeds them, even though the food is meagre and filthy.

For many years when strays approached me I would not yield an inch. I spared not a mouthful, spoke not a word, never extended so much as a friendly finger. But this little bitch took advantage of me while I slept. Before I even set eyes on her she had shared my warmth for several hours one January night. I woke to find her snug in the small of my back, as the wind drove the snow along the pavement. She had nosed her way between my body and the shop-window, under cover of my blanket and my plastic sheet.

I see. So it was the bitch who adopted you.

She joined me in my refuge. My doorway. That doorway has been my home for almost two years. It's one of the best entrances in this part of London. To doss down in, I mean. Such accommodation is keenly competed for by those of us who can't be comfortable in hostels. I tried to get used to hostels, but I failed. There's no freedom in a hostel. No freedom and no privacy. Also, many of them charge money. I never have money because I cannot beg. And I don't apply for benefit. I gave up applying for benefit a long time ago. The clerks in the Benefit Offices could never find any clause in their regulations which would justify them in giving me money. So I stopped attending their offices and made up my mind to rely on charity.

Not begging. Charity. I rely on the volunteers who come out every night, when the streets are quiet, to supply our needs. They do this without interrogation or criticism. They vie with each other to be of use to us. We seem to confer a benefit on them by being there to be helped. They set up their canteens under bridges and flyovers and in the crypts of churches. They lure us in to be fed and clothed. Soup. Sandwiches. Boots. Plastic sheeting. Foam rubber strips for mattresses. Tea. Cigarettes. No alcohol, of course. And no money. I live very well on all this.

So you awoke to find the bitch beneath your blanket?

I did. And she was pleased with her accommodation. As I have said, that doorway is my chosen home. I had my eye on it for many months before I took possession. The entrance is deep and narrow, with room only for one sleeper, but the door is set well back from the pavement. This enables me to stretch my full length and still keep dry. A woman had the place before me. I made no attempt to get her out. But I kept it in view. One morning I found her dead. As soon as she was taken away I made the entrance my home. I was there that evening an hour before the shopkeeper locked up. I stared down all other claimants.

This was before you had the bitch?

Many months before. But when she joined her life to mine she took my doorway as her territory. And she is a terrier bitch. Her bite is as good as her bark. I could not foresee that first morning how useful she would be. All I knew was that I could not drive her away. She felt warm and soft in the small of my back. So I let her stay while I began my daily routine. I always begin by freshening my mouth, so I took a screw of salt from my pocket – I provide myself with this from the evening soup-kitchen – and rubbed my teeth with a salted finger. Then I took a swig from my water-bottle, rinsed and spat. The bitch watched this with deep interest.

From that time my every action has been an object of interest to her. Nobody, not even my mother, ever favoured me with such attention as I receive unceasingly from Malthusa. But of course it has not been easy to fit her into my

economy. To live on the street with dignity it is necessary to
be an economist. Nothing can be wasted. Time, energy, food,
water, boot-leather, string, matches, sunshine – all must be
made the most of. Most of all, I make the most of sleep. Sleep
comes uneasily, in the early hours of the morning, when the
shouting and fighting and wailing stop and the police cars
return to base. Once asleep, I hope to stay asleep until the
caretaker arrives to open the shop. But this is seldom possible.
My bladder wakes me. I make it a rule never to soil my clothes
or bedding. So many street-dwellers are careless in this way.
However hard the weather, when I need to pass water I get up.
I freshen my mouth, comb my hair and beard, roll up my
bedding and make for the public convenience. On that first
morning the bitch followed me, head down, tail up, keen to be
on the move. But the snow and wind were hard on us.

*I can quite see that fending for an animal would strain your
resources.*

I thought at first it would. I was anxious about it. I feed
myself once a day, in the evening, after nine o'clock, when the
Homeless Action van arrives. I know exactly what I need for a
day's subsistence, I ask for it and they give me what I ask for. A
cup of soup, a packet of meat sandwiches, two biscuits and a
cigarette. I never take more than that, because of the problem
of excretion. The calls of nature are a great inconvenience to
the unhoused. To make my way in a hurry to a public
lavatory, to find it occupied, to join a queue, to see the distaste
aroused in other users by my appearance, all that is bad
enough. But then the real obstacles arise, the layers of clothing
to be removed, two coats, two pairs of trousers, long-johns,
underpants, the elastic body-belt provided for my hernia, all
that undressing to release a few turds into a pan. This can't be
undertaken more than once a week. So I restrict my intake.
The doctor at the Social Care unit gives me vitamins when I
see him for attention to my truss. I drink no alcohol, tea or
coffee. All those stimulate the bladder. I drink water from
standpipes. And soup, of course.

Tell me how you feed Malthusa.

Dogs like to scavenge, as you know. She likes to scavenge.

But I stopped her. I could not take the risk of her eating anything foul. A healthy animal I can cope with, but a sick one would be too much to manage. There is no free veterinary clinic in this area. The nearest is six miles away, in the Old Kent Road. To get there costs more than I can spare in energy and boot-leather. So I have to keep the bitch healthy. I leave her in the entrance, keeping watch over my bedding, while I scavenge for her myself.

Yourself!

Yes indeed. I scavenge for her in the backyards of hotels. I get her food from dustbins and pigswill. I found a small plastic bowl, thrown out for being discoloured, and I fill this with waste suitable for a terrier. No bones or pastry or sweet stuff. But stale bread as long as it's not mouldy, pickings of meat from poultry carcases, fat and gristle scraped from plates, meat from stale sandwiches. I rinse all this under a yard tap to get rid of cigarette ash and other contamination. I feed her this at night, when we settle to rest. In the morning I fill her bowl with water at the lavatory. She drinks once a day, feeds once at night. She keeps well. But then, of course, I have to consider her hygiene. I have taught her not to crap on pavements. She is a co-operative creature and soon learnt to contain herself until we reach the graveyard of a deconsecrated church. Every day she leaves her excrement in the long grass of forgotten graves. This is the least possible nuisance. But fleas are a trouble to us. They breed behind her ears and at the base of her tail. I hunt them relentlessly with my fingers. I sometimes spend a whole summer afternoon tracking one flea through the thickness of her coat. Lice are easier, they do not jump. Neither Malthusa nor I are verminous.

Why Malthusa? I must know the reason for her name.

She is named, of course, after the great political economist. I read *An Essay on the Principle of Population* shortly before I lost my home. It was an anxious, stressful time and my state of mind was such as to be deeply impressed by hopeless truth, or true hopelessness. Greed and sexual activity bring disease and death. That was Malthus's teaching. I am glad that I am not guilty either of greed or sexual activity.

But I had not reckoned with the sexual activity of my companion. Six months ago I saw that she was distended. At first I thought that I had overfed her, so I gave her less, but the distension grew. The truth became apparent to me one cold sunrise. An annunciation! (I was born a Catholic.) I knew that I must expect a litter. Blind, hungry mouths. Tender, helpless flesh. She must have gone whoring while I slept. I was appalled. What sort of nursery could I provide, living as I do? The mother herself would provide the milk, but so much more would be needed. Shelter, warmth. A future for each pup. How do human parents face these demands? Home, security, peace, love, how can such needs be met? But the bitch was calm. She ate and drank and groomed herself.

The idea occurred to me that I could kill the pups. Drown them. Smother them. Crush their skulls with my boot. But I knew I could never do such things. I remove worms and slugs from tarmac to save them from motor tyres. I release trapped flies and wasps. I cannot kill or leave to be killed. If I could kill anything I would kill myself. To do that would be easier than to kill my bitch's pups. My heart broke to think of the world into which they were to be born.

I understand. Procreation, subsistence, living space. Malthus was concerned with these themes. And with the regulation of sexual activity.

My poor bitch had no way of regulating the activity of the curs who mounted her. Or of regulating her own desires. A few moments of instinctual pleasure and her nature was trapped! It remained for me to solve the problem by the exercise of human intelligence. I was distraught. As I carried on patiently with our routine, as I disciplined myself and the bitch to my rigid and rational economy, I worried ceaselessly about the coming confinement. I was ashamed of my helplessness. In the event, it was the mother herself who solved the problem.

How did she do that?

She ate the puppies. They were born at night. The street was silent. She was bedded down beside me. She began to lick her genitals. She was anxious but composed. After half an hour the first pup was born. I felt beaten down with dread and despair. She licked the pup. It squeaked. After a minute it stopped squeaking. The mother chewed and gulped. I struck a match and looked. The infant was gone. Nothing left but tail and blood. Six pups were born, all the size of my thumb. All were devoured. Finally their mother cleaned herself. Then she cleaned my blanket of the blood and slime. Then she slept.

Naturally.

My gratitude and relief were intense, almost amounting to happiness. The next few days were spent in a mood of deep content. But I knew that this could not last. Animal nature would assert itself again. The bitch was young. Litter after litter would be born to me and the mother could not be expected to eat them all. As spring drew on to summer and days grew warmer and longer, I realised that the danger was approaching. Dogs sniffed Malthusa. She would soon be ready again. I wished her dead, and myself with her, but as this was a wish unlikely to be granted I turned despair to resolution. I resolved to use human intelligence to counter the brutishness of the natural world. To put the matter plainly, I resolved to walk to the free veterinary clinic in the Old Kent Road.

Absolutely the right decision!

I made up my mind to ask them to spay her, to plead with them to do so, if necessary to force them to do so by threatening to injure myself, or by whatever means of coercion I could devise. For I had no idea at all that as a charity, they would not only be pleased to spay Malthusa, but as determined to do it as I was to get it done. It seemed quite possible to me that I and my bitch might walk all the way to the clinic, 12 miles there and back, and be turned away. So I felt distressed as we set off, undertaking so much with so little hope of satisfaction.

You didn't ask for help? Not even for the bus fare?

I did not. I never ask for help. I value my independence. Food and clothing and bedding I have to ask for. But nothing else. Besides, we would not have been allowed to board a bus. No dogs. No vagrants. No option but to walk. I made her a leash out of soft cord and we set off in the early morning. To go beyond our own territory was an ordeal to us both. I am as attached to my home ground as others are to their homes. The bitch also. As we entered strange streets, heard strange noises, smelt strange smells, she tucked in her tail and her eyes grew anxious. As for me, I felt alien to myself. But we pressed on, burdened by my bedding slung over my shoulder, and by the extra food I had asked for the previous evening, not knowing how soon we could return. The journey took five hours. I carried the bitch through the worst of the traffic. Her legs are short, as you can see. We arrived in the afternoon. The veterinary nurse was pleased to be of use, and the surgeon was available within the hour. The operation was performed. But I was dismayed to hear that Malthusa was to be kept at the clinic for 48 hours! To be nursed.

I was happy to think of the care being taken of her, but how was I to get through two days and nights so far from all that I was used to and comfortable with? My doorway would be taken over within an hour of my being missed. It would be assumed that I was dead. All the same, I had no thought of leaving Malthusa. When the clinic was closed for the night I settled myself in its doorway. I made my bed there and ate one of my sandwiches. From time to time I whistled, in the hope that she could hear me. The second night was spent in the same way. I slept very little, ate the second sandwich, drank from the fountain in the forecourt of a Temperance Hall, and so got through the time. On the third morning Malthusa was released.

How was she?

Weak. I had to carry her the many miles back. But as we reached our own territory she recovered her strength. It was early evening when we reached home. The shop was closed. As I feared, our place had been taken. I turned away to leave it to its new possessor. There is no law securing the tenure of doorways. But Malthusa's laws were not mine. She set about evicting the squatter. His coat was torn and his leg was bleeding as he made off down the street. I put down my bundle and left her to guard it while I went for our food. That night we ate well and slept well. Our lives have been pleasant since.

I thanked the old man for his story. I said that I found it instructive. He was pleased. To give an account of himself, to be understood, to have his story valued, these things perhaps made him feel at home.

North of Nowhere

JANETTE TURNER HOSPITAL

THEY ARE CURIOUS people, Beth thinks, though it is easy to
like them. They consider it natural to be liked, so natural that
you can feel the suck of their expectations when they push
open the door to the reception room and come in off the
esplanade. Their walk is different too; loose, somehow; as
though they have teflon joints. Smile propulsion, Dr Foley
whispers, giving her a quick wink, and Beth presses her lips
together, embarrassed, because it's true: they do seem to float
on goodwill, the way hydrofoil ferries glide out to the coral
cays on cushions of air. Friendliness spills out of them and
splashes you. Beth likes this, but it makes her slightly uneasy
too. It is difficult to believe in such unremitting good cheer.

Of all the curious things about them, however, the very
oddest is this: they wear their teeth the way Aussie diggers
wear medals on Anzac Day. They flash them, they polish
them, they will talk about them at the drop of a hat.

'Got this baby after a college football game,' Lance Harris
says, pointing to a crown on the second bicuspid, upper left.
Lance is here courtesy of Jetabout Adventure Tours and a
dental mishap on the Outer Reef. 'Got a cheekful of quarter-
back cleats, cracked right to the gum, I couldn't talk for a
week. It was, let me see, my junior year, Mississippi State,

those rednecks. Hell of a close fight, but we beat 'em, all that matters, right? Keeps on giving me heck, but hey, worth every orthodontist's dollar, I say.'

Beth never understands the half of it, but in any case, what can you make of people who talk about their teeth? She just smiles and nods, handing Dr Foley instruments, vacuuming spit. American spit is cleaner than Australian spit, that's another interesting difference. Less nicotine, she thinks. No beer in their diets. But Scotch is yellowish too, wouldn't that . . .? and certainly the boats that go beyond Michaelmas Cay for marlin are as full of Johnny Walker as of American tourists with dreams. Champagne too. She's seen them onloading crates at the wharf. She imagines Lance's wife, camcorder in hand, schlurping up into her videotape Lance's blue marlin and his crisp summer cottons and the splash of yellow champagne and the dazzling teeth, whiter than bleached coral. How do they get them so white? Here I go, she thinks, rolling up her eyes for nobody's benefit but her own. Here I go, *thinking* about teeth. What a subject.

She wonders, just the same, about amber spit and clear spit. Is it a national trait?

'Australians don't floss,' Lance mumbles, clamp in mouth, through a break in the roadwork on his molars.

Beth's hand flies to her lips. Has she done it again, blurted thought into the room? Possibly. She's been jumpy, that's why; ever since the dreams began again, the dreams of Giddie turning up. Or maybe she just imagined Lance spoke. Maybe she gave him the words. Her head is so cluttered with dialogue that bits of it leak out if she isn't careful.

'It astonishes me, the lack of dental hygiene hereabouts,' Lance says. 'We notice it with the hotel maids and the tourist guides, you know. As a dentist, it must break your heart.'

'Oh, we manage,' Dr Foley says. He lets the drill rise on its slick retractable cord and winks at Beth from behind his white sleeve. She lowers her eyes, expressionless, moving the vacuum hose, schlooping up the clear American words.

'You see this one?' Lance mumbles, pointing to an incisor. 'Thought I'd lost this baby once, I could barely . . .' but the

71

polished steel scraper gently pushes his consonants aside and only a stream of long shapeless untranslatable vowels grunt their way into the vacuum tube.

If we put all the tooth stories end to end, Beth thinks, we could have a twelve volume set. Oral history, Dr Foley calls it, laughing and laughing in his curious silent way at the end of a day, the last patient gone. Every American incisor and canine has its chronicle, lovingly kept, he maintains, laughing again. Many things amuse him. Beth can't quite figure him out. She loves the curious things he says, the way he says them. She loves his voice. It's the way people sound when they first come north from Brisbane or Sydney. He seems to her like someone who became a dentist by accident.

As he cranks down the chair, he murmurs: 'The Annals of Dentition, we're keeping a chapter for you, Lance.'

'I'm mightily obliged to you, Doctor, mightily obliged. Fitting me in at such short notice.' Lance shakes the dentist's hand energetically. 'And to you too, young lady.' He peers at the badge on Beth's uniform. 'Beth,' he reads. 'Well, Miss Elizabeth, I'm grateful to you, ma'am. I surely am.'

'It's not Elizabeth,' she says. 'It's short for Bethesda.'

'And a very fine city Bethesda is, yes ma'am, State of Maryland. I've been there once or twice. Now how did you come by a name like that?'

'The tooth fairy brought it,' Beth says.

Dr Foley's eyebrows swoop up like exuberant gulls, then settle, solemn. Lance laughs and, a little warily, pats Beth on the shoulder.

'Well, Lance,' the dentist says in his professional voice. 'Fight the good fight. Floss on. Mrs Wilkinson will handle the billing arrangements for you.' He ushers the American out, closes the door, and leans against it. 'Don't miss our thrilling first volume,' he says to Beth, madly flexing his acrobatic brows. His tone has gone plummy, mock epic, and she can hear his silent laughter pressed down underneath. 'Wars of the Molars. Send just $19.95 and a small shipping and handling charge to Esplanade Dental Clinic, Cairns – '

'Ssh,' she giggles. 'He'll hear.'

'No worries. Now if Mrs *Wilkinson* hears me – '

'She might make you stand in the corner.'

'You're a funny little thing,' he says, leaning against the door, watching her, as though he's finally reached a judgment now that she's been working a month. 'How old are you?'

'Eighteen,' she says, defensive. 'It's on my application.'

'Oh, I never pay attention.' He brushes forms aside with one hand. 'I go by the eyes in the interview.' Beth feels something tight and sudden in her chest, with heat branching out from it, spreading. 'You can *see* intelligence. And I look for a certain liveliness. You haven't been in Cairns long, I seem to remember.'

'No.'

'Just finished high school, I've forgotten where.'

'Mossman.'

'Hmm. Mossman. No jobs in Mossman, I suppose.'

'No,' she admits. 'Everyone comes down to Cairns.'

'Does your father cut cane?'

He might have winded her.

'Well,' he says quickly, into the silence, 'none of my – '

'My father *raises* Cain,' she says tartly.

His eyebrows dart up again, amused, and spontaneously he reaches up to touch her cheek. It's a fleeting innocent gesture, the sort of thing a pleased schoolteacher might do, but Beth can hardly bear it. She turns to the steriliser and readies the instruments, inserting them one by one with tongs. 'Sorry,' he says. 'It's not funny at all, I suppose. And none of my business.'

She shrugs.

'I didn't realise Beth was short for Bethesda,' he says.

'It's from the bible. Mum gave us bible names.'

'It's rather stylish.'

'Thanks.'

'I'm pleased with your work, you know.'

'Thank you.' She fills the room with a shush of steam.

'Listen,' he says, 'after I close the surgery, I always stop for a drink or two at the Pink Flamingo before I go home. You want to join me?'

'Uh . . .' She feels dizzy with panic. Anyway, impossible. She'd miss dinner. 'Uh, no thanks, I can't. Dinner's at six. We're not allowed to miss.' She keeps her back to him, fussing with the temperature setting.

'Not *allowed*?'

'At the hostel.'

'Oh, I see,' he says doubtfully. 'Well, I'll drop you home then.'

God, that's the last thing she wants. 'No. No, really, that'd be silly. It's way out of your way, and the bus goes right past.'

'You're a funny little thing, Bethesda,' he says, but she's reaching into the steriliser with the tongs, her face full of steam.

'Girls,' matron says from the head of the table. 'Let us give thanks.'

Beth imagines the flap flap flap of those messages which will not be spoken winging upwards from matron's scrunched-shut eyes. Thank you, O Lord, for mournful meals. Thank you for discipline, our moral starch, so desirable in the building of character. Thank you for stiff upper lips. Thank you for the absence of irritating laughter and chatter at the table of St Margaret's Hostel for Country Girls. Thank you that these twenty young women, sent to Cairns from Woop-Woop and from God Knows Where, provide me with a reasonable income through government grants; in the name of derelict fathers, violent sons, unholy spirits, amen; and also through the urgings of social workers and absurdly hopeful outback schools. Thank you that these green and government-sponsored girls, all of them between the dangerous and sinward-leaning ages of 16 and 24, are safely back under my watchful eye and curfew, another day of no scandal, no police inquiries, no trouble, thanks be to God.

'We are grateful, O Lord,' matron says, 'for your abiding goodness to us, and for this meal. Amen.'

And the twenty young women lift grateful knives and forks. Beth, hungry, keeps her eyes lowered and catalogues sounds. That is finicky Peggy, that metal scrape of the fork imposing grids and priorities. Peggy eats potato first, meat second, carrots last. Between a soft lump of overcooked what? – turnip, probably – and some gristle, Beth notes the muffled *flpp flpp* of gravy stirred into cumulus mashed clouds, that is Liz, who has been sent down from the Tablelands to finish school at Cairns High. Liz's father is a tobacco picker somewhere near Mareeba, and Liz, for a range of black market fees, can supply roll-your-owns of head-spinning strength. That ghastly open-mouthed chomping is Sue, barely civilised, who has only been here a week, dragged in by a district nurse who left her in matron's office. Where's this bedraggled kitten from then? matron asked, holding it at arm's length. From Cooktown, the district nurse said. Flown down to us. You wouldn't believe what we deal with up there. North of nowhere, believe me. In every sense.

'Inbreeding,' Peggy sends the whisper along. 'Like rabbits. Like cane toads, north of the Daintree. If this one's not a sample, Bob's your uncle. Whad'ya reckon?'

What does Beth reckon, between a nub of carrot and a gluey clump of something best not thought about? She reckons that this, whisper whisper, is the sound of matron's own stockinged thighs as matron exits, kitchen-bound.

'Oh Christ, look at Sue,' Peggy hisses. 'Gonna cry in her stew.'

A sibilant murmur circles the table like a breeze flattening grass – *Sook, sook, sook, sook!* – barely audible, crescendo, descrescendo, four-four time, nobody starts it, nobody stops. Stop it! Beth pleads inwardly. Malice, a dew of it, hangs in the air. *Sue wants her Daddy.* Nudge, nudge. *Maybe she does it with her brother.*

'Leave her alone,' Beth says.

Peggy makes a sign with her finger. 'Well, fuck you, Miss Tooth Fairy Queen.'

'Girls,' matron says. 'Jam pudding and custard for those who leave clean plates.'

January presses hotly and heavily on the wide veranda. Beth, in cotton shorty and nothing else, lies on the damp sheet and stares through the mosquito net at a tarantula. How do they squat on the ceiling like that? If it falls, it will fall on Peggy's net. *Please fall*, Beth instructs it. She beams her thoughts along the road of moonlight that runs straight from the louvres to the eight hairy legs.

Night after night, the tarantula will show up in exactly the same spot, but is gone by day. There's another. It has been camped below the louvres, opposite Corey's bed, for six nights. Then suddenly both of them will pick new stations. Or maybe they change shifts. Maybe there are hordes of tarantulas waiting their turn in the crawlspace below the verandas. What do they see from the ceiling? Ten bunks on the east veranda, ten on the west. Do they sidle in through the glass louvres that enclose the verandas? The louvres are always slanted open to entice sea breezes. Is that how the spiders get in? And where do they hide by day?

No one worries about them. Or perhaps, Beth thinks, no one admits to worrying about them, though everyone takes note of where they are before the lights go out. As long as she can still see, by squinting, the filaments of spiky hair on the spider's legs, Beth can stop the tide from coming in. She can keep back the wave that has her name on it.

Beyond the spider, beyond the louvres, she can see the tired palms that bead the beaches together, filing south and south and south to Brisbane, reaching frond by frond by a trillion fronds north to Cape York. She can hear the Pacific licking its way across the mangrove swamps and mud flats, though the tide is far out. God, it's hot. She reaches to her right and yanks at the mosquito net, tucked under the mattress, and lifts it to let in some air. Uhh . . . bite! Bite, bite, bite. God, they're fast little blighters, noisy too, that high pitched hum, it could drive you crazy in five minutes flat. She hastily tucks the net in again and swats at the stings. Greedy bloated little buggers. By moonlight, she examines the splats of blood on forearm and thigh.

'Who's making all the fucking noise?' complains someone, drowsy.

'Can mosquitoes spread AIDS?' Beth asks.

'Ahh, shuddup 'n go to sleep, why don't ya?'

But if dentists can . . . ? Beth wonders. She is fighting sleep, she is fighting the wave coming in.

She fans her limp body with her cotton nightie, lifting it away from herself, flapping air up to the wet crease beneath her breasts. There is no comfort. The tide is coming in now.

Every night the tide comes in. It seems to well up from her ankles. She feels this leaden heaviness in her calves, her thighs, her belly, her chest, it just keeps rising and rising, this terrible sadness, this sobbing, it can't be stopped, it bubbles up into her throat, it is going to choke her, drown her, she has to stuff the sheet in her mouth to shut it up.

Then she goes under the wave and sleeps.

Black water. Down and down and down.

Beneath the black water, beneath the wave, in a turquoise place, the pink flamingos swim. Their breath is fragrant, like frangipani, and when Beth vacuums the bright pink ribbons of their spit, *pouff*, tables appear, and waitresses in halter tops and gold lamé shorts. This way, the waitresses say, and Beth follows, though the sandy path between the tables twists and turns. There are detours around branching coral, opal blue. Here and there, clamshells lurk with gaping jaws. At every intersection, the bright angelfish dart and confuse.

'Where is he?' Beth calls, and the waitresses turn back, and beckon, and wink. 'Is he waiting for me? Is he still here?'

The waitresses smile. 'He is always just out of reach,' they murmur. 'See? Can you see?' The waitresses point. And there he is beyond a forest of seaweed, fiery red. He sips a piña colada that wears a little purple paper parasol like a hat, but when she fights her way through the thicket of seaweed, he's disappeared.

'Terribly sorry,' the waitresses say, winking, 'but he'll be right back. Dental emergency. Floss on, he says, and he'll join you as soon as he can. He really likes your work. He really really likes you, you know.'

And all the waitresses line up and link arms and kick up their legs in a can-can dance. He really really really really likes you, they sing, but they roll their eyes to show it's just a sick joke and then she sees that the waitresses are Peggy and Liz and Corey and matron herself and she throws the piña colada at them and they disappear.

But their laughter stays behind them like the guffaw of a Cheshire cat. *Sook sook sook*, it splutters, hissing about Beth's ears. *We can hear you crying in your sleep*.

No, Beth protests. *Never!* Never ever.

Nevermore, the waitresses sing, offstage. *He's gone for good*.

No, Beth argues. *That isn't true*.

And see, he's coming back, he is, she can't mistake his coat, there it is, yes, white against the brilliant coral, starch against sea-hair flame, but she won't turn her head, she's not going to make a fool of herself, she pretends not to see. She wants to be surprised. She wants to feel a light touch on her cheek and then she will turn and then . . .

And then? And then?

The dream falters. The water turns opaque with thrashing sand. Shark, perhaps? The pink flamingos avert their eyes. There is something they know, it's no use pretending, the suck of the sobbing wave is pulling across the dimpled ocean floor. But still he taps her lightly on the arm. 'It's all right,' he says. 'You're such a funny little thing, Bethesda.'

And so she turns. But it isn't him, it's Giddie.

'Oh Giddie,' she says, resigned. 'I might have known.'

'G'day, Beth.' It's his lopsided grin, all right, and his bear hug, which haven't changed. It's the same old dance. Will you, won't you, will you, won't you? the waitresses sing. We're back again, he's back again, all together now, the old refrain. 'C'mon,' Giddie says, pulling her, and the waitresses twirl. Will you, won't you, will you, won't you, *won't* you join the dance? 'C'mon,' Giddie says, and now they're swimsliding down and around, it's a spindrift sundance ragtime jig, it's the same old tune going nowhere. Shark time, dark time, lip of hell; they are going, going, gone. 'C'mon,' he says, and it's the edge of nothing, the funnel, the whirlpool, he's gone over, he's pulling her down.

'No!' she screams, struggling. 'No! Let me go, Gideon, let me go!'

But he won't let go and she's falling, plummeting, there's no bottom to this, it's forever and ever, amen, though she makes a last convulsive grab at the watery sides – *Gid-ee-oooooon!* – and crash lands on her bed.

She gulps air, trembling, the sheet stuffed into her mouth.

Heedless, the sobbing wave rushes on, noisy, shaming, a disgusting snuffling whimpering sound, the sound of a *sook*.

No, wait. Wait. It's not Beth's wave. It's not Beth.

She listens.

Sue, she thinks.

She must warn Sue: keep the sheet in your mouth. They don't forgive, they're like the fish on the reef. Remember this: the smell of injury brings on a feeding frenzy. They go for blood. You have to keep the sheet in your mouth.

'What are you reading?' he asks, and Beth startles violently. 'Hey,' he says. 'Sorry. What a jumpy little thing you are, Bethesda.' He sits down beside her on the sea wall, the hum of the esplanade traffic behind them, the tide lapping the wall below their feet. 'Is this all you ever do in your lunch hour? Read?'

She says primly: 'I'm watching the tide going out.'

He grins, then offers: 'I've offended you. Would you like me to leave?'

'No,' she says, too quickly. Then, indifferently: 'If you want. It doesn't matter.' She tucks the book into her bag and sets it on the wall between them. 'It's me, I was rude.' She is angry, not with him, but with herself, for the thing that happens in her throat when he says her full name that way. 'You gave me a scare. I didn't think anyone could see me here.' She gestures towards the pandanus clump behind them, the knobbed trunks and spiky leaves rising from a great concrete planter with a brass plate on its rim: *Rotary Club, Cairns District*. She trails her fingers over the engraved letters and says, inconsequentially, 'I used to have to be a waitress at the Rotary dinners in Mossman.' She rolls her eyes. 'Grown-up men, honestly. They sing the stupidest songs.'

'Oh God, I know. They tried to get me to join. One dinner

was enough. They were raffling a frozen chicken and throwing it round the room. Playing catch.'

'In Mossman,' she says, 'they had this mock-wedding. Fund-raising for a playground or something. You should've seen the bride.' She shakes her head, incredulous. 'Mario Carlucci. His father's a cane farmer but Mario's in the ANZ bank, he's the manager already, everyone says his father got it for him because the Carluccis have the biggest account. Anyway, Mario, he's about six-two, and they made this special dress, satin and pearls, with, you know . . .' She gestures with her hands.

'Large mammary inserts,' he says drily.

She laughs. 'Yeah.' She looks at him sideways. 'You seem like you should be an English teacher, not a dentist.'

'What!' he says in mock outrage, his brows working furiously. 'Fie on thee! Out, out, damned spot, you're fired.'

'You're funny.'

'You're pretty funny yourself, Bethesda.' He smiles and she swings her eyes away, nervous. She focuses on the Green Island ferry, in the distance, nosing in towards the wharves.

'Look, Beth,' he says, 'I don't want to pry, but I've been making a few inquiries, and from what I hear, that hostel is pretty awful. I wondered if you'd like me to – '

'It's okay,' she says. 'I don't mind it.'

'And another thing. I've been looking at your application and your references again. God knows, I don't want to lose you at the clinic, but you got a Commonwealth Scholarship, for heaven's sake. Why didn't you take it?'

The ferry is bumping against the pylons now. Men will be wheeling the gangplanks into place. More tourists – people who are free to go anywhere they want, free even to go home again – will disembark and others will board.

'All right,' he says quietly. 'I just want you to know, if you need any help . . . I'm worried about you, that's all.'

'No one needs to worry about me,' she says politely, swinging her legs back over the sea wall in an arc, away from him. 'But Mrs Wilkinson will worry about *you* if we don't get back.'

★

Every Thursday afternoon, last thing, he gives Mrs Wilkinson and Beth their pay envelopes, and every Thursday she saunters along the esplanade, pretending to browse, in the opposite direction to her bus stop until she's three or four blocks from the clinic. Then she crosses over and makes for her spot on the sea wall behind the pandanus palms. She takes the pay envelope out of her bag and opens it. Four crisp fifty-dollar bills, brand new, straight from the bank every time, a miracle that makes her hands shake. She puts them back in the envelope, back in her bag, and takes her bank book out. Its balances, marching forward line by line, entry by entry, shimmer. Already she can see the way the page will look tomorrow morning at the teller's window. She kisses the open book, slips it back in her bag, and hugs the bag to her chest. She can feel a warm buzz against her ribcage.

On Thursday evenings, she feels as though she could walk across the water to the marina. She feels as though she would only need to lift her arms and she would rise, float, up to the decks of the big catamaran, the one that goes to the Outer Reef. And out there on Michaelmas Cay where the seabirds are, where they rise in vast snowy clouds, she would feel the lift of the slipstream, the cushion of air beneath, the upward swoop of it, climbing, climbing, *We are climbing Jacob's ladder* . . .

She is singing the old hymn triumphantly in her head, or maybe belting it out loud – why not? – because here she is, Sunday night in Mossman again, after the minister and his wife have taken her in. Here's the small Sunday night congregation, the ceiling fans turning sluggishly, moths thick around the altar lights, everyone fanning themselves with hymnbooks, singing their hearts out, *Every rung goes higher, higher*, her mother loving every minute of it, one of her mother's favourite hymns, her mother turning and smiling . . . Oh no, wait, this isn't right, she's mixing things up, she shouldn't have thought of this. Wrong track.

She swings her legs over the sea wall and crosses the road and runs all the way to the bus stop, her feet thud thud thudding on the pavement, too noisy for thought. Three people waiting, that's good, and she recognises the woman in the bright pink cotton dress who always catches her bus. She throws herself into bright conversation. 'Thought I'd missed it,' she says. 'We had this little kid this afternoon, an extraction, and it turned out he was a bleeder, you have no idea what a – '

'You *would've* missed it, love,' the woman says, 'except it's running late. I think I see it coming now.'

'You should've heard this kid's mother,' Beth babbles. 'Poor Dr Foley, I thought she was going to – '

'G'day, Beth.' She hears the voice behind her and comes to a dead stop. She hears the voice but she doesn't believe it. Old hymns, her Mum, now this. Someone taps her on the shoulder. 'G'day, Beth.' If I don't turn, she thinks, he'll go away. He isn't really there, he's inside my head.

The bus is pulling into the kerb, and she stares straight forward and gets on. She pays, walks halfway back, and sits down. Someone is following her down the aisle, someone sits down beside her, someone in jeans and white T-shirt and denim jacket, but she won't look, she stares out the window. Her own reflection stares back at her, resigned.

'G'day, Beth. I reckon you're pretty mad with me, hey?'

She sighs heavily. 'How'd you find me, Gideon?'

'Well, you know, I went to Mossman first, natch. And that's how I found out about Mum. Geez, Beth. You should've let me know.'

'And how was I supposed to do that, Giddie?' – given that she hasn't seen him for about two years – 'How was I supposed to know where you were?'

'I dunno,' he says irritably. 'There's ways. For one, you could've told Johnny Coke. It would've got to me. There's links all the way from here to Melbourne, you know. I mean, this is where they bring half the stuff in, for Chrissake, it stands to reason. And the rest of it *grows* up the Daintree. Think about it, Beth. You've always got your head in the bloody clouds.'

She stares out the window, appalled at her own ignorance.

She thinks of all these people, hundreds of them, thousands of them maybe, all hooked, all hooked up to each other, a vast network of arteries and veins and capillaries all bleeding each into each.

'Anyway, the minister says he got you fixed up in this hostel in Cairns, and at the hostel this arvo some grouchy old biddy tells me where you work. So. I plan to be waiting for ya when ya knock off, hugs and kisses, surprise surprise, only nobody's there. Then wham-bam you come racing past me out of nowhere. You mad at me, Beth?'

'Yeah,' she says. 'No. I don't know.' She punches the seat in front of her. 'You stole the money out of Mum's biscuit tin. How could you *do* that to her, Giddie?'

'I didn't *steal* it,' he says, offended. '*Geez*, Beth! I would've paid her back. Geez!' He swivels to look at her better. 'You look pretty good. I hardly recognised you, lipstick and all, and your hair like that. Aren't you gonna give me a hug? Yeah . . . Hey, that's more like it.'

She's smiling in spite of herself. 'Mum always said you could wrap the devil round your little finger, Giddie.'

'Yeah,' he grins. 'She did, didn't she? I went to her grave, Beth, the minister told me where it was. Picked some flowers, an' that.'

She can't speak, and puts her head fleetingly on his shoulder, then straightens up and looks out the window again. There's nothing to see but herself, and beyond that the curl of a breaker coming in, a great fizz of crest turning into foam, a monster wave. She has to get home first, she has to get to the hostel before the wave breaks, she has to lock herself into the loo. 'Hey,' she says brightly, turning. 'So where've you been all this time?'

'Oh, up and down the coast, you know. Brisbane mostly, but.'

'*Brisbane*. You visit Dad?'

'You gotta be kidding,' he says. 'Anyway, I think he's out again. One of me mates got a few weeks in Bogga Road for possession, and he heard Dad got out on good behaviour. That's a laugh, eh? Went out west, Charleville or somewhere, *shearing* is what I heard, can you believe? *Dad?*' He laughs.

'Remember that time he took us fishing on the Daintree?' Beth asks. 'You were 10, I think, and I was 7, yes, that's right, I remember because I had Mrs Kennedy that year, Grade 3, and I wrote a story about it and she read it out to the class and kids told you and you were mad as hell with me. You'd had something on your line and it was pulling like crazy and you wouldn't let go and you went right over the boat. I was screaming because I thought the crocs would get you.'

Gideon frowns. 'I don't remember that,' he says. 'You made that up, Beth. You're always making stuff up.'

She's incensed. 'Dad yanked you back in the boat and walloped you. And you were so mad, you sneaked out that night and stayed at Wally Rover's place just to give Dad a scare. So he'd think you'd run away.'

But it's no use. He can't remember a thing. Gideon's memory is like a little heap of expensive white powder. He bends over it and breathes, and *pouff*, there's nothing but fog.

She stares at her face in the black window. I remember enough for both of us, she thinks.

'I'll tell you something I do remember,' he says suddenly.

'Remember that time Mum made us matching shorts out of *curtains* and we had to wear them to school?'

'Yeah, I remember. We wanted to die.' She smiles and slides her arm through his. 'I miss you, Giddie.'

'Yeah, me too. Listen, Beth, it's great that you've got this job. You couldn't lend me a bit of dosh, could ya? Just enough to get me back to Brissy on the train. I'll pay you back.'

She holds herself very still, then she withdraws her arm. 'Sure,' she says. 'I suppose. How much?'

'Well, I dunno. Fifty should do it.'

She opens her bag and takes out the envelope. 'I'm saving up, Giddie,' she says. 'I'm going to go to Brisbane, go to uni and stuff, and be a teacher.'

'Wow,' he says, but he's looking at the crisp new bills. 'You're doing all right.'

'I bank nearly all of it,' she says. She hands him one of the bills, her eyes following it as though it were a child leaving home. She can feel this pain, this kind of bleating stab, at the edge of one eye. *Knife*, that's what it feels like. Switchblade. When he reaches for the money, palm up, she sees the tracks on his forearm, a dot matrix map. 'Oh Giddie,' she says in a desperate rush, and it's like finding blessed safe words to hold all the blood. 'I hope you use clean needles.' The words feel bottomless. They hold the sadness neatly and nothing spills out.

'What? Oh, yeah, well mostly. Whenever I can.'

She puts the envelope back into her bag and sets it down between them. The black window stares at her, explaining nothing. Gideon begins to fidget in his seat. His ankles, jazz dancers, jiggle violently against hers. The black window says: *Fix it then, Mr Fixit Man.* Beth mouths at the window: *Don't.* Not that it matters. Not that it matters to her.

At the Blue Marlin Shopping Centre, a couple of blocks before her stop, Giddie bounces up like a rocket. 'Hey, this is where I get off. Great seeing you, Beth. Take care of yourself.' He leans down and gives her a kiss on the cheek. He's blinking furiously and his eyes, clear a few minutes ago, are bloodshot.

'Yeah,' she says. 'You too. Take care of yourself, Giddie.' She hangs onto him but he pulls irritably away.

'*C'mon*, Beth, I'll miss me stop.'

She watches his jerky progress to the front of the bus, down the steps, out. She presses her nose to the window to wave, but when the bus moves he's already sprinting across the parking lot, a blur. Unfixed. It isn't until she gets to her own stop that she realises he's taken her bag. She remembers now the way he held his left arm, pressed against his denim jacket, as he stumbled down the bus.

She can feel the wave coming in. It's tidal, a king tide. She stares at the tarantula, the sheet stuffed into her mouth. King tide. There's a watery halo around the tarantula's legs. Sobs are leaking into the room.

She sits up, panicked. So much of the sheet is balled up in her mouth, she's afraid she will gag. But it's Sue again, the next bed to hers. *Damn. I warned her,* Beth thinks, exasperated.

She lifts her mosquito net, slides out, tiptoes to Sue's bed, lifts the net and leans in. She puts her lips against Sue's ear. 'For God's sake, stuff the sheet in your mouth,' she whispers savagely. Her own anxiety is acute. Sue has her hands up over her face, the way Beth's mother used to when her father was drunk. It is always the worst worst thing. '*Stop it*,' she hisses, furious, grabbing Sue's wrists. 'You're *asking* for it, damn it.'

Then she realises Sue's asleep. Sue is flinching and bucking and moaning and crying in her sleep.

Oh God, she thinks. Any second now, someone's going to wake and hear this shit. Show blood and you're dead, that's the rule. Her mind is racing.

Okay, she thinks. Nothing else for it. Swift and efficient, she slides into Sue's bed, jabs the mosquito net back under the mattress, grabs the girl in her arms, and muffles Sue's face between her breasts. 'It's all right,' she murmurs. 'Shh, it's okay, it's okay, everything's going to be all right.' Sue's snuffling sobbing breath is warm against her. With her left hand, she strokes Sue's hair. 'Go to sleep now,' she murmurs. 'Go to sleep. It's all right, baby, it's okay.'

Sue's body shifts slightly, softening, rearranging itself, moving up against Beth's like an infant curling into its mother. Her breathing turns quiet. Beth goes on stroking Sue's hair with one hand, and stuffs the other into her own mouth. At the fleshy place where her thumb joins the palm of her hand, she bites down so hard she tastes blood.

The Master Builder's Wife

LISA JACOBSON

> If you ask, 'Why is Thekla's construction taking such a long time?' the inhabitants continue hoisting sacks, lowering leaded strings, moving long brushes up and down, as they answer, 'So that its destruction cannot begin.'
>
> Italo Calvino, *Invisible Cities*

FIRST, I SHOULD tell you about the house, which was once ordinary enough. It had, as my husband put it, seen better days. When the auctioneer's silver hammer finally fell and the place was ours, he took out his grandfather's pen and signed his name across the creamy sheaf of paper that was the contract. After that, when all the men in their dark suits had departed, we drank champagne and made love in the kitchen on the rough, hard floorboards.

The roof of our house was at this time covered with a tapestry of overgrowth – blackberries, wheat grass, moss. The external walls had been slapped so often by quick coats of paint that even the most recent layer of ivory was already peeling back to reveal earlier colours – apricot, strawberry, aqua, violet. Inside, the walls leant on all angles into themselves, so that none of the doors ever closed properly, and we would wake in the mornings to find great cracks clawing their way over the plaster where the night before there had been none. On top of that, the bathroom was almost unendurable. We were dirtier after we had used it than before. The first time I tried to take a bath there came out of the tap a stream of mud and leaves and tiny unnameable insects. And I was reminded of the princess in the fairy tale who, cursed by a witch, spewed out of her mouth toads and tadpoles every time she tried to speak.

We did not waste an hour or even a minute. We moved into the kitchen as soon as possible. It was the only room not threatening to collapse under the weight of weeds and silt and crumbling rafters. One hundred and twenty-two cardboard boxes lined the hallway, and I had labelled each one so that the material contents of our lives together were as neatly organised as possible into such categories and sub-categories as 'silverware', 'woollen socks', and 'Christmas decorations'. Then we set to work with hundreds of buckets of soap and water. We stirred plaster into a creamy paste, we sank silver nails into the buckled walls. We polished the windows until they disappeared into the clarity of their own surfaces. How our arms ached! At night I would prepare for our supper a little wine, a few boiled eggs, some bread and butter. Then we would lie on the old mattress listening to the sounds of each other's breathing, too tired to talk. Behind us, in the dark, the garden stretched on for miles, and the back fence reached right across the horizon in a thin wooden line.

All of this took place back in the days of the seventy-hour-week, when we had so very few moments to share with each other. After all, the necessary details of life seemed to take up so much time! One stacked up tasks like so much bricks-and-mortar. Even the act of filling up a glass of water and placing it by my husband's bedside table became something which had to be carried out with haste; so precious had the price of a minute become that it assumed the status of an hour, or even a day. Then, you see, my husband was employed as a builder; paid plastic money to build on some bare loamy mound some other person's ordinary dreams. Hallways for the children with their coloured hoops and balls, windows through which the sun blazed like a single yellow eye or the centre of a giant flower. I am sure that some have said we make a curious couple – I, with my careful rounded vowels and he, with a certain roughness in his hands and the corners of his mouth. Yet he never could erect the foundations of cement and wood without seeing in them some far more intricate structure, a palace perhaps, or some sprawling mansion, its roof peaked as a mountain range. He could have been paid in gold and silver coins, or even a paper bill, thin and brown as a leaf, had he been so inclined. The value of such artefacts has soared now that plastic is the common currency. My husband could have been in high demand . . .

He would often bring home for me miniature masterpieces carved from a door handle or window-sill; the hoary head of a lion, a peacock with its tail spread out, and once, a church with turrets, domes and even a bell tower, so tiny I could place it in the palm of my hand! Sometimes, long after everyone else had left the site, he would lean against the new raw wood of a verandah post or an unfilled doorway and wander, trance-like, into the private city of his own ideas. Late at night I would find him there, stiff and cold, with a look of vague surprise in his walnut eyes. But when the new government introduced the fifteen-hour-week and the country was at leisure my husband was the first to go, and it was true that the strain of his occupation was beginning to show. He has worked on building sites for so long that the very extremities of the weather have imprinted themselves upon his body. There are red streaks of sun on his back and arms, and an almost permanent sheen of liquid on his face which might be rain or perspiration. I thought he could do with the rest. I had no idea . . . I am, perhaps, more at ease with leisure, with the hollow hours through which the wind moves like an ocean. He, on the other hand, is not comfortable without his instruments – his battered measuring-rod, still in metric, his ancient levelling pole. The first thing he did with his empty hours was to fill them up.

★

My husband cannot seem to stop building. It is as if the pattern of his working days has been so deeply inscribed into his mind that he cannot help but act them out. No longer must he stand propped against a verandah post dreaming up his imaginary edifices. Now he may build precisely what he wishes. On the first morning after he stopped work I rolled over in our bed and my hand met nothing but the cotton sheets and cold dawn air. Then I saw his dark shape framed for a second by the doorway. He had his overalls on and a hammer in his hand.

Approached from the front, our house is much improved – the paint is a clean, hard white and we coloured the glass in the windows ourselves so that the sky is green as leaves or blood red, depending on which pane you are looking through. If you happened to be walking past and paused, say, while your dog snuffed the grass or your child handed you a chocolate wrapper, you might perhaps see the place as a cottage, as the home of a young couple with no children. We have no children, but that is beside the point. Do not, however, be fooled by first appearances. Our house is no longer what it seems. For a start, it's so much larger than it was. And the back garden, that huge sprawling forest of a garden where once I could wander for hours and not see anything but trees; well, now it's so much smaller. Looking in from the front you'd have no idea. But it is no longer possible, for instance, for me to change my daily clothes for I am unable to find the bedroom closet. Room after room appears – sometimes, it seems, overnight – and often one will take the place of another. I have no idea any more where this house begins or ends.

What was once the laundry is now the lounge room and what was once a bedroom is now a bathroom. I have counted at least twenty-seven separate bathrooms, with their gold and silver, crystal and mahogany taps. Sometimes I am certain that I have walked through the same house twice, only to find a different view out of the windows, for some rooms are completely identical at first sight. But then there will be the slightest change of colour on the walls, from lemon, say, to peach, the almost imperceptible change of pattern on the tiles, from pentagons to hexagons, and I will know that I have moved on. There is an entire wing of nurseries, although, as I have already said, we have no children. And in these rooms everything – the doorways, the built-in wardrobes, the height of the lavatory seats – is scaled down to the size of a child. There are other rooms too, but these ones frighten me; long and narrow as coffins, they are, with all the walls painted black.

Except for our daily breakfast together I often do not see my husband for weeks at a time, though he is no longer at work. We take our breakfast in the old kitchen. It is the only part of the house that is, strangely enough, easy to find and every morning I stumble into it to prepare some kind of meal from the diminishing stocks – tinned tomatoes, spaghetti, chicken soup. On the kitchen wall I mark down each day with the edge of a knife. My husband sits in the yellow chair and eats whatever I put in front of him. I do believe if I were to mix up some dirt with a little water he would eat that too. It may soon come to that. And he will insist upon conducting a normal conversation, as if everything were still the way it once was, as if it were a summer's morning in, say, early February, and he was just about to, any minute now, push his chair out from the table, wipe the bacon fat from his chin, and go off to work. It is impossible to get any sense out of him. 'Is there anything I can do to help you?' I say, meaning the question in several different ways at once. 'The silver could do with a polish,' he says, rustling last month's paper in his dusty hands. 'I cannot find the silver,' I say. 'I cannot find the dining room where the dresser that holds the silver is kept.' 'What do you mean?' says he. 'It's down the hall, where it's always been, first on the right.' But there is no left and right in this house any longer, as I have told you.

What if I were to try and leave here? I have often considered it. But the last time I unbolted a window the air rushed through in such a vertiginous wave that I felt as if I were drowning. Once a bird flew in, just some dun-coloured sparrow, and it took all my energy to chase it about the room. It crashed into the walls, left feathers clinging to the cornices, and splayed its wings up against the green and red glass until at

LISA JACOBSON

last, quietly, carefully, I cupped my two palms over its wings, and felt its heart pound beneath my fingers. Then I opened the window the slightest crack and released it.

I have taken to trailing about with me a long piece of yellow ribbon, like the ones my mother used to tie my sisters and me together at the zoo so we wouldn't get lost. That way I can find my way around, although only yesterday the ribbon caught beneath a doorway and broke, and I lost all sense of direction. North, south, east and west mean nothing in this house any more. Last night, while I lay down to sleep on the floor in a room painted all over with cornflowers, the sun set behind my head; today, it has risen in exactly the same spot. I have a recurring dream in which I tie my yellow ribbon to the leg of an enormous bird the size of a horse. I am outside the house. I am actually outside! There is no fear, no dizziness. The bird soars up above the trees and, suddenly, I am soaring with it. My feet brush the leaves of the tallest oaks. Below me the house sprawls and I can see how it has dug itself deep, deep into the earth. The wooden stumps thrust down through the dust, the soil, like the countless arms of some great wooden beast. Straight through the rock they plunge, and do not stop for breath. But I am thousands of feet above the house, and as long as the cord does not break I am free.

Not long ago (I can no longer be precise about the names of days, the numbers of hours) I discovered a room filled entirely with goldfish. What wonder! The walls in this room were made of glass, double-glazed, and within their narrow confines fish swam like tiny jewelled stars. The sofa, too, was made of clear plastic and there were fish inside it, each with a strip of lightning across its back. Even the crystal vase, the face of the clock and the glass floor were swarming with the things, gold as nuggets and a strong rusted red, like the earth in the centre of this wide country. I lay on the floor with no shoes on my feet and watched them in the water below me. Just like ants they were, making their incomprehensible journeys to and fro in water so clear it seemed they were swimming in air. I have never looked at fish so closely before.

I noticed how the fins on some were eaten away, and how others had several scales missing, so that the skin shone out in a moony silver. I considered my own flesh, I scratched at the dry surface of my forearm so that flakes of skin fell to the floor. I tugged at a fingernail until the crescent of nail itself peeled away. I picked at a loose thread in my shirt, which I have not changed for months now, until the entire sleeve gave way. I began to notice, you might say, the unravelling of things, and the fist of an idea slowly uncurled itself inside me.

I have allowed myself to become the engineer of a plan in which, little by little, I shall take away from this house the most minute amount – say, a single floor tile, a ceramic doorknob, a strip of paint from a bedroom wall – until there is nothing left at all. In fact, I am surprised that I have not thought of it before. I am used to undoing things. As a child, my broad square hands must for some strange reason have signalled the talent of a seamstress to every aunt and uncle in my large family. At Christmas I unwrapped the shiny parcels to find embroidery sets and knitting needles. That's all they ever gave me. They were wrong about my talents, but not about my persistence. For every stitch that I sewed, knitted, or crocheted, I undid another. I was the shy girl sitting cross-legged in the centre of some aunt's drawing room, unpicking a thread of cotton or wool with eternal patience.

The plan that I have engineered swings round and round like some well-greased cog. I like the sound of the word 'engineer'; it brings an oily taste to my lips, and the smart crimson panels of a fire engine or a train. Did you know that you can almost spell the word 'engine' both ways? Forwards and backwards? If you swap the letters 'g' and 'i' around, that is. There is a term for that kind of word, but I cannot recall it now. The plan that I have engineered stops me from sleeping, and it is true that I have been sleeping far too much lately. My dreams slide away from me even before I open my eyes. Their edges are blurred, and all I can recall of them are dark unspecified colours with the texture of an old serge coat. But now I am kept busy day and night.

To begin with, I took the diamond ring from my hand and

made an almost imperceptible crack in the glass wall of the goldfish room. The glass began to emit its drops of water, one at a time, until finally a pool of the stuff had formed, the size of a rose petal, near my right foot. Then I pierced the plastic couch in the goldfish room with the point of a safety pin, so that slowly, slowly, water leaked out of it too. There is no hurry, you see. The speed at which I do these things is not nearly so important as the fact that they are done well. But that is not all. I have also wrenched out all the nails that I can find from the floorboards with a fork from the kitchen cupboard. Later, when I am rested, I shall rip away some of the skirting boards, and that will be enough work for the day. My husband, you see, is a very hard worker. He was never one to break for lunch. But that is what we have in common. And so for every ceiling rose and plasterboard that he puts up, for every strut and prop, lintel and louvre, I will tear one down.

My hands are embossed with cuts and scars. One wound never seems to heal before another one is made. My finger-nails, too, are chipped, and beneath each nail I have a black crescent of dirt which I can never get rid of, no matter how hard I scrub. Amidst the coffee grains and the canned tomatoes my fingernails stand out against the white cotton cloth on the table where we eat. When I passed my husband his plate this morning I left a dark circle, like a bruise, on the white china rim. Meanwhile, the floorboards clank beneath my feet, flakes of plaster stick in my hair. I keep a stack of unhinged doors and broken four-by-twos beneath the beds, behind the sofas, in the cupboards – although the furniture, too, will eventually have to go. The goldfish room must surely be demolished by now. Sometimes I can almost hear the faint tinkle of glass falling into water.

My husband has begun to comment upon my hands. It is the only thing he has noticed about me for what could be months or even years. My husband once had an eye for detail. So I tell him about the garden, though we must have very little garden left, scarcely a patch six feet by five. I tell him that my hands are not used to such hard work, for I must tangle with the thorny stems of roses to make them fat and pink, and plunge my fingers into the rich dark soil so that the daffodils open yellow as butter. I think that he believes me.

Song of Roland

JAMAICA KINCAID

HIS MOUTH WAS like an island in the sea that was his face; I am sure he had ears and nose and eyes and all the rest, but I could see only his mouth, which I knew could do all the things that a mouth usually does, such as eat food, purse in approval or disapproval, smile, twist in thought; inside were his teeth and behind them was his tongue. Why did I see him that way, how did I come to see him that way? It was a mystery to me that he had been alive all along and that I had not known of his existence and I was perfectly fine – I went to sleep at night and I could wake up in the morning and greet the day with indifference if it suited me, I could comb my hair and scratch myself and I was still perfectly fine – and he was alive, sometimes living in a house next to mine, sometimes living in a house far away, and his existence was ordinary and perfect and parallel to mine, but I did not know of it, even though sometimes he was close enough to me for me to notice that he smelt of cargo he had been unloading; he was a stevedore.

His mouth really did look like an island, lying in a twig-brown sea, stretching out from east to west, widest near the centre, with tiny, sharp creases, its colour a shade lighter than that of the twig-brown sea in which it lay, the place where the two lips met disappearing into the pinkest of pinks, and even though I must have held his mouth in mine a thousand times, it was always new to me. He must have smiled at me, though I don't really know, but I don't like to think that I would love someone who hadn't first smiled at me. It had been raining, a heavy downpour, and I took shelter under the gallery of a dry-goods store along with some other people. The rain was an inconvenience, for it was not necessary; there had already been too much of it, and it was no longer only outside, overflowing in the gutters, but inside also, roofs were leaking and then falling in. I was standing under the gallery and had sunk deep within myself, enjoying completely the despair I felt at being myself. I was wearing a dress; I had combed my hair that morning; I had washed myself that morning. I was looking at nothing in particular when I saw his mouth. He was speaking to someone else, but he was looking at me. The someone else he was speaking to was a woman. His mouth then was not like an island at rest in a sea but like a small patch of ground viewed from high above and set in motion by a force not readily seen.

When he saw me looking at him, he opened his mouth wider, and that must have been the smile. I saw then that he had a large gap between his two front teeth, which probably meant that he could not be trusted, but I did not care. My dress was damp, my shoes were wet, my hair was wet, my skin was cold, all around me were people standing in small amounts of water and mud, shivering, but I started to perspire from an effort I wasn't aware I was making; I started to perspire because I felt hot, and I started to perspire because I felt happy. I wore my hair then in two plaits and the ends of them rested just below my collarbone; all the moisture in my hair collected and ran down my two plaits, as if they were two gutters, and the water seeped through my dress just below the collarbone and continued to run down my chest, only stopping at the place where the tips of my breasts met the fabric, revealing, plain as a new print, my nipples. He was looking at me and talking to someone else, and his mouth grew wide and narrow, small and large, and I wanted him to notice me, but there was so much noise: all the people standing in the gallery,

sheltering themselves from the strong rain, had something
they wanted to say, something not about the weather (that
was by now beyond comment) but about their lives, their
disappointments most likely, for joy is so short-lived there
isn't enough time to dwell on its occurrence. The noise, which
started as a hum, grew to a loud din, and the loud din had an
unpleasant taste of metal and vinegar, but I knew his mouth
could take it away if only I could get to it; so I called out my
own name, and I knew he heard me immediately, but he
wouldn't stop speaking to the woman he was talking to, so I
had to call out my name again and again until he stopped, and
by that time my name was like a chain around him, as the sight
of his mouth was like a chain around me. And when our eyes
met, we laughed, because we were happy, but it was
frightening, for that gaze asked everything: who would betray
whom, who would be captive, who would be captor, who
would give and who would take, what would I do. And when
our eyes met and we laughed at the same time, I said, 'I love
you, I love you,' and he said, 'I know.' He did not say it out of
vanity, he did not say it out of conceit, he only said it because it
was true.

His name was Roland. He was not a hero, he did not even have
a country; he was from an island, a small island that was
between a sea and an ocean, and a small island is not a country.
And he did not have a history; he was a small event in
somebody else's history, but he was a man. I could see him
better than he could see himself, and that was because he was
who he was and I was myself but also because I was taller than
he was. He was unpolished, but he carried himself as if he were
precious. His hands were large and thick, and for no reason
that I could see he would spread them out in front of him and
they looked as if they were the missing parts from a powerful
piece of machinery; his legs were straight from hip to knee and
then from the knee they bent at an angle as if he had been at sea
too long or had never learnt to walk properly to begin with.
The hair on his legs was tightly curled as if the hairs were
pieces of thread rolled between the thumb and the forefinger in

preparation for sewing, and so was the hair on his arms, the hair in his underarms, and the hair on his chest; the hair in those places was black and grew sparsely; the hair on his head and the hair between his legs was black and tightly curled also, but it grew in such abundance that it was impossible for me to move my hands through it. Sitting, standing, walking, or lying down, he carried himself as if he were something precious, but not out of vanity, for it was true, he was something precious; yet when he was lying on top of me he looked down at me as if I were the only woman in the world, the only woman he had ever looked at in that way – but that was not true, a man only does that when it is not true. When he first lay on top of me I was so ashamed of how much pleasure I felt that I bit my bottom lip hard – but I did not bleed, not from biting my lip, not then. His skin was smooth and warm in places I had not kissed him; in the places I had kissed him his skin was cold and coarse, and the pores were open and raised.

Did the world become a beautiful place? The rainy season eventually went away, the sunny season came, and it was too hot; the riverbed grew dry, the mouth of the river became shallow, the heat eventually became as wearying as the rain, and I would have wished it away if I had not become occupied with this other sensation, a sensation I had no single word for. I could feel myself full of happiness, but it was a kind of happiness I had never experienced before, and my happiness would spill out of me and run all the way down a long, long road and then the road would come to an end and I would feel empty and sad, for what could come after this? How would it end?

Not everything has an end, even though the beginning changes. The first time we were in a bed together we were lying on a thin board that was covered with old cloth, and this small detail, evidence of our poverty – people in our position, a stevedore and a doctor's servant, could not afford a proper mattress – was a major contribution to my satisfaction, for it allowed me to brace myself and match him breath for breath. But how can it be that a man who can carry large sacks filled with sugar or bales of cotton on his back from dawn to dusk exhausts himself within five minutes inside a woman? I did not then and I do not now know the answer to that. He kissed me. He fell asleep. I bathed my face then between his legs; he smelt of curry and onions, for those were the things he had been unloading all day; other times when I bathed my face between his legs – for I did it often, I liked doing it – he would smell of sugar, or flour, or the large, cheap bolts of cotton from which he would steal a few yards to give me to make a dress.

What is the everyday? What is the ordinary? One day, as I was walking towards the government dispensary to collect some supplies – one of my duties as a servant to a man who was in love with me beyond anything he could help and so had long since stopped trying, a man I ignored except when I wanted him to please me – I met Roland's wife, face to face, for the first time. She stood in front of me like a sentry – stern, dignified, guarding the noble idea, if not noble ideal, that was her husband. She did not block the sun, it was shining on my right; on my left was a large black cloud; it was raining way in the distance; there was no rainbow on the horizon. We stood on the narrow strip of concrete that was the sidewalk. One section of a wooden fence that was supposed to shield a yard from passers-by on the street bulged out and was broken, and a few tugs from any careless party would end its usefulness; in that yard a primrose bush bloomed unnaturally, its leaves too large, its flowers showy, and weeds were everywhere, they had prospered in all the wet. We were not alone. A man walked past us with a cutlass in his knapsack and a mistreated dog two steps behind him; a woman walked by with a large basket of food on her head; some children were walking home from school, and they were not walking together; a man was leaning out a window, spitting, he used snuff. I was wearing a pair of modestly high heels, red, not a colour to wear to work in the middle of the day, but that was just the way I had been feeling, red with a passion, like that hibiscus that was growing under the window of the man who kept spitting from the snuff. And Roland's wife called me a whore, a slut, a pig, a snake, a viper, a rat, a low-life, a parasite, and an evil woman. I could see that her mouth formed a familiar hug around these words – poor thing, she had been used to saying them. I was not surprised. I could not have loved Roland the way I did if he had not loved other women. And I was not surprised; I had noticed immediately the space between his teeth. I was not surprised that she knew about me; a man cannot keep a secret, a man always wants all the women he knows to know each other.

I believe I said this: 'I love Roland; when he is with me I want him to love me; when he is not with me I think of him loving me. I do not love you. I love Roland.' This is what I wanted to say, and this is what I believe I said. She slapped me across the face; her hand was wide and thick like an oar; she, too, was used to doing hard work. Her hand met the side of my face: my jawbone, the skin below my eye and under my chin, a small portion of my nose, the lobe of my ear. I was then a young woman in the early twenties, my skin was supple, smooth, the pores invisible to the naked eye. It was completely without bitterness that I thought as I looked at her face, a face I had so little interest in that it would tire me to describe it, Why is the state of marriage so desirable that all women are afraid to be caught outside it? And why does this woman, who has never seen me before, to whom I have never made any promise, to whom I owe nothing, hate me so much? She expected me to return her blow but, instead, I said, again completely without bitterness, 'I consider it beneath me to fight over a man.'

I was wearing a dress of light-blue Irish linen. I could not afford to buy such material, because it came from a real country, not a false country like mine; a shipment of this material in blue, in pink, in lime green, and in beige had come from Ireland, I suppose, and Roland had given me yards of each shade from the bolts. I was wearing my blue Irish-linen dress that day, and it was demure enough – a pleated skirt that ended quite beneath my knees, a belt at my waist, sleeves that buttoned at my wrists, a high neckline that covered my collarbone – but underneath my dress I wore absolutely nothing, no undergarments of any kind, only my stockings, given to me by Roland and taken from yet another shipment of dry goods, each one held up by two pieces of elastic that I had sewn together to make a garter. My declaration of what I considered beneath me must have enraged Roland's wife, for she grabbed my blue dress at the collar and gave it a huge tug; it rent in two from my neck to my waist. My breasts lay softly on my chest, like two small pieces of unrisen dough, unmoved by the anger of this woman; not so by the touch of her husband's mouth, for he would remove my dress, by first patiently undoing all the buttons and then pulling down the bodice, and then he would take one breast in his mouth, and it would grow to a size much bigger than his mouth could hold, and he would let it go and turn to the other one; the saliva evaporating from the skin on that breast was an altogether different sensation from the sensation of my other breast in his mouth, and I would divide myself in two, for I could not decide which sensation I wanted to take dominance over the other. For an hour he would kiss me in this way and then exhaust himself on top of me in five minutes. I loved him so. In the dark I couldn't see him clearly, only an outline, a solid shadow; when I saw him in the daytime he was fully dressed. His wife, as she rent my dress, a dress made of material she knew very well, for she had a dress made of the same material, told me his history; it was not a long one, it was not a sad one, no one had died in it, no land had been laid waste, no birthright had been stolen; she had a list, and it was full of names, but they were not the names of countries.

What was the colour of her wedding day? When she first saw him was she overwhelmed with desire? The impulse to possess is alive in every heart, and some people choose vast plains, some people choose high mountains, some people choose wide seas, and some people choose husbands; I chose to possess myself. I resembled a tree, a tall tree with long, strong branches; I looked delicate, but any man I held in my arms knew that I was strong; my hair was long and thick and deeply waved naturally, and I wore it braided and pinned up, because when I wore it loosely around my shoulders it caused excitement in other people – some of them men, some of them women, some of them it pleased, some of them it did not. The way I walked depended on who I thought would see me and what effect I wanted my walk to have on them. My face was beautiful, I found it so.

And yet I was standing before a woman who found herself unable to keep her life's booty in its protective sack, a woman whose voice no longer came from her throat but from deep within her stomach, a woman whose hatred was misplaced. I looked down at our feet, hers and mine, and I expected to see my short life flash before me; instead, I saw that her feet were without shoes. She did have a pair of shoes, though, which I had seen: they were white, they were plain, a round toe and flat laces, they took shoe polish well, she wore them only on Sundays and to church. I had many pairs of shoes, in colours meant to attract attention and dazzle the eye; they were uncomfortable, I wore them every day, I never went to church at all.

My strong arms reached around to caress Roland, who was lying on my back naked; I was naked also. I knew his wife's name, but I did not say it; he knew his wife's name, too, but he did not say it. I did not know the long list of names that were not countries that his wife had committed to memory. He himself did not know the long list of names; he had not committed this list to memory. This was not from deceit, and it was not from carelessness. He was someone so used to a large fortune that he took it for granted; he did not have a bankbook, he did not have a ledger, he had a fortune – but still he had not lost interest in acquiring more. Feeling my womb contract, I crossed the room, still naked; small drops of blood spilt from inside me, evidence of my refusal to accept his silent offering. And Roland looked at me, his face expressing confusion. Why did I not bear his children? He could feel the times that I was fertile, and yet each month blood flowed away from me, and each month I expressed confidence at its imminent arrival and departure, and always I was overjoyed at the accuracy of my prediction. When I saw him like that, on his face a look that was a mixture – confusion, dumbfoundedness, defeat – I felt much sorrow for him, for his life was reduced to a list of names that were not countries, and to the number of times he brought the monthly flow of blood to a halt; his life was reduced to women, some of them beautiful, wearing dresses made from yards of cloth he had surreptitiously removed from the bowels of the ships where he worked as a stevedore.

At that time I loved him beyond words; I loved him when he was standing in front of me and I loved him when he was out of my sight. I was still a young woman. No small impressions, the size of a child's forefinger, had yet appeared on the soft parts of my body; my legs were long and hard, as if they had been made to take me a long distance; my arms were long and strong, as if prepared for carrying heavy loads; I was not beautiful, but if I could have been in love with myself I would have been. I was in love with Roland. He was a man. But who was he really? He did not sail the seas, he did not cross the oceans, he only worked in the bottom of vessels that had done so; no mountains were named for him, no valleys, no nothing. But still he was a man, and he wanted something beyond ordinary satisfaction – beyond one wife, one love, and one room with walls made of mud and roof of cane leaves, beyond the small plot of land where the same trees bear the same fruit year following year – for it would all end only in death, for though no history yet written had embraced him, though he could not identify the small uprisings within himself, though he would deny the small uprisings within himself, a strange calm would sometimes come over him, a cold stillness, and since he could find no words for it, he was momentarily blinded with shame.

One night Roland and I were sitting on the steps of the jetty, our backs facing the small world we were from, the world of sharp, dangerous curves in the road, of steep mountains of recent volcanic formations covered in a green so humble no one had ever longed for them, of three hundred and sixty-five small streams that would never meet up to form a majestic roar, of clouds that were nothing but large vessels holding endless days of water, of people who had never been regarded as people at all; we looked into the night, its blackness did not come as a surprise, a moon full of dead white light travelled across the surface of a glittering black sky; I was wearing a dress made from another piece of cloth he had given me, another piece of cloth taken from the bowels of a ship without permission, and there was a false pocket in the skirt, a pocket that did not have a bottom, and Roland placed his hand inside the pocket, reaching all the way down to touch inside of me; I looked at his face, his mouth I could see and it stretched across his face like an island and like an island, too, it held secrets and was dangerous and could swallow things whole that were much larger than itself; I looked out towards the horizon, which I could not see but knew was there all the same, and this was also true of the end of my love for Roland.

Nihon-jin Girls

MATTHEW KRAMER

> *A flowering silk tree*
> *In the sleepy rain of Kisagata*
> *Reminds me of Lady Seishi*
> *In sorrowful lament.*
> (Matsuo Bashō)

TAKAKO AND MIYAKO went different ways. Takako bought a leather jacket and leather trousers and a leather cap. It was a passion. Her hair was allowed to hang in deliberate disorder. She lifted and exposed her cleavage. Barely balancing on new heels, she would totter into Yoyogi Park with a ghetto blaster and scowling make-up, as if someone had delivered a punch to both eyes. Her ordered and well-scrubbed past was jettisoned. She threw away her school uniform and her teddy bears. She daubed black paint, in huge fuzzy lozenges, on the pink walls of her tiny bedroom. Everything had to go. But despite the leather and the brooding make-up, she still could not get rid of what troubled her most, her little red mouth and her syrupy little voice. And round-eyed *gaijin*, amused, would photograph her unsteady rebellion in Yoyogi Park every weekend.

★

Following university, Miyako flew to London. She learned English with enthusiasm while working as a part-time OL (office lady) for a Japanese bank in the City. On occasional long weekends she went shopping in Milan. Italian designs enhanced and befitted her. She knew she was graceful. Not one of those short, awkward Japanese girls with stout cylindrical legs.

Takako was now at college, but never read books. She read *manga*, pulp comics. Not though the cute manga she'd had bought for her as a small, dutiful girl. Now it was hard core, dark, abrupt, syncopated, jagged with sudden lunges and assaults, the teenage girls pinioned and used in all conceivable ways, the brash gang members, the absurd and pitiful parents, motorcycles always swollen and bestial, the city, Tokyo but not Tokyo, ghastly, cold, crazed, chromium, corseted in the pipes and tubes of technology, a metallic and monochrome bondage. She read these manga while quietly eating her noodles, on the underground to her classes, in coffee shops in the evening. She worried about her piping voice, which could intimidate no one. She worried how, unless she could do something about it, she would ever be accepted into a motorcycle gang.

Although renting in Chalk Farm, Miyako avoided the supermarkets in nearby Camden Town. The people living there struck her as dirty, and she didn't trust them to wash themselves properly before handling the food. Instead she went to Selfridges and Fortnum and Mason. From time to time over the telephone she urged her bewildered widowed mother to sell up and move to London. It's so green here, she explained, they have so many parks, thinking of dusty concrete Tokyo.

> *Yet, if there is the slightest*
> *deviation, you will be as far from*
> *the Way as heaven is from earth.*
> (Dōgen Zenji.)

College was easy, and there was no reason to study hard. As it was a Buddhist university, Takako was expected to do *zazen* meditation. While the grizzled *Roshi*, their fearsome teacher, sat watching, ready to bawl out anyone who moved, the snooty assistant priest in his plain dark robe patrolled the motionless lines of students, each seated on a cushion and folded into the lotus position, together presenting to him six rows of ramrod backs. If they slackened, dozed or appeared to sink back into thought, it was his job to silently administer a blow just below the shoulder with his *kyosaku*, a long wooden stick. First the warning touch, so the recipient could steel himself, and then the blow. Sudden, swift, accurate, where nerve ends clustered. The purpose to redirect the body to its true task. She'd sensed, when they filed in, that the assistant priest hadn't warmed to her, to the black rings around her eyes, her chemically red lips and spiked hair. And though she resentfully struggled to focus all attention, as prescribed, below the naval, the *hara*, monotonously counting each time she exhaled, and was further certain her body had betrayed no evidence of banal, subversive thought, still he placed the flattened end of the stick upon her shoulder – and, once her head had tilted, taken the necessary precaution, hit. The undeserved blow passed through her like a hot shiver. She was sure that he'd struck because of her appearance. Not to help her achieve Satori, and all their other mumbo-jumbo of which he was the unsmiling representative, but to slyly remind her of her place. So the next time she went, with the others, to sit silent and with their backs to him in the *zendo*, the meditation room, she wore a big brass stud in her nose, lightning-flash earrings and lipstick black as congealed blood. She had, moreover, worked so much gel into her hair, before brushing upwards, that it resembled a scarecrow's. As he passed, the assistant priest looked at her most peculiarly. (And Takako was also certain that even the veteran *Roshi*'s eyes had fleetingly boggled.) Ignoring them, she made the ritual bow with palms pressed together, then sank down onto her cushion and folded herself into the lotus position. She concentrated. She appeared at peace and, on the surface which the priest saw, properly and obediently focused on their goal, the suppression of the ego and its mundane desires, the harmonisation of body and mind.

But in fact she swam the other way. Not away from thought, but towards it, into it; it churned in her head while the patrolling assistant priest watched their motionless backs, initially quite oblivious to her surreptitious rebellion. Unaware that she was now with the motorcycle gang whom she'd yet to meet, their Japanese bikes spawned from American designs, their Japanese faces frozen in surly homage to English punk *ennui*. But soon after, though, she began to sense, became increasingly certain, that he was now, in particular, concentrating on her. Coldly considering whether she was yet adrift of her goal, and waiting, malevolently, for an opportunity to strike the traditional blow. So she fought to maintain her surface calm, to fool his inquisitorial eyes, while going unconditionally crazy in her head to show him what she really thought of all their hocus-pocus, a chaos of lights and squealing tyres inside her skull, and a band ragged and acned as the *Sexu Pistoru* vomiting filth just behind her soft, placid face. She began now to sense his mounting suspicion. That something was up. She coolly raised the volume, while remaining perfectly still. She knew he knew, and also that he couldn't be sure. Knew his eyes were repeatedly flicking to this one especially troublesome girl, who, even amongst the westernised styles and trimmings of the others, constituted a particular, dark affront. Time passed, but heavily, reluctantly. Somewhere along the petrified and aching lines of upright backs an electronic watch bleeped. The priest's gaze ranged over them. Others were found out, caught dozing, or still secretly paddling in the shallows of consciousness, unable or unwilling to walk up out of them, and away. Oh but this generation was soft. Not one truly fit to raise a Japanese sword. He gently positioned the *kyosaku*. But she, though, only became more like their teacher's metaphors for meditative perfection, a *great pine tree*, an *iron mountain*, or, as she saw herself, immobile as a carving, an ornate and extravagant

109

carving, while inside the noise assaulted and the harsh light strobed her. He suspected but he couldn't be sure. There was not a tremor anywhere on her surface. She felt the burning glow of his frustration. And her charcoal black lips could not but involuntarily stretch in a triumphant secret smile. Without a sound, the tip of the *kyosaku* came softly to rest on her shoulder.

Miyako left her job to study finance and the financial markets at a college in London, having admired the *gaijin* dealers employed by her bank, the ease with which they made money, the dash and vigour with which they spent it. Shortly after, she returned to Tokyo, and was soon at a desk, telephone pressed to her delicate ear, dealing for a foreign bank.

> *We are Ninja. Not Geisha.*
> *We are not what you expect.*
> (Kazuko Hohki)

Arguments at home. Her mother and father wished her to learn the tea ceremony. It was a proper accomplishment for a girl hoping to make a good match. And so they wanted her to take evening classes in its forms and etiquette. Takako's current predilections for music tuneful as a building site and dark, mutilated clothes perplexed them. Young people now were going down the strangest roads. They vaguely hoped the mastering of this traditional skill might somehow reform her. But she didn't want to fall to her knees and learn. What would the *Sexu Pistoru*, Johnny Lotten and Sid Vicious, or even Nancy Spungen, have done? Nancy Spungen would never have had time for *a tea ceremony*. Professional groupie and mistress of her body, she'd have kicked out; proudly desecrated the ancient bowl gleaming with the self-satisfaction of age, splattered across screen and tatami mat the green tea ringed by its own froth. But Takako depended on her father's money for everything. Without it she was naked. So she went. Participated throughout with an extraordinary scowl. It was painful to maintain. She wouldn't talk to the other girls.

Unlike them, craven and blandly obedient, she was a *ronin*, a masterless punk-samurai.

When she'd completed her course, was done with all that kneeling and waiting, all that rustling across tatami mats, and had been handed her diploma, grandpa, with his new girlfriend, came arthritically up from the country to sample his grand-daughter's brand-new accomplishment. Grandpa would not allow himself to be collected from the station. He wanted to impress his new girlfriend with his resourcefulness. So they waited in the apartment for them all day. While they were waiting, her mother pressed her to wear late grandma's ceremonial kimono. Late grandma's *beautiful* ceremonial kimono and *beautiful obi*, sash, garments which late grandma had worn when a girl. She shook her head, emphatically. Her father backed her mother. But no, she wouldn't. Eventually they began to shout at her. Her late grandmother's *beautiful ceremonial kimono* from the days of her young womanhood, and she wouldn't wear it? Had she no sense of shame, nor duty, no feeling for her ancestors, no respect for her family name? Crying, she locked herself in the tiny toilet and stayed there. She didn't want to try to explain. Explain why she could not wear the clothes of a dead person. But the very thought of doing so terrified her. Takako had seen her grandmother immediately after she died. Her white stone face, the mouth marginally ajar. She could not wear that dead woman's ancient, constricting girl's kimono. It would smother her, the musty, patterned silk, lock her into its odour of decay and decrepitude, and haunt her with the memory of a mouth without teeth she'd watched, in horror, mumbling shamelessly to the Buddha. Outside, in the flat, she heard the front door opening. Grandpa's country voice. The high-pitched cooing of his sixty-five-year-old girlfriend while she nervously, frantically bowed in all directions. And again Takako saw her dead grandmother, mumbling emptily to that lump of wood.

The summer grasses!
All that is left of the warriors' dream!
(Matsuo Bashō)

She stayed in the toilet. Her father shouted angrily at her through the door for a while, but then gave up. After a pause, grandpa came up close and recalled in a loud country voice how he'd played with her when she was just a child; and now he was so proud of her, and had brought her some money, it was in his bag, where was his bag? All the time calling her Tako, a diminutive of Takako, meaning octopus, which she hated. She was no one's little octopus. Then the girlfriend timorously introduced herself, calling her Takako-san, and insisted in her high-pitched, girlish way how much it would mean, what a great honour it would be if they were to meet. She didn't answer. She sat there on the toilet seat in the darkness and said nothing. After a while, her father began to shout again.

The dealing room excited her. Equipped with screen and telephone, she dealt in foreign currency, bought and sold money for money. Long hours. Every morning, with her American boss, Miyako plotted which currencies to buy and which to sell. In the evening – perfect simulacra of French restaurants. The quiet respectful voices of the waiters. To be honest, she told him, she didn't really like Japanese food. For amusement that evening, she taught her young boss certain *kanji*. Laboriously, he attempted to copy the character for *pleasure* into her leather-skinned filofax. Not bad. (A pretty smile.) They talked about the foreign banks, the finance houses whose screens now gleamed in cream-carpeted Tokyo offices. Their extraordinary profits. She thought of her poor stupid friends, *office ladies* for dreary Japanese manufacturers, doomed to spend their pre-marriage years bringing tea for the men, on expeditions to the photocopier. She opened her tasselled menu; in roman letters only.

Following the incident with her grandfather, Takako's parents were ready to see her gone, at least for a while. They therefore acceded to her request to go to London – as was now undeniably the fashion – to study English. Her mother packed her suitcase and her father, lips fused to a masculine pout, drove her in silence to Narita airport. To placate them that day, she'd worn a pale skirt and a conservative pullover. She didn't expect to wear either item again in the next six months. She was going to London. But not to post-card London. She was going to do dangerous and disturbing things. Her father's windscreen wipers began to swish. So many grey buildings on either side. Rain always made her sad. She fell again to worrying about her voice and her ridiculous plump little mouth. Why had she been cursed with a Japanese voice and a Japanese mouth? She wanted to cut them out of her.

After their meal, Miyako drove her young boss in her imported car to Yokohama for coffee. Hood down. Night air on their faces. Oh. A bay of lights in the darkness, the bridge drenched in gold. Truly a romantic gesture over water. She wondered briefly why the Japanese engineering students she'd ignored at college had all been so boring, so acned.

Coffee with *Sachertorte*. How do you think Maastricht will affect the Deutschmark?

On the aeroplane, to brief herself, Takako read a Japanese manga set in an English public school. English public schoolboys were tall and willowy, each with a waterfall of fine, wheaten hair that hung dramatically over their cobalt eyes. They had stately homes, servants, arrogant mouths, absolute confidence and addressed each other by their surnames. The school tortured and hardened them, in particular through compulsory cold showers every morning. The hero and his friends, naked save for their veils of hair, lined up across the page to be lashed ferociously by the water. Their own relations were mediated by every conceivable cruelty, physical and psychological, inflicted by the strong on the weak. The older boys, just as they had once been beaten, would beat the younger boys, and sometimes bed them. She hoped very much she would meet an ex-English public schoolboy.

★

She rented a bedsit in Camden Town. In the mornings she went to school, the rest of the day she would drift dreamily amongst the little shops and stalls, excited by the filthy streets, the sound of harsh music from mysterious open windows above, the cramped and fractured façades. Antique shops, richly piled, would gleam and resonate through glass and draw her in. In full regalia – leather, chains, surly and aggressive make-up – she would touch and handle scarred, dilapidated furniture, furnishings, trinkets, cases, stage jewellery, fans, things worked long ago in ivory and ebony, the dust collecting inside her little nose, while the aged proprietors silently watched this bizarre Asiatic apparition. With an inbred politeness she could not get rid of, she would enquire meekly regarding prices, and receive her change and tiny, wrapped purchase with an automatic effusion of respectful thanks. She noticed how foreigners, English people, would look at each other as she softly sang *thankyou-verymuch* – and then smile. It was no good. She had to find a gang. She had to find the most terrifying and disgusting gang in Camden Town . . . and join them. She had never joined a gang before. She speculated how it might be done. In the manga, aspirant members were invariably set tasks to prove themselves worthy. She wondered what might be her task, and whether she would rise to it.

The man was very tall and, Takako guessed, at least thirty-five, maybe even older. Every day as she passed, he sat in the cafe at the formica table against the window. His hair on top clearly now grew with little vigour, chestnut scrubland only, but his sideburns were another matter, a darker, deeper chestnut, they curved aggressively forward, like scythes, as they tapered off. He looked promisingly anti-social, and so, on the fifth or sixth time that she passed him, when he knocked on the glass and confidently beckoned her with a finger, she turned and obeyed. He knew where she was from. He said he often met Japanese girls. She asked him, timorously, if he was in a band. He had been. There was a stud in his left ear. The more she looked at him, the more promising he appeared. She asked, though she anticipated his reply, whether he had been to public school. No, he had not. If he could, he would burn down every public school and shoot every single public schoolboy. Takako continued to examine him. Definitely he was ugly. Not only was his face an unpleasant colour, it was too narrow, and his cocksureness compounded rather than exonerated this ugliness. Takako asked him how old he was. He spoke, vaguely, of being in his early thirties. Yes, she was sure he was at least thirty-five. And sure, also, this was exactly the kind of boy she needed to meet. She realised this meant that she would probably sleep with him shortly. She wondered how he appeared and what he did when he was naked.

In Corrida of Love *two moments strike one with particular epiphanic force . . . In a Japan that is still recognisably the old Japan, indeed the orientalists' Japan, land of rice and paper, two trains, two vast black craggy steam trains, motionless amidst a lattice-work of points and rails, emerge out of thinning, upwardly coiling steam and morning mist. They are Industry. The Machine Age. Glimpsed as they are on a morning satisfyingly vaporous and bright, surrounded by tokens of this old Japan, they appear more mythical than credible, waking monsters slowly exhaling into the cold air . . . Later, down a long, sloping street, come Imperial soldiers, rank upon rank, neurotically regimented. All in silence, in filmic silence. The wordless crowd seethes with flags. Our hero passes them, but going the other way, up the same long, sloping street. He is a little hunched, unclean about the face. Neither acknowledges the other. They pass, going towards their different destinies, in chill and utter silence. He is, at that moment, the very quintessence of the self that will not merge with the mass, that will not compromise, the sexual anarchist, heroic dupe of the*

> *personal obsession he has pitted against the greater (and blander) madness of his times rolling unstoppably, uniformly, the opposite way.*
> (Gavin M. Remarque. *Ashes into Light: A History of the Post-War Japanese Cinema.*)

He took her to pubs to meet his mates. Mostly, they were like him, only not as tall. Their girls dressed like her, but looked as if they were already mothers. They had lined faces, and drab, tired skin. Their short leather skirts exposed their pasty legs. There were liver spots and red spots on the tops of their breasts. She was suspicious as to how often they washed their hair. Still, they tried to be nice, drawing her into their circle. And would loudly, confidently mispronounce her name. Takako told them, if it was easier, to call her Nancy. She said it was her English name. They didn't seem surprised that she should have an English name. The men, though, were more of a problem. She noticed that with her they compulsively acted. It was strange, but in her vicinity they tried very hard to emphasise their sophistication, their experience, their grasp of the world. He would meanwhile stay near enough to her to make clear their connection, but otherwise would rarely address Takako at these pub gatherings. Once she went to the toilet and on returning, waiting patiently to thread her way back through the crush to rejoin the group, heard him describing with considerable precision to two of his mates, while they grasped their manly pints, what she would and wouldn't do in bed.

They spent most mornings at the same cafe. He didn't really seem to have any deep drives. She could find in him no hint of a will to power, or to anything else. He didn't have a motorbike, but had occasional use of a van he sometimes made deliveries with for money. He had never even been to prison. She was losing patience with the terrible smell in his bedsit and was now increasingly certain that he was not dangerous enough, certainly no gang leader, and miles from being the equal of Johnny Lotten and Sid Vicious. Every morning

Takako drank insipid tea while he ate two fried eggs, a pork sausage, baked beans and fried bread. Sometimes he'd glance at the *Daily Express*. He knew the cafe's owner by his first name. Yolk and baked bean sauce would meanwhile slowly collect on his chin. Takako looked at his plate, and thought of green tea, and a scrubbed rectangle of wood bearing fragile slithers of raw fish, pale and clean. While he noisily slobbered his eggs and beans, she made her decision. Nancy Spungen would never have had breakfast with this man.

His abandonment by her perplexed him, but there was no evidence he was upset. She continued to see him each morning, as if on duty, at the little table by the window. She glimpsed the familiar viscous palette of his plate, soiled cutlery at rest, and knew his appetite had not abated.

Miyako's mother told her of that strange and stupid girl, Takako, three years her junior, whom she'd vaguely known at school. She's gone to London. Her mother is very worried. She wears strange clothes. Miyako recalled the last time she had seen Takako, about a year before: passing defiantly along the opposite pavement in Jiyugaoka while supporting with difficulty a monstrous ghetto blaster, cradled with both arms, her eyes like those of a giant panda, seemingly very angry – certainly she'd been scowling. But the portable music centre, into whose carriage she'd invested so much effort, had been playing so quietly that the passing traffic had entirely blotted out its rebellious sound . . . So, that strange and stupid girl was now in London. Her mother would like to give you her address, when the bank sends you back there. She'd like you to find out what's happening.

Takako was adopted by a motorcycle gang. It was her moment of greatest triumph. She realised now the man with the sickle sideburns had been no man at all, a mere tawdry approximation of the real thing. Now that she'd at last found her gang – or rather, they had found her. Its members had become used to seeing Takako, a solitary fixture of the pub

117

MATTHEW KRAMER

opposite Camden Lock where they drank, always bizarrely polite behind the morbid colouring applied to her face. Huge, bearded men with pronounced bellies and leather jackets that stank of their lives, they had gotten into the habit of offering the lonely Japanese girl cigarettes. The gushing gratefulness with which she always declined amused them. As did the way she had lately taken to puffing uncertainly on those she'd purchased herself. They asked her what her grandad had done during the war. Did his teeth protrude? Did he have you know those little round glasses? How many POWs had he bayoneted and thrown into the river Kwai? They asked her if she was looking for work as their comfort woman. I'm sorry. I don't understand. Beneath the funereal make-up, she nodded and smiled at what she couldn't understand, but assumed must be jokes. They showed her their battle scars. They peeled up string vests to reveal the violent and vivid tattoos on their sweating skin. Finally, one evening, they took her outside to where the bikes were. Swollen machines, horned with giant handlebars, dark from oil and use. It was almost night. She was invited to mount. Heart pounding, she obeyed. Told to embrace the wide waist of her escort. Her hands gently linked over the soft cusp of his gut. She looked around. On every side were hairy, obese, leatherjacketed men, gripping with terrible seriousness their handlebars. In unison, engines were kicked alive. No one had told her where she was going. Perhaps into the dark and burning streets – their neat containing rectangles opening up to swallow her like mouths – of that other, manga Tokyo.

Walking in a desolate field
I picked up a woman's comb;
She must have come here
To pluck flowers in spring.
(Sōin)

Miyako met her in McDonald's. Takako's hand, which parcelled out small change to pay for her hamburger, was engrained with dirt. Miyako was luminous in Italian designs,

118

and could not stop staring, in particular at the shapeless bruise under the other girl's left eye. I'm going with a hell's angel, Takako told her proudly. And I'm pregnant. And tomorrow my parents are flying from Japan to collect me, because I won't go home. She giggled. My father will get a big surprise. My boyfriend is going to beat him up.

> *Every force but conservatism was pressing from within at the closed doors: so that when a summons came from without they were flung wide open, and all these imprisoned energies were released.*
> (G. B. Sansom. *Japan. A Short Cultural History*.)

Resplendent in Milanese couture, Miyako waits with a glass of mineral water. She is relaxed in airports. Airports, she knows, are very much part of her world. She is travelling business class. She is wearing a Swiss watch. Her hair was cut in Paris. An Italian handbag is balanced on her lap. On the table in front of her is the *Financial Times*, which she buys every morning when in London, and sometimes reads. A flight to Frankfurt is announced. She has been to Frankfurt, to see the banks and other financial institutions. She is an admirer of the Deutsch-mark. An exemplary currency. But as this is Heathrow, in her handbag there is still mostly sick old Sterling. Announce-ments ricochet. The great international destinations. Their names resonate with wealth and power. Near her, she hears a sobbing. No, she hears people sobbing. Two people in fact are sobbing. More announcements. Rome. New York. Paris. Blue chip destinations. But the weeping continues unabated, vaguely in tandem. She looks across from her restaurant table to the nearby café. In a plain dress, Takako is sobbing into her hands. Beside her is a squat, middle-aged Japanese woman in a cheap English coat, also sobbing into her hands. Next to the woman there sits a Japanese man of similar age, very badly dressed. He looks directly ahead, the colouring in his cheeks somewhere between apricot and strawberry. Intermittently his nose twitches. She cannot see his eyes inside their slits. In front of him, on a small plate, is an uneaten cheese and pickle roll, but he shows no interest in this unfamiliar western thing, even though he presumably, earlier, paid for it. His pullover is V-necked, and a dismal brown. From it emerges the unbuttoned collar of his check nylon shirt. Mass produced and Taiwanese. It is not an impressive sight. She looks away, catches the eye of the restaurant waiter; he approaches: height, looks, dinner-jacket, bow-tie – all there. Do you want anything else, Madam? Miyako thinks for a moment; keeps him waiting, then shakes her head. No, I'll have the bill . . . Of course. Expressionless, he backs away.

Frankfurt. New York. Tokyo. Deutschmark. Dollar. Yen. Including bonus, she now earns $120,000 per annum. In the dealing room, CNN is always on. News is important, anticipating it even more so. If you buy your dollars before war is expected, you can sell at a profit when the bombs begin to fall. We did very well out of the Gulf War. Milanese fashions. Cosmetics from Paris. In bed with an American dealer in his Tokyo penthouse in Roppongi. So many lights below. Introduction to cocaine. Including bonus, $120,000 per annum. Frankfurt. New York. Tokyo. Deutschmark. Dollar. Yen.

A Bed of Roses

EDNA O'BRIEN

LIKE ALMOST EVERYONE Miss Dalton had a secret but, like everyone, she did not wish to know what that secret was. It was not that it got mixed in with other secrets, greater or lesser, it simply got submerged because Miss Dalton did not want to share it with anyone, least of all herself.

She was open and private by turn but, as time went on, she was more inclined to be private except when she had a drink or two, and then told some little story or other relating to the past. Miss Dalton had different stories for different people. She had – again, like most people – godchildren and one whom she liked in particular, a young girl called Emma, whom she had seen in her crib and had thought at once, 'Emma, you have character, you have presence.' To Emma she usually related some escapade, a missed advantage in love; whereas to others she might tell a story about the different places she had lived in, a haunted room, or some spectacular sights, such as the proud, scrolled columns of a shattered temple.

On occasion love and travel overlapped, when she gave rein to the reckless and put a flower in her bodice, and in some strange dining-room made the acquaintance of some gentle-man who sat with her and conversed with her, and then took a stroll with her in the grounds and ventured a kiss. Abroad, these gentlemen possessed an aura and a gallantry which they might not have had at home. Home was eventually England, though Miss Dalton was not English. Sometimes a bouquet arrived next day and sometimes not. She heard from one or other of these men and found herself surprised at the nature of their confidences. Distance and unfamiliarity made them indiscreet. One man who had witten from Vancouver confessed that he had come across her name and had been swept, yes swept, by a wave of nostalgia for her company. She was quite pleased, quite buoyed, and for a moment drawn back to the snowy fortress in the mountains and the warm wine, and this aloof man who had hired a sleigh on Christmas Eve for both of them to go into the forest. Oh yes, she remembered it as she remembered the woodland in Sweden in autumn, the birch leaves like freshly minted sovereigns; a very studious young man, a Marxist, blond, bespectacled, who had actually proposed to her and she had declined, but in a nice way, saying that really the language barrier and the long dark winters might create a difficulty, might erase the sweetness of the heady embraces in the woods.

The one story Miss Dalton could not tell Emma in entirety was the kernel of her secret. It had happened long before. Miss Dalton was married and was having with her husband their first holiday abroad. It was her first taste of Europe and her last week of marriage. As a young student she had married her professor, but after two years of marriage found herself still the student and very trapped. What she saw of Europe was not how she had envisaged it at all. The bus – a bus holiday it was – would pull up outside some unprepossessing inn on the outskirts of a town, disgorge its passengers, while the coxcomb of a driver would holler out arrangements for the following morning. Inside they were allocated to small dingy rooms, one towel per person, and a handwritten note about hygiene in another tongue. In some of these inns there was an ironing room and always a great queue, as the ladies had creased their dresses. On the third evening, while waiting for the iron, she talked to the two ladies who had intrigued her,

A Bed of Roses

who were superior to the other passengers, all of whom knew each other and many of whom worked in the same marmalade factory in Dundee. The ladies looked down on these people, and on the driver with his brilliantined hair who did not even know the names of the lesser cities they drove through.

'The spiv', they called him. It turned out that they were mother and daughter but looked exactly the same age, and the animal that their pinched features suggested was of course the shrew. Yes, two little shrews, Mona and Ivy, who wore the same maroon skirts and matching cardigans and had identical little cysts on their lower eyelids. Their eyes, a very washed blue, looked as if to be holding back tears, but it was not certain if these were tears of scorn or of sorrow. Mona, the daughter, had a heightened sense of smell and was particularly disgusted by the smell of fish, which, as it happened, could be real or imaginary. As they stood in the corridor, watching a half-naked woman iron her blouse, Mona had one of her retchings and insisted on going to the kitchen where her instinct was proved right, because there on a big platter was an inky mass of fish with ink coming out of its pores. Naturally, an argument arose and she was told by a very irate chef not to come into his quarters again. She insisted on a separate table for supper, where she sat with her mother and ate grapes which she dunked in a bowl of water. It was her own china bowl which she carried everywhere, ivory with a motif of roses on the front.

That night Miss Dalton heard rats and, as she heard them scrape and scurry behind the wainscoting, the lunatic thought came to her whether rats in different countries had different appearances, just like people. She was not sure whether she was in France or Holland. Throughout the night she prayed that she could go home. She thought of running away and going to a railway station but she was without money as her husband held the purse. By morning she was herself again, smiling insincerely and making stupid remarks about the scenery.

In the bus, three of the passengers were sick and several complained of nausea. Opinion was united on the fact that it had been the octopus served at dinner. The driver who acted as compère was, as usual, spouting some fanciful facts and pretending not to be aware of the embarrassments going on around him. However, Mona saw to that. She gave him such a wallop of her leather handbag that he stopped the bus on a bend, hurtling them into a stone wall over which a vast willow drooped. The passengers piled out. Those who had up to then been jocular, or even forbearing, now vented their rage – a rage induced by heat and claustrophobia – and it seemed as if he might be assaulted on the roadside by a coven of angry Scotsmen who had drunk heavily the night before. Their floor-manager intervened, said they did not come abroad to disgrace their clan and asked them to tuck their sleeves up and help hawk the bus out of its *impasse*. Mona, meanwhile, with Ivy's help, opened the several windows and then insisted that some men go to the nearest farmhouse and ask for pails of water. There was difficulty in finding volunteers, because few were linguists and the driver refused to go as a matter of pride. A buxom young woman who had been sick offered her services because she could see some nice apples in the orchard beyond.

'I am like the Romans: I am sick and then I eat and then I am sick again,' she said, taking the arm of one of the young men and heading off.

Miss Dalton took her book across to the hayfield and read. It was her husband's book, had his name written on it, and she had to thank him for that. Oh yes, she had to thank him for that, as she read those infinitely sad and infinitely nourishing stories. They were stories that mirrored her own plight – unhappy men and unhappy women in distant Russia, who railed against their situations but were unable to change them. The bundles into which the hay was saved, its very texture and its smell, were different from the haycocks in her native land, and this also made her lonesome for something, but she did not know what.

Soon they were en route again, passing through towns with bells and church spires; then the countryside, the shuttered houses, fields with poppies and workers – mostly women – bent over, their heads covered with scarves or cloth caps. It was all so hot, so monotonous. Others shared her disappointment, complained about the small bedrooms, the cheerless dining-rooms, portions of leaky clotted cheese in little pouches along with black bread and raw sausage for breakfast, and not once a decent cup of tea. Yet, as they said, they must make the best of it and, anyhow, there were only two days to the final destination. In their different ways they elaborated on it.

The resort, at the foot of a high mountain, was not a fairy-tale castle with turreting and painted timbers, but a low complex of wooden chalets skulking under the mountains, which were free of snow except on their summits. There were '*verboten*' signs, two muzzled dogs, and the driveway was freshly cemented so that the bus got stuck, and they had to walk the remainder with their luggage. Inside, a battle-axe with extremely long plaits ordered them to queue until their names were called out. Complaints abounded. Some went to the spiv, tackled him, demanded a refund and were told, not without a degree of insolence, that the head office in London was the place where objections could be lodged. He himself was officially free of them and setting out to meet his girlfriend in Weimar. The prurience with which he repeated this brought extra odium on his head and, in a brisk exchange with the receptionist, he said, 'Don't expect sweetness and joy from this lot.'

The bedrooms were boxrooms and there were bunk beds. The one remark that passed between Miss Dalton and her husband was concerning the bunk beds, as to who should take which bunk. She mentioned her vertigo and, by way of censure, he said he was trying very hard to remember the day he fell out of love with her, but that when he did remember it she would be the first to know. She panicked then. She became afraid of what her husband might do. She lost her marbles to the extent that the blisters on the newly creosoted walls looked like insects that would soon buzz about and crawl over them as they slept. She could feel something pending. She had felt it downstairs when she found the one book in the salon. It was called *Die Elixire des Teufels*. She had gone to the woman with the plaits to enquire what it meant. It meant 'The Elixir of the Devil'. Much as she feared it, she was also intrigued by it, something potent, something dangerous, an elixir that could change a person's character, make for daring. It was syrupy and viscous and quite a new taste on her palate.

Her husband's second comment during their five-day stay was that the brown pencil she applied to her eyebrows was ludicrousness incarnate. It was not a dark brown, but a sort of ochre brown, bought in the kiosk of the hotel which opened for three hours a day so that people could get soap, or occasionally an English newspaper or aspirins or liver salts. Everyone had some ailment or other – headache, stomach-ache, swollen ankles, what have you. Even Mona and Ivy began to mutter spiteful things to each other, using Miss Dalton now both as companion and go-between. She heard of Mona's several, indeed rarefied, allergies and of Ivy's brief fling with another man, litigations they had taken and solicitors who had tricked them out of money. When Mona went off to wash her hands – a thing she did constantly – Ivy hinted at scenes too awful to relate, hysterics, sleepless nights, hostage to a highly strung daughter who could not suffer a rival.

'It was him or her . . . I had to choose,' she would say and shake her head bitterly, and go on to talk of the lurcher who was a figment of Mona's imagination. This lurcher had even been given a name, which was Misty, but in fact had never existed. Mona, who could not stand the stench of an animal, or the heat of animal flesh, would hardly have a pet in the house, would she. Both their hands were raw and pink from repeated washings. Their hands looked frost-bitten in the glare of the sun.

The bedrooms too were cauldrons. Their little room was so cramped and the smell of creosote so stifling that Miss Dalton crept there only to sleep. She could feel her husband's gravity above her, his body shifting around, venting his rage. She avoided him as much as possible and in the daytime, if she had need to get her book or comb her hair, she listened to make sure he was not inside. For the most part he took walks and befriended the young cashier who aspired to sing *Lieder*. She had seen them once at dusk set out for a walk, and she thought how wonderful if he should fall in love with this dark young woman and give her permission to leave him. Idiotically, she felt she needed his permission so that she could go.

The five days dragged along with constant moaning about the food: the black bread, the sour cabbage, the tripe; not to mention the language itself, so fat and guttural to the ears, like the thickly sliced, fatty salamis. Men began to order beers and sit down to cards as soon as they had finished their breakfast. The women, however, were buoyed up by the idea of the last night soirée. Some had even gone to the town and got some finery. There was to be an orchestra, a five-course dinner and dancing.

Miss Dalton had a little bolero crested with jet which she wore over her blue dress, and long gaudy earrings. Mona and Ivy took exception to her appearance at once, as if sensing some intended transgression. The bolero they deemed both ill-bred and skimpy, and so she found herself without a companion on either side. Her husband had taken the car to the town for dinner. Mona and Ivy both wore lilac which gave an unfortunate hue to their skins. All around was a sea of bold bright dresses, brooches lethal as daggers and such a glut of perfumes and talcum powder smells that Mona sat with her handkerchief to her face, and refused the entrée. The whole party was seated at one long table on which there was a regiment of pink candles stuck in wine bottles that were crusted with candle grease from previous farewells. She drank a lot. She had never in her life drunk but she drank red wine and over-sweet white wine and talked a little intemperately to the couple across from her. She talked of a museum where she had gone, and how in her mind the figure in the portrait seemed to pass out of the paint and approach her. She did not mention that he had the leer of a devil. She said, too, that she had learned that many German folktales had originated in the spot where they had been set down. *Wildhaus*. Wild house. They smiled but in a disbelieving way.

As soon as the main course was served, the musicians filed

on and sat by their several instruments. Among them was the
most ravishing man Miss Dalton had ever seen. He was tall,
smooth, dark-haired and dark-eyed, with a cropped beard,
black as soot. He was the violinist. She was not alone in
singling him out. Others remarked on his charm, his spill of
dark hair, his velvet jacket, his eyes with a soft absorbed
quality, looking disinterestedly into the room. Although
brown, they looked to have a glow of orange, but that, she
conceded, could be from the spotlighting. As the music struck
up and strains of a waltz filled the room, people began to thaw
somewhat and enter into the party spirit by donning the paper
hats and becoming saucy with one another. Although sparing
in her glances, Miss Dalton could see the intensity with which
the violinist played and see, too, that his chin seemed to be at
one with it. First he played softly, as if to lure them into a
friendly state, and then far more vigorously, enticing them to
get up. She was not asked to dance, and as she sat alone helping
herself from the wine bottle, she became aware of his glances
in her direction. Ivy was aware of them, too, and came across
and shook her and said, 'Stop dreaming . . . Stop bloody
dreaming.'

'I'm not dreaming,' she said, and thought, 'I don't care . . .
I don't care what they think,' and stared into space, realising
that her breathing was quite rapid and quite fluttery.

When the celebrations ended and the orchestra played both
English and Scottish songs in honour of the guests, she had
this longing to march straight up to him and say something
but her nerves prevented her. She decided to go into the
garden to cool off, but instead found herself in a warren of
passages ending up in a sort of vestibule which was full of
clutter, stepladders, beer-barrels and a mesh of newly born
kittens crawling along the muddy floor. The over-head light
was such that she could see the sleek cat nibble the umbilical
cord and chew it assiduously. Then a footstep. There he was,
facing her, a shy look now as if to say, 'I have come to rescue
you.' Not being able to converse, they simply stood there,
smiling, somewhat surprised, somewhat transfixed.

'Celia . . . Ce . . . Celia,' she heard her name a distance

away, Mona and Ivy saying it imperiously, as if she was a member of their family. Nothing for it but to hide, and he followed her in there, into a fuel shed where they had to crouch. She could feel the heat coming off him, not like the heat of the sun, but a warmer, balmier heat.

'She's here . . . She must be here.'

'You're quite sure you saw her come this way?'

'Quite sure.'

She could feel them prowling about outside, could almost feel them lift back the trap-door and then, with a leap of delight, she heard the scream and the retching as Mona sighted the kittens suckling.

'It's disgusting, it's loathsome,' she shouted to her mother, who led her away.

Crawling out, Miss Dalton made some gestures of apology and a wan attempt at goodbye. He did not want that. He wanted her to stay, the gentle, searching eyes more chivalrous than ever. To try and persuade her, he took out his hotel key and waved it back and forth so that she felt like someone being hypnotised. She recalled the room number and noted that the figures added up to seven.

'*Heimlich*,' he said, and put the key to his lips.

'*Heimlich*,' she said, not knowing what it meant.

Back in the lounge, she sat with a rowdier group and drank liberally, because the men were anxious to get rid of their foreign money. She drank a very strong liqueur which tasted of pears and even had a pear, like an embryo, in the bottom of the bottle. Later in the bunk bed things went askew: the violinist, his jacket, the Dundee accents, the ice-cream with the lit sparklers, rungs of the bed and her husband's haunches above her, hurtled dangerously in and out of her mind and she knew that for the first time in her life she was drunk, very drunk. She feared that something calamitous would befall her. As time went on she felt worse: she felt hot and also that she was expiring and thought that the best thing to do would be to creep out of her room and get some fresh air and wash herself under the outside shower. Reams of mist, white and milky, hung in the atmosphere, masking the few stars that were left in the sky. She sat for a while, then climbed over the low wall and went into a field to pick flowers that she could bring home as a souvenir. She who did not want to go home.

It was on her way back that she decided not to go directly to their boxroom but to find the room that corresponded with the number on the key. The stairs grew shabbier the higher she went, the carpet ran out and gave way to linoleum and soon after were stone stairs and a rope banister. Outside the landing lavatories there was disinfectant the shape of a round biscuit and pink, but with a very acrid smell.

'*Die Elixire des Teufels*,' she said as she climbed and also feared that the man might have a guest with him. It took him several moments to answer. First he called out in German but she was too fearful to answer. His shoes were outside the door and she noticed that he had quite large feet. They were black patent shoes and they had not yet been polished. A dust lay in the creases where his toes had inclined upwards. Opening the door, he did not recognise her for an instant, what with no bolero and no earrings, and then he did.

'*Die Elixire des Teufels*,' she said, and he smiled as if to some sacred password.

Drawing her into the room like a sleep-walker, he led her across to a rocking-chair and she was aware as she sat down of a garment slipping onto the floor. It was his velvet jacket. On the bedside table she noticed his gold watch and an ashtray with a lot of stubs. He had smoked very little of each cigarette. Taking the flowers, he laid them one by one into a tooth-mug, studying them carefully and with infinite tenderness. It was then it happened. She could not put a word to it, she had simply lost the memory of where she had come from or why exactly she had come. She had put herself in his keeping. It was like going on the big dipper except that her mind as well as her body was at sway.

'*Heimlich*,' she said. It meant home. She had asked a waiter in the hotel the night before. She had come home for a few moments to a stranger who was not really a stranger because he seemed to have such a sense of her, sensed her exile and her dread. She seemed weightless in his arms and very safe, as if being led into a niche.

When they departed the next morning, the man seated next to her on the bus waved and she waved too. He was waving, as he said, to Ingrid, the gay girl in polka-dot who had taught him the German dance steps and had given him three boiled eggs for breakfast.

'Lovely lass,' he said, looking down at a photograph of her in a shell frame. She thought of her friend, maybe sleeping, maybe not, but standing by the window smoking one of his black cigarettes; thinking of her, perhaps.

'Changed my life,' the man said, and brought his face closer to the picture. Yes, lives had been changed; hers also, because when they stopped at the first inn for refreshments she marched up to her husband and said, quite confidently, 'I'm leaving you.'

'Leaving me – you won't last a week,' he said. To her amazement, she did not break down as she always had when broaching something difficult to him, or asking him for money. She was quite calm, quite confident, and knew that when they got to Victoria Station in London, she would not be going home with him. And she didn't.

'But what about the stranger?' Emma would say. 'What happened with him?'

'I don't know.'

'How long did you spend in the room?'

'Half an hour . . . less?'

'Did he kiss you?'

'Just the once.'

Always at that moment Emma shivered, an exaggerated shiver summoning a constellation of pleasures and sensations that she had no name for.

'And you came away with your clothes on?'

'Yes, I was carrying my shoes and the stairs felt spongy, like warm sand.'

Twenty odd years went by and Miss Dalton was travelling again, but her travels were of a more agreeable kind. She lectured on the restoration of icons and attracted a reasonable audience in cities throughout Europe. It was in Vienna, after she had given her lecture and prepared to go out to supper with

EDNA O'BRIEN

her hosts, that she sighted a gentleman at the back, hovering,
with a bunch of roses, apricot roses.

'One for every year since we met,' he said.

'Since we met?'

'In the mountains – *Wildhaus.*'

'Wild house,' she said, and felt the blood rising in her neck at
this sudden challenge to her reserve. He bore no resemblance
to her violinist at all, but he was him, older, more harried,
with the same soft, rueful eyes. What had happened to him?
He shrugged, as if to say, 'You see, I have grown older, I have
grown heavier but I have not forgotten.' He only played the
violin occasionally, at some wedding or other. A rose for
every year since they had met. He remembered exactly. How
had he known she was coming? He had read it in the paper.

By the way he looked at her, he was also saying how
pleasant it would be if she could excuse herself and go off with
him for a few hours and talk and perhaps even reminisce. What
would he tell her? What would she learn?

'I can't,' she said, glad that there were people waiting on
her.

'Maybe you'll come back one day?' he said.

'Maybe I will,' she said, thinking it quite unlikely.

He did not kiss her hand, simply bowed, then withdrew as if
he were a spirit, a spectre of the night, except that he wasn't.
He had come in person and had brought this sheaf of roses.

Their secret was safe now, lost without a trace, like a stone
cast into the sea, a stone to be absorbed in the timelessness of
the great currents.

Rum and Coke

JULIA O'FAOLAIN

I EXPECT AT any minute to hear from the nursing home where my wife is due to go into labour. They thought I was making her nervous, which is why they asked me to leave. I can't blame them. After all, what could they know of our – what? Anomalies? So now I sit by the phone, thinking of the boy – we know it's to be a boy – and of how he'll be called Frank in memory of my father: Senator Leary, whose death, to quote the obituaries, was such a sore loss to his country. Soon there will be a new Frank Leary to take his place. Symmetry and *pietas*. He'd have liked that.

He laid out his principles for me on the day, not long after my nineteenth birthday, when I took up my duties as summer barman at the Moriarty Castle Hotel. He'd got me the job. The Knights sometimes held functions there, indeed were holding one that weekend, which was why he drove me down. My mother came in her own car and stopped off for lunch. She was en route to Galway where the League to Save the Unborn Child (SUC) had organised a rally. She's one of their officers.

While she settled my father into his room, I introduced myself to the head barman, who said he'd show me the ropes in the lull after lunch. Then back came my parents and my

133

JULIA O'FAOLAIN

father asked me to pour him a drink: coke and rum. That
surprised me because of his being a teetotaller. He grinned and
so did my mother: a benedictory, parental grin. Declan's an
adult now was what it decreed; then he made his speech. You
could sum it up to sound like hypocrisy – until you remembered about *that* being the tribute vice pays to virtue. Anyway,
his principle was simple – although its workings turn out not
to be! He said he wanted me, during his stay at the castle, to do
what trusted barmen around the country had been doing for
years: slip a sizeable snort of rum into his Coca Cola but charge
whoever was standing drinks for the coke only. Later, he
would drop by and pay the difference. The common interest
came before that of the individual. And he, a man in the public
eye, must neither alienate voters nor weaken his own influence
for good. What the eye didn't see didn't matter.
   'But father, surely drinking wouldn't alienate many Irish
people?'
   'As a politician I can't afford to alienate any. For the sake of
the causes I support.'
   As this was one of the times when the Right-to-Lifers were
making a push to stop creeping Liberalism, I guessed he meant
them. 'But what,' I objected, 'about your conscience?'
   'That,' he cut me off, 'is between me and my God.' Then he
said again about the general good coming first. 'Abide by that
rule and you can do what you like. Obedience,' he smiled,
'makes for freedom!' And raised an eyebrow.
   I laughed.
   He believed in having a sense of humour. The obituaries
quoted him on how disarming it could be. It was, he liked to
say, a tempering mechanism. Also: that conservatives must
strive to surprise and dazzle so as to steal the opposition's fire.
   It's been odd reading about this clever, shifty man. To be
sure, some of the reminiscences went back to his school days –
and how could he have stayed the same? Ironically, though,
change was a bogy of his. One writer described him as 'a man
whose unwavering aim was to preserve on our island a state
faithful to the more orthodox teachings of the Roman
Catholic Church'. To do this, as he told me in the Moriarty

Castle bar, you had to fight unethical innovation. Unchristian practices. Unseemly publications. You needed counter-seductions. Wit and paradox. Nonchalance. Panache.

No one denied he had *that*. Too much? Maybe. Maybe he ended up seducing and bamboozling himself? *I* certainly can't be trusted to judge. He was fifty-seven but looked younger, in a Cary Grant sort of way: silver wings to his hair, white teeth, big frame, flat belly. He had a good tailor and could, as the saying goes, charm the birds off the trees – or, discreetly, pull birds. I was proud of him but apprehensive as to what he expected of me – or believed in really. My eldest brother has for years been a missionary in Ecuador, and it would be a mistake to suppose this pleased my father. According to him, most missionaries nowadays were crypto-Communists. Indeed, now that the official Communists had collapsed, they *were* the last Communists. Priests – which may sound odd from a militant layman – were dangerously gullible and monks worse. He'd sent me and my two brothers to school to the Benedictines with advice to take what they taught us with a pinch of salt. He wanted us to have a grounding in religion, yes, but also to be able to take the world on at its own game. And for this, the Benedictines, he was sorry to say, were insufficiently robust. They were considered classier than the Jesuits, but lacked the nous to spike their coke with rum. Or their red lemonade with whiskey, which I should also be prepared to serve. Likewise tonic with vodka. Doubleness was all. I guessed that the job as barman was meant to sharpen me – and was happy about this. I had been reading Stendhal and thought of Moriarty Castle in terms of his great houses where raw young men learn amatory wit. My second brother was in Australia. As an uncle of ours put it, he and my father were too alike, and two cocks in one barnyard upset the pecking order. My sisters were married, so on whom could my father's hopes focus if not on me? I might have resented this if I had been surer of it. As it was, I was desperate to impress him.

I've rung the nursing home again. They're to let me know just

135

as soon as I'm needed – and are undoubtedly being patient because of whose son I am. In this city, you are never anonymous, so may as well reap the benefits, since there are drawbacks too. It's odd: I haven't thought so much about him for months. Not since the last panegyric was read and folded away. Maybe when the new Frank Leary is hogging attention I'll forget the old one? Come to think of it, I'll *be* the 'old' Leary then. Old, worldly and not quite twenty-one! Maybe, God help me, I'll burst out in my fifties!

The drawbacks? Well with women for a start. Feminists. His name was a red rag to them, so I could never take things on their own terms. Every choice meant being with or against him and I always chose to be 'with'. I had – I admit – a girlish admiration for his manliness and saw women as rivals.

Away from home though – I spent three summers abroad, learning modern languages – all this changed and by my second week in Italy, when I was fifteen, I was sharing a tent with a Danish girl. The tent was a tiny thing and dyed bright orange so that hunters would not shoot in our direction. I loved that: colour of flame and folly! I was over the moon to be out from under my Irish camouflage. Our parents, of course, thought we were in a hostel, but we simply moved out and after that I swear it was the difficulty of communicating – we talked in pidgin Italian to each other – which made it easy to be together. I conclude that the answer to that old conundrum as to which language Adam and Eve spoke in Paradise may be 'none'. Not being able to ask questions eliminates the trip-wires of shyness, class, and wondering whether what you feel for each other is love or lust. As for the one about using 'artificial contraceptives', Vinca was on the pill and had a container with a dial which clicked forward a notch each time she took one. Streamlined and sage, it made me glad I couldn't tell her of the preserved foetus which my mother's colleagues toted to their lectures on the ills the flesh is heir to. Silence was golden in our Umbrian olive grove – and we left chatter to the crickets.

But to return to Moriarty Castle: as I wasn't yet, strictly

speaking, on the staff, my father asked if it would be all right for me to sit down to lunch with my mother and himself. Later, such privilege would be off limits, like the swimming pool and the nine-hole golf course. Teasingly, he made me try a rum and coke.

Then my mother left and, as he and I strolled back through the lobby, he introduced me to the receptionist, a Miss Sheehy.

'This is my son, Declan,' he told her and she gave me a funny look. I told myself that I was imagining it and took her hand in a forthright grip. She was one of those slim, quivery girls who shy like deer and have a curtain of dark hair for hiding behind. I guessed her to be my age or maybe a bit older. More importantly, she was a beauty. My Stendhalian summer partner? Why not?

Later, after the barman had shown me how to mix drinks, I came back to the lobby. She was still on duty.

'How does it feel to be the son of a famous father?'

This annoyed me, so I countered with 'How does it feel to be a knockout beauty?'

That got a blush. I walked off regretting the balkiness of words. With Vinca and her summery successors I had rejoiced in their absence. Maybe it was auricular – Christ, *there's* a word! – confession which poisoned them for me? All that talk of 'bad' thoughts. Maybe I should become an explorer and live in the Amazon jungle: steamy heat, warm mud, bare-breasted Indian girls and, above all, no chat! I kept thinking of Miss Sheehy though. That hair had a tremulous life to it. Like seaweed. Now I'd got myself uselessly excited and should maybe take a run around the tennis courts – unless they were off limits too. I wondered: was Miss Sheehy? As it happened, I had no time to find out because carloads of Knights started arriving and soon the bar was abuzz and I was kept busy. I wondered whether the castle chapel was off limits to staff too? This seemed unlikely, so maybe I'd be able to watch them next day at their mumbo jumbo, robing and disrobing, in imitation of the Crusaders donning armour to fight the forces of darkness and fornication. I wasn't sure how close my father's connection with them was. They favour confidentiality and infiltration and he might be their man in the senate. He didn't appear in the bar.

I finished work after midnight. There was no sign of Miss Sheehy. I fell on my bed and slept.

I was awoken before daylight. My mother wanted me on the phone. Or rather, it turned out, she wanted my father. There was some decision to do with the rally which only he could take. Neither she nor the other Pro-Life ladies took decisions. They were there to make it look as though *women* were opposing the feminists but were puppets really. She apologised for waking me but said she'd been ringing him since last night.

'Your father's not answering his phone,' she told me. 'It's off the hook. I think maybe he knocked it off inadvertently and now he'll miss all his calls.'

So I pulled on some clothes, took the lift to the guests' part of the hotel, and arrived at his door just as Miss Sheehy emerged from it – or rather just as she started to emerge, for when she saw me she ducked back in. That was hard to misinterpret and froze me in my tracks. I mean if she had said 'Hello Declan' and that she had been answering a room-service call, I would have believed her. I would have accepted any plausible story because I was thinking of her in terms of my own designs, not his – but, instead, she turned tail on seeing me. For perhaps a minute, I stood transfixed. Then, as I turned to go, out she bobbed again.

'Declan, can you come here, please. Your father wants you.'

I bolted. Unthinkingly. Or rather what I was thinking was that I didn't want to know any more of his secrets.

Back in my room I started making faces at my mirror and told the clown grimacing back that I was a prize ass. Obviously he was ill and she *had* been answering a room-service call. Why, though, had she bobbed away? Clown, so as to tell him his son was outside. Clown, clown! What would they both think of me now? Worldliness, where were you? I had failed the test! Fallen at the first fence. Could my father, I even wondered, have set the thing up deliberately? I had heard of British Foreign Office candidates being tested like this on country-house weekends.

I wasn't surprised by the knock on my door. It was Miss Sheehy to say that, just as I'd guessed, he was ill. Alarmingly so. Her manner had grown agitated and she was asking for my help. 'He can't walk and we can't have the doctor finding him in my room.'

Her room? I was so flustered that we were at its door before I remembered that, just now, they had been in his. How had he got here?

She brushed away the question. 'Look, he's passed out. We should get a doctor. It could be serious! A heart attack even! But he can't be found *in my room!*' Her voice had an edge of hysteria.

She opened her door and there he was on the carpet, I saw the urgency then. Jesus, I thought. Christ! As far as I could tell, his pulse was all right. Or was it? I tried, clumsily, to compare it to my own – but it's hard to take two pulses simultaneously. Miss Sheehy became impatient.

'Take his shoulders,' she directed. 'I'll hold the door. Can you drag him to the lift? Or hoist him on your back?'

'Supposing we're seen?'

'We'll say he began to feel ill in your room. Then, when you tried to help him back to his, he fainted. I'm here because you rang the front desk.'

Good enough, I thought with relief, and gave myself to a frenzy of activity which kept my feelings in check. He was heavy but I'm strong and was able, like *pius Aeneas* fleeing the wars of Troy, to carry my father down the corridor, into the lift, then down another corridor to his room. By then, she had rung the doctor who was on his way. As I laid him on his bed, she divulged some facts. They had, she admitted, been quarrelling and her invitation to me to enter his room had been a move in the quarrel. When I left, she had rushed off, whereupon he, thinking she'd gone after me, followed her.

'He's terrified of his family finding out about us.'

'Us?' I asked stupidly.

'Him and me.'

You, I wondered dourly, and how many others? I was in a sweat of filial guilt: unfounded, to be sure, but my feelings had run amok. My father's poor, vulnerable, open eyes stared glassily and saw neither of us. Oh God, I prayed, don't let him die. Not here. Not for years! Please, God! At the same time I was furious with him. For what about my mother? Did she know – I recalled her tolerance of the rum-and-coke – that as well as trusted barmen 'up and down the country', he also had – what? What was Miss Sheehy? His heart's love or one of a team? A team of floosies? If so, how big? Basketball five? Hockey eleven? She, no doubt, imagined him to be in love with her. Might he be? I felt obscurely flouted, and confused.

The doctor, when he came, quickly changed my mood.

'It's serious,' he warned. 'He's had a stroke. I'm going to call a helicopter and fly him to Galway.'

He told us to stay in the room while he went to make arrangements. For moments we sat in silence. Miss Sheehy was as pale as paper. My father's eyes were closed now and his face was grey.

'How long have you – been with him?'

'Three years.'

'So why the quarrel now?' He would not, I was sure, have misled her with false promises. He would never leave my mother. A Senator! A militant Catholic layman! Never in this life!

'I'm pregnant,' she blurted and began to cry.

'Don't cry!' I could have slapped her. Hysteria, I thought. Then: could he be such a fool? 'You mean you didn't use anything?' Condoning the use of artificial contraceptives led, said the League to Save the Unborn Child, to condoning abortion. Changing our legislation would open the sluice gates. I knew the arguments by heart. But what about the principle of what the eye didn't see? *Her* eyes were getting scandalously red. 'Don't cry,' I urged. 'The doctor will be back in a moment.'

'And he'll take him away. To Galway. Listen,' she clutched my arm, 'I must see him, get news of him. But he'll be in intensive care. I won't be let in. Only relatives will be. Will you help me?'

Red-eyed, feverish mistress! Outcast, beautiful Miss Sheehy. I kissed her and it was she who slapped me! Ah well, some outlet was needed. The doctor may have heard the slap for he gave us a look as he came in the door. Two paramedics were with him and in no time had my father on a stretcher. We followed them down the familiar corridors and out to the lawn where the helicopter was waiting. They loaded him on. Blades rotated; wind moulded our clothes to our bodies; then up it whirred into a misty dawn, turning silver, then grey, then fading to a speck.

I thought of 'the rapture', the bodily whisking of people up to heaven in which certain Protestants believe – ex-President Reagan for one was, I'd read in some magazine, expecting to be whisked aloft. Holus, bolus, body and bones! It was an inappropriate thought. But then what was appropriate? Maybe I was in shock?

Miss Sheehy's hand was in mine. Would I help her see him, she begged, or at least keep in touch? Yes, I said, yes. I'd be leaving for the hospital as soon as I could explain things to the management here. I'd phone her this evening.

'I have this weekend off,' she told me.

Ah, I thought: they planned to spend it together. Poor father! Poor Miss Sheehy!

'What's your first name?' I asked.

She said it was Artemis. Her parents had wanted her to be a huntress, not a victim. I made no comment.

I've had a call from my mother. From the nursing home. No need for me, she says, to worry. First babies are often slow to arrive. She should know: a mother of five and a four-time grandmother. My sisters have been dutifully breeding. She's in her element and hasn't been in such good spirits since my father's death.

He never regained consciousness. When Artemis came in on the Friday evening, I dissuaded her from seeing him, arguing

–truthfully – that he'd have hated to be seen with drips and needles stuck all over him.

She acquiesced, noting, with an unreadable little smile, that she was used to *not* doing things – not writing to him ever, nor ringing him up. Not at his office. Not at home. Nowhere. She always had to wait for him to make the contact. I looked appalled and she said defiantly, 'When we were together, it was pure delight. Like wartime furloughs. Utterly without ordinary moments. We met sometimes on a friend's barge on the Shannon, once on a yacht in Spain, once in a flat in Istanbul. Never for long. But he was so happy at being able to do what he never ordinarily did . . .'

Christ, I thought, he'd raised negativity to a mystique! He was a one-man cult and had brainwashed her good and proper. I suddenly realised that I disliked him deeply and had, unknown to myself, done so for years. No wonder my brothers had fled to Australia and Ecuador.

By now I had spent three days in the hospital with my mother – the stroke had happened on the Wednesday morning. There was nothing to do but wait, talk to doctors about their scans, filter their pessimism back to her, hold her hand. The staff, predictably, was assiduous, so I had a lot of help.

'Such a fine man,' I would hear them murmuring prayer-fully to her in corridors and guest areas. 'What a tragedy!' Sometimes they went with her to the chapel. One of the nurses was a member of the League to Save the Unborn Child. She, she told my mother, rarely questioned the will of God but found it hard to see a clean-living teetotaller like my father struck down when the town was full of drunks whose blood-pressure seemed not to give them a moment's trouble. 'God forgive me, I'm a desperate rebel!' boasted this docile mouse, trembling under her blue, submissive veil.

These conversations, I admit, gave my mother a lot more consolation than I could provide. Communicating with her has never been my forte. She was younger than my father and totally his creature. They were what's called a fine couple. She's five feet ten, graceful, blonde-speckled-tastefully-with-grey, dutiful, cheerful, plays tennis and bridge, takes pleasure in her volunteer work for his causes and has never, in my presence, revealed a spark of even the mild brand of rebelliousness favoured by the blue-veiled nurse. None. My sisters' opinion is that she's been emotionally lobotomised. By whom?

I went from time to time to look at him. He was semi-paralysed and his face was badly askew: mouth twisted up and down in a vertical, Punch-and-Judy leer. Doubleness had finally branded him. Nobody but me, though, seemed to have had such a thought. At least nobody voiced it, and neither, to be sure, did I. My mother kept putting her hand on his brow, murmuring coaxing endearments and kissing his convulsed grey face. She hoped something might be getting through. This must have drained her emotionally for, in the evenings, she went back to her hotel and was served a meal in bed.

This left me free to dine *en ville* with Artemis Sheehy, whose weekend was, I reminded myself, available and blank. Despite my advice, she yearned to do precisely what my mother had been doing: put her long-fingered hand on my father's brow and kiss him well.

I decided – in retrospect it is impossible to disentangle my motives – to let her. From hope? Pity? As aversion-therapy? How can I say?

We had by now had a row, or rather we had had another. Our relations from the start had been edgy. Why, I queried on Friday evening, as we sat waiting for the baked Alaska – I had, since she refused to drink with me, had a bottle of claret to myself – why had she let my father cast her as Patient Griselda, while he played the Pillar of the Irish Establishment? A P.I.E., I mocked, that was what he was, a po-faced Pie! An escapee from the novels of Zola and nineteenth-century operetta! Old hat! Self-serving! A canting humbug! My jealousy revenged itself on his charm – I now thought of it as smarm – and on his unassailable advantage in the minds of my mother and Artemis: his poignantly stricken state. The new-felled Knight!

'Can you,' I harried, 'deny that he is – was a hypocrite?'

What could she do, in all decency, but throw down her

napkin and leave? I, waiting for the bill, had to let her go – and, anyway, knew I had her on a string. I was her only connection with him and so could let her stew. Greedy from anger – and satisfying one appetite in lieu of another – when the baked Alaska arrived with the bill, I ate her portion as well as my own. It struck me, as I walked morosely back to my hotel, that I was beginning to act like him. Ruthless and masterful. I hated myself. Still – I licked the last of the baked Alaska from my lips – it would be pointless to forgo my advantage by capitulating too soon.

Sure enough, she rang me next morning. Triumphant – but hiding it – I was sweetness itself. And contrite. She must, I begged, see how hard it was for me to hold my mother's hand by day and hers in the evening? I was painfully torn – as no doubt my father too had been. Instinctively, I was blending my image with his: an anticipation of what was to happen when obituaries appeared with photographs of his young self, looking, as was universally noted, disturbingly like me. But, to go back to my conversation with Artemis, I now made a peace-offering, which was that if she really wanted me to, I would take her to see him this evening, after my mother had left the hospital.

She accepted and, as I had tried to dissuade her, could hardly blame me for the shock. His skewed mouth dribbled. There were tubes in his nose. He looked worse than dead. He looked like an ancient, malicious changeling put together from that grey stuff with which wasps build their nests. Or ectoplasm or papier mâché made from old, pulped bibles. These conceits swarmed through my head as I watched, then, from pity, ceased to watch her.

She was devastated, disgusted, guilty: a mirror of myself. Did she also feel that hot rush of feeling which, for days now, had been distracting and perhaps healing me? The urge to fuck, which is a pro-life remedy for death-fears? People get it in wartime and, notoriously, in graveyards and during blackouts and other foreshadowings of mortality. I let her look her fill. I even left her alone lest, like my mother, she wish to kiss him. I don't know whether she did.

I waited in the hospital-green corridor, not hurrying her adieux which, whether she knew it or not, were what they were. He, the doctors had told me, would be a wreck if he lived but was unlikely to last the weekend. I hadn't told her this, but guessed she knew. Then I took her on a drive along the coast, next for a long, twilit walk along a stretch of it, and finally to a small seaside hotel, where we spent the night comforting each other and conjuring away ghosts.

My father died that night, which was just as well for all concerned, especially her. If he had lived, what would she have done? Gone to somewhere like Liverpool to have her child, then given it out for adoption? Or raised it in resentful solitude on the income he would feel frightened – if compos mentis – into coughing up? Taken an 'abortion flight' to London? Instead, once we had faced my mother with the *fait accompli* of our runaway marriage – registry office in London, followed by a conciliatory Church ceremony back home – Artemis became part of the household which, for three years, she had been forbidden to phone. Sometimes, she tells me, she used, in her loneliness, to dial the number anyway then listen, silently, to our irritably convivial voices.

'Hullo! Speak up. Who is it? Oh it's the heavy breather again! What do you want, Heavy Breather? If you're a burglar, we're all at home so there's no point trying to break in!'

Now she *is* in and the noses of my sisters' children – none of them Learies – are put out of joint by the glorious prospect of Frank Junior's birth. Any minute now my mother will phone with news of my new brother's entry under false colours in the Leary clan. Brother-masquerading-as-son, he will be born under the true Leary sign of duplicitous duality.

And I? Well, I'm in Law School and active in the Student Union. People ask whether I'll go into politics and my fear is that I may find myself turning into a carbon copy of my father. I am, after all, living by his principles and can't see quite how to break out. Drinking claret instead of rum and coke seems an inadequate gesture, and my support for Family Planning, Abortion and Divorce has been hailed by some of his cronies as the sort of forward-looking thinking to which he himself

JULIA O'FAOLAIN

might well have subscribed had he lived. Times have changed, they say, and we must march to the European Community's tune if we want subsidies for our farmers. After all, providing the option to use contraception, etc., obliges nobody to avail themselves of it. And anyone who does can repent later. God is good and there's no point being simple-minded. So, they would have me think, opposing the letter of my father's laws is a way of being true to their spirit.

Maybe. It's hard to tell. Double-think is the order of the day.

Of course I rejoice in Artemis's love, though here too a shiver of doubt torments me: does she see him in me? Am I two people for her? To be sure, it's foolish to probe! We're happy and . . . there's the phone! Alleluia! Where are my car keys? Frank Junior must be on his way.

A Prayer From the Living

BEN OKRI

WE'VE ENTERED THE town of the dying at sunset. We went from house to house. Everything was as expected, run-down, a desert, luminous with death and a hidden life.

The gun-runners were everywhere. The world was now at the perfection of chaos. The little godfathers who controlled everything with guns raided the food brought for us. They raided the air-lifts and the relief aid and distributed most of the food amongst themselves and members of their clan.

We no longer cared. Food no longer mattered. I had done without for three weeks. Now I feed on the air and on the quest.

Every day, as I grow leaner, I see more things around us. I see all the dead around, outnumbering the living; I see the dead, all who had died of starvation. They are more joyful now; they are happier than we are; and they are everywhere, living their luminous lives as if nothing had happened, or as if they were more alive than we are.

The hungrier I became, the more I saw them – my old friends who had died before me, clutching on to flies. Now, they feed on the light of the air. And they look at us – the living – with so much pity and compassion in their eyes.

I suppose this is what the white ones cannot understand

when they come with their television cameras and their aid. They expect to see us weeping. Instead they see us staring at them, without begging, and with a bulging placidity in our eyes. Maybe they are secretly horrified that we are not afraid of dying this way.

But after three weeks of hunger the mind no longer notices; you're more dead than alive; and it's the soul wanting to leave that suffers. It suffers because of the tenacity of the body.

Most of us are already in the other world and only the dreadful strength and resilience of life keeps us staring at this world and at flies.

We should have come into the town at dawn. In the town everyone had died. The horses and cows were dying too. The stink in the air was no longer amazing in its horror. I could say that the air stank of death, but that wouldn't be true. It smelled of rancid butter and poisoned heat and bad sewage. There was even the faint irony of flowers.

The only people who weren't dead were the dead. Singing golden songs in chorus, jubilant everywhere, they carried on living their familiar lives. The only others who weren't dead were the soldiers. And they fought amongst themselves eternally, fighting for the dying flesh of our land.

They had split into innumerable factions. It didn't seem to matter to them how many died. All that mattered was how well they handled the grim mathematics of the wars, that is to say of the dying, so that they could win the most important battle of all, which was for the leadership of the fabulous graveyard of this once beautiful and civilised land.

The soldiers weren't interested in us; and we who were dying weren't interested in them. We had come on a quest. I was searching for my family and my lover. I wanted to know if they had died or not. If I didn't find out I intended to hang on to life by its very last tattered thread. I will not die till I know where my companions are. I will die at peace if I know that they too were dead or safe and no longer needed me.

In this life everything has betrayed us: nation, history, notions of God, the future, food, and air. The fabric of life is thinner than we think. And when all is said and done there's not much to distinguish the good and the bad than the way in which they face death. And even that's not wholly true. But maybe as a people we've become too much at home with death and have forgotten the miracle of life. Or maybe we've forgotten how to love. I don't know how we got around to forgetting, but we did.

All my information has led me to this town. Here is where the trail ends: if my lover, my brothers, my family are anywhere, they are here. This is the last town in the world. Beyond its rusted gate, where the vultures of hunger gladly circulate the air, lies the desert. The desert stretches all the way into the past, into history, to the western world, and to the source of all drought and famine – the mighty mountain of lovelessness. From its peaks, at night, the grim spirits of negation chant their awesome soul-shrinking songs. Their songs steal hope from us, and make us yield to the air our energies. Their songs are cool and make us submit to the clarity of dying.

Here is the world's end. Behind us, in the past, before all this came to be, there were all the possibilities in the world, all the potentials for joy, and the building of a new world, and learning to love one another. There were all the opportunities for starting from small things to creating a sweet new history and future, if only we had seen them. But now, ahead, there lie only the songs of the mountain of death, with its spirits of silence. And time's negation.

We wandered about the town at dawn, and wove our ways through the debris of the dead. After a while the geometry of the dead becomes familiar, even quite beautiful, in its simplicity. Everything is clear.

We search for our loved ones mechanically, and with a dryness in our eyes. Our stomachs no longer exist. Nothing exists now except the search. We turn the bodies over, looking for familiar faces. All the faces were familiar; death had made them all my kin.

I search on, without feeling, or hope. I come across an unfamiliar face; it is my brother. I nod. I pour dust on his flesh.

149

Hours later, near a dry well, I come across the other members of my family. My mother holds on tightly to a bone so dry it wouldn't even nourish the flies. I nod twice. I pour dust on their bodies. Feeling my dry eyes sliding off the things of this world, I search on. There is one more face whose beautiful unfamiliarity will console me. When I have found the face then I will submit myself to the mountain songs of pure negation.

I wandered through the town, dragging my own corpse with me like the ancient hero who was weighed down by his cross. I search every alley. I crawl past the white ones with their equipments. They point their television cameras at me and ask me questions, and I nod three times and try to smile. I crawl on, aware that they must see me as bestial now, and pity me as such, but aware also that if they knew the object of my search they might see me as possibly the last hero in this land of heroes, with all the heroes dead all about, and most of them children. For they died every one of them without howling and wailing and self-pity, and without fear.

It is possible that a land of heroes eventually becomes a land of gravestones. Maybe the new heroism of the future will have more to do with the courage to lose, in order to win; to give way, in order to gain ground; to be a little weak, in order to be invisibly strong; to live slowly, and with a low but long-lasting fire. Maybe the future heroism will have more to do with these than with this courage of ours which makes us bear and withstand and ultimately be destroyed by too much suffering. We are too strong for our own good. Our resilience has made a fertile graveyard of this earth.

Sunset was approaching when, from an unfinished school building, I heard singing. It was the most magical sound I had ever heard and I thought only those who know how sweet life is can sing like that, can sing as if breathing were a prayer.

I hurried towards the singing, crawling over the bloated sweet-smelling bodies of the dead, climbing over the shrivelled corpses of sweet young children and babies who had died without a curse on their lips and with flies and worms on their legs. Maybe it takes the dying to see the beauty of the dead.

The singing was like the joyous beginning of all creation, the first chorus of time at its own momentous dawn, the initial amen to the great idea of the universe, the holy yes to the breath and light infusing all things, which makes the water shimmer, the plants sprout, the animals jump and play in the fields, and which makes the men and women look out into the first radiance of colours, the green of plants, the blue of sea, the gold of the air, the silver of the stars. To me the singing was the true end of my quest, the grail I couldn't have known about, the music to crown this treacherous life of mine, the end I couldn't have hoped for, or imagined.

It seemed to take an infinity of time to get to the unfinished school building. I had no strength left, and it was only the song's last echo, resounding through the vast spaces of my hunger, that sustained me. After maybe a century, when history had repeated itself and brought about exactly the same circumstances, because none of us ever learned our lesson, or loved enough to learn from our pain, or took the great scream of history seriously enough, I finally made it to the schoolroom door. But a cow, the only living thing left in the town, went in through the door before I did. It too must have been drawn by the singing. The cow went into the room, and I followed.

Inside, all the available floor space was taken up with the dead. But here the air didn't have death in it. The air had prayer in it. The prayers stank more than the deaths. But all the dead here, in this room, were differently dead from the corpses outside in the town's square and in all the other towns. The dead in this school room were – forgive the paradox – alive. I have no other word to explain the serenity. All I can say was that I felt they had come here, to this room, and had somehow made it holy with the way they had approached their dying. I felt that they had made the room holy because they had, in their last moments, thought not of themselves but of all people who suffer across the length and breadth of the world. I felt myself doing the same thing as I entered the room. I crawled to a corner, sat up against a wall, and felt myself praying for the whole human race.

151

I prayed – knowing full well that prayers are possibly an utter waste of time – but I prayed for everything that lived, for mountains and trees, for animals and streams, and for human beings wherever and whosoever they might be. I felt myself, in that moment, completely at home with the whole of humanity. I heard the great anguished cry of all mankind and heard its great haunting music as well. And I too, without moving my mouth, for I had no energy – I too began to sing in silence. I sang all through the evening. And when I looked at the body next to me and found the luminous unfamiliarity of its face to be that of my lover's – I sang all through the recognition. I sang silently even when a good-hearted white man came into the school building with a television camera, weeping, and recorded the roomful of the dead for the world – and I hoped he recorded my singing too.

It seemed a long time passed in the singing and I weaved in and out of it all. And when I came to briefly I saw, in a radiant astonishment, that the room wasn't full of the dead, but full of the living. The dead were all alive; but they were alive with light, in a way only few of the living are alive – alive with all the shimmering possibilities of life active in their being; alive in such a way that they come close to sublimity.

And the dead were all about me, smiling, serene. They didn't urge me on, they didn't insist; they were just quietly and intensely joyful. They did not ask me to hurry to them, but left it to me, left it to my choice. What could I choose?

Human life – full of greed and bitterness, dim, low-oxygenated, without light, judgmental, and callous, gentle too, and wonderful as well, but – human life had betrayed me. And besides, there was nothing now left to save in me. Even my soul was dying of starvation.

The song started again. I opened my eyes for the last time. I saw the cameras on us all. To them, we were the dead. As I passed through the agony of the light, I saw them as the dead. I saw them gesticulating out of time, without eternal connection, marooned in a world without pity or love.

As the cow wandered about in the apparent desolation of the room, it must have seemed odd to the people recording it all that I should have made myself so comfortable among the dead. I did. I stretched myself out and held the hand of my lover. With a painful breath and a gasp and a smile, I gently let myself go.

The smile must have puzzled the reporters. If they had understood my language, they would have known that it was my way of saying goodbye.

Concerto Grossman

FREDERIC RAPHAEL

I HAVE ALWAYS envied musicians. What could be more virtuously self-serving than to sing for one's supper? Alas, not even when allotted the triangle in my prep school was I ever able to strike the right note at the right time; at Charterhouse, I was definitely branded a 'non-singer' by the choirmaster. It is bad enough to hear that all flesh is as grass without being banished for ever from the number of those who can be trusted to announce it in tune. To one beyond its magic scope, to be a musician is not only an accomplishment, it is to have the entrée to a hermetic and harmonious community. Who would argue with Peter-Paul Grossman when he said, in a recent interview, that he wished that half the time that he had devoted to the cinema had been dedicated to Wagner or to 'the dance'?

Peter-Paul did not disclose exactly what he should have done with the *other* half of his misused time; he left it hazily clear that it was something of even greater cultural significance than taking yet another dip with the Rhinemaidens. It is typical of his determination at all times to renew himself that Peter-Paul chose implicitly to discount the merits of his 1963 Freudian version of *Winnie The Pooh* in which the brilliantly re-thought Eeyore was said to be closely modelled on certain newly discovered material on Carl Gustav Jung. The fact that the imported actor spoke partly in Schweizer-Deutsch irritated some Milne scholars, but I agree that it created a marvellous perspective through incongruity.

It was that seminal 'Winnie Ze Poo', and its explosive critical reception, that convinced Gino Amadei, and Gino who almost convinced me, that we should ask my already famous college friend to direct the script on which I had been working for the last six months. It was based on my own story and, in my pettish way, I was not flattered when Peter-Paul first said that he did not normally do commercial crap. Nor was I wholly placated when, after a persuasive lunch at the Trattoria, he relented, on condition that A PETER-PAUL GROSSMAN FILM appeared above the title. The casting of Rosemary Titchbourne as Lola was another non-negotiable demand. Peter-Paul told us that what he valued about 'Rosie' – as opposed to 'some putative star' – was that she could *sing*.

After the film was finished, Gino Amadei said, 'I'm sorry but I have to tell you one thing: that Rosemary Titchbourne has a voice we never hear and the most audible ankles I have ever seen.' For one reason or another, *The Love of Lola Gerassi* never received a general distribution. As Grossman said in a recent interview, England is a Philistine country in which tolerance is all too often only another name for laziness. Peter-Paul attributed the failure of the film to 'the basically banal *donnée* and, of course, the Bistro-style music'. He had, he said, wanted to create the soundtrack himself, but 'the producer's vulgar and venal considerations had, alas, prevailed'. However, as *auteur* he had the grace to allow that the blame had finally to be his. When Peter-Paul says *mea culpa*, it is the cue for everyone else to redden guiltily.

The first time I ever saw him, he was wearing blue jeans, Moroccan slippers and a tented beige duffel coat with its hood half-latched over masses of that often photographed, and caricatured, curly black hair. He was carrying his breakfast tray across the third court of St John's College on a November morning. His porridge was being kept warm by a lustreless tin lid on top of which a much-flagged quarto volume lay legibly open. As he walked, he was reading with intimidating intensity, his corrugated forehead lined like a manuscript page, ruled and ready for crotchets. There must have been a morning frost, for as he stepped from the paved to the cobbled part of the way to the Bridge of Sighs, his leading foot suddenly went shooting away and up into the raw air. He skittered backwards and forwards, at once, with his tray and his book. Happening to be on the way to the buttery for my own breakfast, I watched and listened, with malicious anticipation, for the clattering comedown of a man whose reputation, even at the beginning of his first year, both promised eminence and prompted spite. Instead, he hopped, tottered, lurched, blundered in a cascade of staggeringly balanced improvisations. Not only did he not fall, not only did he not lose so much as a single lump of his porridge, but he also contrived *both to turn a page of his book and to continue reading*. Was there ever a more manifest annunciation of genius?

As recent studies have shown, my generation at Cambridge was top-heavy with theatrical talent. In the 1950s, the difficulty lay less in finding a prodigy to direct undergraduate productions than in recruiting the troops on whom he might exercise his generalship. Emulous contemporaries who could not hold a candle to Peter-Paul were not always ready to carry a spear for him. My modesty was my salvation; I enrolled to play ignoble Romans and rhubarbing mechanicals in a number of early Grossman successes. In his version of *Macbeth*, I doubled as Malcolm and as a branch manager in Birnam Wood; he schooled me to add a neoteric note (not always spotted by the groundlings) to my interpretation of the part of Cinna the poet; as Osric, I spoke broad Devonshire in a sly, if slightly unintelligible, allusion to Sir Walter Raleigh who, Peter-Paul postulated, was almost certainly in Shakespeare's mind as the courtier's macaronic model.

After being promptly laurelled with a research fellowship to study Comparative Anthropophagy, it argued great courage when Peter-Paul quite suddenly renounced his academic career. Since he had been sponsored by men unaccustomed to having their favours set – let alone chucked – aside,

Grossman's decision to go to Paris in order to become a *clown* struck some of his intellectual Godfathers as picayune, not to say blasphemous. He justified himself, at a meeting of the Apostolic circle to which he had been elected at a younger age than anyone since Bertie Russell, by declaring that it was not some Bohemian caprice which took him to Paris, but an out-of-the-blue opportunity to learn 'the rhetoric of silence' offered him by the great mimetic sage, Touvian, to whom even Marcel Marceau himself conceded the last wordless word. By leaping into a world of pure gesture, Peter-Paul hoped to come back through a door 'on the far side of speech' and gain a new insight into 'the pharmacopoeia of mundane signs'. The effect of this declaration was heightened, as perhaps I should have mentioned, by the red nose, white face, bald wig, orange braces and baggy pants in which he delivered it.

Sylvia and I were living in Paris when word came that Grossman was coming to study with the white-faced master of the *Cirque Muet*. We were shivering that winter in a couple of rented rooms in the working class district of Crimée, while I wrote my first novel, but I heard that a fellow Apostle, with money in furs, had lent Peter-Paul a cosy flat on the Ile de la Cité whence he pedalled to his class in the *Onzième*. I sent him a card saying that we should be glad to hear from him if he were lonely. He must have been studying silence too diligently to be able to respond.

A mere week or two after his unobtrusive arrival in a city where he had announced he knew no one, I saw a full-page interview with Grossman in *L'Express*. Its subject was '*La Musique Totale et la Chose Sociale*'. One phrase was particularly Delphic: '*Pour moi,*' P.-P. G. was quoted as saying, '*la logique est surtout un cri d'alarme!*' When Sylvia said, 'Logic is above all a cry of alarm? What's that supposed to mean?', I replied that I thought that I could give it a sense, but that we needed Peter-Paul for a definitive exegesis. We did not get him until towards the end of that freezing winter in Crimée, when Sylvia and I received an invitation to a '*soirée unique*', directed by Peter-

Paul Grossman, in which a critical history of the world was to be encapsulated, with an interval, in terms of music, mime and movement. If I was touched that Peter-Paul remembered us, I was petty enough to frown when I shook the envelope in vain for the tickets I assumed he had enclosed.

Sylvia and I sat very high up in the Salle André Breton somewhere in the Marais, and were properly chastened as Peter-Paul's little troupe challenged any number of *idées reçues* with a vocabulary, as it were, consisting only of lengths of coloured rope, three beach balls, two window-cleaner's ladders, a bathbrush, a trampoline and a uni-cycle. Some people were so shaken by the iconoclastic acrobatics that they left early, but we stayed to tell Peter-Paul how amused we had been. All at once, his forehead took on immensely responsible corrugations. He looked like a frighteningly polyvalent Labrador who had been threatened with the Nobel Prize for Frivolity.

I chose to think of it as a mark of favour, though it may have been more loyalty, that he agreed to be free to dine with us after the show. It had, of course, taken it out of him. Was Sylvia a little tactless when she raised the question of what had he meant by saying that logic was a sign of alarm? He responded by opening his mouth in an inaudible shriek which, nevertheless, turned every head in the not inexpensive restaurant to which he had led us. He had, as it were, piped ultrasonically like a bat and transformed the whole room into his belfry. When Sylvia made a weary face, I had to admit that my friend had somehow succeeded in making me feel that my wife had failed to see the point. My mood was not lightened when Peter-Paul deferred to me, instantly, after I had gestured to the waiter for the bill. At the door, the *patron* thanked him thoroughly for the old francs I could ill afford to spend.

Despite and perhaps on account of our affinities, Peter-Paul and I have never become close friends. Over the years, our paths have crossed, but we were never true *compagnons de route*. It was something of a surprise, therefore, when I was contacted by young Giles Carpenter, the president-elect of the Cambridge Union, and asked whether I was free on a certain

date in the autumn. The thing was, Giles explained, they were
having a debate about Music. When I muttered sincere excuses
on the grounds of incompetence, the conniving young man
explained that Peter-Paul wanted the word 'music' taken in a
very wide sense, as signifying the domain of the Muses. I said
'Peter-Paul? As in Grossman?' 'Who else?' 'Ah,' I said, 'and
what is the motion exactly?' My question was, of course,
tantamount to acceptance. 'That Today Memory Has Too
Many Children,' Giles said. 'He hopes you'll propose.'

Despite Sylvia's Cassandran warning, I fell for it. As I
started to write my speech, I was surprised at the virulence
with which my first draft was laced. Intent only on the
composition of amiable barbs, I armed more warheads than I
ever guessed my arsenal contained. Only now did I realise
how angry I was at Peter-Paul's perversion of *Lola Gerassi* or at
his appropriation of its *auteur*ship. I had not even forgotten
that he never returned the hospitality we could ill afford at the
Brasserie de l'Hôtel de Ville. Had I, in consequence or merely
in addition, seriously disliked his setting of *Dido and Aeneas* in
a Calcutta knocking shop and of *Adriadne auf Naxos* in the
Betty Ford Institute? My vituperation stopped short of saying
that he had claimed poetic licence without being a poet,
authorship without ever having written a word, and a place in
the pantheon only on the strength of being panned, but you
could hear the squeal of its brakes.

Before the debate, there was a cheerful dinner, with heaps of
mashed potato. When we lined up to go into the chamber, my
opponent affected horror at the sheaf of paper which I revealed
myself to be carrying. 'You've prepared,' he said, quite as if
this were a breach of all civilised precedent. 'You bet,' I said.

Called to speak first, I was nervous, but I did not tremble. I got
early laughs by pouring feline praise on Peter-Paul who, I said,
was the very instance of the only child who made all his
siblings redundant. His books, his paintings, his operatic
productions, his stage happenings proved that the brother of
the Muses had so upstaged his sisters that they would be well-
advised to marry people who could find them jobs in

subsidised theatres. There was a cry of 'ooh' at this below-the-belt reference to Rosie Titchbourne's frequent appearances in Peter-Paul's operatic productions. I sorted my papers quickly and proceeded to what I paraded as a sincere tribute to my opponent, who lay slumped on the bench opposite me in a style possibly owing something to Henry Moore's dying warrior. Willing to wound, but lacking the killer instinct, I ended by saying that I looked forward to hearing how many new art forms the great innovator had conceived during my defence of obsolete forms and old hats. However, I warned the audience not to be too easily seduced by my opponent as he played all the parts in his own Concerto Grossman. He was, I reminded them, a particular virtuoso on his own trumpet.

I sat down to solid applause. When Peter-Paul rose, it was, it seemed, in articulated instalments. He less walked than ramped, like some doomed but dignified caterpillar, to the despatch box. Once there, he groped in an inside pocket and produced a sheaf of paper. So much, I thought, for the sly fox's lack of preparation. He found a pair of glasses – age blights even a prodigy – and piled his script before him. He peered and saw that the sheets were blank. He sighed and turned them the other way up. To his clownish chagrin, he revealed them to be blank on both sides. My feeling of pity was supplanted by apprehension as the audience's rustle of embarrassment turned to a growl of amused complicity. They, and I, had realised that my paper bullets had not even scratched the man whose fire I was now fated to endure.

How shall I describe the fifteen minutes which followed? In front of my eyes, and with gesture alone, Peter-Paul composed cadenzas and improvised riffs in a speechless speech which denounced me as a commonplace novelist, a trudging cinéaste, a commercial traveller, a diurnal and pedestrian reviewer, an uxorious husband and a decidedly overrated tennis player. As for Music, what part had I ever played in its inner counsels? I had, he indicated, after tuning an invisible instrument which still failed to utter a tolerable note, never been better than a futile second fiddle. He had, it seemed, observed me for years and seen nothing he did not despise. My

160

speech had suggested that he had usurped a dominant place in the arts without being an artist. I was now proved to be wrong: his art was that of an assassin; the Concerto Grossman, which I had dared him to compose, was his silent and lethal equaliser.

The Rower

FRANK RONAN

YOU TAKE THE ROAD from New Ross to Kilkenny and cross the Barrow at Mount Garret Bridge, and turn right by the grey house on the corner as if you were going to Graiguena-managh, and if you are not driving too fast you will find yourself passing through The Rower, where you might notice the scattering of houses along the main road, but you will see no people. You will need to ask directions to find the house of Lily Stevens, so it is best to go into the shop, if it is open, and ask there. They will send you towards her by rough lanes and complicated turnings, and no matter how well you under-stand the directions you will be lost once or twice. Be prepared for reversing in narrow dead-ends with your back wheels spinning in the heavy mud. There was one memorably wet winter when Lily Stevens' husband had to pull the harvester through the fields with a bulldozer to save the sugar-beet.

The house is almost square and covered with a lattice of dormant Virginia Creeper. The front door faces a small garden surrounded by a low wall and intersected with neglected bushes of acrid box. In the damp air it is this smell of box which dominates the garden. The door is painted yellow and has not been opened within the span of my memory. Drive into the yard at the back and let yourself in through the porch door, past the rusting, humming freezer and into the kitchen. You may find someone there to make yourself known to, and you might not. Lily Stevens' son and his famly live in a bungalow they have built on the other side of the haggard.

There is not much time left. It has been known for some weeks now that Mrs Stevens is near death, and most of the people who would have done so have come to The Rower to take their leave of her. And prepare yourself. She is so far gone now that she may not recognise you, and you may find it disturbing to hear the noise she makes as she tries to breathe, small and lost in the middle of her bed. She doesn't really speak any more, because of the effort it takes to get the words from her brain to her mouth through the fug of painkillers. Her last words have yet to be recorded, but she has had her last conversation.

'Don't just stand there,' she said. 'Come and sit by me.'

There was no chair, so I made a place for myself among the newspapers and dictionaries and old Penguin paperbacks on the end of the bed, and sat on the pattern of small pink flowers that covered her quilt. Under my weight the bed groaned and the old feathers made a sigh of compaction.

'I didn't think you'd know me,' I said.

A flicker of humour passed across her face. She had never been someone who tolerated false modesty and so, between us, a statement such as the one I had just made could only be taken as a joke. All the same, it was three years since I had last been home; since I had last seen her, and then we had only had the briefest of conversations, in the middle of the street in New Ross. She was still sprightly then, young for her eighty years, still driving herself into town once a week to do her shopping. She had made me promise that I would come out to The Rower to see her before I went away again. I had broken my promise, and I still remember the guilt I felt as the plane flew south from Dublin over the deadening cloudscape that passed for a view.

The bed creaked again with some small movement I made.

'You have a good colour,' she said. 'Are you still in the same place?'

'I've just moved to Lisbon. But the climate's the same.'

'Lisbon,' she said. She was silent for a few moments, not as though she had nothing to say, but more as though she was taking a little rest before continuing. I read the spines in the bookcases while I waited.

She said, 'I have a book of Portuguese poetry somewhere there. I can't remember the man's name, but I suppose you know it anyway. Not good, but very earnest.'

She looked over at her bookshelves, somewhat helplessly.

I said, 'It tends to be a bit like that. I think the Portuguese have been brutal for so long that since the revolution they have found that there is nothing left in them but goodness and earnestness.'

'It sounds very dull,' she said.

'It would be,' I said, 'if it was true.'

She began to laugh at that, but the pain that was brought upon her at the beginnings of laughter was so great that it defeated her amusement.

After a little while I read the clues of the *Irish Times* crossword to her and wrote in the answers she gave. The crosswords of the previous few days were on the bed, each one filled in by the hand of a different visitor.

'You haven't married yet?' she said.

'No.'

'I never thought you would.'

There was no need to give her more information. From the tone of my one word of denial she had divined more than I could divulge.

I was nine years old when I first came into her sphere of influence. She was my schoolteacher for two years. I can't remember any lesson that she taught me, but I can remember having conversations with her in the classroom; talking with her as though the two of us were alone and the thirty other children around me had faded into the gloss-painted walls. I can remember the day I handed her an essay and after she had read it she sent one of the children next door to fetch Sister Philomena. Sister Philomena was Head of the school at the time, and our days were punctuated by the screaming which came through the glass and wooden folding partition between her classroom and ours. The children under this nun's care had a cowed look about them, and scarlet palms where she had beaten them with her leather. Because of the noise from next door we were aware, every day, of the good fortune we had to be taught by Mrs Stevens, whose voice was seldom raised and whose hand never came down on ours in anger.

The messenger returned, followed by Sister Philomena. At the sight of the nun, clutching her leather in the pocket of her apron, my flesh turned to molten tar and my teeth began to chatter with fear. The nun scanned the classroom and rested her eyes on me, knowing by my terror that I was the one for whom she had been called. She drew her leather out as she addressed Mrs Stevens in harsh Irish.

I tried to review all the words I had put in the essay to know where I had transgressed. I couldn't think what sin I had committed that was so grave it made Mrs Stevens summon the Head: a thing she had never had cause to do before. My eyes were fixed on the leather in the nun's hand. The leather was an instrument known to all schoolchildren of the time, since it was invented and manufactured for their punishment and no other reason. Sister Philomena had refined hers by splitting it down the middle for half its length, doubling the pain it could inflict.

We were standing as the nun entered, out of respect, as we were obliged to do. As Mrs Stevens handed her my essay she commanded us to sit down. My legs were too weak to sit down in a controlled way, and I hit the seat with a thud. That was when I looked at Mrs Stevens and saw that she was smiling at me, not just with reassurance but with pride.

After the reading Sister Philomena and Mrs Stevens had a short discussion. Since they were speaking in Irish, as all teachers were obliged to do in front of their pupils, I could only understand one word in ten, but I caught enough of it to know that it was complimentary and that it concerned me. Then the nun bade us good morning and we all rose to our feet again, and just before she swept out of the room she gave me a big condescending smile.

Years later I asked Lily Stevens why she had shown the nun that essay. It was after Lily had retired and after I had left school, in the days when I used to cycle out to The Rower to spend the afternoon with her on Sundays, drinking tea and talking about poetry.

Lily said, 'I had to show her how intelligent you were. I knew, if I did that, she would never put you in her own class. She didn't like pupils who might be a match for her. I didn't want her to be beating the spirit out of you.'

And it was true: before Lily told me that, I had always assumed that in all the class and teacher permutations of my time at school it was luck that had kept me away from Sister Philomena and the lick of her leather.

Lily Stevens was the daughter of two schoolteachers, and her mother's parents were both schoolteachers before that. And they had all spent their whole lives teaching in the same school in the same town. So that for many years it was said that there was no native of New Ross who had not come under the tutelage of one of that family. Lily had broken with tradition by marrying a farmer, and since none of her children had shown any interest in becoming a teacher she was, in some respects, the last of her line.

On her bookshelves there was a first edition of *Ulysses* which Joyce had sent to her mother. The Parish Priest of the time had come to hear of the existence of the book and instructed Lily's mother to burn it. To save a scandal the book had to be hidden, and had to be read in secret. Lily's father was an amateur Greek scholar who had made his own translation of Pindar. This also had to be kept a secret from the town, since it was that part of the Pythian Odes which rejected immortality in favour of possibility. They had less clandestine possessions too; letters to various family members from Yeats and Synge and Mahaffy; letters that were reduced to tattered shreds from being read and re-read.

There were times in the life of the town when Lily's family seemed to be the only thread of life running through the town. Times when the State was young and, for want of an identity, it allowed De Valera to impose his ideal of the Irish as an

innocent peasantry by repression and censorship; times when
the thugs of the Old IRA were allowed to swagger un-
challenged, before the new IRA made that acronym shameful.
There were others, of course, with the courage to think for
themselves. But, by and large, they went away; to fight in
Spain, to live in Russia, to labour in North London, to teach
Portuguese children the English language in my own case. It
was Lily's family who stayed behind and kept the thin-spun
thread of the intellect running through our town. Perhaps
there were others, but that is the family I know of.

'I failed with you,' she said. She said this to me as she lay on
her deathbed, after she had finished the crossword, after I had
said twice that I must be tiring her; that I should be going.

'I failed with you. I wanted you to become a writer, not a
teacher.'

'That's my own fault. Not yours.'

The look she gave me was sceptical. She knew and I knew.
It was because of knowing her that I had come to consider
teaching to be the higher calling of the two. Perhaps if I had
been beaten by Sister Philomena: that might have made a
writer of me; a solitary introspective; each thuck of the
typewriter keys a blow of the leather returned to the nun.

I tried to justify myself. 'There are too many mediocre
writers in the world and not enough good teachers. Hardly
any good teachers at all.'

'Good or bad you might be,' she said. 'Mediocrity isn't in
you.'

She said that she wanted her pills, and gave me instructions,
and I took a pill from each of five bottles on her bedside table,
and held her head, and gave them to her in the right order, one
by one, with a sip of water between each. The back of her head
was soft and light. I realised that, in all the years I had known
her, it was the first time I had touched her. I thought of all the
lovers I had touched more intimately who had not known me
so well.

After the pills, after I had replaced her head on the pillow as
if it was an unconnected object, she closed her eyes, and I
wondered if she had gone to sleep. I waited some minutes,

standing by her head, thinking I should go and leave her to rest. I knew that this was our last conversation and that was why I hesitated. I moved my feet.

'No,' she said. 'Don't go. I'm not finished.'

I sat again on the tracery of pink flowers on the quilt and the bed groaned again under my weight. She smiled.

Without opening her eyes, she said, 'You're getting to the age when you should be minding your weight. Wait till you're like me and you have your work cut out keeping an ounce of flesh about you.'

'Fat chance,' I said.

She opened her eyes.

It must have been the drugs. When she opened her eyes there was an urgency and a vitality in them.

'You're back,' I said.

'I'm back,' she said.

She said, 'Did you notice my Agave? On the window-sill.'

'Yes,' I said. Although I hadn't noticed the plant before, I had turned around as she spoke and seen it: it was a spiny star in a pot, eighteen inches across like any other Agave on a window-sill.

She said, 'You wouldn't think it was twenty years old. I brought it back from Portugal when it was a tiny offshoot. If I'd left it where it was it would be seven feet wide by now. It might have flowered and died this summer. I was only in Portugal the once and the thing I loved most was the sight of flowering Agaves. Monocarpic, is that what you call it? They wait and they grow and when they are ready they throw a flower twenty feet into the sky. And then of course they die. What else could they do? But this one, this unfortunate on the window-sill; this one can only get older and older until it dies of oldness. This is the wrong climate for flowering.'

The thing I said next, the answer I gave, was said with a streak of cruelty in it; with a streak of truth in it.

I said, 'It isn't a question of climate. It is a question of treatment. Physiology is applicable, even in The Rower.'

And her answer was, 'I knew you wouldn't fail me.'

She said, 'I am going to die, and I am not going to die

without saying this to someone, and it is just as well you are here because, of the people I know who are still living, you are the best person I can tell it to. And don't flatter yourself: it is only because I know that you are someone who will write it down. Things must be written down. If Pindar had never written it down, a thousand people might have thought the same thing since and not known that they had thought it. You might consider yourself Jungian, but only because Jung wrote it down instead of keeping it to himself. There you have the greatest contradiction imaginable. If he had such faith in the collective mind, why did he need to tell anyone what he thought? Never mind. The only thing I have to tell you after eighty-three years, after teaching thousands of children to read and write, after reading Shakespeare and Yeats to rows of children's heads, after teaching my own children to use the lavatory and hold their knives in their right hand and their forks in their left, after loving one man exclusively from his youth to his death; the only thing I have to tell you is something you know already and haven't realised. I'm offering you a short-cut so that you can know this now and not wait, like me, until you are a skeleton on your deathbed. The only thing I have to tell you is that almost everyone you will ever meet on this green earth is someone who has spent their whole life with their head stuffed up their backside.'

Having said this, she left a gap for my astonishment and looked at me with drug-wide-opened eyes, challenging me to contradict her. I said nothing.

'Head-in-the-arse is the human condition,' she said, as though the vulgarisation of her philosophy would penetrate further.

I said nothing.

She closed her eyes for four minutes, and when she opened them again she said, 'I know what you are thinking. This is an easy thing to say. Anyone could come to the same conclusion after a casual observation of the human race. You can talk to almost anyone and conclude that the only thing they have ever seen is the inside of their own colon: with your modern mind you are thinking that it is the fault of their nurturing; that every human is an extraordinary creation who could be a Mozart or a Sophocles if they hadn't been irreparably damaged by their upbringing. Once upon a time I thought the same thing. I lived by the same creed. I became a teacher, not because my parents were teachers, but because I thought I could draw the Prometheus out of every child, without liver-damage. It was when I had my own children that I realised I had been wrong. I loved them and I taught them and they grew up with their heads stuffed up their arses. And then I began to have pupils like you. You weren't the only one. You came to me from stupid parents, but still you had the intelligence to see the world around you. Before I ever met you. Before I had the chance to draw it out of you, you knew it already. I kept you from Sister Philomena so that you could write things down. If the only reason for not writing it down is your fear of mediocrity then I have failed you. And the thing that damns you to hell is that you have failed yourself.'

When she had said all this she closed her eyes again, but this time she seemed unconscious. I waited, to be sure she had nothing more to say. Dusk fell in the room. Her daughter-in-law came to see to her needs and I left.

There is still time. You can still go to The Rower and take your leave of her, but she has had her last conversation. She has exhausted the realm of the possible. And I have written it down.

So Far, She's Fine

OAKLAND ROSS

CARMEN LUKOVIC GASTEOZORO returned from the dead at eight twenty-five last Thursday morning, riding in the backseat of a Santiago taxicab. The driver let Carmen off at the corner of the Alameda and Vicuña Mackenna and sped away without a word. He didn't even ask for the fare. Carmen used a public telephone in the Baquedano metro station to call her mother and father, to tell them that she was back and that she was fine. Carmen's father said, oh God, don't move, he'd be there like a shot.

Carmen imagined her father waddling out of the house and thrusting himself into the family's brand-new Peugeot station wagon, forest green in colour because that was what Carmen's mother had said she preferred. As he drove, Señor Lukovic would be perspiring heavily, mopping his brow with a great, white handkerchief, his chins nearly touching the wheel. He was unreliable with a car at the best of times and a threat to all on the road when he grew flustered. Carmen also thought about her mother, who would be hurrying upstairs even now, in a frenzy, to wash her hair. Later, trembling with excitement, she would greet Carmen from the landing with her head wrapped in a towel. Carmen's mother never did anything important without first washing her hair.

171

To pass the time while waiting for her father, Carmen went outside and crossed the street. She balanced herself on a wrought iron bench in the Parque Forestal by the banks of the Mapocho River. The late-winter sunshine spilled over the wall of the Andes to the east, still snow-covered. The shade trees in the park were budding and now shifted to and fro in the cool morning breeze. Nearby, a pair of teenagers wrestled – a boy and a girl, both in blue jeans, bulky sweaters, and plaid scarves. They took turns throwing each other to the grass, where they rolled over and over, nuzzled their cheeks together, rubbed their noses back and forth, licked each other's ears. Then they laughed, got up, and did it all again. The traffic barked and grunted past along the Alameda.

Carmen clasped her hands in her lap, crossed her long legs at the ankles, shifted her feet a little to the side, and watched the day expand. Aside from a rather nasty bruise on her left thigh and a cigarette burn on the inside of her right breast, she bore no physical traces of her ordeal, or none that she could detect. What she felt was a certain numbness, a slight tingly sensation all over her body, rather like a ringing in the ears after a very loud explosion. She felt almost as though she were floating through the air. That was all.

And that was what everyone remarked on. 'She seems . . . fine,' the people whispered to each other. They were neighbours, relations, friends of the family who dropped by the house that morning after hearing the news that Carmen had returned from the dead. They gathered in the dining room.

'How are you, Carmen?' asked one of her aunts, who'd just arrived.

Everyone froze. Idiotic question.

But Carmen simply tossed back her hair and smiled. 'Famished,' she replied.

That was obvious. They all watched as the girl put away three slices of chocolate pie and two large glasses of apple cider. Carmen didn't say another word. She just drank and ate and occasionally looked up with an apologetic sort of grin. Then she picked the crumbs from the plate with her fingers. Señora Lukovic stood behind her daughter, gently massaging her shoulders.

When the older woman eased her grip, started to remove her hands in order to clear the dishes, Carmen reached up and pulled her mother's arms back. 'Please don't stop,' she whispered.

It was a powerful moment. The onlookers in the dining room exchanged glances, nodded at each other. This was such an occasion. Just think – returned from the dead. It started with your name going down on a secret list, with a late night ride in an unmarked car. When people went missing, as Carmen had done, they never came back. Once you lost sight of them, they were gone.

But here was Carmen – a tall, athletic girl of eighteen, splashed with freckles and crowned by a great tangle of dark hair streaked with coppery highlights. She played centre on the women's field hockey team at the Universidad Católica and often, when she strode along a crowded street or hurried through the rooms of the family home, she looked as though she were stickhandling through a maze of opponents, her eyes fixed like twin beacons on the opposing goal. But then she would burst out laughing, over anything, anything at all, and the illusion would be shattered. She was just a girl of eighteen, straightforward, good-hearted, taking the world as it came.

They had a press conference at eleven o'clock, right in the living room. Carmen's father and her older brother pushed the furniture out of the way to make room for the television cameras. The journalists crowded inside, bickering and jostling for space. They fussed with their tape recorders and microphones, set up their cameras, and switched on the TV lights.

Carmen presided from a chair placed behind a refectory table. She crossed her arms in front of her, shook her hair, pushed her caterpillar eyebrows together, and leaned towards the bouquet of microphones in front of her.

'How do you feel?'

At first Carmen said nothing. She seemed to be drawing a

complete blank on this one. She gazed at the speaker and wrinkled her brow, as if she didn't quite understand his accent or hadn't anticipated that there would be questions.

At the back of the room, a man cleared his throat. Somewhere in front, a woman sighed loudly. Anything to fill the silence.

But all at once Carmen straightened her shoulders. She made a what-can-I-say sort of face. 'Savage,' she announced and smiled.

The journalists glanced at each other. She was feeling *savage*?

But it seemed Carmen didn't really mean that. Savage was a new slang expression that young people were using as an all-purpose superlative – tip-top. The journalists went on frowning for a few moments, still unsure, but then relaxed. The word was harmless. They understood now.

'Do you have any idea who abducted you?' someone asked.

'Yes.' Carmen replied promptly. 'In fact, I do. But I'm afraid I cannot go into that part right now. I'm sorry.'

Off to the side, Carmen's older brother, Alejandro, nodded to himself. Before the press conference, he'd warned Carmen about just this sort of question. She had to be careful not to point any fingers – there could be reprisals. The Chilean police, it was well known, responded badly to criticism. Alejandro was a lawyer, and caution was his watchword.

'Were you tortured or beaten?' asked a slim, young man in a tweed jacket, a brown V-neck sweater, and a tie. He was from *La Tercera*. His collar was frayed.

Carmen shifted sideways in her chair, and a muscle started twitching beneath her left eye. She reached up to hold that muscle still.

Alejandro stepped forward. 'I think that will be enough questions for – '

But Carmen put up her hand. 'It's all right,' she said. She looked back at the reporter from *La Tercera*. 'Was I tortured? Beaten?' She swallowed and pushed back her hair. 'Yes. I was.'

Another reporter, from somewhere in the rear. 'Do you have any idea why you were abducted?'

'I think,' Carmen said, more confident now, raising her voice to be heard, 'it was because of Jaime Calderón.' She meant a former boyfriend with whom she had broken up more than a year earlier entirely for personal reasons. Jaime was one of the four men who had been found in a field in Pudahuel out near the airport five weeks earlier. They'd all had their throats slit from ear to ear. Jaime had been a member of the Communist party – so that was the explanation. Everyone had been horrified, Carmen no less than the others. But Carmen herself was not active in politics, never had been.

'Can you,' asked a blonde-haired woman, a reporter for the Universidad Católica TV station, 'tell us a little bit about your ordeal, in general terms?'

And Carmen did exactly that. She didn't hesitate at all, and her voice remained steady. She described her abduction – the two men who had accosted her as she hurried home through the pouring rain after classes. Carmen recalled for the journalists the entangling of arms, the revealed gun, the waiting car, its motor running, the blindfold, the roundabout drive.

But Carmen did not refer to the pawing in the car that night or the crude jokes about the smallness of her breasts. 'Shit, man, you could put these things in an egg cup,' one of her assailants had scoffed. He pinned back her arms with a single hand. 'If all I wanted was a couple of eggs, I could've stayed home and tickled my own balls. Throw her back, man. We want grapefruits. Big ones.' Another of the men had been inspired by this to pluck at Carmen's cheek with his thumb and forefinger, wagging her face and breathing on her a dense fume of *pisco* and onions. 'Where are the big ones, dear heart?'

Then Carmen felt the man slide down to place his mouth at the level of her bare left breast. For a moment she even felt the rasp of his whiskered jaw. 'Where are the big ones?' he growled at her nipple. Carmen could sense the sour heat of the man's breath on her skin. He started to slap at her breast – almost playfully, slap-slap, slap-slap – just the way you'd do across the face of a tongue-tied captive, very early on, to get his attention. 'Talk, you! Where are the big ones? Talk, you! Talk . . . !'

Interrogating a breast! Ha. Ha. Ha.

They all laughed. One man belched, and another changed the subject to soccer. What was the outlook for Colo-Colo, those faggots, this year?

And so, blindfolded, her blouse yanked open, her arms locked behind her, through the night and the constant drumbeat of the rain, surrounded by invisible men, Carmen Lukovic Gasteozoro was carried off to her death.

'Were you raped?' another reporter asked.

And there were a few low whistles and moans of disapproval. People didn't look fondly on this sort of question. Abduction was one thing, but rape was more private somehow, a more intimate pain.

'Yes,' Carmen said. She spoke in a whisper and lowered her eyes. 'More than once.' She hesitated before she looked back up. She started to say something else but stopped herself. She took a deep breath.

It was only then that someone – Emilio Jones, a regular columnist for *El Mercurio* – asked the one question everyone had really wanted to ask all along but had hesitated to pose for fear of seeming morbid. 'What did it feel like?' he asked. He was wearing a navy blue jacket, a red ascot tie. 'What did it really feel like – to be dead?' Apparently this was the angle he proposed to take in his column – the girl had returned from the dead.

Carmen looked down at her hands. On her left wrist she still wore the beaded blue-and-red bracelet that she'd strung for herself when she was twelve years old. It was the one article her captors had not removed from her during five or six separate interrogations. Who cared about a stupid bracelet when they had an eighteen-year-old girl? Carmen looked at those familiar strung beads and remembered her greatest fear as a child. She'd had a horror of being buried in the mud beneath a river, a lake, or the sea.

Now she looked up and tried to explain to the journalists about that fear, what it meant. As a child, it had been her firm belief that all souls were known to God and could be restored unto Him, except those souls that were trapped in bodies buried underwater. Those souls were lost for all eternity. 'It felt,' Carmen said, 'just that way. That was how it felt.' She was silent for a few moments, then looked up and smiled. 'Are there any other questions?' She believed she could handle at least another one or two.

But the journalists had got what they needed. They packed up their equipment and filed out into the street, climbed into their cars and minivans. They headed back downtown, to put together their reports for the evening news or the next editions. SANTIAGO STUDENT RETURNS FROM THE DEAD. As usual, they all hit upon the exact same angle.

Carmen's family was amazed at how well she had handled herself during the press conference. Alejandro had been against it from the start, arching his eyebrows and clucking his tongue, but Señor Lukovic overruled him.

'If Carmen wants to do this,' he had said, 'then we have to let her. Besides, the people have a right to know.'

It was a risk. Señor Lukovic had known it was a risk. He'd worried she might break down. But Carmen had conducted herself with surprising composure, as if she'd barely been through anything at all. What was holding the girl up? Señor Lukovic shook his head. He just didn't know, and that made him uneasy.

In the middle of the afternoon, Carmen and her mother went off to the Hospital El Salvador in a taxi so that Carmen could be examined. But everything seemed to go smoothly there as well, as Señora Lukovic reported to her husband that evening. The couple were talking in their bedroom while they dressed for the small celebration they were to have that night in Carmen's honour.

Señora Lukovic buckled the belt on her dress and twisted in front of the full-length mirror, eyeing her reflection over her shoulder. 'I agree. It's a miracle,' she told her husband. 'But that's what the doctors said. On the whole she's in good shape. Good shape physically.' Señora Lukovic got out two pairs of shoes from the closet and went over to the bed. She said, 'Gus.'

'Yes?'

'Doesn't it seem strange?'

'What does?'

'That she seems so – normal. Or not normal exactly. But she should be a wreck. She should be in bed, taking tranquillisers. She should be speechless.'

Señor Lukovic nodded. It was true. It was what he thought himself.

'Instead, on the way home from the hospital she wouldn't stop talking. She wants to go to Buenos Aires soon. There's some concert there. And she wondered, should she cut her hair? Maybe just a trim? Oh, and of course, we had to stop for ice-cream. She was perishing for ice-cream. And she's not going to be a lawyer, after all. She's going to be a vet. And she plans to read more, too. One book a week. She's thinking of taking up French. And jazz singing. And horseback riding. On and on. I couldn't make her hush. Not that I tried very hard. I just went along. I was glad, of course. But . . . I mean. I don't know. It seems so odd. What do you think?'

Señor Lukovic ran the heel of one hand across his forehead. 'I know,' he said. 'I've been wondering the same thing.' He shifted his several chins in order to get a good look at his collar in the mirror. He clutched the loose ends of his bow tie with large, pudgy hands.

'She's not facing up to it,' his wife went on. 'She's not facing up to what happened. Except for the press conference this morning, she hasn't talked about it at all. Not one word. A couple of times I tried to mention it, but she just changed the subject. She started to talk about clothes.'

'Clothes?'

His wife shrugged. 'Well, she is eighteen after all. She's bound to be concerned about clothes. But still. It was very strange. I'm worried. You can't just get over a thing like this. Gus?'

Señor Lukovic let out a long breath of air. He wanted to say something reassuring but couldn't think of any words that wouldn't seem trite or false. 'We'll just have to stay close to her and see what happens. Maybe she'll be all right. You never know.'

He looked back at the mirror. He wasn't sure what else to say – the things they had done to his daughter! At first he'd been stunned by what he had heard at the press conference, so horrified that he couldn't feel a thing. But later Carmen's words had sunk in. The images haunted him all afternoon until he had to close his eyes to shut them out. Otherwise, he'd go mad.

Yet Carmen had survived, and more than survived. She seemed almost unchanged on the surface, as if nothing had touched her, as if her life had been returned to her, not shattered but whole. Señor Lukovic stared at his reflection in the mirror. What was holding their daughter up? He couldn't say. He didn't know.

He turned to look at his wife, her slender figure and powdered face, her short waves of blue-rinsed hair. She sat on the bed with one leg tucked beneath her, trying to choose between two pairs of black shoes. She looked up to hold her husband's gaze. Then they both smiled and shook their heads and quickly turned away because they both were crying. Who would have dreamed they'd be having a celebration tonight?

Señor Lukovic blinked several times and began to fumble with his tie. In a minute he'd give it up, and his wife would do the knot for him. But he always liked to try.

Immediately after his daughter's disappearance, Señor Lukovic had made the rounds of a number of his associates in the Christian Democratic party – effectively banned, like all the old political parties – in order to organise support for her release. In his younger days, long before the coup, he had been an advisor to President Eduardo Frei, so he was pretty well connected. Almost everyone liked him, which had turned out to be of critical importance following Carmen's abduction.

Even senior military officers tempered their usual contempt for civilian politicians when they dealt with Gustavo Lukovic. He was a good churchgoing family man, they had to admit. There he went – always lumbering about, mopping his brow, seeking appointments with generals and colonels about the issues of the day. He tried to get things done in a reasonable manner. The officers respected that and briefly wondered if they weren't sometimes being a bit too harsh in the way they ran the country.

But when Señor Lukovic had left their gloomy chambers, the officers promptly forgot about him and everything he'd said, and they went right back to ruling Chile in their usual fashion. This may explain why, when the low-level order had gone out to abduct Señor Lukovic's daughter, it just slipped through the system. Carmen's name was jotted down just like all the others. By the time the mistake was discovered and verified, it was too late. She was already gone.

When the news of Carmen's disappearance became widely known, there'd been an outcry. Twice, the Archbishop of Santiago broadcast appeals for her release over the Catholic radio station. All the banned political parties used what little influence they had to get the government to act. Meanwhile, telegrams of protest poured in from outraged officials and solidarity organisations in other countries.

Señor Lukovic barely slept during this period. He talked to everyone he could, drove from one building to the next, called in long-standing political debts. He plodded from office to office, from meeting to meeting, cajoled and pleaded. Perspiration ran down his great, jowly face, and his handkerchiefs got soaked. Alejandro worked the phones, and Señora Lukovic enlisted as many of her friends as she could, to use feminine suasion with the wives of the military officers.

In the end, the question ran right up the chain of command to the very top, to His Excellency General Augusto Pinochet Ugarte, commander in chief of the Armed Forces and president of the Republic. He was the one who had to decide. There were no witnesses to the discussion itself apart from the small, tight-lipped cluster of senior military men who were in the room at the time. But, when the meeting was finally adjourned, the order that was issued and repeated in hushed tones along the dark, carpeted corridors of La Moneda, the presidential palace, went something like this: 'I don't care how you do it but give the girl back to her family. Alive.'

This was unprecedented. It went entirely against the grain. How to begin? Did anyone know where the girl had been taken? Was she even alive? If so, to what extent? In the end it all got sorted out. They had one of their undercover people drive Carmen back in a taxi.

At the dinner party that night in her honour, Carmen almost seemed to float. About two dozen people showed up for the celebration, including some aunts and uncles, Carmen's godparents – Señor and Señora Echeverría – and a few of her closest chums from school. Guests made speeches and proposed toasts. The room erupted in gales of laughter, and Carmen and her school friends linked arms to sing their school anthem. 'Savage!' Carmen exclaimed. She shook out her hair and hugged her friends one by one, then all together. She was wearing a short, black skirt, a black turtleneck jersey, and a lovely vest embroidered with an oriental floral pattern. In addition to that old string of beads, she had gold bracelets on both wrists. She looked beautiful. She seemed perfectly fine.

Everyone stood up together to sing 'Gracias a la Vida', the Violeta Parra song. They all embraced, and there was no shortage of tears. Señor Lukovic sauntered about with a bottle of Napoleon brandy. He grew more subdued as the evening wore on. He kept turning to watch his daughter as she circulated among the guests. He was struck by how tightly she held each person, how she let go, immediately reached out for someone else.

Señor Lukovic could feel a strange pressure in his temples. Carmen was, by her own admission, or boast, a demonstrative sort of girl. What was that appalling phrase she sometimes used? Kissy-face, pressy-body – that was it. Those were her words to describe her penchant for hugs and cuddles – shows of affection that were normal for Carmen, a necessity. But this was different. These weren't embraces. Carmen was holding on.

He noticed that her arms and hands were never still, that she was always reaching to push back a girlfriend's hair so that she could whisper something into her ear, or to clasp an older relative by the elbow, or to draw a pair of friends closer, or simply to hold somebody's, anybody's, hand. She was always clutching at something, as though she might otherwise fall.

And several times Señor Lukovic caught snatches of conversation – his daughter telling her friends about the courses she planned to enrol in or the dance steps she wanted to learn or the trips she hoped to take. Once, when he wandered close to Carmen and several of her friends, she slipped an arm around his back and took his hand in one of hers.

'Here's the man who's going to have to pay for all this educating,' she said and grinned up at him.

Señor Lukovic shrugged, held up the bottle of brandy. It was empty. He looked at Carmen's friends. 'I may, of course, go broke.'

Everyone laughed, and Carmen laughed, too.

'More brandy,' someone shouted, someone who must have overheard. 'You can go broke tomorrow, Gustavo. Tonight we drink.'

More laughter. The snap of cigarette lighters. Señor Lukovic kissed Carmen on the forehead, turned, and trudged out to the kitchen. He opened the liquor cabinet and caught sight of his pale reflection in the kitchen window. Nothing that happened that night had made him any less fearful. He pulled a fresh bottle down from the shelf, ran his handkerchief across its dark green surface to clear the dust. He recalled an anecdote he'd once heard about a man who fell from the top of a very tall building. The man hurtled towards the earth, faster and faster. Along the way, he called to horrified witnesses staring out through the windows, 'I'm fine so far!' Those words began to echo and shift in Señor Lukovic's mind. He thought again of his daughter.

When he returned to the living room, everyone had risen to sing the Chilean national anthem – not for the military government, they sang for la Patria – and he lumbered over to plant himself beside his wife, who was alone with her arms crossed at her chest, near the simmering warmth of the fireplace. She touched her hand to her hair, then smiled at him, and held out her brandy snifter. 'Perhaps just a smidgen,' she whispered. Carmen hurried over and then Alejandro, and they put their arms around each other. The guests all turned to watch and briefly lowered their voices, uncertain what to do. But Carmen and her family looked up, joined right in – and now there was no stopping anybody. They all sang out, loud as they could.

Despite her parents' pleading that she take things slowly, Carmen went straight back to school on Monday. A nice boy, Roberto Sepúlveda, has asked her out on a date for this Saturday, and she has said yes. The two of them plan to go to a movie and afterwards maybe meet some friends in one of the noisy outdoor cafés near the funicular station at the bottom of the Santa Lucía hill.

Yesterday, Carmen even turned out for the Universidad Católica game against the women's field hockey team from Concepción. She scored one goal and had an assist in a winning effort. In the dying minutes, she was jostled by two opponents and went down hard. She gave her ankle an awful wrench. But she climbed back up and kept right on playing, and now she won't admit that she was hurt at all. The ankle has swollen up like a balloon, yet she refuses to rest it. 'Never mind,' she keeps saying. 'It's nothing at all.'

A Respectable Woman

ALAN SILLITOE

TRAVELLING SOUTH, PAUL enjoyed the slow melting of cloud after passing the watershed, *les partages des eaux*: white lines waving on a brown board prominently displayed by the motorway, but the pleasure often had to be paid for with worsening weather on the homeward trip from the Mediterranean. That was life. What you didn't expect, you didn't appreciate. An electric dark blue sky between downpours turned into a threatening decline of the day.

Somewhere beyond Rheims, heading for Calais, white headlights made little impression on swathes of water at the windscreen, wipers sluggish on the fastest rate. He seemed to be driving under the sea, and marvelled at the occasional car overtaking confidently into the slush.

Life was too short to be maimed in such a way, or even killed, so he argued with himself about parting from the motorway at the nearest exit. Eight o'clock meant he would be lucky to get a room in Cambrai, but a sizzle of lightning settled him to try.

He trawled the streets, deserted under heaven's free wash, calling at three places that were full. Coming again out of the main square, onto a road he didn't know, he pulled in at the Hotel de la Paix, and took a room large enough for a family, no option but to pay up and bless his good fortune.

The way had been long from the house in Tuscany. After leaving Wendy at Pisa airport, with their two sons who could not be late for school, he drifted up the motorway through mountains he had always wanted to walk in. Wendy didn't like the car trip, but he enjoyed doing it alone, whether or not he was late slotting back into managing his electronics firm. A long drive was good for mulling on problems he might find on getting there.

He backed into the last vacancy of the courtyard. All other cars faced inwards, but a quick getaway, though rarely a necessity, was always neat to think about. He took his overnight case to the room, washed and changed into a suit, and went downstairs before the restaurant closed. The tourist season lagged on, and he stood between the bar and reception counter waiting for a table, rain at the glass locking his gaze as firmly as had the tarmac sweeping all day under the car.

A dark blue Renault stopped at the door, and he assumed the GB plate because of the side the driver stepped from. She ran in like a goddess coming from the ocean to be born – he couldn't help telling himself – and when she asked at the counter for a room he felt some satisfaction in knowing the answer.

'Damn,' she responded, 'nothing at all?'

The clerk told her.

She had been all over the town – and so have I, Paul thought. 'Isn't there another hotel you can recommend?'

It was no feat to pick up her responses: 'I can't go on in this atrocious weather. What the hell am I to do?' His feeling of guilt was overridden by exaltation at having got there before her.

'They'll all be full,' the clerk said. 'I telephoned around for someone a few minutes ago.'

Paul, no reason to be concerned at her plight – though he was – sensed her annoyance at whoever might be responsible, and he for one wished he knew who it could be. A day on the road sleeved by the rich landscapes of France acted on him like a drug, opening his mind to spaces that made him ready for anything, especially after the relief of finding such an opulent billet. He couldn't think why he said it:

'I might have a solution to your problem.'

She stood in the doorway, a tall woman, in her late thirties perhaps, with short reddish hair and gold-framed spectacles, an opened raincoat showing a pale cream blouse, a loose purple skirt, and short black boots that zipped up the front. 'Well, it's *my* problem. I'll just have to drive on.'

'I took the last room, I'm afraid.'

'I suppose someone had to.' A trace of vinegar indicated that she was too proud to let him assume he might have done her an ill turn.

'I had to take a room far too big for me. It seems a shame for you to go out in that, and me with a large double bed going to waste.'

He told her his name, and held out a hand, French style, which she barely touched, though looked at the card which he took from his wallet and laid on the bar, wondering what he thought he was up to. Of medium height and slender, with thinning dark hair combed drily back above a pale relaxed face, he seemed too well dressed for a holiday bird of passage. Maybe he tried this stunt every night, staying all day in the hotel and waiting to pounce on such as her. She forced a smile as if to show she was embarrassed by such a proposition. 'What do you mean?'

'I've driven up from Italy today, and I'm absolutely done for.'

'You don't look it.'

'I'd be at death's door if I did. But after dinner I'll drop onto one of the beds and won't wake for nine hours. All *you* have to do is fall onto the other and do the same.' He regretted having spoken, since she thought he wanted to make love to her, which he had no intention of doing. 'Have a drink while you're waiting. By the time you've decided against my practical suggestion the rain might have eased off.'

Very smooth, yet she was tempted. After much experience she had evolved the notion that you should think everything but let no one suspect your thoughts. She sometimes wondered why it came so easy, but in that way, common sense – or an instinct for self-preservation – decided your actions. No harm therefore in taking up his offer. 'I could do with a Martini.'

On trips to and from her house in the Haute-Loire she whiled away the miles with a fantasy of such a meeting, and now that something like it was happening she would drink her drink and get back into the weather. Fantasy was one thing, and reality another game altogether.

He eyed his *pastis* as if to make sure every swallow was worthy of the honour. His idea of paradise, he told her, was the smell of pine trees in the hottest sun, subtly mixed with odours of rosemary and olive, preferably while sitting on the terrace with his wife at midday over a bottle of wine and a platter of dark bread and salami. Such an injection of relaxed living, at least once a year, was the best way he knew of keeping sane. In the afternoon – though he didn't go this far – he would dispatch the boys into the hills with map and compass, and a haversack of things to eat, so that he and Wendy could go to bed as in the days of their honeymoon. He hoped that talking about himself would make her feel at ease, and not be so suspicious at what ought to be seen as his generosity in offering to share his room. 'I'm a practical person, basically. I have to be, in my job, so it seems only logical to put the spare bed at your disposal.'

She smiled at his good sense, good for him, anyway, and as if to confirm it even more, rain drummed louder at the windows. She asked herself, during the second Martini, what her thoughts would have been on passing him in the street, and decided she might have found him interesting enough to want to know more. She could even, in a certain mood, have 'fancied' him. Such a judgement had no bearing, but the warmth within reddened her face.

He would have the advantage of a good story, if only to tell against himself, about how he had rescued this very person-able woman in distress, and been correct in not trying to seduce her. 'If you don't accept my suggestion you leave me no alternative but to push on. I'll stop in the first layby, and sleep soundly at the wheel, more than happy in knowing you're well taken care of. Here's my key. I'll have a word with the clerk.'

Occasional dips into the bread-and-sausage bag along the way had left her famished, and the two Martinis, quickly drunk, were having an effect. Though his plan ought to be rejected in no uncertain manner, she heard herself say: 'All right, I'll take it.'

Such an adventure to look back on couldn't be bad: 'This *very* kind chap actually gave up his room for me. Would you believe it? No, he wasn't *that* sort. He was such a gentleman that on thinking about it I rather wish he had been.'

He put his glass down. 'There's just one condition.'

Oh Lord, her grey eyes said, now I've dropped into it. Why are men always so sly? He probably plays chess. If he'd come straight out with it I'd at least know where I was.

'I can see what you're thinking.'

There was too much triumph in his tone for her liking, but he probably knew that, too. She was ready to leave. 'Am I so transparent?'

'Oh no, nothing like that. I only want you to have dinner with me, before I ask the clerk to transfer the room. I always hate eating on my own in a strange place. I hope you won't take too long to decide, though, because here's the waiter coming to say our table's ready.'

What am I doing? – he refilled her glass from the bottle of Côte du Rhône – me, a supposedly respectable woman getting into a situation like this? My name's Margaret, she told him. He reasonably wanted to know about her, so what could she do but say she was a teacher at a girls' school? She couldn't think why such a plain truth seemed so out of place: 'An aunt died and left me enough money to buy a small house near Le Puy. A cottage, really, but I don't imagine you can use such a word in France, can you? There was enough left over to buy a car, so I go when I can.'

On leaving, and putting the key under the earthen flower-pot outside the back door, she drove down the winding cobbled track with bushes scraping the car. On the main road she already thought of her flat in Ealing, and the cat her neighbour was looking after, though she was too much a lover of France not to enjoy the scenery before reaching the more rolling country of the north. 'What delicious onion soup. I'm feeling better already. I was done for when I arrived.'

'So I noticed.' He wanted to touch her wrist, and say how sensible she had been in agreeing to stay, but held back in case she changed her mind. A man and his soignée wife of forty-odd sat at the next table, and she saw him look at their slim daughter who had a rather mousy helmet of hair but an exquisite bust. He was merely noting how each had a plate of open baked potato with grated cheese on top, the whole in a bed of curly lettuce. 'They believe in a healthy diet,' he said, seeing the waiter with his steak tartare and her platter of cutlets, 'which seems such a pity in France.'

He leaned against the rail and levelled his binoculars, but it was hard to see the assembly lines of cars coming onto the boat, so he moved to the loading end, knowing he would curse himself for the rest of his life at not having stayed for breakfast. Hurry was in his bone-marrow, and it was impossible they would meet again. Unable to stop thinking of that warm and womanly figure under her clothes, he had passed half an hour in a layby hoping to see her tuppenny sardine tin trundling along.

Five minutes to sailing, the ship loaded with trucks, buses, caravans and cars, he supposed it was too late now for her to make it. Maybe he would have a cup of coffee at Dover, and wait to see if she was on the next boat.

There were moments on the hundred motorway miles to Calais when she forgot who she was, whereabouts she was, even what she was doing. Everything went, the brain went, the car went from around her. All protection went, but she came back to safety – thinking herself lucky – and ran once more through her adventure of the night.

The smell of wine on their combined breaths filling the shuttered and curtained room had not stopped them falling asleep almost immediately on their separate beds. In the middle of the night she was awakened by him going to the bathroom, flushing whatever it was, and washing his hands. Drifting back into sleep, and wishing it could happen without embarrassment, she felt him beside her, and they moved against each other to find an even greater comfort than oblivion.

When she awoke, more raddled than after an insomniac few hours at the flat or cottage, he had gone, and his lack of politeness in not saying goodbye so that she could at least thank him properly left a sense of injury which didn't dissipate on finding another of his cards with 'Thank you for every-thing' scrawled on the back. At breakfast she felt as if half of herself was missing, the only advantage in being so shamefully maudlin was that maybe he was in the same state.

She made a stupid blunder in asking whether the bill had been paid, as if a man she had picked up had left her to do it. A bit more know-how would have saved her a funny look from the clerk. Carrying her overnight bag to the car, she wondered how far or if at all a respectable woman could be called sophisticated. She had always had so many and such strident opinions as to how 'men' ought to behave that she did not know to within any shade of accuracy what exactly 'men' finally were. Well, now she did, a little more anyway. They were all different, and he was the most different one she had known.

The motorway was visible for miles ahead under high-flowing clouds, landscape hillier than she had previously noted. Every turn of the wheels brought the sea closer. A man who would use an offer to give up his room so as to get into her bed must be given top marks for ingenuity – and skill.

A postcard, in an envelope, to his business address, could do no harm – with her own locations firmly scripted in. When he next came up from Italy he might want to stay at her place overnight, an offer almost as good as his. And the detour shouldn't faze him.

Heavy Weather

HELEN SIMPSON

'YOU SHOULD NEVER have married me.'

'I haven't regretted it for an instant.'

'Not *you*, you fool! *Me!* You shouldn't have got me to marry you if you loved me. Why *did* you, when you knew it would let me in for all *this*. It's not *fair!*'

'I don't know. I know it's not. But what can I do about it?'

'I'm being mashed up and eaten alive.'

'I know. I'm sorry.'

'It's not your fault. But what can I do?'

'I don't know.'

So the conversation had gone last night in bed, followed by platonic embraces. They were on ice at the moment, so far as anything further was concerned. The smoothness and sweet smell of their children, the baby's densely-packed pearly limbs, the freshness of the little girl's breath when she yawned, these combined to accentuate the grossness of their own bodies. They eyed each other's mooching adult bulk with mutual lack of enthusiasm, and fell asleep.

At four in the morning, the baby was punching and shouting in his Moses basket. Frances forced herself awake, lying for the first moments like a flattened boxer in the ring trying to rise while the count was made. She got up and fell

191

over, got up again and scooped Matthew from the basket. He was huffing with eagerness, and scrabbled crazily at her breasts like a drowning man until she lay down with him. A few seconds more and he had abandoned himself to rhythmic gulping. She stroked his soft head and drifted off. When she woke again, it was six o'clock and he was sleeping between her and Jonathan.

For once, nobody was touching her. Like Holland she lay, aware of a heavy ocean at her seawall, its weight poised to race across the low country.

The baby was now three months old, and she had not had more than half an hour alone in the twenty-four since his birth in February. He was big and hungry and needed her there constantly on tap. Also, his two-year-old sister Lorna was, unwillingly, murderously jealous, which made everything much more difficult. This time round was harder, too, because when one was asleep the other would be awake and vice versa. If only she could get them to nap at the same time, Frances started fretting, then she might be able to sleep for some minutes during the day and that would get her through. But they wouldn't, and she couldn't. She had taken to muttering I can't bear it, I can't bear it, without realising she was doing so until she heard Lorna chanting I can't bear it! I can't bear it! as she skipped along beside the pram, and this made her blush with shame at her own weediness.

Now they were all four in Dorset for a week's holiday. The thought of having to organise all the food, sheets, milk, baths and nappies made her want to vomit.

In her next chunk of sleep came that recent nightmare, where men with knives and scissors advanced on the felled trunk which was her body.

'How would you like it?' she said to Jonathan. 'It's like a doctor saying, now we're just going to snip your scrotum in half, but don't worry, it mends very well down there, we'll stitch you up and you'll be fine.'

It was gone seven by now and Lorna was leaning on the bars of her cot like Farmer Giles, sucking her thumb in a ruminative pipe-smoking way. The room stank like a lion house. She beamed as her mother came in, and lifted her arms up. Frances hoisted her into the bath, stripped her down and detached the dense brown nappy from between her knees. Lorna carolled, 'I can sing a *rain*bow,' raising her faint fine eyebrows at the high note, graceful and perfect, as her mother sluiced her down with jugs of water.

'Why does everything take so *long*?' moaned Jonathan. 'It only takes *me* five minutes to get ready.'

Frances did not bother to answer. She was sagging with the effortful boredom of assembling the paraphernalia needed for a morning out in the car. Juice. Beaker with screw-on lid. Flannels. Towels. Changes of clothes in case of car sickness. Nappies. Rattle. Clean muslins to catch Matthew's curdy regurgitations. There was more. What was it?

'Oh, come on, Jonathan, think,' she said. 'I'm fed up with having to plan it all.'

'What do you think I've been doing for the last hour?' he shouted. 'Who was it that changed Matthew's nappy just now? Eh?'

'Congratulations,' she said. 'Don't shout or I'll cry.'

Lorna burst into tears.

'Why is everywhere always such a *mess*,' said Jonathan, picking up plastic spiders, dinosaurs, telephones, beads and bears, his grim scowl over the mound of primary colours like a traitor's head on a platter of fruit.

'I *want* dat spider, daddy!' screamed Lorna. 'Give it to me!'

During the ensuing struggle, Frances pondered her tiredness. Her muscles twitched as though they had been tenderised with a steak bat. There was a bar of iron in the back of her neck, and she felt unpleasantly weightless in the cranium, a gin-drinking side effect without the previous fun. The year following the arrival of the first baby had gone in pure astonishment at the loss of freedom, but second time round it was spinning away in exhaustion. Matthew woke at 1am and 4am, and Lorna at 6.30am. During the days, fatigue came at her in concentrated doses, like a series of time bombs.

'Are we ready at last?' said Jonathan, breathing heavily. 'Are we ready to go?'

'Um, nearly,' said Frances. 'Matthew's making noises. I think I'd better feed him, or else I'll end up doing it in a lay-by.'

'Right,' said Jonathan. 'Right.'

Frances picked up the baby. 'What a nice fat parcel you are,' she murmured in his delighted ear. 'Come on, my love.'

'Matthew's not your love,' said Lorna. '*I'm* your love. You say, C'mon love, to *me*.'

'You're *both* my loves,' said Frances.

The baby was shaking with eagerness, and pouted his mouth as she pulled her shirt up. The little girl sat down beside her, pulled up her own teeshirt and applied a teddy bear to her nipple. She grinned at her mother.

Frances looked down at Matthew's head, which was shaped like a brick or a small wholemeal loaf, and remembered again how it had come down through the middle of her. She was trying very hard to lose her awareness of this fact, but it would keep re-presenting itself.

'D'you know,' said Lorna, her free hand held palm upwards, her hyphen eyebrows lifting, 'D'you know, I was sucking my thumb when I was coming downstairs, mum, mum, then my foot slipped and my thumb came out of my mouth.'

'Well, that's very interesting, Lorna,' said Frances.

Two minutes later, Lorna caught the baby's head a ringing smack and ran off. Jonathan watched as Frances lunged clumsily after her, the baby jouncing at her breast, her stained and crumpled shirt undone, her hair a bird's nest, her face craggy with fatigue, and found himself dubbing the tableau, Portrait of rural squalor in the manner of William Hogarth. He bent to put on his shoes, stuck his right foot in first then pulled it out as though bitten.

'What's *that*,' he said in tones of profound disgust. He held the shoe in front of Frances's face.

'It looks like baby sick,' she said. 'Don't look at me. It's not my fault.'

'It's all so bloody *basic*,' said Jonathan, breathing hard, hopping off towards the kitchen.

'If you think that's basic, try being me,' muttered Frances. 'You don't know what basic *means*.'

'Daddy put his foot in Matthew's sick,' commented Lorna, laughing heartily.

At Cerne Abbas they stood and stared across at the chalky white outline of the iron age Giant cut into the green hill.

'It's enormous, isn't it,' said Frances.

'Do you remember when we went to stand on it?' said Jonathan. 'On that holiday in Child Okeford five years ago?'

'Of course,' said Frances. She saw the ghosts of their frisky former selves running around the giant's spreading limbs and up onto his phallus. Nostalgia filled her eyes and stabbed her smartly in the guts.

'"The woman riding high above with bright hair flapping free,"' quoted Jonathan. 'Will you be able to grow *your* hair again?'

'Yes, yes. Don't look at me like that, though. I know I look like hell.'

A month before this boy was born, Frances had had her hair cut short. Her head had looked like a pea on a drum. It still did. With each year of pregnancy, her looks had hurtled five years on. She had started using sentences beginning, 'When I was young.' Ah, youth! Idleness! Sleep! How disorientating was this overnight demotion from Brünnhilde to spear-carrier.

'What's that,' said Lorna. 'That *thing*.'

'It's a giant,' said Frances.

'Like in Jacknabeanstork?'

'Yes.'

'But what's that *thing*. That thing on the giant.'

'It's the giant's thing.'

'Is it his stick thing?'

'Yes.'

'My baby budder's got a stick thing.'

'Yes.'

'But I haven't got a stick thing.'

195

'No.'

'Daddy's got a stick thing.'

'Yes.'

'But *mummy* hasn't got a stick thing. We're the same, mummy.'

She beamed and put her warm paw in Frances's.

'You can't see round without an appointment,' said the keeper of Hardy's cottage. 'You should have telephoned.'

'We did,' bluffed Jonathan. 'There was no answer.'

'When was that?'

'Twenty to ten this morning.'

'Hmph. I was over sorting out some trouble at Cloud's Hill. T. E. Lawrence's place. All right, you can go through. But keep them under control, won't you.'

They moved slowly through the low-ceilinged rooms, whispering to impress the importance of good behaviour on Lorna.

'This is the room where he was born,' said Jonathan, at the head of the stairs.

'Do you remember from when we visited last time?' said Frances slowly. 'It's coming back to me. He was his mother's first child, she nearly died in labour, then the doctor thought the baby was dead and threw him into a basket while he looked after the mother. But the midwife noticed he was breathing.'

'Then he carried on till he was eighty-seven,' said Jonathan.

They clattered across the old chestnut floorboards, on into another little bedroom with deep thick-walled windowseats.

'Which one's your favourite now?' asked Frances.

'Oh, still *Jude the Obscure*, I think,' said Jonathan. 'The tragedy of unfulfilled aims. Same for anyone first generation at university.'

'Poor Jude, laid low by pregnancy,' said Frances. 'Another victim of biology as destiny.'

'Don't *talk*, you two,' said Lorna.

'At least Sue and Jude aimed for friendship as well as all the other stuff,' said Jonathan.

'Unfortunately, all the other stuff made friendship impossible, didn't it,' said Frances.

'Don't *talk!*' shouted Lorna.

'Don't shout!' said Jonathan. Lorna fixed him with a calculating blue eye and produced an ear-splitting scream. The baby jerked in his arms and started to howl.

'Hardy didn't have children, did he,' said Jonathan above the din. 'I'll take them outside, I've seen enough. You stay up here a bit longer if you want to.'

Frances stood alone in the luxury of the empty room and shuddered. She moved around the furniture and thought fond savage thoughts of silence in the cloisters of a convent, a blessed place where all was monochrome and non-viscous. Sidling up unprepared to a mirror on the wall she gave a yelp at her reflection. The skin was the colour and texture of pumice stone, the grim jaw set like a lion's muzzle. And the eyes, the eyes far back in the skull were those of a herring three days dead.

Jonathan was sitting with the baby on his lap by a row of lupins and marigolds, reading to Lorna from a newly-acquired guide book.

'When Thomas was a little boy he knelt down one day in a field and began eating grass to see what it was like to be a sheep.'

'What the sheep say?' asked Lorna.

'The sheep said, er, so now you know.'

'And what else?'

'Nothing else.'

'Why?'

'What do you mean, why?'

'*Why?*'

'Look,' he said when he saw Frances. 'I've bought a copy of *Jude the Obscure* too, so we can read to each other when we've got a spare moment.'

'Spare moment!' said Frances. 'But how lovely you look with the children at your knees, the roses round the cottage door. How I would like to be the one coming back from work to find you all bathed and brushed, and a hot meal in the oven

197

and me unwinding with a glass of beer in a hard-earned crusty glow of righteousness.'

'*I* don't get that,' Jonathan reminded her.

'That's because I can't do it properly yet,' said Frances. 'But, still, I wish it could be the other way round. Or at least, half and half. And I was thinking, what a cheesy business Eng.Lit. is, all those old men peddling us lies about life and love. They never get as far as this bit, do they.'

'Thomas 1840, Mary 1842, Henry 1851, Kate 1856,' read Jonathan. 'Perhaps we could have two more.'

'I'd kill myself,' said Frances.

'What's the matter with you?' said Jonathan to Matthew, who was grizzling and struggling in his arms.

'I think I'll have to feed him again,' said Frances.

'What, already?'

'It's nearly two hours.'

'Hey, you can't do that here,' said the custodian, appearing at their bench like a bad fairy.

'Excuse me,' said Jonathan, 'But are you aware my wife has read all of Hardy's novels?'

'Not *The Hand of Ethelberta*,' muttered Frances.

'We have visitors from all over the world here. Particularly the Japanese,' said the custodian. 'The Japanese are a very modest people. And they don't come all this way to see THAT sort of thing.'

'It's a perfectly natural function,' said Jonathan.

'So's going to the lavatory!' said the custodian.

'What about hara-kiri? I suppose you call *that* natural?' said Jonathan wildly.

'No need to be offensive, young man.'

'Is it all right if I take him over behind those hollyhocks?' asked Frances. 'Nobody could possibly see me there. It's just, in this heat he won't feed if I try to do it in the car.'

The custodian snorted and stumped back to his lair.

Above the thatched roof the huge and gentle trees rustled hundreds of years' worth of leaves in the pre-storm stir. Frances shrugged, heaved Matthew up so that his socks dangled on her hastily covered breast, and retreated to the hollyhock screen. As he fed, she observed the green-tinged light in the garden, the crouching cat over in a bed of limp snapdragons, and registered the way things look before an onslaught, defenceless and excited, tense and passive. She thought of Bathsheba Everdene at bay, crouching in the bed of ferns.

When would she be able to read a book again? In life before the children, she had read books on the bus, in the bathroom, in bed, while eating, through television, under radio noise, in cafés. Now, if she picked one up, Lorna shouted, 'Stop reading, mummy,' and pulled her by the nose until she was looking into her small cross face.

Jonathan meandered among the flowerbeds flicking through *Jude the Obscure*, Lorna snapping and shouting at his heels. He was ignoring her, and Frances could see he had already bought a tantrum since Lorna was now entered into one of the stretches of the day when her self-control flagged and fled. She sighed like Cassandra but didn't have the energy to nag as he came towards her.

'Listen to this,' Jonathan said, reading from *Jude the Obscure*, '"time and circumstance, which enlarge the views of most men, narrow the views of women almost invariably."'

'Is it any bloody wonder,' said Frances.

'I want you to *play* with me, daddy,' whined Lorna.

'Bit of a sexist remark, though, eh?' said Jonathan.

'Bit of a sexist process, you twit,' said Frances.

Lorna gave Matthew a tug which almost had him on the ground. Torn from his milky trance, he quavered, horror-struck, for a moment, then, as Frances braced herself, squared his mouth and started to bellow.

Jonathan seized Lorna, who became as rigid as a steel girder, and swung her high up above his head. The air was split with screams.

'Give her to me,' mouthed Frances across the awe-inspiring noise.

'She's a mini terrorist,' shouted Jonathan.

'Oh, please let me have her,' said Frances.

'You shouldn't give in to her,' said po-faced Jonathan, handing over the flailing parcel of limbs.

'Lorna, sweetheart, look at me,' said Frances.

'Naaoow!' screamed Lorna.

'Shshush,' said Frances. 'Tell me what's the matter.'

Lorna poured out a flood of incomprehensible complaint, raving like a chimpanzee. At one point, Frances deciphered, 'You always feed MATTHEW.'

'You should *love* your baby brother,' interposed Jonathan.

'You can't tell her she *ought* to love anybody,' snapped Frances. 'You can tell her she must behave properly, but you can't tell her what to feel. Look, Lorna,' she continued, exercising her favourite distraction technique. 'The old man is coming back. He's cross with us. Let's run away.'

Lorna turned her streaming eyes and nose in the direction of the custodian, who was indeed hotfooting it across the lawn towards them, and tugged her mother's hand. The two of them lurched off, Frances buttoning herself up as she went.

They found themselves corralled into a cement area at the back of the *Smuggler's Arms*, a separate space where young family pariahs like themselves could bicker over fish fingers. Waiting at the bar, Jonathan observed the comfortable tables inside, with their noisy laughing groups of the energetic elderly tucking into plates of gammon and plaice and profiteroles.

'Just look at them,' said the crumpled man beside him, who was paying for a trayload of Fanta and baked beans. 'Skipped the war. Nil unemployment, home in time for tea.' He took a great gulp of lager. 'Left us to scream in our prams, screwed us up good and proper. When our kids come along, what happens? You don't see the grandparents for dust, that's what happens. They're all off out enjoying themselves, kicking the prams out the way with their Hush Puppies, spending the money like there's no tomorrow.'

Jonathan grunted uneasily. He still could not get used to the way he found himself involved in intricate conversations with complete strangers, incisive, frank, frequently desperate, whenever he was out with Frances and the children. It used to be only women who talked like that, but now, among parents of young children, it seemed to have spread across the board.

Frances was trying to allow the baby to finish his recent interrupted feed as discreetly as she could, while watching Lorna move inquisitively among the various family groups. She saw her go up to a haggard woman changing a nappy beside a trough of geraniums.

'Your baby's got a stick thing like my baby budder.' Lorna's piercing voice soared above the babble. 'I haven't got a stick thing cos I'm a little gel. My mummy's got fur on her potim.'

Frances abandoned their table and made her way over to the geranium trough.

'Sorry if she's been getting in your way,' she said to the woman.

'Chatty, isn't she,' commented the woman unenthusiastically. 'How many have you got?'

'Two. I'm shattered.'

'The third's the killer.'

'Dat's my baby budder,' said Lorna, pointing at Matthew.

'He's a big boy,' said the woman. 'What did he weigh when he came out?'

'Ten pounds.'

'Just like a turkey,' she said, disgustingly, and added, 'Mine were whoppers too. They all had to be cut out of me, one way or the other.'

By the time they returned to the cottage, the air was weighing on them like blankets. Each little room was an envelope of pressure. Jonathan watched Frances collapse into a chair with children all over her. Before babies, they had been well matched. Then, with the arrival of their first child, it had been a case of Woman Overboard. He'd watched, ineffectual but sympathetic, trying to keep her cheerful as she clung onto the edge of the raft, holding out weevil-free biscuits for her to nibble, and all the time she gazed at him with appalled eyes. Just as they had grown used to this state, difficult but tenable, and were even managing to start hauling her on board again an inch at a time, just as she had her elbows up on the raft and they were congratulating themselves with a kiss, well, along came the second baby in a great slap of a wave that drove her off the raft altogether. Now she was out there in the sea while he bobbed up and down, forlorn but more or less dry, and watched her face between its two satellites dwindling to the size of a fist, then to a plum, and at last to a mere speck of plankton. He dismissed it from his mind.

'I'll see if I can get the shopping before the rain starts,' he said, dashing out to the car again, knee-deep in cow parsley.

'You really should keep an eye on how much bread we've got left,' he called earnestly as he unlocked the car. 'It won't be *my* fault if I'm struck by lightning.'

There was the crumpling noise of thunder, and silver cracked the sky. Frances stood in the doorway holding the baby, while Lorna clawed and clamoured at her to be held in her free arm.

'Oh, Lorna,' said Frances, hit by a wave of bone-aching fatigue. 'You're too heavy, my sweet.' She closed the cottage door as Lorna started to scream, and stood looking down at her with something like fear. She saw a miniature fee-fi-fo-fum creature working its way through a pack of adults, chewing them up and spitting their bones out.

'Come into the back room, Lorna, and I'll read you a book while I feed Matthew.'

'I don't want to.'

'Why don't you want to?'

'I just don't want to.'

'Can't you tell me why?'

'Do you know, I just don't WANT to!'

'All right, *dear*. I'll feed him on my own then.'

'NO!' screamed Lorna. 'PUT HIM IN DA BIN! HE'S RUBBISH!'

'Don't scream, you little beast,' said Frances hopelessly, while the baby squared his mouth and joined in the noise.

Lorna turned the volume up and waited for her to crack. Frances walked off to the kitchen with the baby and quickly closed the door. Lorna gave a howl of rage from the other side and started to smash at it with fists and toys. Children were petal-skinned ogres, Frances realised, callous and whimsical, holding autocratic sway over lower, larger vassals like herself, clay-complexioned, occasionally drunk and whispering rebellious oaths which were punished with immediate sledge-hammer severity.

There followed a punishing stint of ricochet work, where Frances let the baby cry while she comforted Lorna; let Lorna shriek while she soothed the baby; put Lorna down for her nap and was called back three times before she gave up and let her follow her destructively around; bathed the baby after he had sprayed himself, Lorna and the bathroom with urine during the nappy changing process; sat on the closed lavatory seat and fed the baby while Lorna chattered in the bath which she had demanded in the wake of the baby's bath.

She stared at Lorna's slim silver body, exquisite in the water, graceful as a Renaissance statuette.

'Shall we see if you'd like a little nap after your bath?' she suggested hopelessly, for only if Lorna rested would she be able to rest, and then only if Matthew was asleep or at least not ready for a feed.

'No,' said Lorna, off-hand but firm.

'Oh thank God,' said Frances as she heard the car door slam outside. Jonathan was back. It was like the arrival of the cavalry. She wrapped Lorna in a towel and they scrambled downstairs. Jonathan stood puffing on the doormat. Outside was a mid-afternoon twilight, the rain as thick as turf and drenching so that it seemed to leave no room for air between its stalks.

'You're wet, daddy,' said Lorna, fascinated.

'There were lumps of ice coming down like tennis balls,' he marvelled.

'Here, have this towel,' said Frances, and Lorna span off naked as a sprite from its folds to dance among the chairs and tables while thunder crashed in the sky with the cumbersomeness of heavy furniture falling down uncarpeted stairs.

'S'il vous plâit,' said Frances to Jonathan, 'Dancez, jouez avec le petit diable, cette fille. Il faut que je get Matthew down for a nap, she just wouldn't let me. Je suis tellement shattered.'

'Mummymummymummy,' Lorna chanted as she caught some inkling of this, but Jonathan threw the towel over her and they started to play ghosts.

'My little fat boy,' she whispered at last, squeezing his strong thighs. '*Hey*, fatty boomboom, *sweet* sugar dumpling. It's not fair, is it? I'm never alone with you. You're getting the rough end of the stick just now, aren't you?'

She punctuated this speech with growling kisses, and his hands and feet waved like warm pink roses. She sat him up and stroked the fine duck tail of hair on his baby bull neck. Whenever she tried to fix his essence, he wriggled off into mixed metaphor. And so she clapped his cloud cheeks and revelled in his nest of smiles; she blew raspberries into the crease of his neck and onto his astounded hardening stomach, forcing lion-deep chuckles from him.

She was dismayed at how she had to treat him like some sort of fancy man to spare her daughter's feelings, affecting nonchalance when Lorna was around. She would fall on him for a quick mad embrace if the little girl left the room for a moment, only to spring apart guiltily at the sound of the returning Start-rites.

The serrated teeth of remorse bit into her. In late pregnancy she had been so sandbagged that she had had barely enough energy to crawl through the day, let alone reciprocate Lorna's incandescent two-year-old passion.

'She thought I'd come back to her as before once the baby arrived,' she said aloud. 'But I haven't.'

The baby was making the wrangling noise which led to unconsciousness. Then he fell asleep like a door closing. She carried him carefully to his basket, a limp solid parcel against her bosom, the lashes long and wet on his cheeks, lower lip out in a soft semicircle. She put him down and he lay, limbs thrown wide, spatch-cocked.

After the holiday, Jonathan would be back at the office with his broad quiet desk and filter coffee while she, she would have to submit to a fate worse than death, drudging round the flat to

Lorna's screams and the baby's regurgitations and her own sore eyes and body aching to the throb of next door's Heavy Metal.

The trouble with prolonged sleep deprivation was, that it produced the same coarsening side effects as alcoholism. She was rotten with self-pity, swarming with irritability and despair.

When she heard Jonathan's step on the stairs, she realised that he must have coaxed Lorna to sleep at last. She looked forward to his face, but when he came into the room and she opened her mouth to speak, all that came out were toads and vipers.

'I'm smashed up,' she said. 'I'm never alone. The baby guzzles me and Lorna eats me up. I can't ever go out because I've always got to be there for the children, but you flit in and out like a humming bird. You need me to be always there, to peck at and pull at and answer the door. I even have to feed the cat.'

'I take them out for a walk on Sunday afternoons,' he protested.

'But it's like a favour, and it's only a couple of hours, and I can't use the time to read, I always have to change the sheets or make a meatloaf.'

'For pity's sake. I'm tired too.'

'Sorry,' she muttered. 'Sorry. Sorry. But I don't feel like me any more. I've turned into some sort of oven.'

They lay on the bed and held each other.

'Did you know what Hardy called *Jude the Obscure* to begin with?' he whispered in her ear. '*The Simpletons*. And the Bishop of Wakefield burnt it on a bonfire when it was published.'

'You've been reading!' said Frances accusingly. '*When* did you read!'

'I just pulled in by the side of the road for five minutes. Only for five minutes. It's such a good book. I'd completely forgotten that Jude had three children.'

'*Three?*' said Frances incredulously. 'Are you sure?'

'Don't you remember Jude's little boy who comes back

.from Australia?' said Jonathan. 'Don't you remember little
Father Time?'

'Yes,' said Frances. 'Something very nasty happens to him,
doesn't it?'

She took the book and flicked through until she reached the
page where Father Time and his siblings are discovered by
their mother hanging from a hook inside a cupboard door, the
note at their feet reading, 'Done because we are too menny.'

'What a wicked old man Hardy was!' she said, incredulous.
'How *dare* he!' She started to cry.

'You're too close to them,' murmured Jonathan. 'You
should cut off from them a bit.'

'How *can* I?' sniffed Frances. '*Somebody's* got to be devoted
to them. And it's not going to be you because you know I'll do
it for you.'

'They're yours, though, aren't they, because of that,' said
Jonathan. 'They'll love you best.'

'They're *not* mine. They belong to themselves. But I'm not
allowed to belong to *my* self any more.'

'It's not easy for me either.'

'I know it isn't, sweetheart. But at least you're still allowed
to be your own man.'

They fell on each other's necks and mingled maudlin tears.

'It's so awful,' sniffed Frances. 'We may never have
another.'

They fell asleep.

When they woke, the landscape was quite different. Not only
had the rain stopped, but it had rinsed the air free of
oppression. Drops of water hung like lively glass on every leaf
and blade. On their way down to the beach, the path was
hedged with wet hawthorn, the fiercely spiked branches
glittering with green-white flowers.

The late sun was surprisingly strong. It turned the distant
moving strokes of the waves to gold bars, and dried salt
patterns onto the semi-precious stones which littered the
shore. As Frances unbuckled Lorna's sandals, she pointed out
to her translucent pieces of chrysophase and rose quartz in

amongst the more ordinary egg-shaped pebbles. Then she kicked off her own shoes and walked wincingly to the water's edge. The sea was casting lacy white shawls onto the stones, and drawing them back with a sigh.

She looked behind her and saw Lorna building a pile of pebbles while Jonathan made the baby more comfortable in his pushchair. A little way ahead was a dinghy, and she could see the flickering gold veins on its white shell thrown up by the sun through moving seawater, and the man standing in it stripped to the waist. She walked towards it, then past it, and as she walked on, she looked out to sea and was aware of her eyeballs making internal adjustments to the new distance which was being demanded of them, as though they had forgotten how to focus on a long view. She felt an excited bubble of pleasure expanding her ribcage, so that she had to take little sighs of breath, warm and fresh and salted, and prevent herself from laughing aloud.

When she reached the rock pools, she stopped to admire their lucidity. Under water, edges unblurred by air, the plush little anemones waved languidly at passing life. Weed the colour of wine and jewels, limpets, pebbles, violet-black mussel shells, all were stage lit, without shadow or dubiety.

After some while she reached the far end of the beach. Slowly she wheeled, like a hero on the cusp of anagnorisis, narrowing her eyes to make out the little group round the pushchair. Of course it was satisfying and delightful to see Jonathan – she supposed it *was* Jonathan? – lying with the fat mild baby on his stomach while their slender elf of a daughter skipped around him. It was part of it. But not the point of it. The concentrated delight was there to start with. She had not needed babies and their pleased-to-be-aliveness to tell her this.

She started to walk back, this time higher up the beach in the shade of cliffs which held prehistoric snails and traces of dinosaur. I've done it, she thought, and I'm still alive. She took her time, dawdling with deliberate pleasure, as though she were carrying a full glass of milk and might not spill a drop.

'I thought you'd done a Sergeant Troy,' said Jonathan. 'Disappeared out to sea and abandoned us.'

'Would I do a thing like that,' she said, and kissed him lightly beside his mouth.

Matthew reached up from his arms and tugged her hair.

'When I saw you over there by the rock pools you looked just as you used to,' said Jonathan. 'Just the same girl.'

'I am not just as I was, however,' said Frances. 'I am no longer the same girl.'

The sky, which had been growing more dramatic by the minute, was now a florid stagey empyrean, the sea a soundless blaze beneath it. Frances glanced at the baby, and saw how the sun made an electric fleece of the down on his head. She touched it lightly with the flat of her hand as though it might burn her.

'Isn't it mind-boggling,' said Jonathan, 'Isn't it impossible to take in that when we were last on this beach, these two were thin air. Or less. They're so solid now that I almost can't believe there was a time before them, and it's only been a couple of years.'

'What?' said Lorna. '*What* did you say?'

'Daddy was just commenting on the mystery of human existence,' said Frances, scooping her up and letting her perch on her hip. She felt the internal chassis, her skeleton and musculature, adjust to the extra weight with practised efficiency. To think, she marvelled routinely, To think that this great heavy child grew in the centre of my body. But the surprise of the idea had started to grow blunt, worn down by its own regular self-contemplation.

'Look, Lorna,' she said. 'Do you see how the sun is making our faces orange?'

In the flood of flame-coloured light their flesh turned to coral.

Nessun Dorma

ALAN SPENCE

IT'S THE FIRST thing I hear when I step out into the street. Pavarotti at full volume, belting out *Nessun Dorma*. Half past six in the morning, the streetlights on, the sky above the tenements just starting to get light. Three closes along, on the other side, the groundfloor window is wide open, pushed up as far as it can go. That's where the music is coming from. It builds to its crescendo. *Vincero*. It stops. There's a brief silence. Then it starts all over again.

I peer across as I pass by, but I can't really see in. The lights are off in the house. All I can make out is a faint glow that might be from a TV in the corner. The curtains are flapping, whipped about by that freezing Edinburgh breeze, straight off the North Sea.

In the papershop at the corner, Kenny from upstairs is buying his *Daily Record*, his cigarettes.

'Early shift this week?' I ask him.

'That's right. It's a bugger,' he says. 'Wife still away?'

'She'll be back at the weekend. Hey, did you hear that racket in the street?'

'The music?' he says. 'That World Cup thing?'

'Pavarotti.'

'I think it's been on all night. I got in the back of ten and it was going full blast then.'

'Weird.'

'The thing is.' He has pulled open the door, set the bell above it jangling. He stands half in half out of the shop. 'I couldn't help wondering if she was OK. The wifie in the house like. I mean, I looked in the window when I was passing and she was just sitting there in the dark wi the TV on and that music blaring out. Over and over.'

'Could be a video and she's rewinding it.'

'Aye.' He looks uncomfortable. 'Anyway. Maybe somebody should make sure she's all right. I'd do it myself but I've got my work to go to.'

'Sure.'

'So.'

'Right.'

He lets the door go and it closes behind him.

Thanks Kenny.

Christ.

Back along the street with my milk and rolls, the paper, I have to look in and see for myself. The music is still playing, louder the nearer I get. Right outside the window it's deafening. The curtains are still being tugged about by the wind, white net gone grubby. They flap out and I catch their dusty smell.

Inside, the TV flickers bright and harsh. Pavarotti is in close-up, the colours lurid and wrong, his face orange. Silhouetted in the blue light from the screen, I can make out the woman, sitting in an armchair, her back to the window. I lean right in and call out hello, above the music. My eyes adjust to the light and a few things take shape. A stack of newspapers on the table, an empty whisky bottle, ashtray full to overflowing, a carton of longlife milk. And the smell hits me, reek of drink and stale tobacco and somewhere in at the back of it a pervading sourness like old matted clothes in a jumble sale. The room stinks of misery. It's a smell I remember.

I call out hello again, hello there, and this time her head turns, she makes some kind of noise.

210

'Are you all right?'

She heaves herself up in the chair. She's a big woman, heavy. I recognise her, I've seen her in the street. Not old, maybe late forties, fifty. She steadies herself, peers at me blankly, takes a careful step or two towards the window. She looks terrible, her face blotched and puffy. Her hair is flattened, sticks up at the back, the way she's been leaning on it. She wears a thick wool cardigan, buttoned up, on top of what looks like a nightdress.

'What's that?' she says, bleary, looking out.

'Just making sure you're all right.'

'All right?' She has no idea who I am, what's going on. 'Yes,' she says. 'It's all right. Each one that has wronged me will come undone. Nice of you to take an interest. I would offer you a drink but it's not on. They sent for the police you know. But I told them. No uncertain terms. So now they're looking into it. Full investigation. I'll show them. Would you like a drink? No, of course. It's not on.'

She suddenly stops and looks confused, stranded in mid-stream. The voice of Pavarotti swells, fills the room. She lets herself be caught up in it again, lost in it. Her face crumples, folds in a grimace, a tortured smile as she stands there swaying in her stinking kitchen. The aria builds to its climax, again.

Vincero.

She finds the remote control and winds back the tape.

The Chinese dragon I painted on the wall of my room, in Glasgow, all those years ago. Eight feet long in bright primary colours, straight on to the blank white wall.

No reason why it should come to me now, but it does. I see it floating in its swirl of cloud, fire flaring from its nostrils, its long tail curled and looped round on itself like a Celtic serpent.

The room was the first one I'd ever had completely to myself. The twenty-third floor of a highrise block. My father and I had been moved from the room and kitchen where I'd grown up, where I was born. The room and kitchen that had come to have that stink of misery I recognised just now. The smell of hopelessness, my father not coping, myself useless in the face of it.

But all that was past. The tenements were rubble and dust. We had been transported to this bright empty space, high in the sky. I remember us laughing as we walked through it, shouted to each other from room to room, intoxicated by the cleanness and newness. It still smelled of fresh putty and paint. And the view from the windows had us stand there just staring. Instead of blackened tenements, the back of a factory, we could see for miles, clear down the Clyde.

I kept my room simple and uncluttered, a mattress in the corner, straw matting on the floor. And I started right away on painting that dragon. I copied it from a magazine, divided it up with a grid of squares, pencilled a bigger grid on the wall and scaled the whole thing up. That way the proportions would be right, exact. And when I'd drawn in all the lines, traced every delicate curve, I set to colouring it in, with poster-paint and a fine-tip brush.

I worked on it meticulously, a little every day, with total concentration and absolute care. After a week it was finished, except for one small section, the last few inches, the very tip of the tail. I decided to take a break over the weekend, finish it the following week. But I never did. I lived in that house for four years and never completed it. That section of tail stayed blank. When anyone asked me why, I had no idea. I just couldn't make myself pick up the brush. The dragon remained unfinished.

When I head out later along the street, Pavarotti's *bel canto* is still ringing out. *Tu pure, o Principessa nella tua fredda stanza.* Princess, you too are waking in your cold room. Again that smell wafts out as I pass by.

My father had a record of *Nessun Dorma* – an old scratched 78 – sung by Jussi Björling. So I know the song from way back. He used to play it loud when the drink had made him maudlin, sometimes alternating it with records of mine he liked in the same way, records that moved him to tears, Edith Piaf's *Je ne regrette rien*, Joan Baez singing *Plaisir d'amour*. In the years after my mother died, I grew to dread hearing those songs. I would stop and listen on the stair, halfway up the dank close, knowing the state I would find him in, guttered into oblivion.

It must have been those songs that made him want to learn French.

'Got to do something about myself,' he said. 'Haul myself up by my bootstraps.'

So he'd signed up for an evening class at the University, gone along once a week.

'Gives me something to look forward to,' he said.

He made lists of vocabulary in a little lined notebook.

'That tutor's some boy,' he said. 'Really knows his stuff.'

He had told the tutor he was hoping to go to France on holiday, someday.

The night I came home late and that smell hit me as soon as I opened the door. No music playing, but in the quietness the hiss and steady click of the recordplayer, the disc played out, the needle arm bobbing up and down in place. And behind that, my father breathing heavy in a deep drunk stupor. He slept in the set-in bed in the recess. I didn't want to disturb him, but I wanted to turn off the recordplayer. I switched on the light, turned and saw him.

Sprawled across the bed, still dressed, shoes on, his clothes and the bedding covered in blood, a bloodsoaked hanky wrapped round his hand.

I managed to wake him but couldn't get him up on his feet. He had drunk himself senseless, beyond all comprehension and pain, anaesthetised and numb.

I sat up all night, dozed in the chair. A couple of times he shouted out, nothing that made any sense. At first light I shook him awake, took him down to casualty at the hospital. He had lost the tip of a finger, had no recollection where or how. The doctors stitched him up, gave him injections.

'I was on my way to the French class,' he said. 'Met a guy I used to work with, in the yards. Drinking his redundancy money. Just the one, I said. Got somewhere to go. That was it. The rest's a blur.'

'What about your hand?'

'No idea,' he said. 'Except maybe.' He stopped. 'Just a vague memory. Getting it jammed in a taxi door.'

'Where in God's name were you going in a taxi?'

'I haven't a clue, son. Haven't a clue.'

For a while after that he was ill. A low ebb. He never went back to his evening class, never finished the course. He was giving up on everything, until this move to the new place, the high rise. A fresh start.

I like to get settled in the library early, get a good stint of work done in the morning. But today I just can't seem to focus. So I'm glad of the distraction when Neil comes in, sits down at the table next to me.

'How's the mature student?' he asks. 'Working on something?'

'Dissertation,' I tell him. 'Zen in Scottish literature.'

'Wild!'

'Of all the people on the planet, you're the one most likely to appreciate it.'

'Hey, thanks!'

His beard and long hair are grizzled these days. The archetypal Old Hippy.

'Passed these young guys in the street the other day,' he says. 'And they're looking me up and down. And one of them says Hey, man, tell it like it was!' He shrugs, spreads his hands. 'Thing is, I'd have been glad to!'

I hand over one of my sheets of paper to him, point to the passage at the top. It's a story from the legend of Fionn.

Fionn asks his followers, What is the finest music in the world? And they give their various answers. The call of a cuckoo. The laughter of a girl. Then they ask Fionn what he thinks. And he answers, The music of what happens. 'Beautiful!' says Neil, handing me back the page.

'I'm writing about MacCaig at the minute,' I tell him. 'He once described himself as a Zen Calvinist!'

'Ha! He won't thank you for that!'

'Listen. Do you fancy a cup of tea?'

214

'Hey!' he says. 'Is the Pope a Catholic?'

In the tearoom he says, 'Stevenson's your man.'

'Stevenson?'

'Have a look at his *Child's Garden*. Then check out a wee book called *Fables*. It's the two sides, you see. Innocence and Experience. Here, I'll tell you my favourite one of the fables. This man meets a young lad weeping. And he asks him, What are you weeping for? And the lad says, I'm weeping for my sins. And the man says, You must have little to do. The next day they meet again. And the lad's weeping. And the man asks him, Why are you weeping now? And the lad says, Because I have nothing to eat. And the man says, I thought it would come to that.'

Neil throws back his head and laughs. 'There's Zen Calvinism for you!'

'The Ken Noo school!'

'Lord, Lord, we didna ken!'

'Aye, weel, ye ken noo!'

He thumps the table, laughs again.

Over more tea, I find myself telling him about the woman this morning, listening endlessly to *Nessun Dorma*.

'Sad,' he says.

Then I tell him about that dragon I once painted on the wall. And he stares at me.

'Now that is something.'

'How do you mean?'

'There's this Chinese story,' he says. 'About an artist that paints a dragon. And his master tells him he mustn't complete it. He has to leave a wee bit unfinished. The artist says fine, no problem. But sooner or later his curiosity gets the better of him. And he finishes it off. And the dragon comes to life and devours him!'

I stare back at him.

'I've never heard that story in my life. How could I have known?'

'We know more than we think,' says Neil. 'I mean everything's telling us, all the time. Only we don't listen.'

'Sure.' For some reason, his story's disturbed me. 'Better get back to my work.'

'The dissertation!' He looks amused.

Outside in the High Street he asks, by the way, how's Mary? And I tell him she's fine, she's away in the States, she'll be back at the end of the week.

'Good,' he says.

We stop at the corner.

'Right.'

'One last thing,' he says. 'Do you know the story of *Turandot*, where your *Nessun Dorma* comes from?'

'Just that it's set in China.'

'Aye.' He nods, grins. 'Check it out sometime. I think you'll find it interesting.'

Back at the library, I look in the music section, find the libretto.

An unknown prince arrives at the great Violet City, its gates carved with dragons. In the course of the story, he finds his long-lost father. He solves three riddles which grant him the hand of the princess Turandot. The answer to one riddle is the name of the princess. The answers to the others are hope and blood.

The word Tao catches my eye as I flick through the pages. The prince is told, *Non esiste che il niente nel quale ti annulli.* There exists only the nothingness in which you annihilate yourself. *Non esiste che il Tao.* There exists only the Tao.

One last passage jumps out at me, a paragraph in the introduction, explaining that Puccini never completed the opera, it was left unfinished when he died.

I see Neil's grin. Everything is telling us. All the time.

I close the book, put it back on the shelf.

When I'd lived four years in that white room with a view, the painted dragon unfinished on the wall, I met Mary and moved out. We travelled a bit, in France then Italy. We got work teaching English, enough to get by. I sent my father postcards from every new place. When we came back home I went to see him. The flat had come to have the old familiar smell, staleness of booze and fags and no hope. He was listening again to his sad songs. He had lost his job, been laid off. He was months behind with his rent, and we were too broke to bail him out.

In the end he had to give up the flat. I helped him find a bedsit near the University. He liked it well enough, liked the neighbourhood. The bedsit was his home for five years, till he died.

Ten o'clock at night and *Nessun Dorma* still going strong. She's been playing it for 24 hours at least.

At the World Cup, Italia 90, in one of the games Scotland lost, the song was played at half-time, the video shown on a giant screen in the stadium. Someone shouted, 'Easy the big man!' And the whole Scottish crowd started chanting,

> *One Pavarotti*
> *There's only one Pavarotti.*

Scotland in Europe.
Wha's like us?
My old neighbour Archie next door has started up on his accordion. He plays it most nights, runs through his repertoire. *Moonlight and Roses. Bridges of Paris. Spanish Eyes.* A taste for the exotic. He plays with gusto, undaunted by the odd bum note. I find it unutterably melancholy.

The long dark night. This wee cold country.
Ach.

I know the noise has something to do with me as it batters into my awareness, harasses me awake. The phone ringing at 3 a.m. So it must be Mary calling from the States. Still groggy, I pick it up, hear that transatlantic click and hiss, then her voice, warm.

Hello?
'Hi.'
I know it's late, sorry.
It's one of those lines. The person speaking drowns out the other. When you talk you hear a faint, delayed echo of your own voice. Not great for communication. Those little phatic responses keep getting lost. So I just listen as she tells me the

ALAN SPENCE

story. New York's been hit by a hurricane. Roads are flooded, bridges closed, subways off. The airports are shut down, all flights cancelled, no way she can get out.

Sorry.

'So it'll be, what, a few more days?'

Whenever.

I listen to the wash of noise down the line, feel the distance. Then she's telling me about a call she made to the airline, and the woman she spoke to knew nothing about the situation.

So I says, Haven't you been watching the news on TV? And she says, You think I'm sitting here watching TV? I'm working!

I laugh at that, miss the next bit.

and I ask her what I should do, and she says Stay tuned!

'Nice!'

What?

'I said, Nice.'

Yeah, right.

'So.'

So this is costing.

'Who cares?'

What?

'Never mind.'

I'll call when I know what's happening.

'See you soon.'

Take care.

I put down the phone, stare at it. I shiver and realise I'm chilled from sitting. I know I won't get back to sleep, so I pad through to the kitchen, put on the kettle, light the gas fire. Then I hear the commotion out in the street, voices raised, an argument, crackle of an intercom. I pull back the curtain and peer out, see the flashing light on top of the police car. Two young policemen are at the groundfloor window, trying to reason with the woman, and she's screaming out at them, 'I know the score here! I know what's going on!'

Finally she bangs the window shut. Then the music stops, cuts off.

A man's voice shouts out from an upstairs window. 'Nessun bloody dorma right enough! How's anybody

218

supposed to sleep through this lot?' And he too slams his window.

The car drives off, and everything is quiet again, so quiet. For no reason I get dressed and go out, walk to the end of the street. I stand there a while, looking up at the night sky. The winds are high. The way it looks, the clouds stand still, the stars go scudding past.

Somewhere a dog barks. A taxi prowls by.

The music of what happens.

Stay tuned.

That groundfloor window is open again, just a fraction. Smell of my father's house. Things left unfinished. The music is playing, one more time, but quietly now, so I have to strain to hear it. I stand there and listen, right to the end.

Vincero.

Reservations

CARL TIGHE

IT WAS THE YEAR when the Great White Queen sent the Long Knives into the land of the black earth against Flying Hair. And afterwards, through the winter months, many lodges stood empty. The squaws sang their lament, while the children cried with hunger.

Mrs Jones was scraping flour from her fingers. Sion ran in shouting – Long Knives! Long Knives! – Mrs Jones took up a cloth to wipe her hands and went to the door. There were two policemen and a woman social worker in a plastic rain hat standing on the garden path. The sergeant took off his helmet and mopped the inside with a handkerchief. The social worker peeped round his bulk and said:
  – Mrs Jones, it's about your boy, Sion . . .
  – And what do you say he's done this time?
  The social worker fiddled with her rain hat. The sergeant cleared his throat.
  – Well I don't like to keep on at the boy, what with your husband and all, but this is getting serious . . .
  The social worker brought out a large file and flipped through it.
  – First there was the business with the rabbit, and then there

was the business at the school, and after that there was the complaint about the . . .

– And what is it this time? Mrs Jones interrupted. She already knew his misdemeanours by heart.

– We've had a 999 call from a woman down the bottom end of the estate. It seems he, well, tied up a little girl . . .

– My God! He didn't . . .

– No, nothing like that, no. He tied her to a garden fence and he cut off her plaits. Frightened the life out of the kid anyway . . .

– Good lord, Sergeant, I thought he'd committed some real crime the way you were carrying on . . .

– Mrs Jones, make no mistake about this. He may not have . . . well, you know what we feared, but he's still committed an offence. Technically it is aggravated assault, possibly even kidnapping. I don't know, it's for a judge to say, not me . . .

– Must he go to court?

– There were witnesses, the girl is upset and the mother is very angry indeed . . . I wouldn't be surprised if she pressed charges.

They sat in the kitchen. Sion, who thought of himself as Floating Owl, was given a severe talking-to by the Sergeant (Three Stripes). Mrs Jones (Bear Woman) dabbed her face with a tea towel. The other policeman (He Who Follows) and the woman (Rain Hat) listened, but Floating Owl would make no response.

– I don't know if he hears me or what, sighed Three Stripes.

– He's been like this ever since his grandfather passed on. And he's the one I blame. Filling him up with all this Wild West nonsense . . .

– How old is he now, said Three Stripes.

– Sixteen. Nearly seventeen.

– He's too big for me, you see. I can't do nothing with him these days.

Mrs Jones began to cry onto the kitchen table.

– He hasn't done no harm. Not really.

Burly Three Stripes put his hand on Mrs Jones' shoulder.

– Don't you take on now. We'll do the best we can for the lad.

– But my husband . . . he'll never forgive me . . .

– He'll understand, I'm sure. We'll have a word with him. All right?

Bear Woman packed a bag for Floating Owl: a clean set of breech clouts, a buckskin shirt, extra leggings. Floating Owl checked that his medicine bag hung at his throat – its contents were his own private secret and must never be shown to anyone. He clutched the bundle given him by Bear Woman and took a long last look around the tepee. He felt his breath catch in his throat. He would prefer to wrap himself in a buffalo skin, to feel the sturdy bulk of his pony beneath him. He would have preferred to select a couple of travois poles and simply move the tepee in the traditional manner, but his mind fogged on this point. Where was the pony? He told himself the pony must have run off in the night, and as for the travois poles, well, there were no trees for miles around. They escorted him to the buckboard of the Long Knives and he sat in it uneasily. He kissed Bear Woman goodbye through the open window. When she wiped away her tears he said:

– Fear not. It is a good day to die.

When Three Stripes climbed in beside him, Floating Owl said:

– So we go to the stockade?

He offered his wrists for handcuffing, but Three Stripes said:

– Don't be so bloody daft, lad.

Floating Owl had a dream. It was Grandfather who put the dream into words for him. Over the years it had become an established ritual between them: Floating Owl would ask for his dream, and Bright Beads would tell the story, using the same words every time. It was from this dream that Floating Owl took his name.

Fort Hitachi lay at the edge of the Powder River territory – the ancient Cheyenne hunting grounds off the A48 west of Dinas Powys. Upon arrival a squaw dressed all in white led Floating Owl to a white tiled room. He sat cross-legged on the bedstead. When it was quiet he took a deep breath and analysed the smells of the fort. Nothing. He could smell nothing. He waited.

In the silence of the night he could hear the leaping and gurgling of the Sweetwater River.

Next morning all the captive braves were put in the compound. It was cold. They walked briskly in a circle, their breath forming a grey mist. It was the month of the Falling Leaves. To the north there was already snow on the peak of Mount Bighorn. Soon it would be the month of the Frozen Waters. The buffalo were already moving south across the M4. Floating Owl paused in his walk. He could smell the buffalo.

In his mind's eye Floating Owl pictured his Grandfather propped up in his bed. His hair and beard were white and though blind his eyes were a startling blue. Grandfather Bright Beads had said:

– One day Owl decided to explore the far country beyond the Black Hills. It was not the habit of his people to travel far from home, so he was a little nervous. He said to himself: I will just take a look and see what life is like over there. And flexing his wings he beat against the ground and rose up in a cloud of dust. Higher and higher he climbed, and then, turning, he flew towards the Black Hills on the horizon.

Dr Higgins will see you now.

Floating Owl disliked being spoken to unbidden by a woman. It was bad for his magic. But this woman, dressed in white, was not unfriendly. He followed her along the corridor and wondered what to call her. As they arrived at the doctor's door he decided on the name of the messenger – White Bird.

Dr Higgins was a shrivelled little man who sat behind a huge desk as if it were some kind of palisade. He polished his glasses until they were as shiny as his bald pink pate. To Floating Owl the lack of hair denoted cowardice. Single combat with this man would win him no 'coup' since there was no scalp to take.

– Good Morning. Sit down, won't you. Now then, let me see. The file says that . . . well . . . there's all sorts of things. Problems, eh? Something about a rabbit . . . a girl . . . probably nothing at all. Blown up out of all proportion, eh? Do you want to tell me about it . . . ?

Higgins waited. At last Floating Owl spoke:

– White Man, why did you come to the land of The People?

– Pardon?

– We do not need you, White Eyes. The Spirit that is Everywhere has given us everything we need. We have sweet water, the sky and land, and buffalo on the land beneath the arch of the sky, from horizon to horizon. Buffalo darken the planes from the place where the sun rises to the place where the sun rests. They provide us with all a human needs. Who needs more, is none. There is nothing we want from the White Eyes. Go back to the Great White Mother and give her my words.

– Buffalo? I see . . . said Higgins, licking his lips nervously. But what about this rabbit then . . . ?

– We ate it.

– Yes, I'm sure you did. But it wasn't yours to eat, was it?

– I am a hunter. I caught it.

– According to the police report you took it from a neighbour's hutch.

– I caught it.

– It belonged to a Mr Morgan . . .

– Ha! Rain in the Face!

– Rain in the Face? Is that your name for Mr Morgan?

Floating Owl closed up. He had said too much.

– Well, I wonder what you call me . . . ?

Floating Owl said nothing. He had not decided what to call this man. He looked closely at Dr Higgins' face, trying to gauge his opponent. He noted the soft, fleshy chin and the blue bags under the eyes. At first he had thought it was the face of a weak man, but there was something else there too. Perhaps it was not physical strength, but this man had the power of other men at his command.

A few days later Floating Owl was called again to the tepee of the White Eyes' Medicine Man. This time there were no opening pleasantries.

– Tell me Sion, what name do you call yourself?

– It is not good for me to utter my own chosen name. A demon might steal it.

– I see. Well then, tell me about your father.

– Frog that Sings has gone away.

– I know.

– He travels alone to repair his medicine. No one knows where.

– That is not exactly true is it?

Floating Owl looked at the floor.

– I know where he is and so do you. Your father is in prison.

– My father is a prisoner at the Fort. He was tricked with a piece of paper. My people warned him not to touch the White Eyes' pen, but he would not listen.

– Do you miss your father?

– He was warned. It is peaceful without him.

– And how does your mother feel about all this?

– She does not miss him. She has me. I hunt. I provide for her. I am the man of the lodge now.

– What will you do when your father returns?

– He will not return.

– Oh but he will. They didn't put him away for ever. In fact he's due for release any day now.

– No!

– It's true. What with good conduct and all, he'll be out on parole. You have to face it Sion, his time is up. Your father has paid for the business of the embezzlement. He wants to come home to his wife and his son. He wants to be a proper father to you.

– He must not return. He brought shame upon us. He sold his family into slavery. He has no honour.

– But, surely he paid for his mistake . . .

225

– How is it possible to pay?

– He went to prison . . .

– The Long Knives may keep him at the Fort if they wish. The Human Beings do not weaken in the face of White Eyes' trash and trinkets. Frog that Sings was blinded by the gifts and promises of the White Eyes. He is lost to us. He may not return.

In his room Floating Owl spread out his sweat shirt on the floor. He sat cross-legged next to it, closed his eyes and began the necessary chant:

– Spirit that is everywhere, hear me . . .

When he had finished he stood up and commenced moving round the shirt in the slow Cheyenne medicine dance, all the while softly intoning:

– Hey-a-na. Hey hey, hey-a-nah . . .

When he had finished he knew that his ghost shirt with its glittering A-Team logo would make him invisible and would protect him from the bullets of the Long Knives.

Grandfather Bright Beads had said:

– And Owl flew higher and higher until he was way above the Black Hills. But by then his wings ached and his lungs were crying for rest. He decided that he would ride a while on the rising draughts of warm air. So with wings outstretched he floated in long wide circles, all the while scanning the land beneath with his clear, sharp eyes. He asked himself: Why do I go against the habit of my people and travel to another place to see how it is there? Why am I, a creature of the air, so fascinated by the shape of the land? And while he circled high above the mountainside he thought over his question to himself. And finally he answered: I am fascinated by the land and the shapes of the land because the land made me, and because I in my turn help make the land. And when I die I will become the land. And as he thought this his sharp eyes picked out a tiny figure standing on the hillside.

Floating Owl noticed a change in the way they treated him.

226

They were less patient with him. One morning White Bird opened his cell door without knocking and said:

– OK Chief, move your arse. You've got an appointment at Apache Pass.

Floating Owl wrinkled his nose at the mention of Apache. To him Apache were a small, ugly, bandy-legged people, whose women were unnaturally hairy.

– Apache are not Human Beings, he told White Bird, but she did not seem interested.

– No? Well never mind. Big Chief Higgins wants a pow-wow.

Floating Owl had decided to call Higgins Shadow Cloud. Confronted now with his paleness, Floating Owl wondered if Shadow Cloud was in fact a Hopi Indian. The Hopi were famous for the albino among them. Hopi were not Human Beings either. They disgusted Floating Owl with their clammy, wormy whiteness.

– Tell me about this er . . . this War Path of yours. The school, remember?

– A warrior does not sing his own praise-song.

– No. Of course not. I just want you to tell me what happened.

– For that you must listen to the songs of the Human Beings.

– Oh, I see. Well, of course I'd just love to do that, but I don't have the time. And in any case I'm from St Albans, Herts. I don't speak the lingo.

– No. You are not of The People.

Floating Owl remembered the night attack, creeping through the buffalo grass, the bright moonlight, climbing through the window, padding up to the laboratory, and then the joy of smashing test tubes, flasks, fish tanks. Coloured liquids and dying fish covered the floor by the time the Long Knives arrived. Three Stripes stood in the doorway, his hands on his hips. He Who Follows had looked into the room over Three Stripes' shoulder and said: Strewth! Floating Owl had replied: It is a good day to die. He remembered the siren and

the flashing blue light on the buckboard of the Long Knives as
they took him into custody at the Fort.

Shadow Cloud said loudly:

– Are you going to tell me or not?

– Or not.

– Look in two days' time your father will come home from
prison. I don't want to use drugs on you, but if you carry on
like this you leave me with no alternative. Let's talk again
tomorrow, but if we make no progress . . .

– He must not return.

– Oh but he will. He will.

– He must not!

– Why?

– The gew-gaws of the White Eyes.

– You mean the embezzlement?

– I mean the video camera, the TV set, the caravan, the
home computer, the new car, the chalet . . .

– Heap big wampum, eh Chief?

– I am no chief.

– Except in the home. You're Chief there, aren't you? And
since when do Red Men speak about home computers and
videos, eh? I think you're getting a little anachronistic there
Chief. Heap Big Trash, eh? Look, why don't you just drop all
this Red Man speak with Knife and Fork tongue nonsense.
Your father did his best to provide for you. All right, so he
made a mistake, he took a little more than he should. But that's
business: the line between profit and crime is a very thin one.
You must understand that. Your father did what he did
because he loved you. You were his Baby Bunting. He was
out hunting for a rabbit skin to wrap his baby up in. You can't
go on punishing him . . . all this Red Man stuff . . . If you
keep it up they'll put you away, not your father.

– The swallow flies south for the winter. It does not return
to see how the snow lies on the earth.

– Don't give me all that bullshit! I see right through it!
shouted Shadow Cloud. He snatched up a mirror and held it
before Floating Owl's face.

– What do you see there? Do you see a Red Man? I see a little

Welsh tyke who's wasting my time with silly bloody games. That's what I see.

Floating Owl admired himself in the mirror. His single green feather, his hair band, his wind tanned features . . .

Floating Owl sat cross-legged on the bed. White Bird stood awkwardly in the doorway. She was looking at his A-Team shirt hanging from the wardrobe door. She fingered the glittery logo.

– And what's so special about the shirt then?
– It is my ghost shirt. When I wear it I am invisible.
She smiled.
– Chief, not even the A-Team are that good.

Floating Owl was suddenly angry with himself. He had revealed his medicine to a woman, someone who was not a Human Being, who did not believe in his medicine.

Grandfather Bright Beads had said:
– Owl could feel the wind whistling through the outstretched feathers at the ends of his wings. He was curious about the figure on the landscape below, and he said to himself: I'll go down, fly a little closer, just to see what life is like for that person in that place. And swooping in wide circles, Owl descended until he could see that the figure was that of a beautiful girl. She had skin as dark as chocolate, her long hair and her eyes were as black and shiny as coals, but she was crying and the tears poured from the point of her chin. Owl flew closer and settled in a nearby tree. He called to her in his clear flutey voice:
– Little girl, why do you cry?
She said.
– I cry because I hate this place. I feel terrible here. The people don't see how awful they are and they make me terribly unhappy.
Owl, who was a very kind bird, said:
– Don't they treat you well?
At which the girl cried even harder.

229

– No, that's not it. Because I am beautiful they give me everything. I want for nothing. I am so spoiled.

In the morning during his exercise period, Floating Owl paused in his circular walk of the compound to watch the V-shaped formations of the geese as they flew south. He wanted to return to his lodge, to be in familiar surroundings, to be with Bear Woman. But thought of the lodge upset him. Frog that Sings would soon come home – the thought he should not think. He listened to the honking calls of the geese and decided that he must break out of the Stockade and head back along the Sweetwater River as soon as posssible. Like the birds and the buffalo he must be free to wander where his nature and his ancestors told him he must.

White Bird saw him watching the geese.

– Hey, Chief, what's six inches long, red, and got an arrow through it?

Floating Owl looked blank.

– Custer's Last Stand. Get it? Oh you're hopeless, you are.

At lunch Floating Owl refused a knife and fork, spat lumps of gristle on the floor.

– Rattlesnake! he exclaimed. I won't eat it. Give me buffalo hump.

White Bird escorted him to his room.

– You know, White Bird said as they walked, I heard that one of them Red Indian tribes was actually a bunch of Welsh men that got lost. I read it somewhere. Is that what you are? Eh? A lost Welshman? Well you aren't the first, and you won't be the last.

Floating Owl studied her face for a moment. Was she mocking him? He made no reply.

– What's the matter Chief? You're behaving like somebody pissed on your signal fire. And Dr Higgins is getting proper fed up with you.

That afternoon Dr Higgins sent for Floating Owl. The Medicine Man of the White Eyes talked on and on, asking questions, waiting for answers that never came. The more he talked the more taciturn Floating Owl became. He told himself that the White Man's medicine was failing – that was what all the talking was about.

Floating Owl let his mind wander. He thought of Grandfather Bright Beads, of his endless pipe smoking and his tales of travels and adventures. Bright Beads had an ancient picture book – it was the only book in the lodge. Floating Owl loved to look at it. It was about Indians. The pictures showed the various chiefs and the patterns of their head-dresses, the different types of face and body paint. By the time he was nine years old Floating Owl could distinguish over thirty different kinds of tribal arrow. But that was in the Year of the Many Sparrows. Since then Bright Beads had gone to the Happy Hunting Grounds. Floating Owl had turned to his father for tales and stories, but Frog that Sings refused saying that he was too busy. The book, the one book in the lodge, disappeared. Floating Owl suspected that his father had sold it. After that his father had touched the White Eyes' pen, had become involved with the trick of words and numbers they called Accountancy, and with The Embezzlement he had brought shame.

Floating Owl became aware that Shadow Cloud was no longer speaking. The doctor had asked a question and was waiting for an answer.

Bright Beads had said:
– Owl was surprised. He had never heard of such a thing. He thought about the girl's words, and then he said:
– Girl who is a woman, in another place it may be different. In another place they may not consider you to be beautiful at all. Climb onto my back and with my powerful wings I will carry you to the land beyond the Black Hills, to a place where you can be happy, because you must know, I am making a journey to see what life is like in that part of the world.

But this only made the girl cry even harder.
– I can't, she wailed. I belong here. They all tell me this is so. They would never let me go.
– Never let you go? said Owl, his feathers ruffling at the thought. You are a free spirit in the world. You can go as you

231

please. It is easily done. Just climb up on my back and away we go. No one will stop you.

– No, no, said the girl. You don't understand at all. You see although I hate it, I have all my things here. And anyway, there is no other place in the whole world that is so good.

That night Floating Owl slept in his ghost shirt. The moonlight played on the glitter. Soon he fell asleep. He had a dream. In his dream he saw Bright Beads standing over the body of Frog that Sings. Under his arm Bright Beads carried the book, and with his other arm he gestured to the skies. Floating Owl rose up into the air and floated to the clouds in a graceful arc. From this vantage he looked down on the land of the Human Beings. A movement caught his eye. Down among the ravines and gulches of the Badlands he could see himself, walking and singing, his head thrown back. He floated a little lower until he could see that he had a single green feather in his headband and a bow across his shoulders. Three horizontal bands of coal-black war paint were streaked across the bridge of his nose. He called to himself, but Floating Owl did not hear.

In the early hours of the morning Floating Owl broke out of the Stockade. Strangely there were no sentries. He thought of stealing a horse from the Long Knives, but in the dark he could not locate the picket lines. He sneaked out of the main gate unobserved, invisible in his ghost shirt. After a little while he picked up an old hunting trail marked *B4268 Cardiff*. Floating Owl shook his head from side to side to drive out the confusion and to focus on the task in hand.

Bright Beads had said:
– Owl shook his head reluctantly. I can't help you if you won't help yourself little girl. We must all do what we can to be ourselves. Won't you come with me?

A tear-drop ran down her face but the girl did not answer, only shook her head. Owl flexed his enormous wings and rose up into the sky. As he climbed higher and higher he could hear the girl calling to him.

– Goodbye Owl. Goodbye. Please visit me on your return and tell me how it was.

Owl turned to look at her, but even with his sharp eyes he could not pick her out from the landscape, so Owl just called out: Goodbye Black Hills. Goodbye. And turning again on the wind he resumed his journey.

The Cheyenne death chant came softly from the bushes at the side of the Lo-Price Supermarket: Hey hey hey hey; hey hey hey hey . . . Eventually the chant subsided and a voice said: It is a good day to die. Floating Owl shivered until in the grey light of dawn he saw his father, Frog that Sings, walking along the terrace of Council-owned lodges towards the front door of the family lodge. In one hand he still held his prison travel warrant. In the other he carried a small carrier bag with his belongings. He paused at the garden gate, looking at the front of the house, as if comparing his memory with the real thing.

The first arrow hit him in the hand. He stood a moment, looking at the quivering rod in his palm and the point that poked through his knuckles. As he felt the surge of pain, the second arrow hit him in the throat. He toppled over the garden fence with barely a sound. His feet drummed briefly on the garden path, and then his eyes glazed. Floating Owl stood on the tidy lawn. Even in the dawn light he could see blood, black and sticky, on the concrete path. White Eyes! he breathed. He knelt and took Frog that Sings by the hair. Gritting his teeth against the sound he took the scalp.

Three Stripes and He Who Follows found Floating Owl at the weir in Roath Park – The place of the White Waters he preferred to call it. Floating Owl had walked a long way from the Pen-y-Lan Reservation. He was very tired. He let the Long Knives take away his bow and knife without a struggle. His father's scalp was still wet at the waistband of his jeans. Upon being cautioned he said: The day of the Red Man is past. It is a good day to die.

Spirit of a New India

JONATHAN TREITEL

'THE GREAT WHITE queen is dead, sir.'

'Bloody fool.'

'She died three days ago.'

'What?'

'I am telling the whole truth. It is reported in *The Times*.'

'Are you having me on, Gupta?'

'The queen herself, the colossal blanched one, Empress of Magrapore and England and India and innumerable other lesser places, has kicked the bucket.'

'Here, let me see that.'

Dawson, chief tax inspector of the district of Magrapore, seized *The Times of India* from his assistant. The large pages rustled and resisted. The front page, as always, was occupied with numerous small ads: a cheap lot of used horseshoes for sale; tickets to England; an announcement that if relatives of Mr Charles Arthur Packenham (deceased), formerly of Madras, contact a certain London solicitors, they will learn something to their advantage; best imported tinned butter . . . And the death was revealed within. A cortège of boldface twenty-point headlines: HER MAJESTY HAS PASSED AWAY. The stock was rimmed with black.

Dawson's newspaper trembled.

'Her Majesty is kicking up daisies, sir.'

'Bloody fool.' And laughed.

For Dawson, a bachelor in his mid-twenties, Gupta, a few years older, was essential. Not only did Gupta understand the intricacies of the tax system far better than his superior, but he was also a friend. A friend of a limited kind, to be sure; there could be no question of visiting him at home or strolling side by side through the bazaar, let alone inviting him to the club; but he was an office companion. Frequently as they sat over their work, while the new electric fan whined like a mosquito and threatened to blow stray sheets of typescript off the desk and across the dusty floor, they would engage in banter. For example they might be puzzling over some ancient tax return for 1894: Dawson would enquire why the hell DO NOT THROW OUT was scrawled on it in red ink; and Gupta would reply that Olerinshaw (the previous chief tax inspector) had doubtless been off his rocker. This was one of their long standing jokes: that Olerinshaw, after his seven year stint at Magrapore, had ended up in a lunatic asylum. (In fact he had been promoted to a posting in Trichinopoli.) Then Dawson would call Gupta a bloody fool, and laugh. Other jokes included insulting the queen and the royal family; the head office in Delhi; the viceroy; the local maharaja; the English; the Indians, and so forth. Somehow Gupta, though he had never been outside the vicinity of Magrapore, had acquired not merely correct and idiomatic English, but what seemed to be genuine understanding of the irony which underlies everything a true born Englishman says.

Yet Gupta, among Indians, was Indian. During the lunch break he would squat down alongside those of his fellow assistants of the same rank and caste as himself, and they would all cook food together – rice and some antive sauce – over a cluster of charcoal burners. They would chatter in their lingo and nudge. Sometimes Gupta would be frightfully amused – he would emit an open mouthed roar.

And it would be time to get back to work. Soon Gupta would be conversing with Dawson, suggesting perhaps that they should destroy the records of tax owed by Mr Singh or

Mr Mehta or the other Mr Singh (the richest local business-men) in return for a fat bribe; then he and Dawson would run away to Kashmir. 'Why Kashmir?' Dawson would ask.

'I have cousins in Kashmir. It is very beautiful and cool.'

'Yes, but what would we bloody do there?'

'We would fish. We would stand by the beautiful cool lake and go fishing.'

Dawson would pause, open mouthed, as if seriously weighing the suggestion; then say, 'Hang it all Gupta.' And laugh.

Gupta would get back to work.

But, on reading of the queen's death, Dawson was in no laughing mood. Of course it had been long expected: a monarch is not immortal, but even so . . . Once, Dawson's best friend Boswell had dressed up as Queen Victoria. Boswell had put on layers of petticoats and a grey wig, a black dress and bonnet, and much costume jewellery. He had marched, bold as brass, into a party in the gardens of Trinity College, Oxford, held to celebrate a rowing triumph: the first Trinity eight had 'bumped' three rival eights. Dawson had taken on the role of herald: skipping through the lavender bed and shouting, 'Three cheers for Her Majesty!' Originally Dawson had planned to do himself up as the ghost of Prince Albert, but in the end he hadn't had the nerve. 'Hip, hip, hooray!' The upshot was that Boswell had been gated for one term, and as for Dawson, the dean had told him he was very lucky to have been let off with a severe reprimand, very lucky indeed.

Dawson pulled open the shutters. A lizard flickered on the mosquito wiring. The window was cut into the door that led to the seldom used back stairs which descended into a squarish yard. Beggars squatted there, and from time to time a woman sold spices from big baskets; occasionally a sacred cow would wander through and doze in the shade of the banyan tree – Dawson would have to send a junior clerk down to chivvy the beast away. In the middle of all this, on a solid cement plinth, Queen Victoria was located. (She had been intended to go in front, beside the main entrance, but the delivery boy had made a mistake on the occasion of the erection, during the Diamond

Jubilee, back in the era of Olerinshaw. Too late to change things now.) Unfortunately the twice life-size statue was sculpted of some orange sandstone too weak to stand up to the ravages of the Indian climate. After each monsoon season the modelling would be less precise, the features more eroded. By the time the real Queen died, on a four-poster bed in Windsor Castle, the imitation had become blobbed with an impasto of bird droppings, streaked with red and yellow, and was reduced to a vague androgynous dummy.

'Tragic,' said Dawson, looking out through the mosquito wiring.

'It is a catastrophe, sir. The end of the world is nigh.'

'Bloody fool.'

A calendar was hung on the wall with past days crossed off in black ink and future important days circled in red. Dawson kept a mental tally of the number of days to go till his home leave: one thousand three hundred and eighty-four to go. He had been in India one thousand one hundred and seventy-two days already. It had all been his friend's idea. Back at Oxford, Boswell and he had planned on being poets. To love and to fight and to die in exotic places, leaving one's name writ on water. They had often communed with the white marble statue of Shelley in University College: the poet reclines on his back, young and handsome and dead and polished to a superb shine. How splendid to publish a pamphlet entitled *The Necessity of Atheism* whilst an undergraduate, how simply shocking. Shelley had conceived a passion for geology: consider the slow growth of mountains, the gradual creation of seas, the glory of it . . . so he had attended a mineralogy lecture. He had run out after twenty minutes screeching, 'Rocks! The man does nothing but talk about rocks!' Another time he had drunk a curse to Newton for having explained away the mystery of the rainbow. So in due course he had been sent down and become a genius. And Boswell had suggested they might as well take the Indian Civil Service exam, in as much as one may be a poet and atheist and genius in India as well as anywhere, and the job paid rather nicely. Boswell had failed the interview but Dawson had ended up in the

Magrapore tax office. Boswell was now doing something in the City: insurance, actually; he was married and had a baby girl, Geraldine. He wrote each Christmas. But what larks the two of them had got up to! They hadn't in fact placed a chamberpot on the cross on top of the college chapel, but they had talked about doing so tremendously!

The queen is dead. Long live the king. The following year Dawson was officiating at a ceremony in honour of the coronation. He was standing by the open door at the back of the office, looking down the stairs into India. His right hand was burrowing in his trouser pocket, turning over a brand new penny, and passing his thumb over the markings as if reading Braille. He knew what it depicted: the bearded chubby profile, and some lettering around the edges: EDWARD VII. D G. FID DEF. IND IMP. As he turned the coin this message cycled indefinitely. The Latin abbreviations served not to obscure the meaning but to understate it delicately, as one must. *Edward VII, By the Grace of God, Defender of the Faith, Emperor of India*. The image of Britannia was on the obverse, and the date, 1901. This was the first year of the new century. (Many people supposed the century had begun on the First of January 1900 – he had had quite a to-do about it with some fellows at the club – but they were wrong.)

Below, in the yard, the employees of the tax office were lined up according to their status and seniority, behind a representation of the Emperor. Actually it had proved impossible to obtain a statue at short notice – the local sculptors were all booked up, due to the sudden spurt in demand, and the petty cash account wouldn't cover the expenditure anyway – so Dawson had authorised a brass name plate to be affixed on the plinth of what had used to be Queen Victoria, covering up her name and inserting that of the new monarch. Dawson felt rather proud to have come up with such an economical (Gupta knew a chap in the bazaar who did the whole job for five rupees) and ingenious solution – only a poet would have thought of it. Indeed, the statue resembled Edward at least as much as it did his mother – just an effect of dumpiness, a crown, a crumbling hairline, a streaky complexion, and the, yes, definite suggestion of a beard.

The sun was shining directly on the king, exacerbating the violence of the sandstone coloration.

Dawson cleared his throat. He spoke without notes, fluently.

'It gives me great pleasure to stand before you today, on such a day, which gives us all pleasure, surely, and pride. All British subjects, all 'neath the crown which sways on high. And when we consider, one cannot help but feel, from the farthest corners of Africa to the northern shores . . .'

As he orated he surveyed his domain: his subordinates were static and dignified as if posing for a photograph. He felt the burden and the pride and the loneliness of being at their head, much as the king must feel when brooding on his empire. Only once before had he experienced such glory, such a sense of leadership, and such a conviction he was doing the right thing. It had been a night of the full moon. Running up to the fence which separates Trinity from its arch-rival, Balliol College, he had spontaneously bellowed, 'Bloody Balliol!' Soon a hundred students had been gathered on both sides of the fence, their heads tilted up, baying, 'Bloody Balliol!' or, 'Bloody Trinity!' as the case may be. Gupta was standing at the far end of the front row with his head slightly bowed. Dawson wondered if he was recalling the many conversations they had had concerning Prince – later King – Edward over the years; Dawson had referred to him as, 'that fat boy . . . gambler . . . womaniser . . . bloody fool.' No observable expression now on the assistant's face.

'. . . And finally, as a tribute to His Majesty. And this is, is it not, the way we all would wish. From the bottom of our hearts. Sincerely. It is my privilege. An ode dedicated to the King-Emperor . . .'

Dawson had worked hard composing a kind of Shakespearian sonnet. His method was first to write out lists of rhyme-words, then to arrange them at the ends of the lines, like this:

      day

woe
sway
O
stay
rest
best
foe
away
lest
excellentest
go
night
light

He recited his poem in a deep, sonorous voice. An intense silence followed, disturbed only by the cawing of an alien bird, the whine of the fan within the office, and some strangers arguing far away. Meanwhile Dawson contemplated his sonnet. He was indeed satisfied with its rhythm and alliteration, its air of wistful melancholy, its play of imagery (the seasons – all must pass – nevertheless some hope remains . . .). He was not wholly sure, however, about the enjambment at line seven . . .

Suddenly a voice was proclaiming: 'India shall be independent!'

'What?' Dawson said. He descended the stairs into the yard.

Gupta didn't move or raise his head. 'India shall be independent, sir,' he repeated in a conversational tone. 'And India *will* be independent. I have discussed the matter with several of my colleagues and we have come to the identical conclusion.'

Then the Indian jumped up onto the plinth and stood with his back against the back of the statue. He boomed, 'All who are with me, follow me! We will overcome fire! We will destroy our enemies! We will liberate India! None shall be able to withstand us!'

'Fool,' a brief chocking guffaw. 'I could have you hanged for bloody treason.'

'Yes, sir.'

Obviously the following action had been plotted before-hand. Without saying a word, several members of the accounting staff, accompanied by six junior clerks, dragged the charcoal stoves into the space between the statue and the banyan tree. They upturned the stoves, scattering the charcoal on the ground. They added extra charcoal from the store at the side of the building. They raked the coals into a rough path, about five foot wide and three or four times that in length. Definitely the coals were glowing.

Gupta proclaimed, 'Behold the sign of our power!'

He took off his shoes and socks and jumped down on the ground in front of the smouldering coals. A dozen or a score of his colleagues lined up behind him. Then others, perhaps thinking there is safety in numbers, or perhaps caught up in the emotion, joined the rebels. And soon the entire staff of the Magrapore tax office – apart from its chief – was standing patiently in a queue, waiting to follow the example and command of Gupta.

Dawson was surprised by his own calmness. It was as if he had always expected this to happen. Some smoke rose from the charcoal, and a heat haze occupied the air above it. Now the employees were vague blurry creatures; India itself was unclear.

It may have been the heat that disturbed the bats that roost in the banyan tree. Or the noise. Or perhaps they too are sensitive to feelings of excitement and abandon. Anyway, the bats – which hang there every day, so that after a while one pays no more attention to the furry shut-eyed shut-winged upside-down creatures than to leaves or fruit – flapped away, one after the other in a chain of blackness . . . making for the eaves of the police station on the far side of the maidan.

An image flashed into Dawson's head. The great iron gates of Trinity College used to be closed every evening at dusk, and students weren't allowed in afterwards unless they had permission, and not at all after midnight. So it was the custom for those students who had been out on the town to climb in over the railings – fifteen foot high and painted black. Now, proctors (nicknamed 'bulldogs') were hired by the university to prevent this. So the trick was: lurk in the alley between The White Horse and the second-hand bookshop until the proctors have gone past, heading down Broad Street – then clamber over quick. One night, just as Dawson and Boswell were heaving themselves up onto the first cross-bar of the gate, the warning cry rang out: 'Bulldog!' Suddenly a host of fellow students – ten or twenty – came rushing past them, scampering wildly upwards. Their black gowns fluttered like bats' wings. Boswell leapt after the crowd, and soon disappeared from sight. Dawson did his best to follow. He lifted and manoeuvred himself up the gate – which was swaying now, due to the shifting weights of the many students on it – and reached the top just as a panting pair of proctors arrived beneath. They shone their torches on him. He saw them from above: the crowns of their bowler hats, the shining ferrules at the tips of their furled umbrellas, the twin glares of their torches like the eyes of some giant beast. He was the sole unescaped prey, still clinging to the top bar of the shaking gate, breathless, unable to descend on either side.

He was standing on the lowest step of the back stairs with his arms folded, patiently watching the rebellion unfold. There was no mystery. Science has explained everything. Old Murchison at the club had told him when he had first arrived in Magrapore how the natives get up to their tricks. 'It's the sizzle effect,' Murchison had said. 'The sweat on the soles evaporates, causing a thin layer of steam to separate the foot from the fire.' Gupta was walking barefoot across the glowing coals. He was not hurrying, simply striding like a man who has somewhere to get to. 'Three cheers for India!' he called. In his pinstripes he seemed the picture of a businessman who keeps his mind firmly on the job. And after him, one by one, his comrades proceeded across the fire. Observed from behind, Indians do not look so Indian: indeed, in their cheap trousers and shirts and haircuts (excusing their shoelessness; and adding imagined hats), they might pass for a crowd of Englishmen going home after work, crossing London Bridge.

A head half-turned – it could have been Boswell's. But no, it was Gupta.

'Hip, hip, horray!'

This was Dawson's finest hour. He declaimed, 'Fools! You will never beat us with your mumbo-jumbo! For I too, an Englishman, can walk on fire!'

He stepped closer to the heat.

What happened next is unclear since no one was standing near by; the chief tax inspector's courage had intimidated the Indians – even Gupta – causing them to retreat to the very edge of the yard. A few beggars and a spice seller were watching from the opposite side of the road. A cow was sloping away.

The following facts have been established. First he undid his left shoelace and pulled the shoe off; then he balanced on his right foot (presumably to avoid getting cinders in his socks) and eased off the left sock. He put his bare foot down and repeated the process on the right side. He placed the two shoes side by side and stuffed the socks tidily inside the shoes.

Then he walked five or six paces, of average length, along the charcoal path. He sat down. He stretched out full length supine on the coals. There are differing accounts as to which part of his clothing caught fire first: some say the seat of his trousers; others his collar; but certainly within two or three minutes he was well aflame. One cannot mistake the stench of burning hair. Somebody claimed to have heard him mutter, 'Bloody fool.'

Now at least the Indians approached. They sprinkled his body with the contents of tax files – those of Mr Singh, Mr Mehta, the other Mr Singh, and many more – encouraging the flames. Soon the yard had turned into a giant pyre. King Edward himself was speckled with soot and ash.

Gupta fled and was never seen again. Some say he became a holy saddhu, traipsing around India for many years. Others claim he jumped into the pyre like a widow committing suttee, dying with his immediate superior. Still others insist he was hanged for treason (though his name is not listed on the official records). Or perhaps he went fishing in Kashmir.

And as for Dawson? Well, we have all the stories. How he was a martyr, secretly dedicated to freeing India. How he was

possessed by a jinn. How he was an avatar of Shiva the
destroyer . . .

The tax office survives to this day. Should you be visiting
Magrapore, and – having entered through the yard where
beggars ply their trade, a spice woman displays her wares, an
occasional sacred cow slumps, bats hang from the banyan tree,
and the remnant of the flame-hued sandstone sculpture (which
might represent a lingam or a shell or something figurative or
a pure abstraction) survives on a plinth engraved SPIRIT OF
A NEW INDIA – happen to climb the back stairs and press
your ear to the door shutters, you might still (it is said)
overhear two men bantering. One man will speak quietly so
you will not be able to catch his precise words; then the other
will respond, 'Bloody fool,' and laugh.

The Potato Dealer

WILLIAM TREVOR

MULREAVY WOULD MARRY her if they paid him, Ellie's uncle said: she couldn't bring a fatherless child into the world. He didn't care what was done nowadays; he didn't care what the fashion was; he wouldn't tolerate the talk there'd be. 'Mulreavy,' her uncle repeated. 'D'you know who I mean by Mulreavy?'

She hardly did. An image came into her mind of a big face that had a squareness about it, and black hair, and a cigarette butt adhering to the lower lip while a slow voice agreed or disagreed, and eyes that were small, and sharp as splinters. Mulreavy was a potato dealer. Once a year he came to the farm, his old lorry rattling into the yard, then backed up to where the sacks stood ready for him. Sometimes he shook his head when he examined the potatoes, saying they were too small. He tried that on, Ellie's uncle maintained. Cagey, her uncle said.

'I'll tell you one thing, girl,' her uncle said when she found the strength to protest at what was being proposed. 'I'll tell you this: you can't stay here without there's something along lines like I'm saying. Nowadays is nothing, girl. There's still the talk.'

He was known locally as Mr Larrissey, rarely by his

Christian name, which was Joseph. Ellie didn't call him 'Uncle Joseph', never had; 'Uncle' sometimes, though not often, for even in that there seemed to be an intimacy that did not belong in their relationship. She thought of him as Mr Larrissey.

'It's one thing or the other, girl.'

Her mother – her uncle's sister – didn't say anything. Her mother hadn't opened her mouth on the subject of Mulreavy, but Ellie knew that she shared the sentiments that were being expressed, and would accept, in time, the solution that had been offered. She had let her mother down; she had embittered her; why should her mother care what happened now? All of it was a mess; in the kitchen of the farmhouse her mother and her uncle were thinking the same thing.

Her uncle – a worn, tired man, not used to trouble like this – didn't forgive her and never would: so he had said, and Ellie knew it was true. Since the death of her father she and her mother had lived with him on the farm on sufferance: that was always in his eyes, even though her mother did all the cooking and the cleaning of the house, even though Ellie, since she was eleven, had helped in summer in the fields, had collected and washed the eggs and nourished the pigs. Her uncle had never married; if she and her mother hadn't moved on to the farm in 1978, when Ellie was five, he'd still be on his own, managing as best he could.

'You have the choice, girl,' he said now, the repetition heavy in the farmhouse kitchen. He was set in his ways, Ellie's mother often said; lifelong bachelors sometimes were.

He'd said at first – a fortnight ago – that his niece should get herself seen to, even though it was against religion. Her mother said no, but later wondered if it wasn't the only way out, the trip across the water that other girls had gone on, what else was there? They could go away and have it quietly done; they could be visiting the Galway cousins, no one would be the wiser. But Ellie, with what spirit was left in her, though she was in disgrace and crying, would not agree. In the fortnight that passed she many times, tearfully, repeated her resolve to let the child be born.

Loving the father, Ellie already loved the child. If they turned her out, if she had to walk the roads, or find work in Moyleglass or some other town, she would. But Ellie didn't want to do that; she didn't want to find herself penniless because it would endanger the birth. She would never do that was the decision she had privately reached the moment she was certain she was to have a child.

'Mulreavy,' her uncle said again.

'I know who he is.'

Her mother sat staring down at the lines of grain that years of scrubbing had raised on the surface of the kitchen table. Her mother had said everything she intended to say: disgrace, shame, a dirtiness occurring when people's backs were turned, all the thanks you get for what you give, for sacrifices made. 'Who'd want you now?' her mother had asked her, more than once.

'Mind you, I'm not saying Mulreavy'll bite,' Ellie's uncle said. 'I'm not saying he'd take the thing on.'

Ellie didn't say anything. She left the kitchen and walked out into the yard, where the turkeys screeched and ran towards her, imagining she carried meal to scatter, as often she did. She passed them by, and let herself through the black iron gate that led to the sloping three-cornered field beyond the outbuildings, the worst two acres of her uncle's property. Ragweed and gorse grew in profusion, speckled rock-surfaces erupted. It was her favourite field, perhaps because she had always heard it cursed and as a child had felt sorry for it. 'Oh, now, that's nice!' the father of her unborn child said when she told him she felt sorry for the three-cornered field. It was then that he'd said he wished he'd known her as a child and made her describe herself as she had been.

When it was put to Mulreavy he pretended offence. He didn't expostulate, for that was not his way. But as if in melancholy consideration of a personal affront he let the two ends of his mouth droop, as he sometimes did when he held a potato in his palm, shaking his head over its unsatisfactory size or shape. Ash from his cigarette dribbled down his shirt-front, the

WILLIAM TREVOR

buttons of a fawn cardigan open because the day was warm,
his shirt-collar open also and revealing a line of grime where it
had been most closely in contact with the skin of his neck.

'Well, that's a quare one,' Mulreavy said, his simulated
distaste slipping easily from him, replaced by an attempt at
outraged humour.

'There's a fairish sum,' Mr Larrissey said, but didn't say
what he had in mind and Mulreavy didn't ask. Nor did he ask
who the father was. He said in a by-the-way voice that he was
going out with a woman from Ballina who'd come to live in
Moyleglass, a dressmaker's assistant; but the information was
ignored.

'I only thought it was something would interest you,' Mr
Larrissey said.

Their two vehicles were drawn up on the road, a rusting
Ford Cortina and Mulreavy's lorry, the driving-side windows
of both wound down. Mulreavy offered a cigarette. Mr
Larrissey took it. As if about to drive away, he had put his
hand on the gear when he said he'd only thought the
proposition might be of interest.

'What's the sum?' Mulreavy asked when the cigarettes were
lit, and a horn hooted because the vehicles were blocking the
road. Neither man took any notice: they were of the neighbourhood, local people, the road was more theirs than
strangers'.

When the extent of the money offered was revealed
Mulreavy knew better than to react, favourably or otherwise.
It would be necessary to give the matter thought, he said, and
further considerations were put to him, so that at leisure he
could dwell on those also.

Ellie's mother knew how it was, and how it would be: her
brother would profit from the episode. The payment would
be made by her: the accumulated pension, the compensation
from the time of the accident in 1978. Her brother saw
something for himself in the arrangement he hoped for with
the potato dealer; the moment he had mentioned Mulreavy's
name he'd been aware of a profit to be made. Recognising at

first, as she had herself, only shame and folly in the fact that his niece was pregnant, he had none the less explored the situation meticulously; that was his way. She had long been aware of her brother's hope that one day Ellie would marry some suitable young fellow who would join them in the farmhouse and could be put to work, easing the burden in the fields; that was how the debt of taking in a sister and a niece might at last be paid. But with a disaster such as there had been, there would be no young fellow now; instead there was the prospect of Mulreavy, and what her brother had established in his mind was that Mulreavy could ease the burden too. A middle-aged potato dealer wasn't ideal for the purpose, but he was better than nothing.

Ellie's mother, resembling her brother in appearance, lean-faced and with his tired look, often recalled the childhood he and she had shared in this same house. More so than their neighbours, they were known to be a religious family, never missing Mass, going all together in the trap on Sundays and later by car, complimented for the faith they kept by Father Hanlon and his successor. The Larrisseys were respected people, known for the family virtues of hard work and disdain for ostentation, never seeming to be above themselves. She and her brother had all their lives been part of that, had never rebelled against these laid-down *mores* during the years of their upbringing.

Now, out of the cruel blue, there was this; and as far as brother and sister could remember, in the farmhouse there had never been anything as dispiriting. The struggle in bad seasons to keep two ends together, to make something of the rock-studded land even in the best of times, had never been lowering. Adversity of that kind was expected, the lot the family had been born into.

It had been expected also, when the accident occurred to the man she'd married, that Ellie's mother should return to the house that was by then her brother's. She was forty-one then; her brother forty-four, left alone two years before when their parents had died within the same six months. He hadn't invited her to return, and though it seemed, in the circumstances, a natural consequence to both of them, she knew her brother had always since considered her beholden. As a child, he'd been like that about the few toys they shared, insisting that some were more his than hers.

'I saw Mulreavy,' he said on the day of the meeting on the road, his unsmiling, serious features already claiming a successful outcome.

Mulreavy's lorry had reached the end of its days and still was not fully paid for; within six months or so he would find himself unable to continue trading. This was the consideration that had crept into his mind when the proposition was put to him, and it remained there afterwards. There was a lorry he'd seen in McHugh Bros with thirty-one thousand on the clock and at an asking price that would be reduced, the times being what they were. Mulreavy hadn't entirely invented the dressmaker from Ballina in whom he had claimed an interest: she was a wall-eyed woman he had recently seen about the place, who had arrived in Moyleglass to assist Mrs Toomey in her cutting and stitching. Mulreavy had wondered if she had money, if she'd bought her way into Mrs Toomey's business, as he'd heard it said. He'd never spoken to her or addressed her in any way, but after his conversation with Mr Larrissey he made further enquiries, only to discover that rumour now suggested the woman was employed by Mrs Toomey at a small wage. So Mulreavy examined in finer detail the pros and cons of marrying into the Larrisseys.

'There'd be space for you in the house,' was how it had been put to him. 'Maybe better than if you took her out of it. And storage enough for the potatoes in the big barn.'

A considerable saving of day-to-day expenses would result, Mulreavy had reflected, closing his eyes against the smoke from his cigarette when those words were spoken. He made no comment, waiting for further enticements, which came in time. Mr Larrissey said:

'Another thing is, the day will come when the land'll be too much for me. Then again, the day will come when there'll be an end to me altogether.'

Mr Larrissey had crossed himself. He had said no more,

250

allowing the references to land and his own demise to dangle in the silence. Soon after that he jerked his head in a farewell gesture and drove away.

He'd marry the girl, Mulreavy's thoughts were later, after he'd heard the news about the dressmaker; he'd vacate his property, holding on to it until the price looked right and then disposing of it, no hurry whatsoever since he'd already be in the Larrisseys' farmhouse, with storage facilities and a good lorry. If he attended a bit to the land, the understanding was that he'd inherit it when the day came. It could be done in writing; it could be drawn up by Blaney in Moyleglass.

Eight days after their conversation on the road the two men shook hands, as they did when potatoes were bought and sold. Three weeks went by and then there was the wedding.

The private view of Ellie's mother – shared with neither her daughter nor her brother – was that the presence of Mulreavy in the farmhouse was a punishment for the brazen sin that had occurred. When the accident that had made a widow of her occurred, when she'd looked down at the broken body lying there, knowing it was lifeless, she had not felt that there was punishment in that, either directed at her or at the man she'd married. He had done little wrong in his life; indeed, had often sought to do good. Neither had she herself transgressed except in little ways. But what had led to the marriage of her daughter and the potato dealer was deserving of this harsh reprimand, which was something that must now be lived with.

Mulreavy was given a bedroom that was furnished with a bed and a cupboard. He was not offered, and did not demand, his conjugal rights. He didn't mind: that side of things didn't interest him; it hadn't been mentioned; it wasn't part of the arrangement. Instead, daily, he surveyed the land that was to be his inheritance. He walked it, lovingly, at first when no one was looking, and later to identify the weed that had to be sprayed and to trace the drains. He visualised a time when he no longer travelled about as a middle-man, buying potatoes cheaply and selling at a profit, when the lorry he had acquired

251

with the dowry would no longer be necessary. On these same poor acres sufficient potatoes could be grown to allow him to trade as he'd traded before. Mulreavy wasn't afraid of work when there was money to be made.

The midwife called down the farmhouse stairs a few moments after Mulreavy heard the first cry. Mr Larrissey poured out a little of the whiskey that was kept in the wall-cupboard in case there was toothache in the house. His sister was at the upstairs bedside. The midwife said a girl had been born.

A year ago, it was Mr Larrissey, not his sister, who had first known about the summer priest who was the father of this child. On his way back from burning stubble he had seen his niece in the company of the man and had known from the way they walked that there was some kind of intimacy between them. When his niece's condition was revealed he had not, beneath the anger he displayed, been much surprised.

Mulreavy, clenching his whiskey glass, his lips touched with a smile, had not known he would experience a moment of happiness when the birth occurred; nor had he guessed that the dourness of Mr Larrissey would be affected, that whiskey would be offered. The thing would happen, he had thought, maybe when he was out in the fields. He would walk into the kitchen and they would tell him. Yet in the kitchen, now, there was almost an air of celebration, a satisfaction that the arrangement lived up to its promise.

Above where the two men sat, Ellie's mother did as the midwife directed in the matter of the afterbirth's disposal. She watched the baby being taken from its mother's arms and placed, sleeping now, in the cradle by the bedside. She watched her daughter struggling for a moment against the exhaustion that possessed her, before her eyes closed too.

The child was christened Mary Josephine – these family names chosen by Ellie's mother, and Ellie had not demurred. Mulreavy played his part, cradling the infant in his big arms for a moment at the font, a suit bought specially for the occasion. It wasn't doubted that he was the father, although the assumption also was that the conception had come first, the marriage later, as sometimes happened. There'd been some surprise at the marriage, not much.

Ellie accepted with equanimity what there was. She lived a little in the past, in the summer of her love affair, expecting of the future only what she knew of the present. The summer curate who had loved her, and whom she loved still, would not miraculously return. He did not even know that she had given life to his child. 'It can't be,' he'd said when they lay in the meadow that was now a potato field. 'It can't ever be, Ellie.' She knew it couldn't be: a priest was a priest. There would never, he promised, as if in compensation, be another love like this in all his life. 'Nor for me,' she swore as eagerly, although he did not ask for that, in fact said no, that she must live her normal life. 'No, not for me,' she repeated. 'I feel it too.' It was like a gift when she knew her child was to be born, a fulfilment, a forgiveness almost for their summer sin.

As months and then years went by, the child walked and spoke and suffered childhood ills, developed preferences, acquired characteristics that slipped away again or stubbornly remained. Ellie watched her mother and her uncle aging, while they in turn were reminded by the child's presence of their own uneasy companionship in the farmhouse when they were as young as the child was now. Mulreavy, who did not go in for nostalgia or observing changes in other people, increased his potato yield. Like Mr Larrissey, he would have preferred the child who had been born to be a boy since a boy, later on, would be more useful, but he did not ever complain on this count. Mr Larrissey himself worked less, in winter often spending days sitting in the kitchen, warm by the Esse stove. For Ellie's mother, passing time did not alter her belief that the bought husband was her daughter's reprimand on earth.

All that was how things were on the farm and in the farmhouse. A net of compromise and acceptance and making the best of things held the household together. Only the child was aware of nothing, neither that a man had been bought to be her father nor that her great-uncle had benefited by the circumstances, nor that her grandmother had come to terms with a punishment, nor that her mother still kept faith with an improper summer love. The child's world when she was ten had more to do with reading whole pages more swiftly than she had a year ago, and knowing where Heligoland was, and reciting by heart *The Wreck of the Hesperus*.

But, without warning, the household was disturbed. Ellie was aware only of some inner restlessness, its source not identified, which she assumed would pass. But it did not pass, and instead acquired the intensity of unease: what had been satisfactory for the first ten years of her child's life was strangely not so now. In search of illumination, she pondered all that had occurred. She had been right not to wish to walk the roads with her fatherless infant; she had been right to agree to the proposal put to her. Looking back, she could not see that she should, in any way whatsoever, have done otherwise. A secret had been kept; there were no regrets. It was an emotion quite unlike regret that assailed her. Her child smiled back at her from a child's innocence, and she remembered those same features, less sure and less defined, when they were newly in the farmhouse, and wondered how they would be when another ten years had passed. Not knowing now, her child would never know. She would never know that her birth had been accompanied by money changing hands. She would never know that, somewhere else, her father forgave the sins of other people, and offered Our Saviour's blood and flesh in solemn expiation.

'Can you manage them?' Ellie's husband asked when she was loading sacks on to the weighing scales, for she had paused in the work as if to rest.

'I'm all right.'

'Take care you don't strain yourself.'

He was often kind in practical ways. She was strong, but the work was not a woman's work and although it was never said he was aware of this. In the years of their marriage they had never quarrelled or even disagreed, not being close enough for that, and in this way their relationship reflected that of the brother and sister they shared the house with.

'They're a good size, the Kerrs,' he said, referring to the produce they worked with. 'We hit it right this year.'

'They're nice all right.'

She had loved her child's father for every day of their child's life and before it. She had falsified her confessions and a holy baptism. Black, ugly lies were there when their child smiled from her innocence, nails in another cross. It hadn't mattered at first, when their child wouldn't have understood.

'I'll stop now,' Ellie said, recording in the scales book the number of sacks that were ready to be sealed. 'I have the tea to get.'

Her mother was unwell, confined to her bedroom. It was usually her mother who attended to the meals.

'Go on so, Ellie,' he said. He still smoked forty cigarettes a day, his life's indulgence, a way to spend a fraction of the money he accumulated. He had bought no clothes since his purchase of the christening suit except for a couple of shirts, and he questioned the necessity of the clothes Ellie acquired herself or for her child. Meanness was a quality he was known for; commercially, it had assisted him.

'Oh, I got up,' Ellie's mother said in the kitchen, the table laid and the meal in the process of preparation. 'I couldn't lie there.'

'You're better?'

'I'd say I was getting that way.'

Mr Larrissey was washing traces of fertiliser from his hands at the sink, roughly rubbing in soap. From the yard came the cries of the child, addressing the man she took to be her father as she returned from her evening task of ensuring that the bullocks still had grass to eat.

All the love there had been, all the love there still was – love that might have nourished Ellie's child, that might have warmed her – was the deprivation the child suffered. Ellie remembered the gentle, pale hands of her lover who had given her the gift of her child, and heard again the whisper of his voice, and his lips lingered softly on hers. She saw him as she always now imagined him, in his cassock and his surplice, the embroidered cross that marked his calling repeated again in the gestures of his blessing. His eyes were still a shade of slate, his features retained their delicacy. Why should not a child have some vision of him too? Why should there be falsity?

'You've spoken to them, have you?' her husband asked when she said what she intended.

'No, only you.'

'I wouldn't want the girl told.'

He turned away in the potato shed, to heft a sack on to the lorry. She felt uneasy in herself, she said, the way things were, and felt that more and more. That feeling wasn't there without a reason. It was a feeling she was aware of most at Mass and when she prayed at night.

Mulreavy didn't reply. He had never known the identity of the father. Some run-away fellow, he had been told at the time by Mr Larrissey, who had always considered the shame greater because a priest was involved. 'No need Mulreavy should know that,' Ellie had been instructed by her mother, and had abided by this wish.

'It was never agreed,' Mulreavy maintained, not pausing in his loading. 'It wasn't agreed the girl would know.'

Ellie spoke of a priest then; her husband said nothing. He finished with the potato sacks and lit a cigarette. That was a shocking thing, he eventually remarked, and lumbered out of the barn.

'Are you mad, girl?' Her mother rounded on her in the kitchen, turning from the draining-board, where she was shredding cabbage. Mr Larrissey, who was present also, told her not to be a fool: what good in the world would it do to tell a child the like of that?

'Have sense, for God's sake,' he crossly urged, his voice thick with the bluster that obscured his confusion.

'You've done enough damage, Ellie,' her mother said, all the colour gone from her thin face. 'You've brought enough on us.'

When Mulreavy came into the kitchen an hour later, he guessed at what had been said, but he did not add anything himself. He sat down to wait for his food to be placed in front of him. It was the first time since the arrangement had been agreed upon that any reference to it had been made in the household.

'That's the end of it,' Ellie's mother laid down, the statement made as much for Mulreavy's benefit as for Ellie's. 'We'll hear no more of this.'

Ellie did not reply. That evening she told her child.

People knew, and talked about it now. What had occurred ten years ago suddenly had an excitement about it that did not fail to please. Minds were cast back, memories ransacked in a search for the name and appearance of the summer priest who had been and gone. Father Mooney, who had succeeded old Father Hanlon, spoke privately to Ellie, deploring the exposure she had 'so lightly' been responsible for.

With God's grace, he pointed out, a rough-and-ready solution had been found and disgrace averted ten years ago. There should have been gratitude for that, not what had happened now. Ellie explained that every time she looked at her child she felt a stab of guilt because a deception of such magnitude had been perpetrated. 'Her life was no more than a lie,' Ellie said, but Father Mooney snappishly replied that that was not for her to say.

'You flew in the face of things once,' he fulminated, 'and now you've done it again.' When he glared at her, it showed in his expression that he considered her an unfit person to be in his parish. He ordered Hail Marys to be repeated, and penitence practised, with humility and further prayer.

But Ellie felt that a weight had been lifted from her, and she explained to her child that even if nothing was easy now, a time would come when the difficulties of the moment would all be gone.

Mulreavy suffered. His small possession of pride was bruised; he hardly had to think to know what people said. He went about his work in the fields, planting and harvesting, spreading muck and fertiliser, folding away cheques until he had a stack ready for lodgement in Moyleglass. The sour atmosphere in the farmhouse affected him, and he wondered if people knew, on top of everything else, that he occupied a bedroom on his own and always had, that he had never so much as embraced his wayward young bride. Grown heavier over the years, he became even heavier after her divulgence, eating more in his despondency.

He liked the child; he always had. The knowledge that a summer priest had fathered her caused him to like her no less, for the affection was rooted in him. And the child did not change in her attitude to him, but still ran to him at once when she returned from school, with tales of how the nuns had been that day, which one bad-tempered, which one sweet. He listened as he always had, always pausing in his work to throw in a word or two. He continued to tell brief stories of his past experiences on the road: he had traded in potatoes since he was hardly more than a child himself, fifteen when he first assisted his father.

But in the farmhouse Mulreavy became silent. In his morose mood he blamed not just the wife he'd married but her elders too. They had deceived him. And knowing more than he did about these things, they should have foreseen more than they had. The child bore his name. 'Mrs Mulreavy' they called his wife. He was a laughing-stock.

'I don't remember that man,' he said when almost a year had passed, a September morning. He had crossed the furrows to where she was picking potatoes from the clay he'd turned, the plough drawn by the tractor. 'I don't know did I ever see him.'

Ellie looked up at the dark-jowled features, above the rough, thick neck. She knew which man he meant. She knew, as well, that it had required an effort to step down from his tractor and cross to where she was, to stand unloved in front of her. She said at once:

'He was here only a summer.'

'That would be it so. I was always travelling then.'

She gave the curate's name and he nodded slowly over it, then shook his head. He'd never heard that name, he said.

The sun was hot on her shoulders and her arms. She might

have pointed across the ploughed clay to the field that was next to the one they were in. It was there, below the slope, that the conception had taken place. She wanted to say so, but she didn't. She said:

'I had to tell her.'

He turned to go away, then changed his mind, and again looked down at her.

'Yes,' he said.

She watched him slowly returning to where he'd left the tractor. His movements were always slow, his gait suggesting an economy of energy, his arms loose at his sides. She mended his clothes, she kept them clean. She assisted him in the fields, she made his bed. In all the time she'd known him she had never wondered about him.

The tractor started. He looked behind to see that the plough was as he wanted it. He lit another cigarette before he set off on his next brief journey.

Wasted Lives

FAY WELDON

THEY'RE TURNING THE City into Disneyland. They're restoring the ancient façades and painting them apple-green, firming up the medieval gables and picking out the gargoyles in yellow. They're gold-leafing the church spires. They've boarded up the more stinking alleys until they get round to them, and as State property becomes private, the shops that were always there are suddenly gone, as if simply painted out. In the eaves above Benetton and the Body Shop, cherubs wreathe pale, cleaned-stone limbs, and even the great red McDonald's sign has been especially muted to rosy pink for this, its Central European edition. Don't think crass commerce rules the day as the former Communist world opens its arms wide to the seduction of market forces: the good taste of the new capitalist world leaps yowling into the embrace as well – a fresh-faced baby monster, with its yearning to prettify and make the serious quaint, to turn the rat into Mickey Mouse and the wolf into Goofy.

Milena and I walked through knots of tourists, towards the famous Processional Bridge, circa 1357. I had always admired its sooty stamina, its dismal persistence through the turbulence of rising and falling empire. It was my habit to stay with Milena when I came to the City. I'd let Head Office book me into a hotel, to save official embarrassment, then spend my nights with her, and some part of my days, if courtesy so required. I was fond of her but did not love her, or loved only in the throes of the sexual excitement she was so good at summoning out of me. She made excellent coffee. If I sound disagreeable and calculating, it is because I am attempting to speak the truth about the events on the Processional Bridge that day, and the truth of motive seldom warms the listener's heart. I am generally accepted as a pleasant and kindly enough person. My family loves me, even my wife, Joanna, though she and I live apart and are no longer sexually connected. She doesn't have to love me.

Milena is an archivist at the City Film Arts Institute. I work for a U.S. film company, from their London office. I suppose, if you add it up, I have spent some three months in the City over the last five years – before and after the fall of the Berlin Wall and the Great Retreat of Communism, a tide sweeping back over shallow sand into an obscure distance. Some three months in all spent with Milena.

Her English was not as good as she thought. Conversation could be difficult. Today she was not dressed warmly enough. It was June, but the wind was cold. Perhaps she thought her coat was too shabby to stand the inspection of the bright early-summer sun. I was accustomed to seeing her either naked or dressed in black – a colour, or lack of it, that suited the gaunt drama of her face – but today, like her city, she wore pastel colours. I wished it were not so.

Beat your head not into the Berlin Wall but into cotton wool, machine-pleated in interesting baby shades, plastic-wrapped. Suffocation takes many forms.

'You should have brought your coat,' I said.

'It's so old,' she said. 'I am ashamed of it.'

'I like it,' I said.

'It's old,' she repeated, dismissively. 'I would rather freeze.'

For Milena the past was all dreary, the future all dread and expectation. A brave face must be put on everything. She smiled up at me. I am six foot three inches and bulky: she was all of five and a half foot, and skinny with it. The sweater was

FAY WELDON

too tight: I could see her ribs through the stretched fabric, and the nipples, too. In the old days she would never have allowed that to happen. She would have let her availability be known in other, more subtle ways. Her teeth were bad: one in the front broken, a couple grey. When she wore black, their eccentricity seemed a matter of course; a delight, even. Now she wore green, they were yellowy, and seemed a perverse tribute to years of neglect, poverty, and bad diet. Eastern teeth, not Western. I wished she would not smile, or trust me so.

The Castle still looks down over the City, as does the extension to that turreted tourist delight – the long, low stone building with its rows of identical windows, tier upon tier of them, blank and anonymous, to demonstrate the way brute force gives way to the subtler yet more stifling energies of bureaucracy. You can't do this, you can't live like that, not because I have a sword to run you through but because Our Masters frown on it. And your papers have not risen to the top of the pile.

Up there in the Castle that day, a newly-elected government was trying to piece together from the flesh of this nation and the bones of that a new, living, changing organism, a new constitution. New, new, new. I wished them every luck with it, but they could not make Milena's bad teeth good, or stop her smiling at me as if she wanted something. I wondered what it was. She'd not used to smile like this: it was a new trick: it sat badly on her doleful face.

We reached the Processional Bridge, which crosses the river between the Palace and the Cathedral. 'The oldest bridge in Europe,' said Milena. We had walked across it many times before. She had made this remark many times before. Look left down the river, and you could see where it carved its way through the mountains that form the natural boundaries of this small nation; look right, and you looked into mist. On either bank the ancient city crowded in, in its crumbly, pre-Disney form, all eaves, spires, and casements, spared from the blasts of war for one reason or another, or perhaps by just plain miracle. But Emperors and Popes must have somewhere

262

decent to be crowned, and Dictators, too, need a background for pomp and circumstance, crave some acknowledgment from history: a name engraved in gold in a Cathedral, a majestic tomb in a gracious square still standing. It can't be all rubble, or what's the point?

I offered Milena my coat. It seemed to me that she and I were at some crucial point in not just our story but everyone's – that the decisions we made here today had some general relevance to the way the world was going. I could at least share some warmth with her. My monthly Western salary would keep her in comfort for a year, but what could I do about that? If she wanted a new coat from me, it would have nothing to do with her desire to be warm; she would want it as a token of my love. She didn't mind shivering. Her discomfort was both a demonstration of martyrdom and a symbol of pride.

'I am not cold,' she said.

The City is a favourite location for film companies. The place is cheap, its money valueless in the real world, and its appetite for hard currency voracious, which means good deals can be had. The quaint, colourful locations are inexpensively histori-cised – though the satellite dishes are these days becoming too numerous to dodge easily. And there are few parking problems, and highly trained post-production technicians, efficient labs, excellent cameramen, sensitive sound men, and so on – and cheap, so cheap. Those who lived in the City had escaped the fate of so many of the hitherto Russian-dominated lands – the sullen refusal of the oppressed and exploited to do anything right, to be anything other than inefficient, to be sloppy and lazy, in the hope that the colonising power would simply give up and go away, shaking the dust of the conquered land from its feet. And the power it had amassed lay not of course in the strength of the ideology it professed, as the West in its muddled way assumed, but in the strength of arms and organisation of that single, colonising, ambitious nation Russia. Ask anyone between Budapest and Samarkand, Tbilisi and the Siberian flatlands, and they would tell you whom they feared and hated. Russia, the motherland, announcing itself to a gullible world as the Soviet Union. Harsh mother, pretending kindness, using Marxism-Leninism as the religious tool of government and exploitation, as once in the South Americas Spain had used Christianity.

In the City they kept their wits about them: too sophisti-cated for the numbing rituals of mind control ever quite to work, for the concrete of the workers' blocks quite to take over from the tubercular gables and back alleys, to stifle the whispers of dissent, to quieten the gossip and mirth of café society. McDonald's has achieved that now, with its bright, forbidding jollity, and who in the brave new world of freedom can afford a cup of coffee anyway, has anything interesting or persuasive to say, now that everyone has what they wanted? Better, better by far, to travel hopefully than to arrive, to have to face the fact that the journey is not out of blackness into light but from one murky confusion into another. Happiness and fulfilment lie in our affections for one another, not in the forms that our societies take. If only I were in love with Milena, this walk across the bridge would be a delight. I would feel the air bright with the happiness of the hopeful young.

Be that as it may, the City was always better than anywhere else for filming. Go to Romania and you'd find the castles still full of manacled prisoners clanking their chains; try Poland and you'd have to fly in special food for your stars; in Hungary the cameraman would have artistic tantrums. But here in the City there would be gaiety, fun, sometimes even sparkle – the clatter of high heels on cobblestones, sultry looks from sultry eyes, and of course nights with Milena in the fringy, shabby apartment with the high, white-mantled brass bed, and good strong coffee in porcelain cups for breakfast. Milena, forever languidly busy, about my body or about her work, off to the Institute or back from it. Women worked hard in this country, as women were accustomed to all over the Soviet Union. Equality for women meant an equal obligation to work, the official direction of your labour, sleeping with your boss if he so required, the placement of your child in a crèche, as well as the cultural expectation that you get married, run a home, and empty the brimming ashtrays while your husband put his feet up. Joanna would have none of that kind of thing; for the male visitor from the West the Eastern European woman is paradise, if you can hack it, if your conscience can stand it – if you can bear being able to buy affection and constancy.

I hadn't been with Milena for three months or so. Now I found her changed, like her city. I wondered about her constancy. It occurred to me that it was foolish of me to expect it. As did the rest of the nation, she now paid at least lip service to market forces: perhaps these worked sexually as well. Rumour had it that there were now twenty-five thousand prostitutes in the City and an equal number of pimps, as men and women decided to make the best financial use of available resources. I discovered I was not so much jealous as rather hoping for evidence of Milena's infidelity, which would let me off whatever vague hook it was I found myself upon. Not so difficult a hook. She and I had always been discreet: I had not mentioned our relationship to a soul back home. Milena was in another country; she did not really count: her high, bouncing bosom, her narrow rib cage and fleshless hips vanished from my erotic imagination as the plane reached the far side of the mountaintops – the turbulence serving as some rite of passage – to reimprint the attraction only as I passed over them once again, on my return.

The cleaning processes had not yet reached the bridge, I was glad to see. The stone saints who lined it were still black with the accumulated grime of the past.

'Who are these saints?' I asked, but Milena didn't know. Some hold books, others candles; noses are weather-flattened. Milena apologised for her ignorance. She had not, she said, had the opportunity of a religious education: she hoped her son Milo would. Her son lived with Milena's mother, who was a good Catholic, in the Southern Province – a place about to secede, to become independent, to ethnic-cleanse in its own time, in its own way.

'I didn't know you had a son,' I said. I was surprised, and ashamed at myself for being so uncurious about her. 'Why didn't you tell me?'

'It's my problem,' Milena said. 'I don't want to burden you.

FAY WELDON

He's ten now. When he was born I was not well, and times were hard. It seemed better that he go to my mother. But she's getting old now, and there's trouble in the Southern Province. They are not nice people down there.'

Once the City's dislike and suspicion had been reserved for the Russians. Now it had been unleashed and spread everywhere. The day the Berlin Wall fell, Milena and I had been sitting next to each other in the small Institute cinema, watching the demonstration reels of politically sound directors available for work, in the strange, flickering half-dark of such places. Her small white hand had strayed unexpectedly onto my thigh, unashamedly direct in its approach. But then exhilaration and expectation, mixed with fear, were in the air. Sex seemed the natural expression of such emotions, such events. And perhaps that was why I never quite trusted her, never quite loved her, found it so easy to forget her when she wasn't under my nose – I despised her because it was she who had approached me, not I her. If Joanna and I are apart it's because I'm so conditioned in the old, prefeminist ways of thinking that I'm impossible for a civilised woman to live with, or so she says. I am honest, that is to say, and scrupulous in the investigation of my feelings and opinions.

'Why didn't you put the child into a crèche?' I asked. It shocked me that Milena, that any woman, could give a child away so easily.

'I was in a crèche,' she said bleakly. 'It's the same for nearly everyone in this city under forty. The crèche was our real home, our parents were strangers. I didn't want it to happen to Milo. He was better with my mother, though there are too many Muslims down there. More and more of them. It's like a disease.'

I caught the stony eye of baby Jesus on St Joseph's shoulder – that one, at least, I knew – and one or the other sent me a vision, not that I believed in such things, as I looked down at the greeny, sickly waters of the river. I saw, ranked and rippling, row upon row of infants, small, pale children, institutionalised, deprived, pasty-faced from the atrocious city food – meat, starch, fat, no fruit, no vegetables –

266

and understood that I was looking at the destruction of a people. They turned their little faces to me in despair, and I looked quickly up and away and back at Milena to shake off the vision; but there behind her, where the river met the sky, I saw that nation grown up, marching towards me into the mists of its future, a sad mockery of those sunny early Social Realist posters that decked my local, once Marxist, now leftish bookshop back home: the proletariat marching square-jawed and determined into the new dawn, scythes and spanners at the ready. Here there were no square jaws, only wretchedness: the quivering lip of the English ex-public-school boy, wrenched from his home at a tender age, now made general; the same profound, puzzled sorrow spread through an entire young population, male and female. See it in the easy, surface emotion, the facile sexuality, the rush of tears to the eyes, uncontrolled and uncontrollable, pleading for a recognition that never comes, a comfort that is unavailable. 'Pity me' – the unspoken words upon a nation's lips – 'because I am indeed pitiable. I have been deprived of freedom – yes, of course, all that. And of proper food and of fancy things, consumer durables and material wealth of every kind, all that. But mostly I have been robbed of my birthright, my mother, my father, my home. And how can I ever recover from that?' Then there is a murmur, as a last, despairing cry, the latest prayer – 'Market forces, market forces.' Say it over and over, as once the Hail Mary was said, to ward off all ills and rescue the soul, but we know in our hearts it won't work. There is no magic here contained. Wasted lives, lost souls, unfixable. Pity me, pity me, pity me.

'I think the fog's coming down,' said Milena, and so it was. The new dawn faded into it. A young man on the bridge was selling black rubber spiders: you hurled them against a board and they crept down, leg over leg; stillness alternating with sudden movement. No one was buying.

'Well,' I said, 'I expect you made the right decision about Milo. What happened to his father?' I turned to button her jacket. I wanted her warmed. This much, at least, I could do. Perhaps if she was warm she would not feel so much hate for the Southern Province and its people.

'We are divorced,' she said. 'I am free to marry again. Look, there's Jesus crucified. Hanging from nails in his hands. At least the Communists took down the crosses. Why should we have to think about torture all the time? It was the Russians taught our secret police their tricks: we would never have come to it on our own.'

I commented on the contradiction between her wanting her son to have a Catholic upbringing and her dislike of the Christian symbol, the tortured man upon the cross, but she shrugged it off: she did not want the point pursued. She was not interested in it. She saw no virtue in consistency. First you had this feeling; then that: that was all there was to it. No parent had ever intervened between the tantrum and its cause; no doubt Milena, along with the rest of her generation, had been slapped into silence when protesting frustration and outrage. She was wounded; she was damaged: not her fault, but there it was. What I'd seen as childlike, as charming, in the early stages of a relationship was in the end merely irritating. I could not stir myself to become interested in her son or in a marriage that had ended in divorce. I could not take her initial commitment seriously.

'I'm pregnant,' Milena now says. 'Last time you were here we made a baby. Isn't that wonderful? Now you will marry me, and take me to London, and we will live happily ever after.'

Fiends come surging up the river through the mist, past me – gaunt, soundlessly shrieking. These are the ghosts of the insulted, the injured, the wronged and tortured, whose efforts have been in vain. Those whose language has been taken away, whose bodies have been starved; they are the wrongfully dead. All the great rivers of the world carry these images with them; over time they have infected me by their existence. They breathe all around me. I take in their exhalations. I am their persecutor, their ruler, the origin of their woes: the one who despises. They shake their ghoulish locks at me; they mock me with their sightless eyes, snapping to attention as they pass. Eyes right! Blind eyes, forever staring. They honour me, the living.

'Is something the matter?' asks Milena. 'Aren't you happy? You told me you loved me.'

Did I? Probably. I remind her that I've also told her that I'm married.

'But you will divorce her,' she says. 'Why not? Your children are grown. She doesn't need you any more. I do.'

Her eyes are large in their hollows: she fears disaster. Of course she does. It so often happens. I can hardly tell whether she is alive or dead. To have a child with a ghost!

Milena is perfectly right. Joanna doesn't need me. Milena does. The first night I went with Milena she was wearing a purple velvet bra. It fired me sexually, it was so extraordinary, but it put too great an element of pity into what otherwise could have been love. There seemed something more valuable in my wife's white Marks & Spencer bra with its valiant label, 40A. Broad-backed, that is, and flat-chested. I supposed Milena's to be a 36C. English women lean towards the pear-shaped; the City women towards the top-heavy. It's un-fashionable, dangerous even, to make comparisons between the characteristics of the peoples of the world – this tribe, that tribe, this religion or that. The ghouls that people the river, who send their dying breath back, day after day, in the form of the fog that blights the place, mists up the new Disney façades with mystery droplets, met their end because people like me whispered, nudged, and made odious comparisons, and the odium grew and grew and ended in torture, murder, slaughter, genocide. Nevertheless, I must insist: it is true. Pear-shaped that lot, top-heavy this. And if I suspected Milena's purple velvet bra of being some kind of secret-police state issue, or part of the Film Arts Institute's plan to attract hard currency and Western business, an end towards which their young female staff were encouraged, even paid, it is not surprising. Had I been of her nationality, I knew well enough, her hand would not have strayed across my thigh in the film-flickering dark. I was offended that the Gods of Freedom, Good Health, Good Teeth, Good Nourishment, Prosperity, and Market Forces, whom I myself did not worship, endowed me with this wondrous capacity to attract. I could snap my fingers and all the girls in Eastern Europe would come trotting and fall on their knees.

'Milena,' I said, and I was only temporising, 'I have no way of knowing this baby is mine, if baby there be.'

Milena threw her hands into the air, and cried aloud – a thin, horrid squeal, chin to the heavens, lips drawn back in a harsh grimace. There were few people left on the bridge. The fog had driven them away. The seller of rubber spiders had given up and gone home. Milena ran towards the parapet and wriggled and crawled until she lay along its top on the cold stone, and then she simply rolled off and fell into the water below; this in the most casual way possible. Between my straightforward question and this dramatic answer only fifteen seconds can have intervened. I was too stunned to feel alarm. I found myself leaning over the parapet to look downwards; the fog was patchy. I saw a police launch veer off course and make for the spot where Milena fell. No doubt she had seen it coming or she would not have done what she did – launched herself into thick air, thin, swirling water. I had confidence in her ability to survive. Authorities of one kind or another, as merciful in succour as they were cruel in the detection of sedition, would pull her out of the wet murk, dry her, wrap her in blankets, warm her, return her to her apartment. She would be all right.

I walked to the end of the bridge, unsure as to whether I would then turn left to the police pier and Milena or to the right and the taxi rank. Why had the woman done it? Hysteria, despair, or was it some convenient local way of terminating unwanted pregnancies? I could take a flight back home, if I chose, forty-eight hours earlier than I had intended. The flights were full, but I would get a priority booking, as befitted my status, however whimsical, as a provider of hard currency. The powerful are indeed whimsical: they leave their elegant droppings where they choose – be they Milena's baby, Benetton, the Marlboro ads that now dominate the City: no end even now to the wheezing, the coughing, the death rattling along the river.

I turned to the right, where the taxis stood waiting for stray foreigners anxious to get out of the fog, back to their hotels. 'To the airport,' I said. The driver understood. 'To the airport' are golden words to taxi drivers all over the world. This way, at least, I created a smile. To have turned left would have meant endless trouble. I was thoroughly out of love with Milena. I wanted to help, of course I did, but the child in the Southern Province would have had to be fetched by the Catholic mother, taken in. There would be no end to it. My children would not accept a new family: Joanna would be made thoroughly miserable. To do good to one is to do bad to another. But you don't need to hear my excuses. They are the same that everyone makes to themselves when faced with the misery of others; though they would like to do the right thing, they simply fail to do so and look after themselves instead.

Bank Holiday

JONATHAN WILSON

WE TAKE THE 226 bus from Dollis Hill to Golders Green
Station. Along the way the houses expand and beautify. Then
we hop on the single-decker 210 to Hampstead Heath. Dennis
asks me, 'How many ears has Davy Crockett got?' I shake my
head. 'Three,' he says. 'His left ear, his right ear, and his wild
front ear.' As soon as we're off the bus we cross the no man's
land near the Whitestone Pond and enter the wild frontier of
the Heath. No fooling around with the coconut shy, the penny
roll, or even the bumper cars. We head straight for the Rat
Woman. It is August, 1967, and you can still catch a freak
show at the funfair.

At the entrance to the tent stands a throwback to the
previous decade, a pointy-faced, vicious spiv, hair slicked
back, Teddy-boy jacket, black drainpipe jeans, winkle-picker
Chelsea boots covered in mud. He wants half a crown from
each of us. Dennis says, 'Who are you – the Rat *Man*?' El Spivo
doesn't like this. He mentions something about slicing our
fucking noses off. Dennis is extremely tough, so it's O.K. to
laugh in his face and enter the tent.

It's very hot under the canvas, and there's a pungent odour
coming from the cage. At first we can't see her, because there's
a whole crowd of men (and a few women) standing in front of

272

us, trying to get a look. O.K., here she is, lying stretched out in this brown wire thing that looks as though it's been together from old fire guards. 'What? Not even tits?' says an old geezer next to us, to no one in particular. 'Shut your *fucking* mouth,' the Rat Woman replies from her supine position.

She's in a full-body leotard: the top half is sheer, with tufts of brown hair glued over her nipples. The bottom is fake rat skin with a long tail attached. She has narrow, sharp-looking, protruding front teeth, which may have got her the job in the first place. It's not the tail that gets me, or the brown and white rats crawling all over her, as if she were in a sewer – it's her long, brown, varnished, witchy nails. 'Imagine being scratched by those,' I say to Dennis, nudging him and pointing.

'Nasty,' Dennis replies.

We're up close now, with our faces almost pressed against the wire. I feel some bastard trying to pick my back pocket, but as there's nothing in it, he's going to be out of luck. 'Can I *do* something for you gentlemen?' asks the Rat Woman, giving a heavy stare and daring us to linger.

'Bite their balls off,' yells some loud-mouth from the back of the crowd.

I say to the Rat Woman, 'Want some cheese?'

'I'll give you cheese,' she screams. 'I'll give you fucking cheese.'

Before I can get out of the way she scoops up a handful of rat shit and sawdust and throws it through the cage at my face. I try to duck but get caught behind the ear. I can feel little pellets in my hair.

We get down on our hands and knees and crawl to the side of the tent. Some kid is lying there, trying to saw through one of the guy ropes with a tiny penknife. 'What are you doing?' Dennis asks him, stupidly.

The kid jabs the knife at us. 'Watch it,' I say. (He's very small.)

We roll out of the fetid tent and into some muddy caravan ruts. Behind our heads the generator for the merry-go-round is giving off a high-pitched whine, as if it's going to explode. '*Fun*fair – they call this a *fun* fair,' says Dennis.

273

'Well,' I reply, 'aren't you having fun?'

We scramble down the Heath to the lower part of the fair. Outside the Big Wheel, we bump into beautiful Pat McNally from our school, and her new boyfriend. 'This is Lemberg,' she says in her Wembley whine. 'He's an artist.'

Dennis looks at me. I know what he's thinking. Pat's last boyfriend, Slim, was a consummate mod: scooter, parka, big Who fan, the whole thing. But he's dead. Done in by the Chinese heroin that blew through our school last year like a fat death wind. This guy, Lemberg, looks like a poor substitute for Slim. 'Wanna see his studio?' Pat asks us. She doesn't bother to tell him our names.

We stand in front of this huge canvas that is a portrait of naked Lemberg, giant size, thick brushes in his hand, long thick tube of a penis hanging down. A black scrawl in the bottom-right-hand corner of the painting reads 'Drive your cart and your plough over the bones of the dead'. Lemberg sits at a table in the middle of his studio, rolling a joint. He's about thirty, maybe thirty-five. 'What's this, then?' says Dennis, pointing at the penis. 'You've been using your imagination a little, haven't you?'

'Oh no,' says Pat, matter-of-factly, 'he does have a big one. Don't you?' Lemberg doesn't respond. He keeps sorting through his bag of grass. He's humming a little song to himself, like Winnie-the-Pooh:

> What you don't need
> stalks and seeds.

We respect almost anything Pat says (1) because of her recent bereavement, and (2) because she knows Twiggy. I have a third reason for respecting her. For some months she has been the object of all my fantasies, in most of which she is naked and hard at work.

Dennis starts to wander around the studio, picking up tubes of paint and squeezing blobs of colour onto his hands. Then he wipes them on his jeans. 'Look,' he says, pointing at his trousers. 'Art.'

It seems all right to be thirty-five and an artist in trendy Hampstead. You get a big bed in the middle of an open space (it's rumpled, and a not-so-small patch of dry brown blood is on the undersheet), and this gorgeous sixteen-year-old girl whom we're all, me especially, dying for, and you get to paint yourself naked. 'Leave the paint alone,' says Lemberg. Ah, he speaks. And what do you know? He's one of us. He's from our part of town. So there's not a lot we can do now, because he knows who we are, and we know who he is. That's all it takes in London, really – someone opening his mouth.

We smoke the dope. 'This is home-grown,' says Lemberg.

'You should see his set-up,' Pat adds. 'There's a whole little room covered in tinfoil, with studio lights he got from a closed-down theatre.'

'Ever try hash oil?' asks Lemberg. 'This is coated in hash oil. Makes for a trippy experience.'

'What?' Dennis asks. 'Are you telling me we can expect to hallucinate?'

'What you expect and what you get may turn out to be two different things entirely.'

'Very meaningful,' Dennis replies.

After about ten minutes Dennis says to me, 'It's big-socks time.' He's referring to that moment when the dope effects start to creep into your knees, then down towards your calves, where they irritate the area just above where the sock line would be if you were wearing big socks. Lemberg has moved over to Pat and is trying to kiss her. She keeps pushing his face away, but only in a kind of 'Just wait until they've gone' way. We go.

Outside, I look at the normally invisible hairs on the back of my hand and see a waving cornfield. 'That's a hash-oil magnification you're experiencing,' says Dennis when I describe what's going on. 'Your powers of perception have been heightened.'

Soon after, I have this idea about running up an Israeli flag on our school flagpole. I use my sharpened powers to imagine a huge blue-on-white Star of David whipping in the wind over Brondesbury, and Queens Park and Paddington. Last week,

Owen (Religious Instruction) beat me badly with the 'kosher cosh' for talking in class. I have a deeper grudge against Beaglehole for humiliating me during gym. I was wearing red shorts instead of regulation black. 'Wolfson,' he said, 'this isn't a Jewish fashion show.' This kind of thing ('Cohen, stand in the wastepaper bin – you're rubbish') goes on all the time in our school, which mingles semi-intelligent socio-paths from Kilburn with recidivist Jewish kids from Willesden and Wembley.

The question is: Where to get the flag? Dennis, who has an agile but generally impractical mind, immediately suggests that we steal one. But where from? We stand outside a house with a blue plaque, where John Keats lived two hundred years ago. Dennis says, 'When was the last time you saw an Israeli flag? I mean one within graspable distance.'

I totter around on some blurry edge in my mind. I know where I'm going, but I don't quite want to get there. Eventually, I say, 'In synagogue, when your cousin Norman was bar mitzvahed. Don't you remember? They unfurled it behind him when he got his J.N.F. trees.'

'What's the problem?' Dennis yells up, in what he thinks is a whisper. I'm lying, like a fish on a platter, on one half of a huge hexagonal stained-glass window that we have managed to push open with a pole. I've scaled the concrete wall, and the friable paint job is all over my hands and clothes. My face is up against the mane of a tawny Lion of Judah. The glass, bonded in metal, feels like it's going to shatter at any minute. Meanwhile, I'm tipping forward but can't slide through. I'm thinking about the fulcrum, and how poorly I did in Physics –'26% (Highest in Form 97%); Diligence C; Comments: Lazy and incompetent' – when suddenly I'm head first on the padded seats of the temple.

Someone has been here before us. The whole place is a mess. There are prayer books with pages torn out and strewn all over the place, and ripped prayer shawls on the floor. One of the red velvet curtains in front of the ark has been slashed, as have the puffy seats where the synagogue wardens sit in their shiny top hats and tails.

I let Dennis in through the side door. He looks around. 'Someone's been enjoying themselves,' he says. 'Any sign of the flag?'

Even I am appalled by his insouciance. 'This is a serious thing,' I say.

We take a quick tour. It's mostly slashing and ripping. There is one piece of nasty art work – a black swastika on one of the side walls – but it looks as if they ran out of paint. It occurs to us both, at about the same time, that if anyone were to come in now we would have a lot of explaining to do.

We're on our way out (sans flag) when we hear the noise. It seems to be coming from the pipes in the organ loft. It's a tenebrous, adult-male groaning. When we get up there, we find the janitor. His face is blotchy and bruised; there's a crescent of half-dried blood under each of his nostrils. 'I tried to stop 'em,' he says. 'Those bastards. They come in out of the park. What do they want to do a thing like this for?'

Dennis looks around – he's developing a volcanic glow in his eyes. I've seen it before; it merges anger and impatience, and is sometimes a prelude to violence.

'Do you know where the flag is?' he asks.

'Who cares about the fucking flag?' I say, and for a moment it looks as if the two of us might get into a fight (not good for me).

For a while, the janitor and I try to clear up the mess. Dennis goes into the back office to look for the flag. I stuff a lot of the torn pages under someone's seat. Then I get fed up, and I sit down and start reading. 'Lust not after her beauty in thine heart; neither let her take thee with her eyelids. For by means of a whorish woman a man is brought to a piece of bread.' What piece of bread? I try to think about Pat McNally's eyelids, but they're impossible to visualise. Eyebrows, yes – average thickness, blonde. A guide to her pubic hair? Could be.

The janitor says he's going to phone the police. Dennis appears with the flag (not quite as big as I'd hoped). He's already attached it to its staff. I ask the janitor, 'Mind if we borrow this for a while?'

277

He shrugs, as if to say 'Makes no difference now.'

Beyond the synagogue are the open fields of Gladstone Park. We unfurl the flag and run with it streaming behind us like a medieval banner. A couple of stray dogs chase us for a while. Dennis sends them off by aiming kicks towards their faces. Kids are on the swings, and forming lines up by the stone fountain. In the distance, past the muddy duck pond, a rainbow arches over the weeping willows and the high, thin branches of the silver birches. It must have rained while we were inside. A small girl comes up to us. She says, 'I know how doggies talk.' She gives a few yelps, then a growl, followed by a heavy bark.

Outside Electric House, on Willesden Lane, we wait a long time for a bus. Then they don't want to let us on with the flag. There's an inspector on board. 'Suppose we stop suddenly,' he says. 'You could lance that right through someone's lungs.'

The conductor adds, 'More like driving a stake through a person's heart.'

Dennis says, 'Or sticking a javelin up your arse.'

We walk.

On the way I try to get Dennis to talk about something that matters. What I want to get at is this: Why would an attractive sixteen-year-old girl give herself over – body and possibly soul – to someone like Lemberg? Now, from Lemberg's point of view it's all very clear – he wants to crush her bones. But from Pat's?

Of course, I have this special interest. In the immediate post-Slim mourning period ('Drive your cart and your plough over the bones of the dead') I had one slow dance with Pat at the Starlite Ballroom, Greenford. She wore a black miniskirt with a semi-transparent pink blouse that revealed something she told me was called a 'no-bra bra'. Her body's imprint lasted all night, as if I were sand.

When I broach the subject with Dennis I quickly discover that he has no interest in the whys and wherefores of anything. He is all business and to the point. The solid rope of dailiness is what he likes to climb. If I were to say now, as I feel like saying, 'I'm losing my enthusiasm for this flag adventure, because the day has already served up more than I can digest,' he would turn on me.

Once, Dennis brought an axe to school. During lunch break he chopped up his desk. At first, I thought this was a familiar, if extreme, assault upon the seat of learning. Then I realised he was trying to break the frozen sea within him. We stuffed the splintered wood in our gym bags and took the afternoon off to ride the tube. As we came to the semi-deserted stations at the northern end of the old Bakerloo line, Kingsbury, Queensbury, and Canons Park, we waited until the doors were about to close, then threw the wood onto the rails.

But is this what I really want? Vandalism and adventure? All summer I have been carrying around the possibilities for change, for shifting my allegiances. They rise and fall, like unexpected adolescent erections, and, appropriately, converge on issues of hardness and softness. I am awed by the former, embodied in Dennis, but generally inclined by temperament and character, towards the latter. Somewhere inside I want to surround a girl – well, Pat McNally – with the most insipid and conventional accoutrements of love.

Now, don't get me wrong – I had seen the brown-red stain on Lemberg's bed, and I knew all about the body's betrayals. What is more, almost my entire education in the sex area derived from dirty jokes, poorly photographed barbershop magazines, and badly drawn graffiti. The previous year, in order to counterbalance my developing vulgarity, my father had dragged me, one Friday night, to a small Sephardic synagogue in London's East End. He wanted me to hear a group of old men chant the Song of Songs – or Canticle of Canticles, as it was called in the prayer book. (I read this, of course, as 'Testicle of Testicles'.) But even though I had listened and learned about the little foxes, the breasts like young roes feeding among the lilies, and the importance of eating the honeycomb with the honey, the notion of a higher love had not really sunk in. It is not until now, walking down Salisbury Road with this stupid flag, that the weak sun of consideration and love, hidden all season long, begins to penetrate the thick clouds of boorishness and lust that are gathered around me.

What I want, I now realise, is more Pat Woman than Rat Woman. Lemberg's bed has been a reminder that you can't have one without the other, but I have reached a decision to approach the hybrid with poetry rather than teenage aggression. I begin this excursion into 'softness' by saying to Dennis, 'Do you know whose house we were outside back in Hampstead?'

'No.'

'Keats's.'

'So fucking what?'

This is no more than I expect, but the fact that I have raised the subject is, in itself, a significant beginning.

We arrive at the school. It is late afternoon. The turbulent sun is sending a bright glare to heat things up. Dennis has red hair, and because, at this moment, it matches the colour of the sun, I start to feel oppressed by Dennis's head. I say, 'Why don't you go and raise the flag yourself?'

'What?' he replies. 'After coming all this way?' He tries to fire me up by reminding me of some heinous teacher acts. 'Do you remember when Fanny wouldn't let Sless go home early on Friday nights? How about when Fogwell threw you against the wall after your father wrote that bar-mitzvah-lesson note?' But this is second-division stuff, and Dennis knows it. He hadn't cared himself that Sless walked five miles to his Orthodox home instead of catching the bus. He had laughed, along with all the others, when I had my encounter with the wall.

'No,' I say. 'You go up there. I've had it.'

Dennis starts to move very fast. For a moment I feel as if I'm a part of observed Nature. Offscreen, someone is whispering, 'The alpha male, by displaying resolution and a sense of urgency, wishes to indicate that his companion is a coward.' Dennis throws the flag over the fence and climbs after it. I figure he'll have to get up on the gym roof, which may take him a while, and then make his way along to the crenellated turret that houses the flagpole. I've got at least twenty minutes.

I head into Queens Park and start walking towards the bandstand. I think I'll find some shade, stretch out, meditate. Considering it's a holiday, the place is oddly deserted. Then I see why. About twenty teenagers are standing near the Pitch and Putt. They're carrying bicycle chains, golf clubs that they have stolen out of the shed, and some long sticks. They're on me before I can even think about running. I recognise a couple of them from the school for psychopaths a hundred yards down the road from our own.

First, it seems, they want to play. One of them, *Homo Kilburnus stupidus*, says, 'I didn't know Jews were allowed in this park.' His chief mate, a boy with a deceivingly innocent-looking outbreak of summer freckles on his face and a peacock tattooed on his bare chest, says, 'They're not.'

'So, what are you doing here?' the first says. 'Because you are a Jew. You are a *fucking* Jew, aren't you?'

I say, 'Yes.' This isn't bravery or defiance, because it absolutely doesn't matter what I say. 'A thing of beauty is a joy forever' or 'Fuck you, I'm Episcopalian.' – the consequences are going to be the same.

In case you think I'm taking all this with an air of cool detachment, I'm not. I shake and sweat and wait to get hit. There's a short interval while Freckles chivalrously challenges me to fight. I say, 'No, thanks.' Then he belts me in the face with a set of brass knuckles. I make myself fall down, and cover my head with my hands. I can feel the kicks coming in: nasty, sharp ones in the kidneys, and one to the head that feels as if it has broken my fingers. I'm praying that they lay off with the driving irons. I cry, choke, and bleed. For a moment I think they've stopped. I cough, and each breath brings a dragging, boiling, bubbling sound. But they're not done. Two of them pull out my arms while a third presses something into my back. A knife! I scream. They laugh. The bastards are all laughing. Someone says, 'Fuck off out of here.' I run, dribbling blood and mucus from my nose. Obviously, I haven't been stabbed. I feel my back – nothing. I reach a water fountain, sip, spit, and sip again. It is only when I take off my T-shirt to wipe my face that I see what they've done. Where once there was a blank, white space, the word 'Joo' is now inscribed; the two 'o's – jocularity or ignorance? I pull the stained, soaking T-shirt back on. It's hot enough to walk bare-chested, but I've been exposed, and I want to cover myself.

In the shade of a grey slate roof my bodyguard is asleep. The Israeli flag which I had imagined rippling in waves of triumph, a shiny point of resistance in a constellation of hostility, droops in the windless early dusk. I can't blame Dennis for what has happened to me, although I sort of want to. We are thrown unprotected on the free, spinning world, and we have to take the blows when they come. They do come.

I try to think my beating through, and, on the way to the bus stop, I half manage it. I feel angry and impotent, no doubt about that. For a while, though, I affect a wounded-soldier aspect towards what I have been through. I say to myself, 'This is not all that unpleasant' – it's like the bruised fatigue that follows a hard soccer game. Then my kidneys start to ache, and I touch my swollen lips. Suddenly, I find myself in tears. There is nothing redeeming about my pain. It is hurt and humiliation, pure and simple, with its own vectors and swoops.

By the time I get back to Lemberg's, which takes a while, because I have trouble remembering where he lives, it's dark. There are iron clouds stamped in a blue-black sky, and all the warmth of the day has gone down with the sun. When she opens the door Pat looks at me, fails to register any shock, and says, 'Been fightin'?' 'Sort of,' I reply. Over her shoulder I see Lemberg at work. He's directing a nude model, a skinny girl with long black hair, and conical breasts like saltshakers. I suppose he's going to sketch her. As I move in through the door the girl takes up a pose, and Lemberg moves close and adjusts her limbs.

Pat leads me past the artist at work. 'You'd better come into the bathroom,' she says. 'I'll wash your face.' There's a bright, naked light bulb hanging over the sink. She touches a cold sponge to my lips and washes the caked blood from my face. I think I might lie and tell her that Dennis and I vanquished a bunch of hard nuts, but instead, I submit to her ministrations. I look in the mirror and review the copper bruises on my jaw and around my cheekbones. The door of the bathroom is open and behind me I can see Lemberg leaning forward to kiss the model. Pat says, 'Wanna go to the pictures?'

In the Hampstead Everyman I think, for about an hour and a half, that I might take hold of her hand, but in the end I don't.

Mr Applewick

TAMAR YELLIN

Mr Applewick finished dinner early and drove out to see his client. He put on his brown check suit for the occasion.

The Metro was still gleaming. It barely came out of the garage these days. Business was slowing down, but he didn't mind. It left him more time to himself.

He glanced at his image in the rear view mirror. His face was very clean, very pink. The pale blue eyes stared back at him, magnified through the thick lenses like marbles in a glass of water. His silver hair stood up very short and harsh, and when he put a hand to the back of his head there was nothing but bristles. He disliked the slight heaviness around his lips, for he did not consider himself a sensual man, but in all respects – the tightly buttoned waistcoat, the severely knotted tie, the spotless trousers – he was refined and harsh. He had in fact, Mr Applewick noted with satisfaction, become what he really was.

His client lived only a short drive away, on the Moorcrofts. The address turned out to be one of those big, mock-Georgian houses without symmetry or grace, surrounded by hideous shrubs. He walked up, as always, with deliberation and without hurry, and rang the bell.

A sulky child answered the door and was swiftly removed

by its mother. She fussed Mr Applewick into the dining-room, steering his bulk around the draylon furniture and precarious knick-knacks, until they reached the object of attention.

Mr Applewick put down his attaché case and summed it up. It was a Broadwood, upright steel frame, walnut casing, probably made around 1910, after the firm had moved from Great Poulteney Street. The casing was in extremely good condition, polished to a high lustre which clashed with the oak veneer of the dining suite. It was remarkable how many people kept their pianos in the dining-room these days, where they wouldn't be a nuisance or interfere with the television.

He sat down, adjusted his seat and took possession of the instrument with a few chords. It was badly out of tune, some of the notes were sticking and strange resonances wheezed from within.

'It hasn't been played for a while,' his client explained.

Mr Applewick stood up.

'If you would mind clearing the top,' he said. She hastened to do so. Mr Applewick helped her, transferring the bric-à-brac to the table piece by piece. He had little respect for people who used their pianos as sideboards. The ornaments interfered with the resonance and even rattled when playing appassionata. But he removed them gently and would not have dreamed of showing his distaste, for he was a man of impeccable politeness.

He opened the top, put one knee on the piano stool and peered inside. The hammers needed refacing, the tapes replacing, it would want new check leathers and a general clean at least. Then, it was so long since it had been tuned that wires were liable to snap when the action was refitted.

He came off the piano stool.

'It was my mother's,' the woman apologised. 'I've never played it much, but now that Samantha's going to start lessons I thought we might as well – '

Involuntarily his eyes wandered to her hands. No indeed: no one with nails that long could be a serious pianist. He glanced up. The sulky child was peering round the dining-room door, sucking its thumb and looking none too pleased at the prospect of learning to play the Broadwood.

Mr Applewick moved a hidden lever and the front of the piano came off. Mother and child started back in alarm.

'Oh! I didn't know you could do that,' she said.

Mr Applewick struggled under the weight of the front panel.

'If I might put this against the wall there – ' he gasped.

'Of course – sorry –' The woman scurried out of the way.

The piano tuner returned to his closer inspection of the interior, testing notes and examining the condition of the hammers and dampers. The inside was beautifully decorated with scrolls and leaves, now faded and dusty. There was a good deal of burnishing to be done.

'It will be a big job, an expensive job,' he said at last. And he began to explain what needed doing.

'But is it worth it?' she wanted to know. 'I mean – is it a good piano?'

'Oh yes,' said Mr Applewick. 'It's worth doing. I wouldn't suggest it otherwise.' She did not know what a Broadwood was. He would have liked to abscond with the action.

'We'll do it, then,' the woman compromised; and Mr Applewick opened his attaché case to reveal a gleaming array of tools, each lying in its own specially shaped well. He set to work removing the piano's action, taking each section out to the van, until the casing stood derelict and every footstep made a ghostly echo.

'I suggest you clean out the dust from there,' Mr Applewick said matter-of-factly, indicating the filthy ledge where the keyboard had been. The woman's face looked exactly as though she had failed to vacuum under the bed. Very gently, Mr Applewick let down the lid, which sloped in now like lips do when the teeth are gone.

'I'll get in touch in about a fortnight,' he said at the door, and gave the woman his card: A. J. Applewick, Piano Tuning and Reconditioning. (Caterer to the Musical Profession)

Mr Applewick took the action through to his workshop at the

286

back of his house and set it up on the bench. The workshop was a single-storey extension built by his father, with a large window overlooking the garden. The light was going now, and he switched on the fluorescent strip which drenched the white walls and threw everything – bench, shelves, trays, tools, Mr Applewick himself – into high relief. Nothing was out of place, and there was not a speck of dirt. The metal trays he had fixed to the walls himself were all neatly labelled: Clip Felt, Wedge Felt, Check Leather, Loops, Tapes. A sweeping brush stood in one corner: he always swept up immediately. His cutting board was clean, his knives sharp. He never ate or drank in the workshop.

Perhaps he took things to extremes, but his was a precise, clean craft and he had his father's standards to maintain. Every element of his drill had been ingrained before the age of twenty.

Once, a long time ago, he had stepped inside an artist's studio, and been horrified at the apparent chaos: the dirty palettes lying here and there, the used rags and unwashed brushes, the half-eaten cake and festering coffee cup. He felt that nothing refined or clean could be created in such a place; and true enough, the paintings turned out to be chaotic daubs, without recognisable form or content, without, even, any recognisable talent or skill. They just broke the rules, and Mr Applewick saw no benefit in that.

He should have waited till morning, but he had a sense of urgency about the Broadwood. It would be a big job. And he enjoyed working on it. He looked forward to seeing all the hammers fresh and firm, the springs responsive and the new tapes snapping back and forth. Even after forty years he had not lost that sense of achievement.

The first time he had finished a restoration entirely on his own he had hardly wanted to return the piano to its owner. He sat in the workshop, gazing at the fresh hammer felts which looked like the eyes on a peacock's tail, searching for any speck of dirt or adjustment still to be made, until his father came in smiling and said it was time to go. They had the Bedford then; the Moorcrofts hadn't even been built yet.

287

Mr Applewick went to the window and took a look at the sky. It would be a clear night. Good. It was dark enough for the whole room to be reflected into the garden. His own face hung amongst the irises like a ghost.

He returned to the workbench, removed his heavy glasses and rubbed his eyes. Perhaps he was tired, after all, and should leave the job until morning. He laid the action face down and began unscrewing the hammers, placing them in a small box marked 'Hammers'.

A faint familiar odour of leather and glue hung in the workshop. He thought of his father, as he often did when he was at work because it often seemed to him that he was standing in his father's skin, performing his actions, wearing his expressions and even grunting the same grunts. They were of an age, now, too, and that thought gave him a little shiver.

They were both perfectionists, both of a scientific turn of mind, with a passion for order. Neither of them spoke much. In the workshop, talk consisted of: 'Pass me the bushing now, please,' 'Set the glue on, would you?' 'Steady, now, and lift!' They were always extremely polite to each other, as if in deference to the fine instruments on which they worked.

His father was religious. He believed that he had been given certain abilities by God, and no more. And so he taught his son a craftsman's pride in building pianos but a layman's humility in playing them. Mr Applewick knew he had no musical ability. He could produce the necessary chords for testing the piano's tone and tuning; perhaps a few commonplace songs. The Knight in his living room was barely ever opened.

As he unscrewed the hammers, he thought, this Broadwood is certainly a noble thing. Mozart and Handel had played at the Broadwoods' concert hall in Great Poulteney Street and Chopin had given his last London recital there. Mr Applewick did not care for Chopin. He admired Bach, Vivaldi and Handel. For him, elegance in music was everything. It stuck to the rules. Now that composers had broken the rules the result was chaos and it was certainly not music. Indeed it was not even composition.

Mr Applewick often wished that he had lived in a previous

century, when life was altogether more elegant, manners more courteous and customs more ornate. Either that or in the future, which had its own endless possibilities; but he certainly didn't care for the shabby little place the world was now.

In the old days, his father had subscribed to a number of educational magazines in an effort to improve himself. He had inquired into the world with a sort of wide-eyed wonder, marvelling at the works of God and man. He had the enthusiasm of a child running loose in the Garden of Eden, knowing that God has made everything for his investigation and delight.

Mr Applewick was not religious and he knew that the garden was not full of serpents but full of other people trampling on the flowers. He did not believe in God and he never had done and secretly he despised his father for being so naive.

When he was eleven years old he had become interested in astronomy. He saved up his pocket money and with some help from his father he managed to buy himself a second-hand telescope, a three-inch refractor which was hardly better than a pair of powerful binoculars, but it was a start all the same. He went through the usual teething troubles, leaning out of the bedroom window with no mount, going out into the frozen garden in the middle of the night with his pyjamas on, trying to make sense of over-detailed star maps by the light of a torch. But gradually he had become proficient, he kept his equipment in the garden shed and worked from there, he bought a decent tripod mount and began to learn the skies. And the more he learned the less he was able to believe in God.

His father had the exactly opposite response. Mildly impressed by his son's new avenue of knowledge, he allowed himself to be initiated, patronised and introduced to the mysteries of the tube. The boy half hoped that when he put his eye to the telescope, atheism would strike him like a revelation. Instead, Mr Applewick senior adjusted his position, gazed long and silently, slowly panned the heavens and whispered in awe: 'How many are thy works, O Lord! In wisdom hast thou made them all.'

The son could not help himself: he snatched his father by the shoulder and grabbed the telescope with a look of fury. It was the only time he showed such anger, and it was the only time his father looked through the telescope.

It had grown late. Mr Applewick got up, switched out the light and went into the kitchen to make himself a cup of tea. Night hung at all the windows; he went around drawing curtains while the kettle boiled. He would not do any more work on the Broadwood tonight. Automatically he reached for his quilted jacket from the back of the kitchen door and put it on, then took his cup of tea and a biscuit into the back garden.

Just behind the workshop was a run-off shed he had built himself. Inside was a sturdy five-inch refractor on a large tripod. It was Mr Applewick's observatory.

He pulled out a stool and balanced his cup and saucer on a nearby ledge, adjusted the telescope and began focusing it on Ursa Major. It was so cold that the bristles on the back of his head seemed to ripple. He smiled to himself. This was the moment of his reward: no one could now enter the small circle which contained him and his telescope.

What he knew, what he had learned – not just the constellations and the planets, but the advent of meteor showers, the existence of distant galaxies, the positions and magnitudes of almost ten thousand stars – all this streamed within his blood like a kind of love, and revolved in his brain like a kind of hope. The limitless possibilities of the universe intoxicated him. He wished he could fast forward time and know what was to be discovered: the exploration of other worlds, the sun's death and earth's destruction, the wonderful contraction of the universe into cosmic egg and big bang and cosmic egg, the pulsating of a universe reborn over and over again, as new, with no previous knowledge. He wanted to see it all! If there was a God, he imagined him working with a piece of clay, moulding it into a universe, then rashly impacting it once again, never satisfied with his production. But there was no such God, for not even God could survive such cataclysm.

Because he was a scientist and a lover of detail, he kept careful diaries of his observations. He had several notebooks now, immaculately written, though he did not pretend to himself that they were of any great usefulness. The useful work an amateur could do now was negligible, he accepted that. He had once met another enthusiast who wore his eyes out in a nightly hunt for comets. He yearned to discover one and have it named after him. Mr Applewick thought the man conceited and absurd. One did not have to justify astronomy by sensationalising it.

He had, in fact, himself discovered a comet some while back. It was in the year his father died, so it was an unusual year in more ways than one. He had made his recordings conscientiously and written to the BAA. As it turned out, a mathematician had already computed its orbit and the comet was named after her instead, but whenever Mr Applewick looked it up in the Handbook he felt an affection towards it.

The practice of astronomy, which seems so broad-sweeping and expansive, is in fact a science of tiny details and pedantic calculations. In this sense it did not sit so uncomfortably with the restoration of pianos. As Mr Applewick measured and cut the leathers for his jacks, as he painstakingly glued each one in place, his nature was in harmony with his work. But in his mind he may well have been considering the primeval matter from which all things come, and the cosmic dust to which jacks, glue, leather and piano will ultimately return.

Whatever his thoughts just now, Mr Applewick made a sudden movement, caught the teacup with his elbow and sent it clattering onto the concrete floor of the shed. He straightened up; all his joints were stiff with cold, and his back ached. He picked up the broken pieces of the cup, laboriously wheeled back the shed and stumbled indoors.

The next day he was up before dawn. Standing in the kitchen he sipped his tea; he would make an early start.

This morning, more than usual, he felt how his clothes were a little too tight under the arms and around the crotch, and as he ran a comb through his minimum of hair he became

291

transfixed by his own reflection. Strange and impassive, the magnified eyes stared at him.

He was at his bench by six o'clock. That morning he dismantled the dampers and found that during cleaning he had mislaid the tray. It was large and difficult to lose, but he could not see it anywhere. He made a careful reconnaissance of all his work surfaces; he found the hammers and levers nestling quietly where he had placed them the night before. He started to look in unlikely places; sweat prickled under his arms and on the back of his neck. Then, just as he was about to lose his temper, he found the offending tray on the floor beneath his workbench, just where he was most likely to put his feet. He could not understand how he had done anything so stupid, and picked up the tray with something like hatred.

He selected those dampers which required recovering and began to scrape off the old felts with a knife. He was still a little angry and he cut away at the felt with some ferocity. The red backing would not detach itself from the wood of this damper, but instead of fetching some methylated spirits to loosen it, he vented his frustration on it with the knife. He cut himself, and blood deepened the redness of the felt.

Among his labelled drawers were those marked 'Clip', 'Wedge', 'Split Wedge' and 'Parallel'. These were the four types of felt used on damper heads. He bought them ready cut from the suppliers, and had only to glue them in place.

It was something peculiarly concordant with that day, that first day, that he opened the drawer marked 'Clip' to find wedge, and the drawer marked 'Wedge' to find it full of split. He said aloud: 'Someone's been messing about in my workshop'; but since it was obvious that the only person to have been in his workshop was himself, he choked on the final word and coughed.

He solved the problem very simply, by removing the labels from their metal frames and changing them round. Now all was in order once again. He took what he needed and returned to work.

He concentrated harder than usual during the glueing of the felts, checking several times that he was fixing the correct type to the correct head, ensuring that no glue dripped where it was not wanted. The day was getting on by the time he finished and he realised that he had not eaten. He would leave the dampers to dry and go and get a bite to eat.

It was odd, however, that despite having counted carefully, he now found that he had one wedge felt left over. He hunted the workbench and tray to see if there was a stray damper anywhere. But it seemed that he had accidentally brought over an extra felt, so he would just have to pop it back in the drawer and go for some lunch.

Now he found that the drawer marked 'Wedge' contained clip; opening the drawer marked 'Split' he found it full of wedge. The Parallel drawer held split and the Clip drawer parallel – in fact, all the drawers were as they had been before someone had changed the labels round. Mr Applewick began to suspect that some kind of jinx was on. He grew cunning. This time he changed the labels back steathily, then made as if to walk away. Next he wheeled round and tore open the drawers, half expecting to catch them in the act of transferring their contents. All were exactly as he had left them. He stared into them for a few moments, his eyes huge and watchful behind their thick glasses, then slowly pushed the drawers shut with his fingertips. He left the room backwards, half swaggering, and shouted as if to some unseen presence: 'I'm going to finish this job if it's the last thing I do!'

He did no more work that day.

From that time on, battle was engaged. The glue pot would fall to the floor and need wiping up; he would cut a piece of bushing wrongly and it would tear out of true. He seemed unable to tie a knot in a piece of string or to smooth out a length of tape. Impatience brought more mistakes. He broke the head off a rusty screw when he tried to force it with his screwdriver, and scorched himself with the casting lamp when he was loosening the tail.

A few moments of peace came with the burnishing of the jacks. With a piece of check felt and some black lead, Mr Applewick felt once more in possession of his territory.

He was making the Broadwood shine, and a burst of love passed through him. He was saving it from decay; he was saving himself from decay. In effect they were serving each other. He became convinced that so long as he concentrated on this restoration, chaos was held at bay.

His nights he spent in observing the stars. He tried to imprint their discipline on his disordered brain. Yet it seemed to him that all the stars were speeding away from him at tremendous velocities, leaving him alone, a mere fragment of life circling a doomed sun.

This was strange, because the universe had always seemed a friendly place to him, with its rules and regulations. Only now, it began to seem rather impersonal, and for the first time in his life he felt lonely.

Back in the 'fifties, when the Russians launched Sputnik and cars had rocket fins, there had been a girl called Eileen who lent him science fiction and listened to Bach. They went to the pictures together and exchanged ideas on the future of the universe. At one time they had almost been engaged; but he had broken it off. He returned the books. He blotted out books, films and Eileen from his mind.

Mr Applewick had no memory of love.

He sat alone in the middle of the night with his telescope, his workshop and the Broadwood, and the stars were all racing away from him.

Sixteen days later he was ready to return the action to its casing. Mr Applewick took a bath and put on a clean shirt. He fitted himself into his brown check suit and his shiny shoes. He felt sweet.

It was exactly six o'clock when he rang the bell of the asymmetric house.

'Ah! Mr Applewick. I'm so glad you've come to put the innards back in this thing,' his client said cheerfully. 'Every time you walk past it echoes as if it's got a ghost inside.'

Mr Applewick got down to work. Not a sound came from the rest of the house. Not so much as a cup of tea appeared. When he began tuning a dog started to howl somewhere in the distance, but that was all.

When he was tightening the strings, one snapped with a sound like a bullet. Mr Applewick put a hand to his heart. No blood. A terror was growing inside him. When all was reassembled and tuned and he began to play, perhaps the Broadwood would produce a cacophony, a travesty of music, exposing the chaos within him? Perhaps he had botched the entire job, made a farrago of the Broadwood's insides, something that could never function?

As he sat down to play the regulation chords his fingers trembled. He closed his eyes. The chords rippled out. He worked his way up the scale. It was a beautiful instrument. He had restored it.

Mr Applewick began to play one of the tawdry songs which were the only pieces he knew. He longed to be able to draw something meaningful from the throat of the instrument.

Hearing the music, his client dared to re-enter the dining-room.

'That does sound good,' she said. 'What a difference!' She hovered behind him. 'Are you all right?' For Mr Applewick looked ill.

Mr Applewick closed the top for the last time and invited his client to try it out.

'Oh – well – I don't think – !' She sat down stiffly and played a few wandering notes with one hand.

'Yes – oh, yes, that's fine. That's lovely, thank you.' She got up again quickly. 'I suppose it'll want tuning every so often?'

'Well, regular tuning does retard deterioration of the action, you see.' He began to explain why, speaking slowly and using terms she did not understand.

'How often, then?' she asked impatiently.

Mr Applewick regarded the Broadwood with a mixture of sadness and affection. 'I wouldn't leave it longer than a year,' he said at last.

When Mr Applewick was found, cold in his bed, an examination of the house was made to rule out any possibility of accident or foul play.

The house was in a dirty state, and the soiled linen in the

bathroom spilled over the floor. The kitchen sink was full of unwashed dishes and a thick odour of rotting vegetables hung about the downstairs rooms. The shelves held worn piano makers' manuals, bound copies of educational magazines and dusty piles of astronomical journals, star charts and calendars.

The workshop itself appeared to be the domain of an untidy and disorganised man: the floor and work surfaces were covered in odds and ends, tools lay scattered and dangerously concealed, drawers were torn half-open, their contents spilling onto the floor. Spiders had woven their webs in every corner, and the once beautiful felts and leathers were full of moth and mildew. All inside was confusion, chaos and decay; while outside in the overgrown garden, the run-off shed when pushed back revealed, rusted to its tripod, an old telescope with a broken lens.

Biographical Notes on the Authors

WILLIAM BOYD was born in Accra, Ghana, in 1952. He is the author of six novels and a collection of short stories that have been published around the world in over two dozen languages. In addition, eight of his screenplays have been filmed, the most recent of which is *A Good Man in Africa*, based on his first novel. He is married and lives in London.

MADDO FIELD was born in Australia in 1953 and lives in Switzerland. Susan Hill and John Murray awarded 'Sentiment in Drag' first prize in the *Stand* 1993 Short Story Competition.

MAVIS GALLANT was born in Montreal and worked as a feature writer there before giving up newspaper work to devote herself to fiction. She left Canada in 1950 and after extensive travel settled in Paris. She is a regular contributor to *The New Yorker* and is currently working on a novel. She has written eleven books the most recent of which is *Across the Bridge*.

NADINE GORDIMER was born and lives in South Africa. She has published ten novels, and eight collections of short stories. Her new novel, *None to Accompany Me*, will be published by

Bloomsbury in September. Amongst many literary awards, she has won the Booker Prize for *The Conservationist*. In 1991, she was awarded the Nobel Prize for Literature.

RUSSELL HOBAN was born in 1925 in Pennsylvania. He was an illustrator before becoming a writer. He has written many books for children and his adult novels are *The Lion of Boaz-Jachin and Jachin-Boaz*, *Kleinzeit*, *Turtle Diary*, *Riddley Walker*, *Pilgermann* and *The Medusa Frequency*. He has lived in London since 1969 and is currently collaborating with Harrison Birtwistle on an opera entitled *The Second Mrs Kong*, which will open at Glyndebourne in October 1994.

MARGARET HORNER was born in Bournemouth in 1925. She was educated at the Bournemouth School for Girls and later at St Hugh's College, Oxford, where she read English. After teaching English in various state schools for twenty-five years, she retired to Clun in Shropshire, where she reads a lot and writes a little. 'Political Economy' is her only publication so far. It won the *Observer*/Penguin short story competition in June 1993.

JANETTE TURNER HOSPITAL was born in 1942 and grew up on the steamy north-eastern coast of Australia, which is still home. After 1967, however, her life became unintentionally nomadic, and she can no longer remember what it is like to live in only one country for an entire year. She is frequently writer-in-residence at universities in Australia, Canada and the USA. Her most recent novel, *The Last Magician*, was shortlisted for Australia's Miles Franklin Award, the Adelaide Festival Award, and Canada's Trillium Award.

LISA JACOBSON is an Australian dramatist, poet and fiction writer. She has received the Harri Jones Memorial Prize (for a young Australian poet) from the University of Newcastle, New South Wales, and her story, 'The Master Builder's Wife', recently won second prize in the international competition run by *Stand Magazine*. She holds an MA in Writing and Literature from the University of Melbourne and is currently completing her first collection of poetry.

JAMAICA KINCAID was born in St John's, Antigua, in the West Indies. She is the author of the three highly praised works of fiction, *At the Bottom of the River*, *Annie John* and *Lucy*, as well as a non-fiction portrait of Antigua, *A Small Place*. She now lives in New York and is a staff writer for *The New Yorker*.

MATTHEW KRAMER with born in 1961 in north London, where he still lives. He read Law and Politics at Cambridge University and now practises as a lawyer in central London. His story 'The Sandcastle' appeared in *Best Short Stories 1992*. He is currently completing a collection of short stories and working on a novel and a play for television.

EDNA O'BRIEN is the author of five collections of short stories and twelve novels, including *The Country Girls*, *A Fanatic Heart*, *Lantern Slides* (which won the *Los Angeles Times* fiction prize), *Time and Tide* (winner of the 1993 Writer's Guild Prize for Fiction), and, most recently, *House of Splendid Isolation*. She has written several plays, including *Virginia* (a life of Virginia Woolf) and *A Pagan Place*. Edna O'Brien was born in the west of Ireland and now lives in London.

JULIA O'FAOLAIN was born in London, brought up in Dublin and educated in Rome and Paris. After living for several years in Florence and in Los Angeles, she now lives in London. Her novels include *The Obedient Wife* and *No Country for Young Men* for which she was short-listed for the Booker Prize and, most recently, *The Judas Cloth*. She is married to the historian Lauro Martines, and is currently working on a collection of short stories.

BEN OKRI has published seven books: *Flowers and Shadows*, *The Landscapes Within*, *Incidents at the Shrine*, *Stars of the New Curfew*, *The Famished Road* which won the Booker Prize in 1991, and *Songs of Enchantment*. His most recent collection of poems is *An African Elegy*. He has been a Fellow Commoner in Creative Arts at Trinity College, Cambridge. His books have won several awards including the Commonwealth Writers Prize for Africa, the *Paris Review* Aga Khan Prize for Fiction, the prestigious International Literary Prize *Chianti Rufino-Antico Fattore* 1993 and the Italian Premio Prize, Grinzane Cavour. He lives in London.

FREDERIC RAPHAEL was born in Chicago in 1931 and was educated at Charterhouse and St John's College, Cambridge. He has had published numerous novels and short story collections including *The Glittering Prizes* (for which he won the Royal Television Society's Writer of the Year Award), *Heaven and Earth*, *Oxbridge Blues*, *After the War* and most recently, *A Double Life*. A new collection *The Latin Lover* is to be published later this year. He is a frequent contributor to the *Sunday Times* and to BBC Radio, is married, has three children and lives in France.

FRANK RONAN's first novel, *The Men Who Loved Evelyn Cotton*, won the 1989 *Irish Times*/Aer Lingus Irish Literature Prize and was followed by *A Picnic in Eden* and *The Better Angel*. He has written a number of short stories which have been published in the UK, Ireland, Australia and the USA. He is the editor of *In My Garden*, a collection of Christopher Lloyd's *Country Life* articles. His fourth novel *Dixie Chicken* was published earlier this year.

OAKLAND ROSS was a newspaper correspondent in Latin America for five years in the 1980s and later reported for three years from Africa. He now lives in Toronto. A collection of his short stories, called *Guerrilla Beach*, will be published in autumn 1994 by Cormorant. He is currently writing a non-fiction book about his travels, to be published next year by Knopf (Canada).

ALAN SILLITOE was born in 1928, and left school at fourteen to work in various factories before becoming an air traffic control assistant with the Ministry of Aircraft Production in 1945. He enlisted in 1946 into the RAFVR and spent two years on active service in Malaya as a wireless operator. He was invalided out in 1949. He began writing, and lived for six years in France and Spain. In 1958 *Saturday Night and Sunday Morning* was published, and *The Loneliness of the Long Distance Runner*, which won the Hawthornden Prize for Literature, came out the following year. He has published several novels and eight volumes of poetry. His latest novels are *Her Victory*, *The Lost Flying Boat*, *Down from the Hill*, *Life Goes On*, *The Open Door*, *Lost Loves* and *Leonard's War*.

HELEN SIMPSON's first collection of short stories, *Four Bare Legs in a Bed* (Heinemann 1990), won the *Sunday Times* Young Writer of the Year and the Somerset Maugham awards. Her suspense novella, *Flesh and Grass* (Pandora 1990) appeared with Ruth Rendell's *The Strawberry Tree* under the general title *Unguarded Hours*. Last year she was chosen as one of *Granta*'s twenty Best Young British Novelists. She has just finished a play, *Pinstripe*. Her second volume of stories will be published next year.

ALAN SPENCE was born and raised in Glasgow. His published work includes poetry, fiction and drama. He has been writer-in-residence at the universities of Glasgow and Edinburgh, at the Traverse Theatre, and with Edinburgh District Council. His novel *The Magic Flute* (Black Swan) won the 1991 People's Prize. His short story collection *Its Colours They Are Fine* (Black Swan) is widely regarded as a modern Scottish classic. Three of his playscripts are in print – *Sailmaker*, *Space Invaders* and *Changed Days* (all Hodder & Stoughton). In 1993 he won the Macallan/*Scotland on Sunday* short story competition with 'Nessun Dorma', the title story of a forthcoming collection.

CARL TIGHE was born in Handsworth, Birmingham in 1950. He was educated at Swansea and Leeds universities and lived in Wales for nearly twenty years. His plays *Little Jack Horner* and *Baku!* were broadcast by BBC Radio. His first book, *Gdansk* appeared in 1990. *Rejoice! and Other Stories* was shortlisted for the *Irish Times* First Fiction Prize in 1993.

JONATHAN TREITEL was born in London in 1959 and educated at the universities of Oxford, Cambridge, Stanford and Johns Hopkins. He has lived in San Francisco, Tokyo, Paris, Jerusalem, and has travelled in seventy countries. He is a hard working fiction writer. Stories by him have appeared in five of the six most recent *Best Short Stories* anthologies.

WILLIAM TREVOR was born in Cork in 1928, and educated at Trinity College, Dublin. He has spent much of his life in Ireland. His novel, *The Old Boys*, won the Hawthornden Prize in 1946, since when he has received many honours for his work including the Royal Society of Literature Heinemann Award, and the Whitbread Prize for Fiction. He edited *The Oxford Book of Irish Short Stories* (1989), and his *Collected Stories* were published in 1992.

FAY WELDON was born in England and raised in a family of women in New Zealand. She took degrees in Economics and Psychology at the University of St Andrews in Scotland and then, after a decade of odd jobs and hard times, began writing fiction. She is now well known as novelist, screenwriter and critic; her work is translated the world over. Her novels include, most famously, *The Life and Loves of a She-Devil* (a major movie starring Meryl Streep and Roseanne Barr), *Puffball*, *The Hearts and Lives of Men*, *The Cloning of Joanna May*, *Darcy's Utopia*, *Growing Rich* and *Life Force*. She has four sons and lives in London.

JONATHAN WILSON was born in London in 1950. He was educated at the universities of Essex, Oxford and the Hebrew University of Jerusalem. He is the author of a book of stories, *Schoom*, and his first novel will be published next year by Secker & Warburg. He lives in Newton, Massachusetts with his wife and two sons. He teaches at Tufts University.

BIOGRAPHICAL NOTES ON THE AUTHORS

TAMAR YELLIN grew up in Leeds and studied at Oxford, where she received the Pusey and Ellerton Prize for Hebrew Studies. After teaching in Bradford, she lived in Toronto for two years. She has now returned to Yorkshire to pursue her writing. 'Mr Applewick' is her first publication.

ACKNOWLEDGEMENTS

Higham Associates, 5–8 Lower John Street, Golden Square, London W1R 4HA.

'Political Economy', copyright © Margaret Horner 1993, was first published in the *Observer*, 27 June 1993, and is reprinted here by permission of the author.

'North of Nowhere', copyright © Janette Turner Hospital 1994, was first published in *Nimrod*, University of Tulsa, Vol. 36, No. 2, spring/summer 1993 and in *Critical Quarterly*, June 1994, and is reprinted by permission of the author and Sheil Land Associates, 43 Doughty Street, London WC1N 2LF.

'The Master Builder's Wife', copyright © Lisa Jacobson 1993, was first published in *Stand Magazine*, autumn 1993, and is reprinted by permission of the author.

'Song of Roland', copyright © Jamaica Kincaid 1993, was first published in *The New Yorker*, 12 April 1993, and is reprinted by permission of the author and Aitken, Stone & Wylie Ltd, 29 Fernshaw Road, London SW10 0XF.

'Nihon-jin Girls', copyright © Matthew Kramer 1993, was first published in *Panurge*, April 1993, and is reprinted by permission of the author.

'A Bed of Roses', copyright © Edna O'Brien 1993, was first published in the *Spectator*, 18/25 December 1993, and is reprinted by permission of the author and Aitken, Stone & Wylie Ltd, 29 Fernshaw Road, London SW10 0XF,

'Rum and Coke', copyright © Julia O'Faolain 1993, was first published in *Scripsi*, Vol. 9, No. 1, and is reprinted by permission of the author and Rogers, Coleridge & White Ltd, 20 Powis Mews, London W11 1JN.

'A Prayer From the Living', copyright © Ben Okri 1993, was first published in the *New York Times*, 29 January 1993, and is

ACKNOWLEDGEMENTS

reprinted here by permission of the author and A. P. Watt Ltd, 20 John Street, London WC1N 2DR.

'Concerto Grossman', copyright © Byronic Investments Ltd, was first broadcast on BBC Radio 3 on 31 August 1993 and first published by *BBC Music Magazine*, September 1993. It is reprinted here by permission of the author and Rogers, Coleridge & White Ltd, 20 Powis Mews, London W11 1JN.

'The Rower', copyright © Frank Ronan 1993, was first published in *Scripsi*, Vol. 8, No. 2, and is reprinted here by permission of the author and Rogers, Coleridge & White Ltd, 20 Powis Mews, London W11 1JN.

'So Far, She's Fine', copyright © Oakland Ross 1993, was first published in *Story* (US), winter 1993, and is reprinted here by permission of the author and Vardey & Brunton Associates, 8 Eel Brook Studios, 125 Moore Park Road, London SW6 4PS.

'A Respectable Woman', copyright © Alan Sillitoe 1993, was first published in the *Illustrated London News*, December 1993, and is reprinted here by permission of the author and Sheil Land Associates, 43 Doughty Street, London WC1N 2LF.

'Heavy Weather', copyright © Helen Simpson 1993, was first published in *Granta* 43, spring 1993, and is reprinted by permission of the author and Peters, Fraser & Dunlop, 503/4 The Chambers, Chelsea Harbour, London SW10 0XF.

'Nessun Dorma', copyright © Alan Spence 1993, was first published in *Scotland on Sunday* and is reprinted here by permission of the author and Sheil Land Associates, 43 Doughty Street, London WC1N 2LF.

'Reservations', copyright © Carl Tighe 1993, was first published in *Metropolitan* 1, winter 93/94, and is reprinted here by permission of the author.

306

'Spirit of a New India', copyright © Jonathan Treitel 1993, was first published in *Ambit*, spring 93, and is reprinted by permission of the author.

'The Potato Dealer', copyright © William Trevor 1993, was first published in the *Spectator*, 18/25 December 1993, and is reprinted here by permission of the author and Sheil Land Associates, 43 Doughty Street, London WC1N 2LF.

'Wasted Lives', copyright © Fay Weldon 1993, was first published in *The New Yorker*, 19 April 1993, and is reprinted by permission of the author and Sheil Land Associates, 43 Doughty Street, London WC1N 2LF.

'Bank Holiday', copyright © Jonathan Wilson 1993, was first published in *The New Yorker*, 11 January 1993, and is reprinted by permission of the author.

'Mr Applewick', copyright © Tamar Yellin 1993, was first published in *London Magazine*, December 1993/January 1994, and is reprinted here by permission of the author.

We are grateful to the editors of the publications in which the stories first appeared for permission to reproduce them in this volume.

Anyone wishing to reprint any of the stories elsewhere or in translation should approach the individual authors through their literary agents as indicated above or care of William Heinemann Ltd.